MW01294156

The Lost Baker of Vienna

The Lost Baker of Vienna

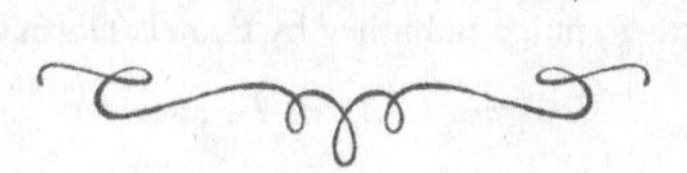

Sharon Kurtzman

PAMELA DORMAN BOOKS / VIKING

VIKING
An imprint of Penguin Random House LLC
1745 Broadway, New York, NY 10019

A Pamela Dorman Book/Viking

The PGD colophon is a registered trademark of Penguin Random House LLC.

VIKING is a registered trademark of Penguin Random House LLC.

First published in paperback in Australia and New Zealand by Headline Review, an imprint of Headline Publishing Group Limited, in 2025
First published in paperback in Great Britain by Headline Review, an imprint of Headline Publishing Group Limited, London, in 2025
First United States edition published by Pamela Dorman Books, 2025

Designed by Alexis Farabaugh

ISBN 9780593830864

Printed in the United States of America

In memory of my parents

My mother, Evelyn Rothspan, for showing me how to love unconditionally

and

My father, Herman Rothspan, for teaching me that every day is a bonus

Chapter One

Zoe

Raleigh, North Carolina
February 2018

On this starless winter night, wind howled through the street and cold wicked up from the ground, burrowing into Zoe Rosenzweig's bones. Not that she minded; she preferred winter. Sweltering summer days often set her on edge. She fumbled in the dark to slip her key in the door. The porch light was out again. She tucked the bag with the snow globe under her arm, turned the lock, then jabbed the doorbell twice. The kitschy souvenir of the Chicago skyline was for her grandfather, as was the double ring; the latter to signal he needn't rush to greet her. Not that he rushed anywhere since his stroke.

"It's me," she called, stepping inside his tidy Raleigh bungalow, and leaving her keys in the misshapen ceramic bowl on the foyer table, the one she'd made for Grandma Tess twenty years ago.

"Zoe, you're back from your trip?" Katherine called from the kitchen. Strong, kind Katherine was a fleshy woman with a tight cap of gray curls, and was Zoe's favorite of the home health aides who cycled through Grandpa Aron's days.

"I came straight from the airport." Zoe dropped her coat and backpack on a kitchen chair. "We need a new bulb on the porch." Katherine was wearing one of Grandma Tess's aprons. The green one with lemons. Zoe's grandmother had been gone for a year, and seeing her apron on the aide made her cheeks feel flush. She wanted to tell Katherine to take it off. Instead, she forced a smile. Katherine was a godsend, she reminded herself, and this was just an apron.

"How is he today?" Zoe asked. The aide didn't answer right away. "What's wrong?"

"He was more confused today than usual."

"Anything specific?" Grandpa Aron's doctor had assured Zoe his condition should remain stable during her trip.

Before Katherine could answer, Grandpa Aron called, "Is that my Zoe?" His footsteps made the stairs creak, followed by his slippers scuffing against the floor. He appeared in the kitchen in navy pajamas with neat comb lines in his damp gray hair. His stroke-crooked smile pinched her heart.

"You showered already." Zoe kissed his cheek, inhaling pine-scented soap.

"Did you enjoy Chicago and the rodeo?"

"The food was amazing. One truck served only dishes with cheese. Mac and cheese, mozzarella sticks, grilled cheese sandwiches, and quesadillas." She ticked them off on her fingers.

"*Meshuga*," he said. "Are you staying for dinner?"

She checked the microwave clock. It was after nine.

"Aron, you ate dinner three hours ago," Katherine said kindly.

"Right. I forgot. I don't know *vhat's* going on in this noggin." He tapped his head. The older he got, and as his dementia worsened, the more pronounced his accent became.

Zoe pulled out the snow globe. "For you."

"Ha!" He shook the souvenir, a blizzard obliterating the silver skyline inside. Wonder cast a childlike glow on his face that faded once the glitter settled. "I learned as a boy that in *var* the *vorld* disappears this *vay*, only it never returns to how it *vas* before."

His comment startled her. Grandpa Aron hardly ever talked about that time. Maybe this was what Katherine meant when she said he was confused.

He turned to the aide. "Did you find my phone?"

"Sorry, no," Katherine said.

"I *vonder vhere* it got to." Grandpa Aron placed the snow globe with a line of others on a shelf above the stove. Ones from Los Angeles, Philadelphia, New York, Texas, and London—all the places work had taken Zoe over the past few years. It had become a part of them, like the keychains her grandfather used to bring her from his Grocers Association conferences. In middle school, she'd hung her collection on her backpack. Her favorite, from Seattle, featured the Space Needle against a cerulean sky. Grandpa Aron had told her the Seattle landmark had a restaurant at the top. "One can dine and see forever. Maybe even wave to your parents in heaven." Though she knew her grandfather meant well, she told him, "I'm not a baby, Grandpa. I know that's impossible." Still, a tiny part of her wished it was possible.

Grandpa Aron sat at the kitchen table and said, "There's cream soda for you in the fridge."

Zoe grabbed a can, loving how he still made it a point to stock her favorite drink, even though she didn't live here anymore. About to shut the refrigerator, she spied his phone beside a bottle of Caesar dressing. "Look what I found." She handed him the phone.

"Ah, you're a genius." He stared at the screen, eyebrows furrowed.

"What's wrong?"

"I think I hung up on Chana. She called from the airport."

She froze with the can at her lips, and Katherine nodded as if to say, *See?*

"No, Grandpa." Zoe touched his arm. "You spoke to me. I called from the airport to tell you I'd landed."

His focus bounced between her and the phone as he worked to remember. "Right, you did."

This wasn't the first time her grandfather had confused Zoe with his older sister, despite the fact that Chana died long before Zoe was born.

Zoe sat. "How are you feeling, Grandpa?"

"The *vay* an old man feels." He batted away her concern. "You know, you look more like Chana every day. Two beauties."

Zoe never tired of hearing how she'd inherited her curly blond hair and amber eyes from the great-aunt for whom she'd always had a strange affinity.

"Do you have a photo of her?" Katherine asked.

Aron gazed at Katherine as if trying to understand the question.

"Unfortunately, no," Zoe said.

Grandpa Aron's attention drifted to the snow globes on the shelf. Zoe stood, motioning for Katherine to join her outside the kitchen.

In the hall, Zoe quietly told the aide, "My grandfather, his sister, and mother were Holocaust survivors. Photos and family mementos were lost in the war. He's never talked about it much. I know they survived two Jewish ghettos in Poland and a concentration camp. After the war, they'd lived in a displaced persons camp, then in Austria." Zoe whispered, "A week before they were to immigrate to the United States, Chana died in a fire at a hotel in Vienna."

"How awful." Katherine pressed a hand to her chest.

"Zoe?" her grandfather called.

"Coming . . ."

"You two visit and I'll get his bed ready," Katherine said.

"There you are," Grandpa Aron said as Zoe rejoined him at the table. He leaned toward her. "I have a secret. Can I trust you?"

"Of course. What is it?"

Aron's eyes grew glassy as he said, "Chana and I *vill* see each other soon. She says *ve're* safe and she's going to bake me her *Cremeschnitte*." He tipped closer. "My sister is the best baker in the *vorld*. She created pastries like art in one of the finest hotels in Austria. The best there *vas* in Vienna!"

Boy, he was really fixated on Chana tonight. Zoe knew her great-aunt had liked to bake as a girl, and that Grandpa Aron's father had owned a bakery before the war. She had never heard that Chana had baked professionally, though. "Your sister worked with food, like you?"

"It was nothing like me. I spent my life peddling goods to mom-and-pop restaurants and shops." Perspiration wet his forehead. "My sister baked like our papa."

Did she work for the hotel where the fire had happened? "When, Grandpa? Before the war or after?" How, in all these years, had her grandfather never mentioned those details?

"*Shhh.* Chana's baking had to be a secret." He put a finger to his lips.

Zoe knew she should gently bring her grandpa back to reality, only . . . There he sat, his grayish-blue eyes shining, looking happier than he had in months. Her shoulders slumped. The weekend had wiped her out. Her schedule covering the Midwest Food Truck Rodeo had been jam-packed and the weather in Chicago had stayed below freezing. She'd worked through the entire flight back, drafting, revising, and submitting two articles to her editor. All she wanted now was to visit with her grandfather and relax. Was it so wrong to let him go on uncorrected?

"I won't tell anyone. Your secret is safe with me," she finally said.

His brows pulled together. "Are you Chana's daughter?"

She gathered his hands in hers. "I'm Zoe. Your son Steven's daughter. I'm your granddaughter."

He searched her face. "Yes, Zoe." He touched her cheek, then pointed to the soda can. "I bought those for you. Cream soda's your favorite."

"You're the best." Zoe kissed the back of his hand. She had known plenty of sorrows in her twenty-eight years. Unrequited crushes. Friendships grown apart. And the most cataclysmic sorrow of all: the death of her parents when she was eleven. She hated having to add her grandfather to the list—her only family, forgetting who she was.

"It's nine thirty," Katherine said, returning.

"Bedtime." Grandpa Aron struggled to his feet.

"I'll come say good night in a minute," Zoe said.

When they'd gone, Zoe checked his phone's call log. There were two incoming calls: hers after landing at RDU, and an international number a few hours earlier. If someone in Europe had called her grandfather, it could be what triggered today's confusion. She hit redial.

"*Hallo*," answered a man. "*Die Kaiserin Hotel, wie kann ich ihnen behilflich sein?*"

The fellow's German greeting surprised her. "Do you speak English?"

"Yes. This is the Empress Hotel. How can I help you?"

"This number called my phone and I'm trying to figure out why," she said.

"Perhaps a guest of ours called."

"Where is your hotel located?"

"On Kärntner Ring in Vienna."

She couldn't imagine who would call her grandfather from Vienna. She'd lived with her grandparents since she was eleven and knew all their friends. There was no one in Europe. She switched the call to speaker and pulled up the hotel's website. A photo of a regal, cream-colored building filled the screen. *Fancy.* More like a palace than a hotel.

"Is there something I can assist you with?" He sounded impatient.

Her pulse quickened, and she couldn't believe what she was about to ask. "Would you put me through to Chana Rosenzweig?"

"One moment, please." Then, "We have no guest by that name. Is there anything else I may assist you with?"

Of course there was nothing else. What she had asked was insane. "I'm sorry," she said. "I'm sure it was a wrong number."

She found her grandfather upstairs settled in bed, reading glasses perched on the end of his nose as he read an article she'd written for *Savouries*, the venerable culinary magazine where she was a staff writer.

"It's terrific," he said. "Who knew a roasted chicken could change someone's life?"

"Is that what you took from it?" She laughed.

"I'm proud of you." He dropped the magazine on the bed. A bottle of Ambien stood on his night table, prescribed for his insomnia.

She knew he was proud of her. He used to tell her that her writing was *beshert*. Her destiny, though lately she wasn't so sure. Breaking into *Savouries* had boosted Zoe's career, yet, for the past two years, the magazine's managing editor, Wes Donnelly, had stuck her with writing soft stories like "The Best Roasted Chicken in America." The idea of pushing for more serious assignments made her gut twist. After losing her parents, Zoe avoided conflict. Though, occasionally, she pushed the matter. Recently, she'd pitched a story on the effect climate change had on oyster harvesting. Wes told her, "Stick with lifestyle pieces. You're good at them."

She smoothed her grandfather's covers. "I should go." His eyes were closed, and she dimmed the lights the way he liked them.

"Chana?" he said softly.

Her breath hitched. *Tell him you're Zoe!* her thoughts cried, but when his watery gaze met hers, she couldn't bear to break the spell.

Grandpa Aron tapped two fingers twice against his chest and looked at her expectantly. She tapped her fingers twice against her chest, and he relaxed into the pillows. Zoe and her grandfather had been exchanging this gesture for as far back as she could remember. It was their shorthand for *I love you*, and now she wondered if it was something he'd also shared with his sister.

Zoe left his door ajar and found Katherine in the living room, folding laundry. "His confusion is worse," Zoe said.

Katherine folded a white undershirt and flicked sympathetic eyes at Zoe. "He was working on the jigsaw puzzle and mumbling to himself while I was making lunch." She gestured to the corner table, where half of the Tottenham Hotspur Stadium puzzle was assembled. "From the little that I heard, he was in a different world."

"I'll call his doctor tomorrow. Thanks, Katherine." Zoe grabbed her coat and backpack and left.

Worry about her grandfather stalked her on the five-block walk to her studio apartment in the same Oakwood neighborhood. A place that had never felt like home. She wished, not for the first time, that she could stop Grandpa Aron's decline, while knowing she was powerless to do so.

The next morning, Zoe was in Walgreens picking up Grandpa Aron's prescription and the lemon hard candies he liked when Phyllis, the morning health aide, called.

"I'm sorry, I have bad news," Phyllis said.

Zoe's fingers tightened around the candy. "Please don't tell me he fell again." He'd missed a stair last month and, fortunately, he'd only incurred a bruise on his hip. No broken bones.

"No, it's not that." The aide hesitated and Zoe's mind raced. Had he somehow wandered away from the house and gotten lost? She needed to get over there. "I'm so sorry." Phyllis's voice was somber. "Zoe, he's gone. He passed during the night. Probably another stroke."

In the seconds between hearing the news and grief swallowing her whole, the world quieted and Zoe experienced a strange sense of peace. Grandpa Aron had died believing he'd spoken to his dead sister and that he was safe—though from what Zoe couldn't even begin to imagine.

Chapter Two

Zoe

Raleigh, North Carolina
March 2018

Three weeks after Grandpa Aron's funeral, Zoe stood in his kitchen and scowled at the two stuffed garbage bags in the living room. For days, she'd been sifting through her grandfather's paperwork, searching for any overlooked investment or bank account. So far, she'd turned up nothing.

She tapped the Hicks Realty brochure on the counter. The one and only Linda Hicks, who lived up the block, had dropped it off a few days after Grandpa Aron's shiva.

"I don't think I want to sell," Zoe had told the agent.

"Consider it, dear," Linda said. "This area is hot."

Since her grandfather's death, Zoe had inherited everything her grandparents had owned, including the home's outstanding sixty-thousand-dollar mortgage. Grandpa Aron's funeral costs had eaten half his savings, leaving her with a few bonds worth less than fifteen thousand dollars. Wanting to keep the house, Zoe had asked her landlord to let her out of her apartment lease, to no avail. She'd placed a Craigslist ad to sublet it, also with no luck. Her job didn't earn her enough, not even with her side hustle tutoring high school English students. She'd consulted her grandfather's accountant, who told Zoe, "If you were my daughter, I'd tell you that unless you find a forgotten investment or savings account, you should sell."

But selling the house felt like trading the last link to her family for some cushioning in her bank account. Zoe shoved the brochure into a drawer.

In the living room, she paused by the bookcase filled with family photos—the sepia-toned picture of her grandparents' wedding, a goofy picture of Zoe and her parents at the Bronx Zoo, others when Zoe was an infant, and several framed shots of her grandmother with the Snazzy Gals, her senior dance troupe. Zoe smiled, recalling their elaborate costumes. Sequined gowns, tuxedo jackets, and *dear God*, a veritable flock of pink and red feather boas. She ran a finger along the shelf of her grandfather's books, touching the well-worn spines. He'd always loved a good mystery. A collection of Agatha Christie's novels filled two shelves, aligned from her first book, *The Mysterious Affair at Styles*, to her last, *Postern of Fate*.

Zoe climbed the stairs to her grandparents' room.

The stillness scraped her heart raw. Her grandparents' dark mahogany bed, night tables, and dresser still dominated the room. She traced a finger over a rose carved into the headboard, the wood smooth as a flower petal.

She opened the closet, her gaze catching for a moment on his shirts and pants hanging lifelessly from the rod. Zoe brought a sleeve to her cheek and caught the faint smell of nutmeg and cloves, remnants of

Grandpa Aron's favorite aftershave. She teared up remembering how she and her grandfather had packed away her grandmother's things together. Grandpa Aron's clothes could wait for another day.

Zoe slid three full boxes from the back of the closet, intent on sifting through them. Most of the contents were likely trash. The first box she emptied held random bits—stacks of old receipts, envelopes with photos from a time long before cell phones, and even a chipped kiddush cup.

Zoe plucked a manila envelope from another box, sat on the floor, and flipped it over. Her name appeared on the front in her grandfather's block handwriting. He'd dated it *February 26, 2018*. The day Zoe had returned from Chicago. The day he'd died.

Her body buzzed as she shook out the contents, finding several stapled computer pages and a smaller yellowing envelope.

Written in black marker across the top of the first printout was: *Important! For Zoe's future.*

After Grandpa Aron's stroke, he'd leave himself reminder notes. He'd scrawled them across envelopes and on Post-its stuck to the fridge and kitchen counters. Zoe flipped through the pages. They were magazine articles. According to the corner date, Grandpa Aron had also printed these on February 26. Confusion and curiosity braided together in the pit of her stomach as she scanned a three-page profile, published in 2017, on Martin Baking Company, a business from Australia. The story focused on their move last year from privately held to employee owned, and how the company became a global success from their home base in Sydney.

She picked up another printout, keen to understand why her grandfather had wanted her to have these. The second article was from *Life* magazine's archives. Published in 1960, it was also about Martin Baking Company and their popular Fudgies, a chocolate-coated biscuit. A Google search of Fudgies filled her phone with pictures of the familiar chocolate-wafer cookies' blue packaging.

Grandpa Aron had worked in sales for a food distributor, and at least once a year, he brought home Fudgies from a specialty grocer in his territory. She flipped to the article's only photograph of a man in profile with a pageboy cap pulled low over his brow, leaning against a Martin Baking Company truck and holding a cigarette. Smoke made the picture hazy. The description read: *Henri Martin, beside a Martin Baking Company delivery truck, 1960.*

Zoe couldn't fathom what these articles or this company had to do with her.

She turned her attention to the smaller envelope, wondering what was inside. Of course, she hoped for some kind of message from her grandfather. Instead, she unfolded three sheets of yellowing paper. The first sported a small black-and-white picture, like a passport photo.

Certificate of Identity in Lieu of Passport—GOOD FOR ONE JOURNEY ONLY was stamped across the top. Below that was the name Aron Rosenzweig.

"Oh, my." She brought the page closer. This was an official document, and the small photo was of her teenage grandfather. The date leapt off the page: July 25, 1946.

These were Grandpa Aron's traveling papers for use after the war. Her hand trembled. Zoe had never seen a picture of her grandfather as a child or teenager. She was holding a piece of history. The other documents were also traveling papers, one for her great-grandmother Ruth, and another for her great-aunt Chana.

Chills rolled up her spine.

It wasn't exactly like looking in a mirror, but as her grandfather always claimed, there was an undeniable resemblance. Zoe and her great-aunt both had heart-shaped faces, wide-set eyes, and petite noses. Zoe brought the photo closer. Chana's mouth was wider, her lips more bow-shaped, but not that different. And they were both blond.

Her great-aunt stared out from the picture with determination.

The document came from the American Consulate General in Wien. *Vienna.* The departure dates matched on all three documents: July 25, 1946. Zoe searched her memory, recalling what Grandpa Aron had told her about her great-aunt's death. She'd died a week before they were supposed to leave Vienna. That meant Chana had died around July 18. She read the rest:

Name: Chana Rosenzweig

Height: 5'4" Hair color: Blond Eye color: Hazel

Distinguishing marks: Scars on chest

Birthdate: January 21, 1927 Place of birth: Vilna, Poland

They had the same eye color, though Zoe considered her own eyes as amber. She already knew that Vilna was now called Vilnius and was in Lithuania, though during World War II it had been part of Poland. The document's last line read: Accompanied by: Aron Rosenzweig-Brother, Ruth Rosenzweig-Mother, Meyer Suconick-Husband, and included birthdates for each.

Husband?

Grandpa Aron had never mentioned his sister was married. According to the document's dates, she was nineteen. Not too young for marriage in the forties. In a Jewish Studies course, Zoe had learned how Holocaust survivors in the displaced persons camps married in exceedingly large numbers, and the birthrate in the camps skyrocketed in the first half of 1946.

If Chana *had* married, where was Meyer Suconick now? He could have died with her in the fire. Or not? Zoe stared out the window at the oak tree sporting new buds. It was possible he might be someone who could shed light on her family's history. Did Grandpa Aron mean for her to find this man? She scanned Chana's paper again, noting the birth dates listed for her traveling partners.

According to the listing for Meyer's birthday, he had been twenty-one years old, meaning today, he'd be . . . Disappointed, she set the paper down. He'd be ninety-three. Grandpa Aron had died at eighty-seven.

She checked the other traveling papers and found a separate black-and-white photo stuck to the back of one page. Carefully, she peeled it off.

There were three people in the grainy shot: Chana, looking as she did on her traveling papers, a teenage Grandpa Aron holding what looked like an old soccer ball, and another man who she didn't recognize. The man was taller than Aron and Chana, perhaps in his early twenties, and with a wrestler's build, his defined biceps visible in a long-sleeved shirt. Where Grandpa Aron boasted a wide, boyish grin, and Chana had a faint smile, this man's expression was somber.

The picture's background was an empty lot with mounds of rubble around the perimeter, and a bombed-out building in the background. The man's square jaw jutted forward.

She flipped the photo over and found a notation: Aron, Chana, and Meyer. Vienna, 1946.

Meyer. The same name on Chana's traveling papers.

Zoe picked up the *Life* article, thinking there was a resemblance. "What do you know?" she said. She'd be damned if she didn't see a likeness now to the man against the truck in the magazine's article.

She compared them side by side. Both pictures were slightly fuzzy, and with Martin's cap pulled low, it was hard to make out all his features. But there were similarities between Henri Martin and Meyer. Their height. Their build. Their determined square jaws. She snapped photos of both with her phone, enlarging them to analyze, but they were too distorted.

This was crazy. These photos were taken fourteen years apart, and a gazillion men had broad shoulders and square jaws. Yet her instincts told her there was a resemblance. It was the same sense she got when she was pitching stories for *Savouries* and landed on an idea that she knew would be *the one.*

Why hadn't Grandpa Aron handed her this envelope when she'd returned from Chicago? Had he intended to, but forgotten? Or had he believed he had more time? If only that were so. She would have asked questions and maybe he would have answered.

Her thoughts traveled back to a time in school when she had first learned of her grandfather's war stories. She'd interviewed him for her fifth-grade social studies project on family histories.

Together at her grandparents' kitchen table, and when Zoe's parents were still alive, Grandpa Aron had talked about how in June 1941 he and his family had fled toward the Soviet Union as the Germans were invading Vilna.

"Bombs dropped all around us," he said. "Many died. After two days on the run, the German army drew near, forcing us to return to Vilna. Eventually, the Nazis herded us into a ghetto. They controlled the city."

He told Zoe how his family had shared a cramped apartment with others starting in September 1941 until the ghetto's liquidation in fall 1943. Then the Rosenzweigs hid in an attic with three other families.

"My sister, Chana, helped the resisters," he said proudly, "and they told her that if *ve* reported to the courtyard, *ve vould* either be taken by train to the camps or killed in the Ponary Forest. People *vere* learning *vhat* happened *vhen* other ghettos *vere* emptied. My family didn't report to the courtyard." He clasped his hands together, his knuckles white. "*Ve vent* to our *malina*."

Zoe heard Grandpa Aron's accent become more obvious as he grew upset. "What was that?" she asked.

"The name for our hiding place."

"How old were you, Grandpa?" She gripped her pen tighter and forced an encouraging smile, even though tears burned in her eyes. She wanted to model her interview style after Katie Couric, who quizzed guests on the *Today* show with a friendly smile. It wasn't working.

"I *vas tvelve.* It *vas* fall 1943."

He had been only a year older than Zoe was when she interviewed him. She imagined being in her grandfather's place and queasiness crept up her throat. Her eyes fell on her cream soda, but she didn't touch it. If she drank, she'd surely vomit.

Grandpa Aron pinched the bridge of his nose and continued. "In late 1943, the Nazis discovered our *malina. Ve vere* arrested. It was lucky they didn't shoot us." His voice had quieted to barely a whisper. As if he feared capture even now. "Instead, they transported us to a second ghetto in Kovno. Life *vas* a *bisl* easier there. Though *ve* lived in an apartment with a dozen others, the gentiles outside the ghetto tried to help by smuggling in food." Grandpa Aron told her that in the summer of 1944, the Nazis liquidated Kovno and forced the Jews into cattle cars. "They *vere* sending us to the camps," he said bitterly. "My mother and sister *vere* taken off the train at Stutthof." His gaze fixed on the hood of the stove. "The soldiers ordered me to stay on. The train took me to Dachau. I believed I *vould* never see my mother or sister again. They made me *vork* in a munitions factory."

After the war, Grandpa Aron reunited with his mother and sister in Foehrenwald, a displaced persons camp.

"What happened to your father?" she asked.

"Papa never made it out of Kovno." Zoe looked up from writing, and her grandfather was wiping his eyes. "I think *ve're* done, *maideleh*."

A knock on the doorframe made Zoe jump. Her father stood there. "I think you have enough for your report," he said. "We should head home."

"But I have more questions." Zoe looked tentatively at Grandpa Aron.

Her grandfather scraped his chair back. "Your father is right. It's enough."

When Zoe and her dad climbed into the car, she fell back against the seat. "I didn't mean to upset him."

"I know. With your grandfather, it's often better to leave the past alone."

This advice felt wrong to Zoe. "But this is for school." She faced him. "Last month, a woman who'd survived just like Grandpa spoke to our class. She *tells* her stories so people will remember, and so it won't happen again." Zoe's voice had gotten loud. The woman had grown up in Poland and had talked about how, for months, she never went outside because she was afraid the Nazi soldiers would hurt her. As the woman spoke, Zoe had imagined herself in the woman's place, and how awful it would be to always be afraid. Even now, it made her stomach hurt. "We need to talk about it," she told her father, leaving unsaid, *so it doesn't happen to me*.

"It's not your grandfather's way." He keyed the ignition, signaling the conversation was over.

Strange, how after her parents had died, and she'd gone to live with her grandparents, she'd adopted her father's protectiveness over Grandpa Aron. If the war came up, the second he grew teary, she squashed down even her own curiosity.

Now she pondered over the photo of Chana at nineteen. Love and admiration had always colored Grandpa Aron's comments about his sister. Her great-aunt had worked with the resistance. That meant she was brave. Zoe knew there was a deeper story here.

Returning to Chana's traveling papers, Zoe focused on the name Meyer Suconick. Despite his being ninety-three now, he could still be alive. Meaning there might be a *living* someone related to her (even if by marriage), and maybe this person could tell her information about her family.

Zoe picked up the *Life* article. It was too hard to believe that her dead great-aunt might have been married to the eventual head of a global baking company.

She dug through the box, past outdated coupons, canceled checks, and a worn dictionary. The only curious items were four postcards of Vienna landmarks with messages in a Slavic language. She opened a translation app on her phone. The messages were in Russian and all read: Stay in touch, K. The postmarks were from Brooklyn, and dated in June of 2002, 2006, 2011, and 2015. She shrugged and left them in the box. The next hour flew by as she tried to gather information. She googled *Meyer Suconick.* A handful of people turned up on ancestor tracking sites, though none with his exact name.

She grew frustrated by the lack of details on Meyer Suconick, Henri Martin, and Martin Baking Company. The company's website contained a little more information than what she'd found in the printed articles, but the only pictures on the site were of baked goods—none of their management or employees. When she clicked on the ABOUT tab, she found a paragraph describing the company's transition to employee-owned last year, a move prompted by Eveline Martin's lung cancer diagnosis. Before her death, Henri and Eveline had been the company's co-CEOs. Apparently, Eveline had been the culinary genius behind the company's success and had died in February. Three weeks ago. Like Grandpa Aron.

A search for the woman's obituary turned up no new information. Zoe found a bit of chatter on the company's Twitter page after her death, mostly condolences from fans of their baked goods.

The company's contact page comprised a box for consumers to send a message, and a separate email address for media inquiries belonging to their director of communications—Liam Martin-Eastman.

Further internet sleuthing turned up only one article that shed new light on the company, from a 2005 Sydney publication.

> Martin Baking Company is one of the largest privately owned businesses in Sydney and yet, it is the company most locals do not know sits right under their noses. Housed in a nondescript concrete building in suburban Putney, most don't have a clue that inside is where their favorite biscuits—Fudgies—are made. NO TRESPASSING signs adorn the fences.

The article explained how the Martins went to great lengths to maintain their anonymity, despite their success and scads of journalists from around the world seeking interviews. Stories gave estimates of the couple's wealth and equated them to a combination of Willy Wonka and Howard Hughes. The only photo Zoe could find was the same 1960 magazine photo of Henri Martin against the truck. There were none of Eveline Martin.

Zoe suddenly remembered the phone call her grandfather had received from Austria—a wrong number. But what if it related to all of this? What if it was some long-lost relative?

Impossible.

Other family members of her grandparents had been older and had passed away by the time Zoe was a little girl. If there were any distant cousins, she had never met them. Her frustration built as her thoughts ran in circles. There had to be a simpler explanation for why her grandfather had left her these documents. If only he had lived to tell her. She stuffed everything back into the envelope. Oh, how she missed him! Zoe dabbed her eyes. Grief was a bitch.

It was late, and she was exhausted. Zoe tucked the envelope under her arm, gathered her purse and keys, and left the house, locking the door behind her.

In the plum light of the fading day, she regarded the house from the sidewalk, taking in the flagstone path, the shady oak tree in front, and the bronze basket door knocker that Grandma Tess had kept filled with blue hydrangeas in summer.

Wind swept by and Zoe hugged the envelope to her chest, feeling certain it held information of great significance. *Important! For Zoe's future,* her grandfather had written.

But how was it important?

Zoe walked up the block, ruminating over what she had found. If even for a short while Meyer Suconick had been her great-aunt's husband, he must know things about her family—details her grandfather clearly believed were pertinent. Even if Meyer Suconick wasn't alive, perhaps he had a family with whom he'd shared his stories. The details of tragically losing a young wife shortly after the war could be among them. A fresh idea formed: perhaps Henri Martin was a relative of Meyer Suconick? His brother? A cousin? That could explain the resemblance.

She stopped to pull up Martin Baking's contact page. Liam Martin-Eastman was the company's director of communications.

"Let's communicate," Zoe whispered, tapping on his email address.

From: ZRosenzweig@gmail.com

To: LiamME@MartinBaking.com

Subject: Questions for Henri Martin

Dear Mr. Martin-Eastman,

My name is Zoe Rosenzweig, and I am the granddaughter of Aron Rosenzweig. He recently passed away, and among his belongings I found articles about Martin Baking Company and a 1946 photograph taken in Vienna. The picture was taken with his sister, Chana, and another man named Meyer Suconick, who I believe bears a strong resemblance to a photo of Henri Martin published in *Life* magazine in 1960.

I'm interested to learn if Henri Martin knew my grandfather or great-aunt Chana or Meyer Suconick? I would welcome the opportunity to speak to Henri Martin directly about this possible connection.

Thank you in advance for your help.
Zoe Rosenzweig

She attached snapshots of the old photograph and the *Life* magazine article. Then she hit send before she could chicken out. Her next breath was shaky as she walked toward her apartment. Grandpa Aron must have wanted her to find Meyer Suconick, and Henri Martin was a lead. She was certain. Zoe vowed to dig until she unearthed the right information. After all, she was a journalist, and if there was a way to piece this story together, she would find it.

Zoe woke early the next morning to send emails and text messages to her public relations contacts, wanting to find out who represented Martin Baking Company. While she waited for replies, she searched *Life* magazine's online archives. After, she combed through the Australian government's business registrations, hoping for a shred of new information on the company or the Martins. She even popped *Meyer Suconick* and *Henri Martin* into fresh Google searches, though she doubted they would yield new information. She simply couldn't help herself. Her mood ran the gamut from fizzy optimism to gloomy despair. Every so often, she shook one of her grandfather's snow globes aligned on the windowsill by her bed; she'd brought only a few of his belongings to her apartment. As the glittery snow settled, she heard the echo of her grandfather's words: *In* var *the* vorld *disappears this* vay, *only it never returns to how it* vas *before.*

Taking her laptop from the bed to her desk in her sparse studio apartment, she set up a Google alert for anything to do with Eveline Martin, Henri Martin, or Martin Baking Company. She checked the time. Seven. She had about ninety minutes before she needed to head to the office. Then she opened an article she was revising on last weekend's barbecue festival in Amarillo, Texas. Her phone rang. Though she didn't recognize the foreign number, she picked up quickly.

"May I speak with Zoe Rosenzweig?" asked a man's gruff voice after she'd answered.

Dare she hope this was a response from Martin Baking Company's communications director? "This is Zoe."

"This is Henri Martin."

She straightened and checked the number. This couldn't actually be *him*? *Could it?* "Thank you for responding so swiftly to my email, Mr. Martin. I appreciate it."

"Right. So, I understand you want to know if I knew your grandfather?" He spoke with an air of authority and in the most interesting accent. Vaguely Eastern European, but with some British inflection.

Silence stretched between them until she realized he was waiting for her to speak. "Yes, sir." She picked up a pen. "His name was Aron Rosenzweig."

"I knew him. I also knew your great-aunt."

"Wow! That's great news." She glanced at the list of questions she'd prepped the night before. "May I ask how you knew them?"

He fell silent. After years of interviews, Zoe knew to wait; this wasn't her first time working with a reluctant source. Eventually, he would respond.

"I prefer not to say at this time."

"Okay," she said. "We can circle back to it. Did you also know a man named Meyer Suconick?"

"Meyer Suconick." He pronounced it with a mix of reverence and contempt. "There's a name I haven't heard in a long time."

It was a nonanswer. She downed the dregs from her water bottle before asking, "Can you elaborate?"

"I'd rather not discuss it over the phone." He paused. "But I would like to talk with you. Are you familiar with the Boucher Foundation?"

"Um . . . yes! I'm a professional food writer." The Boucher Foundation was the largest nonprofit food foundation in the world, founded in the 1920s to celebrate master chefs and bakers around the world. Most considered it the international equivalent to the James Beard Foundation.

He told her, "It's not public knowledge yet, but they're awarding me and my wife, posthumously—the Lifetime Achievement Award. I'll be accepting the honor at their upcoming conference and giving their opening keynote."

She put him on speaker and checked Boucher's website. The conference was to be held in Vienna at the beginning of April. Two weeks away.

"Come see me there, and we'll talk," he said.

Zoe stared at the phone, surprised by his request. She waited for him to continue, perhaps invite her to the conference as his guest. But he made no such offer. She struggled to find a polite way to phrase her response. "Mr. Martin—forgive me, but to clarify—you're saying if I come to Vienna, you'll tell me how you knew my family?"

"I promise to tell you more than just how I knew them. And I keep my promises."

Zoe wished she had a roommate so she could silently high-five someone. She eyed the conference dates. Traveling to Vienna would be expensive, and money was tight. Zoe needed some assurance from Henri Martin, but didn't want to come off sounding transactional. "With all due respect, sir"—she waited a beat—"this would be a big trip for me. Is there anything specific you'd be willing to share about my family . . . now?"

He was quiet, but then said, "A fair question. Are you familiar with your family's war experience?"

"My grandfather told me they'd lived in two Jewish ghettos and were later sent to a concentration camp. He didn't go into details." She popped in earbuds and opened a blank document on her laptop to take notes.

"Many didn't want to talk. In the early years after the war, some who hadn't been in Europe were impatient with the survivors and their stories. 'Move on,' they would say. People grew silent and ashamed." His voice had grown rough. "When the war started, Aron and Chana were in Vilna. People knew the city as 'the Jerusalem of Lithuania.' The Nazis invaded Vilna in 1941."

"Are you from there as well?"

"No." He sounded annoyed. "Do you want to hear this or not?"

She took that to mean not to interrupt. "Forgive me. Yes, I do." Zoe twirled her silver charm bracelet, a gift from her parents on her last birthday with them. Her finger traced the medallion engraved with *We Love You*.

He continued, "After surviving the Vilna ghetto liquidation, they were sent to another ghetto, Kovno in Poland. By then it was winter 1943. Six months later, the Germans sent Aron to Dachau, and Chana and their mother to the Stutthof concentration camp." His story echoed the details her grandfather had told her long ago. He went on to tell her about their reunion after the war in the DP camp named Foehrenwald, then months later they'd arrived in Vienna.

Zoe created a timeline on a legal pad in order to keep track:

Vilna ghetto (Poland) 1941–1943 →
Kovno ghetto (Poland) 1943–1944 →
Dachau & Stutthof (Germany and Poland) 1944–1945 →
Foehrenwald displaced persons camp (Germany) 1945–1946 →
Vienna (Austria) 1946

Henri said, "Though the Allies were heroes for liberating the concentration camps, a number of the DP camps they put the refugees into caused more misery. Some Jews were forced to live with the neighbors who had persecuted them during the war. The conditions in Foehrenwald were particularly awful. There wasn't enough food or housing. Typhus was rampant."

"How did they end up in Austria?" Zoe's hand flew to her mouth. "I'm sorry, sir. I didn't mean to interrupt." She prayed she hadn't broken the spell that had opened this floodgate.

"An organization called Brihah brought them there," he said. "Meyer Suconick worked with Brihah, and he had agreed to transport the refugees from Vienna's train station to trucks that would carry them the rest of the way to Italy's ports and boats out of Europe. Chana and Aron met Meyer when they first reached the city." He quieted.

Zoe waited. "Sir?" she said. "Hello?"

"Yes, I'm here." His tone had softened. "I've brought you up to March 1946. We can go a bit further." He paused. "Picture a beautiful girl, an apprentice baker, and a black-market dealer. Their names were Chana, Elias, and Meyer. You see, it was a love triangle . . . a love story, and they were all survivors in one way or another." He fell quiet, then said, "Do you have time to hear more?"

"If you could give me one second, Mr. Martin." She glanced at the clock, then dashed off an email to Wes that she was revising her article from home and would be in the office by eleven.

Next, she told Henri Martin, "Yes, sir, for this, I have all the time in the world."

Chapter Three
Chana

Munich, Germany to Vienna, Austria
March 1946

At the Munich train station, Chana Rosenzweig pushed a strand of blond hair off her forehead and held tight to her younger, teenage brother's hand. It was impossible to tell whose palm was sweatier. Their mother was on his other side, her arm linked through his, her expression hard and impenetrable as usual.

It was strange to be out in the world this way. Moving around freely with no one in charge of you, threatening you, pointing a gun at you.

"It will be good, you'll see," she said to Aron.

"I know. We'll be together," he said.

"Always." With two fingers, she tapped her chest twice, right over her heart.

He did the same. It was how they conveyed *I love you* without words. During months spent hiding in an attic after the Nazis liquidated the Vilna ghetto, silence saved their lives.

Chana wondered how they looked to the other passengers, gaunt as they were and dressed plainly, but neatly. Both she and their mother, Ruth, wore dark wool skirts, sturdy black boots, and white blouses under their coats; the same garments distributed upon entry to every woman housed in Foehrenwald. Aron wore dark pants and a gray sweater and kept his head down.

The station smelled mostly of fumes, soot, and people. Then Chana caught a whiff of perfume as she passed a well-heeled woman in a fur coat. She couldn't remember the last time she'd inhaled something so lovely.

As they found the train to Wien, Chana was grateful to at last be free from Foehrenwald. After the war, Chana and her family, like many surviving Jews, took shelter in displaced persons camps because they had nowhere else to go. Their homes had either been destroyed by bombs or taken over by locals. Even if her family's home had been empty, Chana's mother refused to live beside neighbors who'd abused them, or in the country that had oppressed them. But they weren't free to go just anywhere. DP camp officials distributed no traveling papers, trapping refugees like Chana, her mother, and brother. They were a forgotten lot.

For months in Foehrenwald, Chana had heard whispers about a group of men organizing these escapes. They called themselves Brihah, and she learned their aim was to smuggle Jewish refugees out of Europe.

"They're former resistance fighters," some said.

"They're ex-soldiers from Britain's Jewish Brigade," others claimed.

She heard most of those smuggled out were on their way to Palestine, though some headed to Canada or America. All traveled illegally, violating those countries' immigration quotas.

For this trip, Chana and her family had been instructed to stay together, but to ignore the others in their group. From the corner of her eye, Chana caught sight of a scattered baker's dozen, those they'd traveled with on the back of a truck, all on the same clandestine trip. A few she knew from Foehrenwald—like her friend Shifra. Others Chana had never seen before. From the bits they'd shared on the ride to the Munich train station, she'd learned they were all Jewish refugees fleeing Europe. They couldn't appear to be traveling as a large group; it could draw the scrutiny of their forged papers. If they were discovered, they'd be sent back to the DP camp.

A loud whistle blew. Now Chana, Aron, and their mother boarded the train for Wien and found adjoining seats. Chana forced a smile, pretending ease, while her nerves skittered around her chest. She tried to call upon the confidence she'd used delivering messages for the Vilna ghetto's resistance.

She remembered the day Natan had recruited her.

"You look Aryan," Natan had said. "It's the perfect disguise."

Chana had jumped at the chance to fight back. Papa had long been involved with Vilna's resistance, mainly smuggling in food for the starving population.

Chana's task was to deliver books with hidden messages, first to locations within the ghetto, then beyond the wood-planked gate and barbed-wire fence into the gentile section of the city, where some partisans hid. Natan gave her the code name "Wren" because of the songbird's ability to survive in a variety of habitats. Every time she went out, she had to pretend she belonged, yet be invisible. Somehow, she'd managed it.

The train jerked, and panic washed over her. During the war, she'd stood in packed cattle cars, hurtling between places. Never knowing what she would meet when she arrived. *Work? Death?* Would she ever be able to go through daily life without reminders of all that she'd suffered?

She told herself that the thin-padded seat where she now sat was a luxury compared to what she'd once endured. Aron was beside her, his face ashen. Their mother stared off, lost in her own world.

"Chana," Aron whispered.

"*Shhh*, it's okay." She bent close. "Remember, we're on our way to Vienna. Someplace good. Take my hand." He hesitated. At fifteen, he often shrugged off her attempts to baby him. Finally, he grabbed her hand. "Breathe with me," she said, inhaling and exhaling. He followed, and the steady rhythm soothed them both.

A conductor made his way up the aisle, and the three of them gave him their tickets. Behind the conductor, two American soldiers stopped to question a group several seats away. Chana pretended to look out the window, absorbing nothing of the city that went by. Herr Schumacher, their Brihah contact, had instructed them to speak German if questioned, or Polish. Anything but Hebrew or Yiddish, which could get them sent back to the DP camp. Schumacher had been a former resistance member in Vilna and a friend of her papa's. Sweat trickled down Chana's back. Thankfully, the soldiers passed, and after they'd crossed to the next car, she relaxed a little.

An associate of Herr Schumacher's, named Meyer Suconick, would meet her family and the others in the Vienna station and escort them to lodging. Chana pictured the map Herr Schumacher had shown them prior to this trip. After one night in Vienna, they'd ride in a truck to the port in Bari, Italy. There, they'd board an illegal boat to America. Herr Schumacher had told her they'd travel on an old cargo ship. It would be crowded. When Chana relayed this to her mother, she'd said, "I'll stand on my head for the entire journey as long as it brings us to America."

The five-hour train ride passed through Germany and into Austria, trundling by big cities and average-sized towns. When they rumbled through Rosenheim, she and Aron smiled, enjoying the similarity to their surname. The land they covered alternated between beautiful and ugly. Miraculously unscarred woods, soon followed by the remnants of homes after bombs had blasted away roofs and walls.

At last, framed in the window, was a sign that read: WIEN. The train screeched as it pulled into the station.

She whispered, "We're here."

"Vienna," Aron said with a smile.

For the first time, Chana felt like the war had indeed ended. She pictured her life in America. Not being afraid all the time. Finishing her schooling. Making friends. She saw a flash of her father's bakery before pogroms and war forced its closure. In America, she wanted to become a baker. It was Papa's dream for her, and she hoped to make that dream come true.

The train doors opened, and she was on her feet, ready to take the first steps toward the rest of her life.

Chana entered the bustle of Vienna's Südbahnhof train station and hooked her arm through Aron's, who grew wan and shaky, overwhelmed by the crowd. Mama came up on his other side.

"Where is this Meyer we're supposed to meet?" Mama asked.

"We'll find him," Chana said with authority she didn't truly feel. So much could still go wrong, even at this point.

"Herr Schumacher told us he'll be wearing a bright green pocket square," Aron said. "And we should look for repairs happening in the station."

Chana scanned the packed concourse. Most of the train station appeared in good condition, save for some black burn marks on the walls and many broken windows. Glass panes were almost nonexistent since the war. She spotted a few others from their group, who searched around nervously. They looked as lost as Chana felt. Several yards away, Chana's friend Shifra bounded toward scaffolding at the right corner of the station, a section being rebuilt.

"Over there," Chana said, tying her scarf over her hair. "Head toward the scaffolding."

Their threesome slipped into the current of bodies, until a man bumped into Chana, and she lost her grip on Aron. The crowd swallowed him and her mother. Someone shoved her as she tried to go after them. The crowd thickened. Her fear ramped up as she shouldered her way out to a wall. The scaffolding was on the other side of the station.

A man stepped in front of her. "What's your hurry, Fräulein?" he asked in smooth German.

She looked into his pale, oblong face, his dark hair slicked back and accentuating an expansive forehead and widow's peak. He wore a gray suit and a dark overcoat. Though he'd said nothing alarming, a deadness to his pitch-black eyes made her step back.

"*Sprechen Sie Deutsch*?" he asked.

He must think her Austrian. "*Ja*," she said in German. "I'm with my family."

"They can wait." He touched a blond curl that had come loose from her kerchief. "Pretty."

A bald, squat, younger man joined him, his lips peeling back into a sneer, revealing several missing teeth. "Very pretty," this other man said.

Chana tucked the hair away.

The taller one said, "See, my brother likes you. My name is Kirill, and if you need work, I can find you work." His fingers snaked around her upper arm, and instinct told her he was a black-market dealer. She'd seen such men moving in and out of Foehrenwald. The dealers she knew of represented all nationalities and were both gentile and Jews. A few were trying to cobble together extra money for their futures. Some were altruistic in their intent, trading goods like food, clothes, and cigarettes to help those with nothing. But there were others who were greedy, in it solely for personal gain. Some dealers encouraged women to use their bodies as payment. Chana didn't trust a single one of them.

In an alcove a few yards away, three Soviet soldiers watched them. She recognized their wolfish grins. Her breath quickened as she worked to push away her fear. They would not help her. In fact, she suspected these two men intended to feed her to the soldiers. Had they struck some kind of bargain in advance? Herr Schumacher had warned the women in their group to be on guard for such attacks.

She yanked free. "I don't need work." She tried to move past him, but he cut her off.

"Kirill," someone yelled from behind him.

Kirill turned, and Chana ducked away, but not before glimpsing the approaching man's nice suit and broad shoulders.

"What do you want?" Kirill said, his angry voice rising above the din. "Is she another of your filthy refugees?"

Chana didn't stop to hear the rest of their exchange, not that she could make out much over the sound of her heart thundering in her ears. Grateful the crowds had thinned, she rushed to join the others in their group, who lingered in clusters near the scaffolding.

"Where'd you go?" Aron asked as she slipped in beside him. "You were there and then you weren't."

"I'm here now." She hung on to his arm to quell her shaking.

Out of the corner of her eye, she saw the man who had intervened; he strode toward them, stuffing a green handkerchief into the breast pocket of his suit.

He stood in the center of their small groups. "I'm Meyer Suconick. You can keep together now," he said in Yiddish, his tone harsh. "Come." He quickly guided them toward a nook behind a wall and out of sight of the rest of the main room. Everyone followed, though a few glanced around, including Chana, clearly remembering their warning about appearing as a large group.

Meyer noticed and said, "We're out of view as a precaution. The Allied soldiers shouldn't bother you while you're with me."

Chana's breath eased. Hopefully, this man to whom Herr Schumacher had entrusted their fate would indeed get them to Italy and off this godforsaken continent.

"Not everyone can be trusted," Meyer said once they were tucked in the alcove. "Don't be naive or careless. Some will rob you, or worse. Cross them or deny them, and you'll be sorry. And a word of warning"—he wagged a finger over them—"especially you women. Don't go out alone. If you have a male relative or friend, ask them to walk with you. Day or night. The Red Army's soldiers are hungry for revenge."

"But we're not their enemies," said a man with bushy gray eyebrows, who held up his hands as if already surrendering.

Meyer glowered. "When they have their fist in your face or their hands under your clothes, tell them that. See if it makes a difference."

Head down, embarrassment and anger set her cheeks aflame. He meant this scolding for her, and though Chana appreciated his intervening, she was neither naive nor careless.

He paused, assessing them one by one, and she stole a better look at him. Meyer Suconick's clothes appeared new, nary a fray or tear visible. He'd paired his black suit with a crisp white shirt and a wide-striped red, white, and blue tie. American colors. This lifted her hopes. The American GIs were her heroes. Meyer's biceps strained against his jacket's sleeves. She pegged him as a few years older than her, though his sharp features made him appear even older. Hadn't war aged them all? Still, she had to admit his looks were striking, though in the rough, exhilarating way of a man who was always game for a fight.

Shifra cut in beside Chana and whispered, "Meyer's handsome, isn't he?"

An unsurprising comment from her friend. Like Chana, Shifra was nineteen, but had lost her parents and sisters in the Warsaw ghetto. She was eager to marry and gushed with optimism at any new man she met.

Shifra cast her longing brown eyes at Meyer and smoothed her dark wavy hair attractively around her jaw. Others saw Shifra's oval face and described her as plain looking, but Chana couldn't disagree more. Her friend's perpetually bright spirit brought a rosy glow to her cheeks. Chana thought her lovely.

"He is good-looking, but in a rugged way," Chana said quietly.

"There was talk before we left Foehrenwald," Shifra whispered.

"Meyer Suconick was with a partisan group in the Białowieża Forest that smuggled Jews out of the Bialystok ghetto. Now he's one of the most successful black-market dealers in Austria."

Before Chana could respond, Meyer said, "You made it this far. *Shalom* to you all."

A few of the refugees broke into tears. An older woman kissed Meyer's knuckles. "Bless you," she said.

Meyer rubbed his cheek, clearly uncomfortable. "I want all of you to come closer."

The group shuffled in.

"I have unfortunate news," Meyer said. "While you were on the train, word came—the British army captured several ships full of refugees outside the port in Bari. They ordered everyone on board to another DP camp. It's too dangerous for you to go to Italy right now. You'll stay in Vienna until it's safe to travel to the ports again."

Disappointment surged through Chana. She looked to her mother, whose frown matched her own. Others protested.

Meyer held up his hands. "I'm only the messenger. I don't deserve your anger. I'm your salvation." He smiled proudly, as if they should welcome this devastating news.

"Why should we believe you?" Chana asked, stepping forward. "Herr Schumacher told us we would be here for one night."

Several others voiced agreement.

He glanced at Chana, his eyes the color of roasted chestnuts, and utterly fearless. Suddenly, and uncharacteristically, shy, she dropped her gaze to her boots.

Meyer cleared his throat. "Herr Schumacher and the others who put you on the train were arrested." Some murmured concern. Meyer kept talking. "There will be no more refugees leaving Foehrenwald. *I* am your only hope. Of course, you are free to leave. Take your chances alone in Vienna. Or get on the train and go back. Let them take away your traveling papers. Perhaps someday you'll get out of Europe."

He was flippant regarding their plight, and Chana didn't appreciate it.

"I'm not giving anyone my papers," Chana's mother said, an edge in her voice. "They may be forged, but at least they work."

Chana smiled with pride at her mother's defiance.

Meyer raised an eyebrow. "A smart decision."

"What will we do until the ports are safe?" one man asked.

Meyer drew near. "Today, I'll find you jobs and a place to live. Then you're on your own." He tilted his head. "You'd be wise to avoid others promising simple work or easy money."

Chana sensed he meant the man named Kirill. His words hit her as another rebuke, and as Meyer turned toward her, she looked away.

He told them, "In time, the ports will reopen. There are Brihah members working across Europe to reestablish routes. Once they contact me, you'll be on your way. So decide what you want to do."

Chana and her family didn't have enough money to buy a train ticket; she doubted any of them did. Besides, returning to Foehrenwald was out of the question. She would not go back. She turned to Aron and her mother. "I don't fully trust him," Chana said. "But I don't see any other way."

Her mother shot her a look. "We should have stayed in Foehrenwald."

"Mama, you said yourself you want to keep your papers," Aron said.

"What good are they if no country will take us? *This* was your sister's idea."

Chana stiffened at her mother's scolding. "You agreed we needed to take matters into our own hands."

"We shouldn't have left Zvi," Mama said while wringing her hands. "He would have made a fine husband for you and he wanted to take care of us."

Everyone in the DP camp knew Ruth Rosenzweig wanted to make a *shidduch* for her daughter. They would smile and wink at Ruth's attempts to match Chana with any single Jewish man willing to show up under a chuppah, as though it was something Chana wanted. Better still if the fellow had a shred of influence. Chana didn't want to marry yet, but went along with Mama's wishes, because her mother was desperate for them to reach Papa's family in America. When they were in the Vilna ghetto, Papa would buoy Chana's spirits with stories about his parents and brother and their grocery store in a place called New Jersey. When Chana pictured them, she saw endless shelves of food, and imagined herself there with their family, fed and safe.

Mama had arranged for Chana to marry Zvi Baitman, the newly appointed Jewish police captain in Foehrenwald—a man as old as her father. Her mother believed Zvi's position and proximity to the American soldiers in charge of the camp would help them gain visas to the United States.

Chana found Zvi polite, and with a decent sense of humor, and in a short time, despite her reluctance to marry so soon after liberation, she grew fond of him. However, a week after she'd accepted his proposal, he changed their emigration plans.

Now Chana told her mother, "You want us to go to America, don't you? Zvi only wanted us if we would abide by his wish to settle in Belgium." When Zvi had told Chana this, she'd approached Brihah operatives, seeing the opportunity as two escapes in one.

It had been a cold winter morning before dawn as Chana snuck out of Foehrenwald and trekked two miles to the yellow building, where it was rumored Brihah's men were staying. Her heart had raced as she walked. She had no identification papers and no permission to leave the DP camp.

Chana found the building and knocked. When the door opened, stale air hit her nostrils, and before she could make out any of the features on the wide, shadowy man in front of her, he jerked her inside.

She found herself in a dark room, struggling to make out the man gripping her arms. His fingers dug into her skin, and she cried out. Her sight adjusted, and she saw him glowering at her, unkempt brown hair sticking out all over.

"Who are you?" he demanded in German, shaking her so hard her kerchief fell back. "How did you find us?"

She struggled to speak. Having heard from others that these men were Jewish, she answered in Yiddish. "I've heard you're helping Jews leave Europe." He stopped shaking her. "We're in Foehrenwald. My family and I need to get out."

He smacked her across the face. Hard. Her cheek throbbed. If not for his hold on her arms, her rubbery legs would have given out.

"Tell me who sent you." The man had switched to Yiddish as well, but was no less menacing. He tugged her hair. "Blond. You're not a Jew, and I am no one's fool. Are you working for the British?" Two more men appeared in the doorway at the back of the room; they said nothing, but she could feel them watching.

"No one sent me. I'm a Jew who wants out of the DP camp."

"You're a spy. You want to shut us down." He struck her again, and she felt as if her eye had exploded.

Stand! her mind barked, the way it had when she and the other prisoners stood in the yard at the Stutthof concentration camp. It didn't matter about the temperature or how long the guards forced them to stand. If you didn't stay on your feet, the guards would whip you to death, then let their dogs rip you apart. "I'm not a spy. My name is Chana Rosenzweig, and all I want is my freedom."

A sharp breath came from the doorway. "What's going on here?" asked a gruff voice.

Before Chana could see which of the other men had spoken, the brute shook her again. "This one pounded on our door. She's working with the British."

One fellow stepped out of the shadows. He was a bear of a man with a white scar running through one eyebrow.

Chana gasped. "Herr Schumacher? Is that you?"

"Chana, I can't believe it," he said. "Let her go," Herr Schumacher ordered.

The man released her with a shove. She held back from cradling her cheek; she wouldn't give him the satisfaction.

"Child, it's hard to believe you're alive," Herr Schumacher said.

Child. The word was in equal measures an ode to her youth and a eulogy for who she'd once been.

Herr Schumacher ran a hand over her head. "Your hair."

"It's coming back." Progress from when the concentration camp guard had razored it to her scalp, leaving gashes as well.

"How is your papa?" he asked.

"He—" She shook her head. "Papa was killed in Kovno."

Herr Shumacher's eyelids drooped. "I'm sorry to hear that."

She fought back tears.

"Chana is my good friend's daughter," Schumacher told the other men. He scratched his cheek. "What brought you to us?"

In a rush, she told him how her mother wanted them to go to America, to her father's family. "We've been trying to find our relatives through the Red Cross and other agencies, so they can sponsor us. We've had no luck. There are so many in our situation, and I fear our requests are buried among them. Can you help us?"

Herr Schumacher walked to the paper-covered windows facing the street, while the other men left the room. "I know the conditions in the camp are difficult, and slowly, we've been getting people out." He turned toward her. "But, Chana, we're focused on *Aliyah Bet*."

They were helping people immigrate to Palestine. "I read the British aren't letting Jews in."

"They're not, and the Brits have intercepted six of our boats. It's why my comrade was so hard on you."

She brought her fingers to her face; her cheek was hot to the touch. "What about America? Do you have boats going there?"

"A few. But it's just as risky."

She grabbed his hands. "Please, I beg you, help us."

He turned her hands over in his. His calluses and scars matched her own, making it hard to tell whose hands belonged to the old man and whose were that of a young woman. He sighed. "All right. There's a ship departing in two weeks. I should be able to include your family. I'll be in touch with instructions."

Chana embraced Herr Schumacher. "Thank you."

She didn't linger, and once she was back at Foehrenwald, she convinced her mother this would be their swiftest chance to reach America.

Now, in the Vienna train station, Mama sniffed. "Belgium. Zvi should have known that would never do!"

Chana grasped her mother's hand and the older woman's rough skin scratched against her palm. Before the war, her mother's hands had been smooth as butter. "I know you want what's best for us, Mama. We're closer to America than we were before." She gestured at Meyer. "Did you hear the man? We're still on our way."

"I hope so." Mama squeezed Chana's hand.

Over the next few minutes, Meyer asked where they were from and where they'd been during the war. People answered in hushed tones about the camps, the ghettos, and loved ones murdered.

When his attention turned to Chana and her family, a clot of emotion filled her throat. Horrors from the past six years flashed in her mind as her mother stepped forward.

"We are from Vilna," Mama said. "I am Ruth Rosenzweig and these are my children, Aron and Chana. The Nazis killed my husband when they marched us out of the Kovno ghetto."

Chana dug her nails into her palm and blinked back tears, grateful for Mama's ability to summon her voice.

Her mother glanced at the others before continuing. "My daughter and I were sent to Stutthof and my son went to Dachau."

"And you found each other?" Meyer asked.

"Yes. At Foehrenwald." She lifted her chin. "My husband has family in America. Parents and a brother. That's where we want to go. How long will it be until the ports are safe?"

"If I could predict the future, I'd be a rich man. How many times did you ask when the war would end?" Meyer said.

"There must be different ports," Mama said.

Meyer took full measure of Chana's mother. "Different ports? Do you think they fall from trees?"

"Of course not. I'm not a child!" Mama's nostrils flared. "Still, isn't there another way? Another route?"

He stepped closer, so close that Chana could feel the heat radiating off his body. "It's too dangerous. You'll wait."

Her mother's lips flattened into a firm line, but she stayed quiet.

Meyer turned to Shifra, and Chana took a fresh look at him, this man who stood his ground with her mother. He was well-dressed and handsome—that was undeniable. She also appreciated his confidence and frankness, qualities she valued in herself.

"Europe has become a continent of mourning," he said. "None of you are special. Everyone has lost family, including me." He straightened. "I'm a Latvian Jew, from Riga. I joined the Soviet army when I was sixteen, thinking I would keep my family safe. My family died anyway. After the Germans ambushed my battalion, I lived in the forest for the rest of the war."

There were murmurs of condolences.

"I don't want your pity," Meyer snapped. "Build your lives back. That will be your sweet revenge." Then he clapped once. "Let's go." Meyer strutted from the station, and they straggled behind him.

Chana fell in between Aron and Mama and replayed Meyer's words in her mind.

Build your lives back. That will be your sweet revenge.

She couldn't agree more.

Chapter Four

Chana

Meyer breezed through the streets like he owned them, and everyone else obliged by moving out of his way. Two of the older refugees walked beside him, and from Chana's position at the edge of their ragtag group, she listened to them peppering him with questions. He barely looked at them when he answered; it probably wasn't the first time he'd heard these queries.

Where will we live? Will we be paid for our work?

Will there be other Jews nearby? Is there food?

And the most pressing question of all: *Are we safe here?*

Chana took in the city, and despite their dashed plans, she clung to her hope that better days were on the horizon. She tried to imagine what Papa would think of this postwar Vienna. As in other parts of Europe, war had hit this city hard. Bombs had blasted apart buildings. Fire had scorched countless walls. Rubble littered the sidewalks and streets. A filthy doll stuck out from a pile of bricks. Yet, in the city's skeletal remains, she saw strong bones. In time, these buildings, and this city, could become whole again.

At one point, they passed window boxes holding fresh blooms, beneath windows covered by wood. A sudden gust of wind tickled the pink and purple petals, emitting hope. Papa once told her how when a person smells something sweet, their body leans toward it as if yearning to eat the air. Chana had seen this prove true repeatedly when customers came into his bakery. Chana filled her lungs with perfumed air and tried to taste hope.

She spotted a shuttered bakery, the sign's lettering worn away, and she wondered if any remnant of her father's store in Vilna still existed.

"We'll be baking together full-time when you turn twenty," Papa would say. "You'll be my partner. A woman business owner."

The group turned onto Argentinierstrasse—one of the few roads with an actual street sign. Meyer pointed out a redbrick cathedral with a bell tower clock. "That's Pfarre St. Elisabeth. If you need the time, check the clock. It's always right." He tapped his watch crystal, his lips lifting into a smile.

Even when Chana looked back at the clock from several blocks away, she could still make out the time—noon on this first day of her new life.

A gray-haired man with a scraggly beard called to them in Yiddish from the middle of the block. "Suconick, I need to talk to you." He sounded as though he'd swallowed a handful of rocks.

Meyer signaled for them to wait as he told the man, "Feingord, I'm busy."

"A minute only . . . I missed you at the Karlsplatz this morning."

"What is it?" His impatience mirrored that of a teacher with a pestering, yet favored, student.

"I need a carton of Chesterfields and two cans of meat."

"And what do you have for me?"

The man held up a flashlight in a hand that was missing three fingers. Chana touched the top buttons on her blouse, the white cotton concealing her cigarette burns. The Nazi soldier had used an identical flashlight to find her in the camp barrack that night. Hatred ricocheted through her to the point she feared she would blow apart.

Meyer checked the flashlight, which failed to come on. "It's not working."

"It needs new batteries." Feingord let out an innocent chuckle. "If anyone can fix it, it's you, Meyer Suconick."

Meyer pocketed the flashlight and clapped a hand on the man's back. "Go see Vlad. Tell him I said to give you the cigarettes and meat. Don't tell anyone I gave in on the price."

"Not a soul." The man brought a finger to his lips.

"Did you go to the Jewish soup kitchen on Kleine Pfarrgasse like I told you to?"

"It's been a godsend."

Meyer gave Feingord a satisfied nod, then told the rest of them, "Follow me."

They were on the move again, Feingord telling them as they passed, "You're in good hands."

Chana repeated the street name for the soup kitchen, as she and her family might need it.

After a few blocks, Shifra was beside her again. "He's wonderful, don't you think?" Her eyes flitted to Meyer.

Chana shrugged. "I don't think, and neither should you. We know next to nothing about him."

Still, she had a clearer picture of Meyer now. He was a black-market dealer, like the man who'd accosted her in the train station.

"So serious and keeping yourself wrapped up. It's no way to live."

Shifra gave Chana's kerchief an affectionate pat. "Has your mama given up making a *shidduch* for you?"

Chana smiled at her friend's light teasing. "We both know my mother means well."

"Well, I hope that by the time we're sent to Italy, I'll be traveling with a new husband at my side." Shifra hugged Chana's arm. "And why shouldn't he be someone powerful, like Meyer?"

"And I'll be overjoyed for you," she told Shifra. "But as for me, I'm headed to America, not the chuppah." The Nazis had stolen her girlhood, and she would not let any man dictate the rest of her life. She'd seen enough young women marry before the war, their work or ambitions laid to rest after marriage. Chana had other plans for her life, the ones she and her father had stoked for years. Her seriousness was an asset.

A few blocks later, they stopped outside a café with its awning partially torn away.

Meyer said, "The café needs waiters and dishwashers." He pulled several men from the group and led them inside.

Over the next few hours, Meyer herded them through the streets, stopping at several other places, mostly dilapidated cafés where a few gained jobs. Those with work either billeted above the cafés or went to boardinghouses.

Chana froze when they arrived at a tailor shop with paper-covered windows. The business resembled a tailor's window from the Kovno ghetto—its faded Polish sign had read: WYKONANY RĘCZNIE. This one claimed: HANDGEMACHTE. Both meant handmade. Meyer pounded on the door.

A memory came back to her.

"Handmade, like all our bread and cakes," Papa had whispered when he saw the sign in Kovno. "A good omen."

"Yes," Chana had agreed, and she didn't need to see inside her father's mind to know he was picturing his bakery.

Now standing on this street in Vienna, Chana closed her eyes, trying to force away any thoughts of their last days in the Kovno ghetto, the place they'd been sent after two years in the brutal Vilna ghetto. After arriving in Kovno, they'd lived in an apartment with a dozen others. Yet, conditions had been better in Kovno than in Vilna. Kovno's gentiles secretly tried to help their imprisoned neighbors, sneaking them food, and at times, even medicine. Chana's family had clung to the hope that they would remain together in Kovno until the war ended.

Unfortunately, that wasn't to be. The night before the final *Aktion* emptying the Kovno ghetto, Chana had told Papa about a shuttered tailor shop where partisans were hiding people.

Mama was against it. "You'll get us killed," her mother said.

"They're killing people anyway," Chana said.

"We should listen to Chana," Papa said. "We could die, or this could be what saves us."

It was 1944, and they believed the whispered horrors about people who were taken away. Torture. Executions in the woods. Concentration camps, where a large number of Jews were being murdered.

In the morning, they proceeded through packed streets with hundreds of other Jews. Dozens of SS soldiers and Einsatzgruppen aimed machine guns at the crowd and barely restrained their snarling German shepherds as they herded everyone toward the ghetto gate. Papa whispered to Chana as they walked, "If we get separated, if something happens to me, look after Mama and Aron. Mama will need your help."

"Hardly," she said.

"She's not as tough as she seems. And one last thing . . ." He smoothed an affectionate hand over her hair. "Remember everything I've taught you, and all your gifts. You will live a glorious life, *shayna maidel.* Promise me this."

"I promise . . . but nothing will separate us. The war will end, and you'll open a new bakery. A better bakery. We'll do it together."

He squeezed her hand so tight it hurt. "Yes, we will."

When they arrived on the street with the tailor shop, she tugged on Papa's sleeve and he put a firm grip on Mama and Aron. They stole away from the crowd unnoticed.

Paper covered the shop's windows. Papa nodded, and Chana knocked hard. The door opened, revealing the sliver of a man's face. "Let us in," she said. "It's my parents, my brother, and me."

"There's no room," he said.

"You must, please." She kept her hand against the rough wood.

The man pressed against the door, but Papa stepped around her, sandwiching his leg in the narrow space. "Please, I'm begging you," he said.

Seconds ticked by, but the door didn't close. Finally, the man said, "We'll take your wife and children."

Papa flinched, then said, "Thank you." He shoved the door open and pushed them all inside. "Papa, no," Chana said.

Her father took several steps back from the alcove. Shots rang out from the street, followed by screaming and shouting. Papa crumpled to the ground. Chana's body went numb. He was face down in the street, blood pooling around his head. People stepped around him, not even looking.

The door slammed shut behind them. "Papa," she whispered. The room was too dark to see.

"Shut up," the man said.

Aron clung to her arm, and Mama whimpered. Chana wanted to scream. Papa was bleeding? They needed him. They were supposed to stay together.

A man tugged her into a narrow storage closet that spanned from one wall to the other, and with a tall ceiling. There were at least a dozen people crammed inside. It smelled of body odor and fear. She had a metallic taste in her mouth.

"Don't talk," the man said. "Not a word."

She trembled, unable to speak. She didn't know if Mama and Aron had seen what happened to Papa. Silently, she wept and stood with the others.

The Gestapo caught them a few days later and put them on a train to the concentration camps.

A lorry backfired, jolting Chana back to Vienna. Her body was damp with perspiration, her blouse sticking to her skin under her coat. Papa had saved them. She owed her life to him. But she regretted telling her father about the tailor shop. If she hadn't, maybe he would be here with them today. She would never know. All she could do now was keep her promise to look after her mother and brother. She was fortunate to have survived and to be standing on this street today, and in time, she hoped to bake again, using her talents to honor Papa.

Meyer took a fellow from their group into the tailor shop. After a couple of minutes, Meyer alone joined them on the street again as the tailor handed him an envelope. Chana glimpsed money stuffed inside before Meyer slipped it in his jacket pocket. She didn't know what it meant, only that she didn't like it.

"What is that for?" Chana asked.

The group quieted. Meyer stared at her for a long minute, letting her know he didn't appreciate being questioned.

"A previous delivery and a finder's fee for a good worker," he said. "I don't put my neck on the line for nothing."

She met his gaze, unwilling to back down. "Will the people you placed in jobs be paid?"

"You mean will *you* be paid." He smirked. Before Chana could protest, he told her, "If I place you in a job, you'll earn a fair wage."

She was meant to take him at his word, but if war had taught Chana anything, it was to be cautious and not to believe everything she was told.

By late afternoon, the refugees in Meyer's care had dwindled to five—Chana and her family, Shifra, and one of the older men. They plodded along exhausted and hungry. The familiar rawness in Chana's belly shot acid into her throat and she longed for the day to end.

Meyer directed them deep into an alley alongside the Empress Hotel. It was a grand place, the tall cream building looking like a palace and noticeably unscarred by the war. Chana surmised only Nazi favor had allowed such a large building to go unscathed.

"Whoever works here will be lucky," Meyer said. "Prince Philipp von Württemberg built this as a palace for his bride, the Archduchess Maria Theresa, in the mid-1800s. A few years later, he sold it and it became the Empress Hotel. Later, it was owned by a Jew." A cloud blotted out the sun, and Meyer's eyes grew as dim as the alley. "During the war, this place was popular with high-ranking Nazis."

Meyer told them this section of Vienna, Innere Stadt, was in the first district and was an international zone, controlled by the Inter-allied police force. "This hotel is mostly filled with GIs and American officers. The chef needs two people. Herr Heiss runs the kitchen, and he's a decent man. You'll eat more than mere rations. Whoever is left will work in the laundry. But if you work here, remember to be careful—some of these employees catered to the Nazis."

Meyer knocked on a door and Mama whispered to Chana, "The laundry will be backbreaking work. Take off your scarf."

"I don't want to," Chana said.

Shifra unbuttoned her coat, revealing her blouse straining across her bosom.

"Listen to me," her mother said. "Show your hair."

Chana shook her head and felt a jab of guilt for her disobedience. Getting a job because of her looks or blond hair would only bring trouble. She lowered her eyes, too. In the past, men had referred to their gold color as everything from *enchanting* to *bewitching.* A rough voice pierced her thoughts. *You have the eyes of a demon*, the Nazi soldier had said, his liquored breath causing her to gag as his lit cigarette hung menacingly close to her skin. *I should slice them out of your head.*

She squeezed her eyes closed. *The soldier is dead*, she told herself. *You are the one who survived!* Two sturdy legs kept her upright in this alley, and her body was mostly intact. Chana was lucky to be alive. Everyone told her so. Others who'd survived. The Red Army soldiers who'd liberated Mama and her from their hiding spot in Stutthof. American officials running Foehrenwald. The DP camp teachers who'd schooled her in English.

A thin-faced cook opened the alley door.

"What do you want?" the cook asked Meyer in German. Flour dusted his cheeks, and behind him, the kitchen buzzed with activity.

"Chef Heiss is expecting me," Meyer said in slightly accented German.

The cook wiped his hands on his apron and Chana could see he was a little younger than Meyer, and though he matched the black-market dealer in height, his frame was slighter.

"Is that Meyer?" a gravelly voice asked from inside.

"It is, Herr Heiss." The cook adjusted his white chef's hat, exposing front locks of light brown hair.

"Let him in," the chef said, followed by the violent thump of something being hacked apart.

Chana flinched.

The cook grudgingly moved aside, and Meyer shoved past him, motioning for the rest of them to wait in the alley.

Clearly, this young cook and Meyer didn't like each other.

The open door afforded Chana a view of the kitchen and a hefty chef standing by a worktable that held a partially cut-up goat carcass. He was a large, barrel-chested man, and in his beefy hand, he held a bloody cleaver. Behind him was another chef icing a cake. *The pastry chef.*

The young man who'd opened the door joined the pastry chef, pressing his palms into a mound of dough. A smile lit his soft-featured face, and he wore a look of pure joy as he kneaded. Chana longed to step in beside him.

"Have you brought me the wine?" the heavyset chef asked, leaving bloody streaks on his apron as he wiped his hands.

"Next week, Herr Heiss. A shipment's coming." Meyer pointed. "Where'd you get the goat?"

"Kirill," Heiss said. "You're not the only man selling meat. Are you jealous?"

Meyer flashed a smile, though Chana detected the strain in his jaw. It did not differ from Foehrenwald, where various dealers competed against each other. There had been fights, and as a volunteer in the hospital, she had seen her share of black eyes and broken bones.

Meyer said, "Kirill Volkov sells subpar goods. That animal is a skeleton. I hope you didn't pay much."

Heiss suspiciously eyed the carcass. "Why have you come today?"

Meyer smoothed his lapels. "I have workers. You said you needed two."

"Ah, yes." He grabbed a skinny cook with an eye patch. "Finish the goat."

Aron stepped closer to Chana. "I hope we get to work in the same place. I don't want us separated."

His cheeks were pink, and she didn't know if it was the city itself or the walk in the fresh air, but she was grateful to see his coloring improved.

"We'll always be together." She sounded more confident than she felt. Their fate was out of their hands, and her indignation made her fidget. Chana needed to take control of the situation.

Meanwhile, the young man who'd opened the door crossed the kitchen, bumping into Heiss. "Elias, watch where you're going." The chef jabbed his finger at the pastry chef. "Trolfe, keep your damn apprentice out of my way!"

The pastry chef's gray mustache twitched, and he swatted away the order.

Heiss stepped out to the alley to regard the group of potential workers.

Lounging against the wall, Meyer lit a cigarette.

Shifra pinched her cheeks and smiled. Heiss's eyes caught briefly on Shifra's chest before he strode to the man in their group. In German, the chef asked if the fellow had ever worked in a kitchen. The man struggled to answer, butchering the language.

Mama patted her brown hair, flattened by the kerchief and patchy in spots. Heiss pivoted away from the man, and her mother turned pleading eyes to her. Chana let out a breath and relented, removing her scarf. She, Mama, and Aron needed to stay together above all else.

"Good girl," Mama whispered.

Gravel ground under Chef Heiss's shoes as he looked them over, his belly protruding over his apron. "You brought me one man, and he can't speak German. I need workers who I don't have to coddle."

Meyer crushed the cigarette under his heel, then kicked a metal pipe out of his way. "I won't have anyone else for at least a few weeks."

The ends of Chana's hair grazed her chin, and she smoothed them back. "*Ich spreche Deutsch*," she said.

The chef hooked his thumbs through his apron strings. "You're a pretty one, but you're nothing but bones." He looked to Meyer. "A wind will knock her over."

Chana couldn't abide the chef's dismissiveness. "*Ich bin stark*."

Meyer stayed silent, but regarded her with a mix of curiosity and . . . admiration.

"Strong? Is that what you said?" Heiss's eyes bore into her.

"*Ja*."

"See?" Meyer perked up. "Her German is excellent. You should hire her."

"What's your name?" Heiss asked.

Meyer shifted closer, as if intending to answer for her. She shook her head, and his lips curved into an intrigued half smile. He was a man unaccustomed to being quieted. She paused, buying time to line up

German answers. "Herr Heiss, I am Chana Rosenzweig." She gestured to Mama. "This is my mother, Ruth. I want you to hire her and my brother, too. His name is Aron. We're hard workers." She planted her feet apart, showing the chef it would take much more than a strong wind to bring her down.

"Ah," Heiss said with an impressed smile. "All right. I'll hire the three of you." He turned to Meyer. "We're desperately short-staffed for dinner. They can start now. Come back for them in a few hours."

Her eyes sought Shifra's. Chana mouthed, *I'm sorry*, feeling a twinge of guilt that she and her family had been hired over Shifra. Her friend gave her a forgiving nod.

"As you wish," Meyer said, buttoning his suit jacket. He told them, "When I come back, I'll take you to the boardinghouse." His gaze lingered on Chana.

She nodded, enjoying having surprised him.

"Good. The lot of you, inside," Heiss ordered.

"*Gehen*," Chana said, guiding Mama and Aron to the door. Thanks to her papa, kitchen work was familiar to all of them. They would prove to Chef Heiss that he had chosen well.

Chapter Five
Chana

Chana's confidence wobbled once she'd tied on an apron, despite having spent her girlhood in her father's kitchen. His bakery had been a hatbox compared to the size of this place. A dozen people rushed about, slicing, sautéing, and running from oven to stove. She smelled cooked onions, melting butter, and roasting meats. Her mouth watered, and she was certain others could hear her stomach rumble even over the noise of waiters crashing in and out of the double doors leading to the dining room.

Heiss steered Chana and her mother to two large sinks. "You'll load the dishes into the machine. Wash the pots and pans by hand. Understand?"

Chana eyed the dishwasher; she'd seen one before, while delivering bread to a Vilna restaurant with Papa. The machine could wash fifty dishes at a time!

"We understand," Chana told Chef Heiss, though she'd never operated such a contraption.

"Good." Heiss handed Aron a large black tray. "You'll clear dirty dishes off tables as fast as you can."

Aron pursed his lips, and Chana winked at him behind the chef's back, signaling her confidence in his ability. Her brother had only recently gotten his health back. In Foehrenwald, they'd feared he had caught typhus. Thankfully not. He no longer coughed at night, though he still wheezed. He would need all his strength to haul a tray full of dishes.

After Heiss left them, Chana whispered to her brother, "Don't stack the plates too high. Keep them in an even layer. It'll be easier to carry." He scratched the back of his neck. "It's only our first day," she said, hoping to alleviate his worry.

"If I drop the dishes, today could be our last," Aron said.

She couldn't argue with that fact. "You can do it." Chef watched them. "Go ahead."

They were so busy Chana would have sworn only a few minutes had passed when she looked at the clock and saw two hours had gone by. She and Mama had loaded the machine, and when the wash cycle finished, they'd removed scorching dishes and cups, which were put to use again. Attacking the sink's ever-growing stack of pots and pans, Chana washed and her mother dried. Aron might as well have been riding on a carousel for the many times he'd rounded through the dining room and kitchen with his tray either full or empty. When waiters slammed through the kitchen doors, Chana saw mostly American soldiers in their olive-green uniforms eating in the dining room. She also spotted a handful of British soldiers in their telltale lighter khaki uniforms.

Her station at the sink also allowed Chana a clear view of the other side of the kitchen, where the pastry chef, Herr Trolfe, an old man with a long, gray mustache and sour demeanor, prepared dough with his apprentice, Elias—the young man with the flour-dusted cheeks who'd first opened the door to them. She licked her lips as Elias pulled rolls from the oven.

Trolfe caught her looking and snarled in disgust. Then he spat into a sink, returning hateful, narrowed eyes to her. Chana quickly focused on the frying pan filling with soapy water and recalled Meyer's warning that some hotel staff had happily catered to the Nazis.

She scrubbed muck from the side of the pan, surreptitiously checking on the bakers. They were making *Striezel.* Chana thought the Austrian sweet bread resembled challah. She noted Trolfe's kneading technique, the way he folded the dough and focused his weight into the heels of his hands to flatten it. Those less skilled could be timid when facing a mound of dough. Not Herr Trolfe. He was aggressive, grunting as he folded. Elias dumped raisins into a bowl of watered-down rum, then began slicing almonds. Chana already knew they'd add the raisins after kneading, and the slivered nuts were for sprinkling on top after braiding the dough. At least that's how she and Papa made *Striezel.*

Chana's eyes filled. She found it torturous to stand so close to something she loved, unable to cross the room and take the sweet mound of dough into her hands. But if the scalding look from Herr Trolfe had conveyed anything, it was for her to stay on her side of the room.

It was near seven o'clock by the time the kitchen calmed. Heiss instructed four women to take their evening meals. "You two take turns," he said, nodding at Chana and her mother.

"You go first," Mama said, moving to the faucet to scrub the next pot.

Chana's stomach rumbled, and she appreciated her mother letting her eat first. She followed another woman, grabbing a bowl from a worktable and filling it with stew from a simmering pot. Next, she took a slightly charred roll from a basket.

The other woman whispered, "The apprentice left them in the oven too long. Their loss is our gain. My name's Gita." The woman looked to be in her late twenties. At first glance, her appearance was severe with a ruler-straight part in her red hair that was pulled into a tight bun. Then Chana noticed the freckles dappled across her nose, as well as how her pretty smile softened her looks.

"I'm Chana."

"Good to meet you."

Chana followed the women to a long bench against the wall. She ate hungrily, barely tasting the food, and was half done with her roll and stew, while Gita had barely eaten a few spoonfuls. Her stomach grumbled even louder than before.

The other women snickered, except Gita, who glowered at them. Shame stabbed at Chana, but she tossed it off. They were thin, but nothing like the hollow eyes Chana saw in her own reflection, or in the people she'd passed on the street while Meyer had guided them around Vienna. Most of Europe was existing on insufficient rations, but the women in this kitchen appeared better fed than most.

Chana glanced across the room as Trolfe smacked Elias on the back of the head. She inhaled sharply, but the apprentice took the blow with no complaint, as if he were used to it.

Trolfe said, "When you bake tonight, don't you dare use any of my ingredients."

"I bought my own, sir," Elias said.

"Good. And you leave this space spotless. I don't want to know you even breathed in here."

"You won't. I promise."

"Try to use what I've taught you." Trolfe's face softened, and he tapped the boy's cheek. "Go eat."

Elias ended up on the bench beside Chana with a bowl of stew. She bit into her roll.

"How is it?" he asked, eyeing her bread.

The crust was dark brown and black in spots, but the inside was pillow-soft. "It tastes fine."

"I'm glad." A medallion dangled from around his neck, and he held it for a second.

"What is that?" She gestured to the necklace.

"This is St. Honoré. The patron saint of bakers." He smiled and tucked the medallion under his shirt. "My . . . my mother gave it to me after Chef Trolfe hired me."

Chana dipped the rest of her roll into her stew and finished it. He then gave her his roll.

"Don't you want it?" she asked.

"No. They came out wrong." He stirred his stew, but didn't eat.

Ah, he reminded her of Aron. When her brother was upset, he lost his appetite. Until the war, of course, when Aron learned to eat whenever food was offered, as the Nazis rarely offered it. Clearly, this gentile boy hadn't learned such a lesson.

"It's still food." She bit into the roll.

"I suppose." He ate a spoonful of stew. "I'll get them right next time," he said, determined.

She asked, "Do you enjoy baking?"

At this, his eyes brightened to the color of cinnamon. "I love it."

Her mood lifted. "My father was a baker. He taught me how to make many things." *Medaus Tortas* came to mind. The multilayered honey cake with lemon-flavored cream was her favorite, and was the treat Papa had always made for her birthday. "I often helped him in his bakery."

The fellow looked at Chana as if he were seeing her for the first time. "You were an apprentice like me."

She smiled, appreciating his describing her as an equal. "Yes, I suppose I was."

"I'm Elias," he said. "Elias Bohm."

She found his formal introduction charming, and amusing, because they'd been working in the same kitchen for the past few hours and Trolfe had called his name several times.

"I'm Chana Rosenzweig." She paused. "Does the pastry chef often ask you to work late into the night?"

"There are times." He quickly added, "And I don't mind. Tonight, though, I'll bake for practice after the kitchen closes. I'll have it all to myself . . . with Herr Trolfe's permission, of course."

A wad of jealousy hit her chest. She envied this young man, who will have this grand kitchen at his disposal to bake whatever he wants. What Chana wouldn't give for such an opportunity.

Clapping drew her attention. It came from an American soldier, who'd entered the kitchen and was applauding.

"Another fine meal you've made for us, Chef Heiss!" the tall-as-a-tree serviceman said in garbled German. The three stripes on his uniform meant he was a sergeant. His short hair was even lighter than Chana's, and a full mustache camouflaged his top lip. He sauntered toward the chef. "Tonight's stew was delicious." He kissed his fingers, showing his pleasure.

"You're too kind, Sergeant McManus." Chef Heiss grinned broadly.

"But I don't mind the compliment." He cast a hand around the kitchen. "It's good for morale, too."

The sergeant's gaze traveled around the room until it landed on Chana and the other women on the bench.

"*Oof*, here he comes," said Gita, tensing as the sergeant swaggered over.

"Fräuleins," he said, throwing his arms wide.

Gita forced a smile, as did the others.

Sergeant McManus's eyes fell on Chana. "Someone new in your ranks. What's your name, blondie?"

"Chana." She followed the lead of the other women and smiled, too.

The soldier pulled a chocolate bar from his pocket with the flourish of a magician. "Welcome to the Empress Hotel." He handed her the bar, and after she thanked him, he winked as if their exchange meant something more. The sergeant bent so they were eye to eye. "If you need anything, sweetheart, come find me."

"Sergeant," Elias said, standing, "Herr Trolfe and I have a new cake we want you to try." He set his stew on the bench. "Come, it's quite a treat."

McManus lingered for a moment, then straightened. "I don't know what could be sweeter than this gal, but sure, kid, lead the way."

The others on the bench relaxed as the sergeant followed Elias.

Gita leaned toward Chana. "Elias did you a favor. That one waltzes in with his candy bars, but expects something in return." The way her eyes drilled into Chana, her meaning was clear. "He gives the rest of the soldiers a bad name. They're not all like him."

Chana readily agreed, having met many kind and generous soldiers since the Red Army liberated her and Mama from Stutthof. It was

American GIs who had guided them to the Red Cross, before they were transferred to Foehrenwald. She and Mama stayed in the DP camp's hospital for several weeks, and American soldiers often visited. They'd inquire about her life before and during the war, and when she talked, tears often gathered in their eyes. When she and Mama reunited with Aron, hugging and sobbing outside the DP camp dining hall, a group of American GIs had cheered. At Foehrenwald, she also overheard soldiers discussing liberating concentration camps and their heartbreak over the condition of the prisoners. They spoke in hushed tones about the nightmares that plagued them ever since. Chana viewed this sergeant as one rotten apple among an enormous bushel of heroes.

Elias came back to his stew and sat beside her again.

"I believe I should thank you," Chana said.

He lifted one shoulder. "I wish Chef Heiss wouldn't allow outsiders in our kitchen."

He glanced over at her, meeting her gaze. "What color are your eyes?"

"Excuse me?" she said, pretending she hadn't understood the question.

"They're like those of a tiger."

She ate the last of her stew, unsure of how to answer. His was a kinder description than others she'd heard. "My father called them amber."

"They're remarkable." Now their eyes met, and pink circles appeared on his cheeks. "When I was a boy, my father read me a book about a tiger. There were pictures."

"My father used to read us books, too. They were about everything... history, mysteries, and love stories."

"Chana," came her mother's sharp call, slicing through the kitchen noise like a hot knife through soft butter.

She looked up into Mama's stern face by the sink. "I'm finished eating." Chana quickly rose.

Elias said, "It's nice to meet you, Chana Rosenzweig."

She bit back a smile. She'd enjoyed their companionable conversation. As if they'd known each other for a while, instead of having just met. At the sink, Chana handed her mother half of the extra roll and the chocolate bar. "I saved these for you."

Mama broke the candy bar into thirds, handing one part to Chana. "We'll save a piece for Aron." Then her mother nodded at Elias. "That gentile boy has no reason to talk to you."

"We're working in the same kitchen, Mama."

Her mother left to eat, but not before pinching Chana's arm hard enough for her to know that by morning she'd have a bruise.

Chapter Six

Chana

By the time Meyer returned, it was dark out and after eight o'clock. When Chana, Mama, and Aron joined him in the alley, she tied her kerchief over her hair.

"Well done speaking German," Meyer said to Chana in Yiddish. "You impressed Herr Heiss. Difficult to do."

"I'm glad he hired us," she said, answering in Yiddish, the language she'd spoken for most of her life. "My father was a baker. Do you think there's any chance I could help the pastry chef?"

"Ha!" Meyer scoffed. "I tried to get Trolfe to hire the son of a friend as his apprentice. They'd owned a bakery in Hamburg. The boy would have made a fine helper, but Trolfe isn't like Heiss. He tolerates the Jews working in the hotel, but he would never hire one."

Chana recalled the disgust on the pastry chef's face when he'd looked at her. She hid her disappointment by busying herself with checking the knot on her kerchief.

"It's a shame to cover such pretty hair," Meyer said.

Chana caught the triumphant curve of her mother's mouth.

"My daughter is a beauty and was the apple of her father's eye."

Chana didn't argue with Mama's comment, and it wasn't because of vanity. She had grown up knowing that, as a Jewish girl, her wavy blond hair and gold eyes set her apart.

Mama said, "Thank you for helping us, Herr Suconick. We will work hard until we go to America."

"Call me Meyer." He cast a glance at Chana. "You have chutzpah."

It wasn't the first time Chana had been told this either, but coming from him—a man who seemed to embody the word—it piqued her interest. "Why do you say that?"

"You didn't cower when you faced Kirill in the train station. Heiss is tough, and you held your own." He ran a palm over his chin. "You remind me of someone." His tone was both admiring and melancholy, telling her this *someone* had been dear to him.

Though curious, she didn't pry; it was none of her business. Yet, she stole another look at him while he focused up the street—his face was equally as striking in profile. She found it hard to look away. After another block, she thought to ask him, "Where's Shifra?"

"At the laundry. For the time being, she's billeting in their basement. It's also in the first district, close to where I'm taking you."

Since they'd arrived, Meyer had taken them to Vienna's first, second, and ninth districts—according to him, these sections of the city were where most Jews had lived and worked before the war, and where some had resettled.

Chana imagined Shifra alone at the laundry and regretted not suggesting Chef Heiss hire a fourth worker. She hoped the washing job wasn't too hard. Knowing Shifra, if anyone could find a bright spot in laundering, it was her. Chana promised herself that she would check on her friend in the next few days.

Fifteen minutes later, Chana and her mother and brother were shown their quarters in Nachmann's boardinghouse.

"This one's yours," said Herr Nachmann, a middle-aged man with a gap-toothed smile, as he limped to the door on the third floor of the four-story building. The door swung open. The room held a bed on one side, two thin mattresses on the floor, a table and chairs, and a bureau.

"There's a shared bathroom at the end of the hall. The kitchen and parlor on the first floor are for all the tenants," Nachmann said.

"Thank you," Mama said gratefully.

Chana looked around. The space was small, but it was all theirs. For the first time since the war, she, Mama, and Aron would live alone as a family. She hugged herself. It was wonderful, but oh, how she ached for Papa.

Meyer hung back in the hall with their new landlord, and Mama said, "It's clear Meyer is an important man with contacts all over the city. He can help us." Her eyes darted to the hall, then back to Chana. "Do you see how he looks at you? Be friendly."

Aron traced a finger over a dent in the wood bureau, pretending he couldn't hear what their mother had said.

"Please, Mama. Let's just get settled in the city."

"Didn't you hear Meyer's warning?" Mama said. "In Vienna, we women can't even walk alone. There is danger here, as there was in the ghetto. We need a man's . . ." She searched for the right word. "Protection."

"I can protect us," Aron said.

Mama regarded him fondly. "You're a good boy."

He frowned. "I'm fifteen, Mama. Not a baby."

"I can't have anything happen to you." Mama turned to Chana.

"I'm still mourning your father." Her voice shook. "Otherwise, I would consider remarrying to spare you."

Was she still mourning? Chana was thirteen when the war had started, but she'd noticed things about her parents and their marriage; their relationship had always confused her. The two frequently argued over Papa's work. Mama thought he worked too much, and she disapproved of the *ideas* he put in Chana's head about school and the bakery.

But occasionally, her parents had held hands as they walked home from *Shabbos* services. Sometimes Papa stole a kiss from Mama when he thought Chana and Aron weren't looking. Mama had viewed the bakery as Papa's domain, and their home was hers. She complained Chana didn't help enough around their apartment, and there were moments Chana suspected her mother had been jealous of the long hours she spent with Papa in the bakery.

Chana told her mother now, "Please, Mama, Papa and I had plans. You remember, don't you?"

The question eased the tension on her mother's face. "I do."

In 1933, when Chana was six, Papa had saved enough to open his small shop, even hiring another man to help. Two years later, word had spread that Jacob Rosenzweig produced the best bread and cakes in Vilna. Even gentile families bought from him. Chana loved helping her father, and he had taught her how to mix and knead dough, as well as many of his recipes.

"You're a natural," Papa had said.

It was true. Chana instinctively knew the correct proportions of flour, yeast, water, and salt. She knew when the dough had risen enough, and how various kinds of weather affected that rise. She could always tell when it was time for the bread to come out of the oven. But, by the time she was eleven, vandalism and rising antisemitism had strangled Papa's business. She was twelve when the war started and fourteen when the Nazis marched into Vilna and her father had to shutter the bakery.

Mama took Chana's hands in her own. "I loved Papa, but our safety is what matters most. *Hertzeleh*, marriage is your duty to this family now." It wasn't often her mother used that endearment. "I'm not saying you have to marry Meyer Suconick, but be nice. Smile. A man with connections could help us."

Her mother's pleading eyes saddened Chana. Perspiration beaded on her neck as the room grew unbearably stuffy. Of course she wanted to keep her family safe and get to America. "I'll be nice."

Mama kissed Chana's knuckles.

"There're clothes in here," Aron said. A bureau drawer hung open and her brother held up a man's coat.

Their mother went over and poked through several garments. "Whoever had lived here must have left in a hurry."

"I think we should keep them," Aron said.

"Yes, why not?" Mama closed the drawer.

Footsteps from the hallway grew nearer. Chana unfastened the top two buttons of her blouse.

"What are you doing?" Mama asked, dismay filling her eyes.

"It's stifling in here." Chana opened her collar, which would reveal three circular burns clustered below the base of her neck.

"Cover that up," her mother insisted. "Aron, open the window."

Aron tried to crack it open. "It won't budge. I think it's nailed shut."

Chana rubbed her nose, her nostrils itching at the memory of the Nazi soldier's sour breath mixing with the smell of burnt skin. The beast had meant to leave her damaged forever. In Foehrenwald, she had shown Zvi soon after he'd proposed.

Repulsed, Zvi had averted his eyes and told Chana, "You'll cover that in my presence."

His reaction had hurt her deeply. As he'd courted her, she'd grown to depend on him. Most nights, he escorted her and her family to the dining hall and proudly introduced her to the soldiers and other policemen. She expected he would call off their engagement. Instead, a week later, he told her, "I don't want to go to America. I plan to return to Belgium."

"Is it because . . . ?" She placed a hand on her chest.

"Of course not," he said brusquely. "I'm not shirking my commitment to you. Visas for America are next to impossible. We'll have no trouble securing papers to go to Belgium. The camp director has urged everyone to return to their home country."

When Chana told Mama of Zvi's plans, she'd cursed and yelled. That was when Chana contacted the Brihah.

Now, in their room at Nachmann's, her mother whispered, "Button up."

Chana didn't have a chance to before Meyer came in. "Nachmann's isn't a palace," he said, "but it is better than most." He crossed to the window, which faced a crumbling brick wall. "This is the only boardinghouse in the district with glass panes."

Chana felt her mother's eyes on her.

"Thank you, Herr Suconick," Chana said. "We're grateful."

"Good." He looked at her, his gaze drifting to her open collar.

Chana stayed perfectly still, though her insides quivered. It was never easy exposing herself in this way. But after what had happened with Zvi, Chana had vowed not to hide again. She didn't need a mirror to know how the three angry red welts looked. Five more remained concealed by her blouse. When Meyer's eyes lifted, she searched them for a squint of revulsion or pity. She found neither and was startled by the heat unfurling in her chest.

"I will see you three soon. I'm at the Empress Hotel often," Meyer said, and gave them a smile worthy of a pirate, one she would bet had captured plenty of ladies' hearts. Chana touched her throat, and her cheeks grew warm. He headed toward the door, but stopped. "I don't know how long it will be until the ports become safe again, but if you truly have family in America, there are others who might help you."

"Who?" her mother asked.

Meyer took out a notebook and pencil and wrote as he spoke. "The Hebrew Immigrant Aid Society might be of assistance. The American consulate and the American Jewish Joint Distribution Committee, too." He tore off the paper and handed it to Mama. "Here are the addresses. Of course, there's also the Red Cross."

"The Red Cross tried, but couldn't find our family while we were in Foehrenwald," her mother said in a voice filled with woe.

He pointed to the list. "Those others should be of help." His gaze flicked to the door. "A bit of friendly advice," he said quietly. "Nachmann is a decent enough fellow, which is why I put you here. He was lucky to get his building back after the war. If he'd been a Jew, he wouldn't have been so fortunate. But . . ." He paused. "He'll rent to anyone with money. He doesn't care about political beliefs."

His steady gaze conveyed everything they needed to know—former Nazis boarded here. Chana's stomach turned sour.

Mama said, "Thank you for telling us."

Meyer patted Mama's arm. "Chana, once you're settled, let's you and I have tea at one of the cafés."

He had a nervous tilt to his head. It was both boyish and endearing, and the invitation pleased her. Until she looked at the list in her mother's hand. Meyer Suconick had given them contacts, and now he might expect something in return. Like the sergeant and his candy bar. If she refused him, would there be consequences? It was often that way with powerful men. Injure their pride and they would injure you. Though, as she met his eyes and took in his tentative smile, she didn't want to refuse. Her mother believed Meyer could be helpful to them. So why shouldn't they be friends? One could never have enough friends.

"That would be lovely," Chana said.

"Then I'll see you soon." He clapped a hand on Aron's shoulder and left.

Chapter Seven

Zoe

Raleigh, North Carolina
March 2018

"Have I enticed you to come to Vienna?" Henri Martin asked, sounding confident.

"Yes, I believe you have." Zoe saved her notes document. "When you have an itinerary, email it to Liam."

"I will," she said, and before he could hang up, she added, "Excuse me, Mr. Martin . . ."

"What is it?"

"How will I find you, sir?" She left unsaid, *I don't know what you look like*, because *no one knows what you look like.*

He chuckled as if he'd heard her thought. "I'll find you." He ended the call.

Zoe sped through *Savouries*' office, past the ad sales department, and into the Pit—the maze of cubicles housing the staff writers. At her desk, she found a Post-it on her chair from Wes.

I need the BBQ piece by one.

She settled into her desk with her laptop, put the finishing touches on her article, and hit send. While she waited for Wes to tell her if the piece needed more edits, she pulled up the Boucher conference website and tapped the link for the conference hotel. She immediately recognized the regal facade. The Empress Hotel. The same place she'd called after finding the incoming number on her grandfather's phone.

Zoe had to go to Vienna. She just had to. The problem was pulling together the money to pay for the trip.

On SonicTravel.com, a tally of airfare and the cheapest room at the Empress Hotel would cost her close to three thousand dollars, putting her checking account in the red. She'd be forced to tap into the money she'd inherited, funds earmarked for her grandfather's mortgage. Weeklong apartment rentals were also pricey. Conference registration would tack on another thousand. But if she was at Boucher, she'd want to see Henri Martin's keynote address. There had to be a way to manage this.

She checked in with the Secret Scribblers—a private Facebook group for journalists. This online community offered insights on everything from public relations contacts for celebrities to the correct editor to pitch on any topic imaginable. She typed *Henri Martin* into the group's search box and found posts with the common theme of journalists seeking to interview Eveline or Henri Martin. Efforts that never panned out. Over the years, reporters tracked rumors that the Martins planned to attend various conferences or events, only to be no-shows.

A rock of anxiety landed in her belly. Even if Zoe made it to Vienna, there was no guarantee Henri Martin would be there. A comment about a charity event from two years ago caught her eye.

> Gus Varhy: Eveline and Henri Martin will never show up! It would be easier to photograph a unicorn eating a Big Mac than to snag a picture or interview with the Martins.

But Henri Martin had asked her to come. He'd promised to talk to her, emphasizing, *I keep my promises.* It was weird, but Zoe believed him. What he'd already told her about her family was profound.

She stared at the screen. Other reporters would lose their minds over Henri having called her. That's when an idea hit. If she talked to Henri Martin, she could write about it. His connection to her family would include part of his history, too. Facts no one else had written about because the man didn't give interviews.

She could write about him for *Savouries.*

That was it! She would convince Wes to send her to the conference for the magazine. Her inbox dinged with an email from Wes.

> WES: Good job on the barbecue piece, especially on expanding the competitive nature of the festival.
>
> ZOE: Thanks. Any chance I can get a few minutes with you today?
>
> WES: I'm traveling tomorrow and my schedule is tight. What's it about?
>
> ZOE: A story idea. It'll be quick.

She rolled her chair toward the hall, gaining a view through the glass wall and into Wes's office. He stared at his computer screen. Did he look interested or annoyed? She couldn't tell which. He glanced over and waved for her to come.

Zoe shot up. Wes wasn't prone to granting last-minute meetings, and she took this as a good sign. A Google alert hit her phone as she left her cubicle. It was for a press release from the Boucher Foundation. She walked and read.

For Immediate Release

Boucher Foundation to Honor
Martin Baking Company

Paris, France—This year's annual Boucher Conference will mark the organization's twentieth year honoring contributions to the world of food. The 2018 Lifetime Achievement Award will be presented to Eveline and Henri Martin of Martin Baking Company.

Martin Baking began as a single bakery in Sydney, Australia, in 1950. Today, the company's worldwide sales of their ever-popular Fudgies are in the billions.

Martin Baking Company is an ardent champion of women, investing in training and education to shepherd female employees to management- and executive-level positions. Their philanthropy includes support of women's charities around the world, as well as medical research and donations to end food insecurity.

Eveline Martin will receive the award posthumously.

> However, Henri Martin has agreed to attend the April conference in Vienna, Austria, and will deliver the keynote address.
>
> "Having spent time in Vienna as a young man after the war, it would be an honor to accept this award in person on behalf of Eveline and myself," Martin said.

Henri Martin had spent time in Vienna after the war, like Grandpa Aron and Great-aunt Chana. She wondered how he fit into the stories he'd already told her about her family.

"Give me a second," Wes said as Zoe settled in the chair in front of his desk.

"Sure."

He typed, then combed his fingers through his sandy hair, the gray at his temples more noticeable than usual. Wes was ten years older than Zoe, and today the lines around his eyes and mouth seemed deeper. He sat back, gulped from a large coffee, then devoured half a sesame bagel loaded with cream cheese and lox. The take-out bag was from Bagel'ish, a restaurant up the block, and a former client of Grandpa Aron's. The owner had also been a survivor, and the two men had been friends. Zoe inhaled the mingled scents of baked dough and briny, smoked fish, and her nerves settled. She and her grandfather used to spend every Sunday morning at Bagel'ish while her grandmother attended dance practice. Over bagels for breakfast, they'd talked about everything. She told him about school and any drama with friends. If she had a big test coming, they'd tote along flash cards or textbooks, and her grandfather would quiz her. Grandpa Aron had been her favorite person, and those breakfast dates with him had been sacred.

Wes set down his coffee. "You called this meeting. What's going on?"

She tipped forward. "It's about the Boucher conference."

"I saw the press release." Wes tilted back in his chair. "People are losing their shit over this. The Martins are the culinary world's Sasquatch and Loch Ness monster rolled into one. Every journalist at that conference will angle for an interview."

"That's why I'm in here. I want you to send me for *Savouries.* I'm going to interview Henri Martin."

Her request dangled between them for a tense minute. "Come on, Zoe," he said. "Henri Martin is the *get* of the decade."

Zoe scooched forward. "You don't understand. I have an edge. Henri Martin knew my grandfather. I just found out. He called me this morning. That's why I was late. He told me all sorts of things about my family."

He studied her. "How does he know them?"

If only Henri had told her. "I don't know yet, but I'll find out, and then I can write about Henri's history. He *wants* to talk to me in Vienna."

Wes's eyebrows hiked up. Her idea intrigued him. Until he frowned. He either didn't believe her or didn't believe she could handle such a big-time interview. Wes was an easy person to read.

Dejection made Zoe want to shrink into her chair. *Time to back off,* her thoughts chided. Then, from somewhere deep inside, another voice said, *No!* The girl Zoe had been before losing her parents would never have backed off. Her grandfather used to say, "My Zoe has chutzpah." She had buried that part of herself, but now it was climbing to the surface. She sat straighter. "Give me a chance, Wes."

Wes steepled his fingers together. "Martin knew your grandfather and called you? Explain how this happened, please."

She told Wes about the envelope she'd found, the articles, traveling papers, the old photograph, and Henri's call. She handed him her phone, showing him her email to Liam Martin-Eastman, the incoming international number from that morning, and then let him swipe through the photos.

He handed back her phone. "The photos are fuzzy. You can't be certain Henri Martin is related to that Meyer guy."

"Even if they're not, he promised if I came to Vienna, he would talk to me about how he knew my family and more. There's history there—Henri Martin's history—something no one has ever written about." She pressed a hand against her chest. "I can feel it."

Wes checked his watch. "I have another meeting in a few minutes." He drained his coffee as *please, please, please* reverberated in Zoe's mind.

"You pitched a good case," Wes said, "but this quarter the pressure is on to boost the magazine's readership and ad sales. If there's an article to be had on Henri Martin, *Savouries* needs it. Which means I must send my best reporter, and that's Virgil. His piece last year on destination restaurants ruining European villages was brilliant."

Virgil's article had been a finalist for a Pulitzer. That let the air out of her hopes.

Wes kept talking, but she didn't hear him. Defeat ate up all her attention. This was her story, not Virgil's. She couldn't let it end here. She had to go to Vienna.

"Wes, please send me." She swallowed. "There's a connection between Henri Martin and my family, which means I'll bring something to this story that no other journalist can." Conviction rushed through her. "Henri Martin told me my family wanted to get to America, but ended up in Vienna. According to the press release, Martin was also in Vienna after the war. It was dangerous . . . there were people dealing on the black market and it all felt . . . bleak. My great-aunt worked as a baker. A baker!" Whatever the envelope contents had meant to her grandfather, Zoe had to find out. "This is personal for me, which will make for the best kind of story."

Wes looked at her long and hard. "I don't want to regret this."

She perked up. "I swear you won't."

A knock on his door made them both look. A guy from accounting leaned in. "Ready for me?"

Wes put up a finger. "Give us a minute."

This was it. Zoe had either convinced Wes to send her to Austria or he was going to assign her a story on the South's best peach cobbler or hummingbird cake.

He stood. "I need a story I can print."

She shot to her feet as a giddy buzz filled her chest. "I understand."

He wagged a finger at her, a familiar gesture when he was serious. "If you don't get the interview, I won't cover your expenses."

She would conduct this interview no matter what.

"It's probably best if you stay at the hosting hotel," he said, continuing with his instructions. "Book the cheapest room. We're trimming our expenditures."

She assumed cost cuts were why the accountant was impatiently tapping his foot. "Cheapest room. Done."

"One more thing." He paused. "As soon as the press release dropped, word quickly spread that other magazines are offering three dollars a word to freelancers for a piece on Martin."

Her mouth fell open, and she quickly closed it. "What's the word count?" she asked.

"Five thousand max."

Zoe coughed. *Too bad she wasn't a freelancer.* Only a few feature interviews conducted by top-tier journalists earned $2.50 a word. She quickly did the math and realized a piece on Henri Martin could fetch the writer a fifteen-thousand-dollar payday.

Wes moved to the door. "That's why I'm willing to give you, as a staff writer, a five-thousand-dollar bonus if you deliver. And I'll promote you to senior editor."

The amount startled her. She scrambled to total what this meant for her. Five thousand dollars plus an almost fifteen-thousand-dollar bump in salary to a senior editor. She would for sure be able to keep her grandfather's house. The invitation from Henri Martin was turning out to be a true golden ticket.

Wes added, "Realize that because you contacted him about your family, he might assume he's talking to you off the record. Identify yourself as a journalist and get him *on the record*."

"I will." A fist of doubt punched her in the gut. Henri Martin could bail on the conference. Or change his mind about talking to her. *One step at a time*, she told herself, while remembering that he had already confided in her. "Thank you, Wes. This is going to be a great article," she said with more confidence than she felt.

"Okay. Now, get out of my office." He motioned to the door.

"Right." Zoe hurried to her cubicle with her entire body wired, understanding how it felt to leap from a great height into the unknown.

Chapter Eight

Zoe

Vienna, Austria
April 2018

On a Monday, ten days after Zoe's meeting with Wes, she stared up at the Empress Hotel, a seven-story buttercream-colored building with baroque architecture, and whispered, "Whoa."

According to her pretravel research, the building had been home to a prince and archduchess in the 1800s. But most interesting to her was a July 1946 fire at the hotel. This was where her great-aunt had worked. Did she die here? Her skin tingled.

Once Zoe was past the hotel's large gold-framed glass door, she gaped at the interior. The opulent lobby boasted a cavernous, mural-painted ceiling, gold-veined mirrored panels, and crystal everywhere. The place was packed with sharply dressed men in slacks and blazers, and women in pantsuits or dresses, accessorized with scarves and funky statement jewelry. Neon-green conference lanyards hung from almost every neck.

The reception check-in line switchbacked among velvet ropes. Zoe checked her phone. No new emails, messages, or calls. Last week, she'd sent her itinerary to Liam, Martin Baking Company's communications director. He'd acknowledged her note with a laconic *Will be in touch when you arrive.*

Now Zoe breezed past the reception line—she didn't have the patience for it—and headed first for the concierge desk, where she stored her suitcase for a later check-in, then on to Boucher's registration table for her conference packet.

As she draped her name tag around her neck, someone at her shoulder said, "Zoe Rosenzweig?"

She looked up to find a fair-haired man in a navy suit. "Yes," she said.

His lips formed a tight line. "I'm Liam Martin-Eastman," he said, offering his hand.

She gave his hand a firm shake. "You weren't kidding when you said you'd be in touch when I arrived."

He gave her a stone-faced response and dropped her hand. "I'd like you to come with me," he said, pronouncing *like* as *loik*, the way Australians did. He sped away, and she followed. Could he already be taking her to meet Henri Martin? She caught sight of herself in the mirrored hallway. She looked a bit worn from traveling; her hair frizzing and shadows under her eyes, but overall, she was presentable. She was glad she'd made the trip in black slacks and a blazer instead of track pants or jeans.

"Where are we going?" she asked as Liam tapped the call button by a private elevator.

"To meet my grandfather, Henri Martin."

Grandfather. Of course. Martin was part of Liam's surname. She should have realized he was family.

The elevator carried them to the penthouse, where Zoe followed Liam into a luxurious living room. Gilded molding, chintz sofas, ornate vases, and an abundance of flowers declared the space a veritable palace. She had never seen a hotel room this grand, if it could even be called a hotel room.

Her eyes moved past the room's glitz to a wall of floor-to-ceiling windows, where an elderly silver-haired man looked out at a breathtaking view of the city and St. Stephen's Cathedral. He turned. This older fellow was dressed in casual tan trousers and a powder-blue oxford shirt. He had a creased, weathered face, was medium height and thickset, even soft around the middle, where his shirt buttons pulled slightly.

"Welcome, Zoe Rosenzweig. I am Henri Martin." His voice and accent matched what she remembered of their call.

"It's a pleasure to meet you, Mr. Martin." She stepped forward, offering her hand. They shook, and when he let go, excitement pumped through her. Here, in the flesh, was Henri *freaking* Martin. This meeting could be the key to everything she wanted. Insights into her family's story. A major byline. A bonus. A promotion. And the ability to stay in her grandfather's house indefinitely. Right then, her future sparkled brighter than the room's elaborate multibranch crystal chandelier.

"Call me Henri." He settled into an armchair. "Come." He beckoned her to the sofa.

As Zoe sat on the couch, Liam placed a folder on the coffee table. The two men shared a look, and Zoe detected tension in their wordless exchange.

"Grandfather, are you sure you don't need to rest? The keynote starts in two hours."

"I'm fine." Henri waved dismissively.

"Of course," Liam said, a muscle pulsing along his jaw. "I'll be back soon."

Liam's curt demeanor unnerved Zoe.

When the elevator doors closed and they were alone, Henri turned to her. "I'm pleased you're here."

"Thank you for meeting with me, Mr. Martin. As you might imagine, I'm eager to hear more about my grandfather and great-aunt. Can you tell me when you met them?" She wanted to quickly pin down if he was with them in Vienna or if he had known them prior to their arrival.

"Aron was a teenager when we met. A good kid. He ran errands around the hotel." He gestured at the room and gave her a crooked smile.

Zoe took in the windows and doorways as if her teenage grandfather would magically step into the room. How she missed Grandpa Aron. "What about my great-aunt Chana? When did you meet her?"

"Your great-aunt was . . ." His voice had taken on a faraway quality. "Chana Rosenzweig was extraordinary. Unforgettable."

It was a lovely sentiment, but it didn't answer her question. "I'm named after her," Zoe said, attempting another way to open the conversation. "My middle name is Chana." Zoe's parents had followed the Jewish tradition of naming babies to honor dead relatives.

Henri folded his arms across his chest and slowly nodded, looking every inch a titan of business. But, after a beat, he slid the folder toward her. "For you."

"What is this?" She picked it up, hoping it held information.

"A nondisclosure agreement."

She touched her neck. "Oh?"

If Henri registered her surprise, he didn't let on. "It's standard practice for me. I can't discuss anything unless you sign." He placed a pen on the coffee table. "There's a rumor about my *wanting* to do an interview. Money is on the line, too. Top dollar per word. I don't appreciate a bounty on my head." He locked his eyes on hers. "I was glad that you didn't write about my award before Boucher announced it. As a journalist, I imagine that went against your nature."

She fought to keep her voice relaxed when she said, "With all due respect, sir, you didn't request to be off the record when we last spoke."

"You're right."

She sensed this had been a test. One she'd passed only because he didn't know she'd used bits of his story to pitch Wes.

Henri tapped the folder. "Look over the papers and decide."

Her intuition told her to approach Henri with the same caution one used with an animal in the wild, fearing he could bolt. Yet she couldn't help asking, "And what happens if I don't sign?"

"You can make use of the elevator, and I'll practice my speech."

The prudent response would be for her to take the document back to her room and carefully go over it. Possibly consult with Wes, who had explicitly instructed her to identify herself as a journalist and state her intention to conduct an interview. But what if this was her only chance to meet with Henri? The way she looked at it, their objectives partially aligned—the conversation about her *family* was personal. As for the article, maybe there was a way around the NDA. Wes would know what to do.

Her boss's warning rang in her mind. *If you don't get the interview, I won't cover your expenses.*

Stress made her right eyelid pulse as she read through the document's standard language. It stated that everything discussed between them would be off the record. She signed it anyway.

Henri put the document in a side table drawer. "Now that the paperwork is out of the way, don't disappoint me."

Another warning. Zoe's mouth went dry as she retrieved the old photo and *Life* article from her bag. "As you know from my email, my grandfather died in February. I found these with his things." She was relieved her words came out steadier than she felt. "He wrote they were important for my future, but I have no idea what that means. Might you?" Henri had squinted at the mention of Grandpa Aron's passing. She thought he looked sad, but he donned reading glasses to check the pictures, and she couldn't tell for certain.

Henri tapped on the old photo by the delivery truck. "They took this without my knowledge," he said, ignoring her question. "It was the last time we granted anyone an interview."

Next, she handed him her great-aunt's traveling paper. "I found this, too. Meyer Suconick is listed as Chana's husband. My grandfather never told me that his sister was married."

He stared at the paper. "Chana and Meyer were never married."

"But were they meant to be married?"

"They were." He leaned forward. "Where did we leave off when we last spoke?"

She couldn't tell if he didn't remember or if he was testing her. "My family had been hired in the hotel kitchen, and Meyer found them a room in a boardinghouse."

"Right . . . Nachmann's."

Zoe took out a pen and pad, then pulled up a recording app on her phone, setting it on the table.

"No recording." He pointed to her pad. "No notes, either."

It wasn't ideal, but she didn't argue. She put the items in her bag, knowing she'd have to type up the stories later.

His eyes drifted to the windows, and she followed his gaze.

The nearest buildings were beige, topped with terra-cotta roofs sporting gold peaks, and a few green-patinated domes. St. Stephen's Cathedral was in the distance with its glazed-tile roof creating an inverted-W pattern. It was hard for Zoe to picture the bombed-out city Henri had described in their phone call. Even in its postwar ruin, the size and scale must have swallowed Grandpa Aron and Chana after their years of hiding and running.

He turned back to her. "Let's begin."

Wind rattled the tall windows, as if the past were trying to break into the room.

Chapter Nine
Chana

Vienna, Austria
April 1946

Their first week in Vienna went by in a blur as Chana and her family acclimated to the city. For Chana, this new life was exhilarating and terrifying in equal measure. There was a rhythm to their days, where Chana, Mama, and Aron would work at the hotel and spend their evenings at Nachmann's. In the boardinghouse, they often stayed in their room, where Mama would mend their worn garments, and Chana and her brother would read; Chana preferred the magazines and newspapers the GIs left behind at the hotel, and Aron borrowed books from the American Jewish Joint Distribution Committee's library. An organization everyone called the *Joint.* A few times, they'd gathered in the shared parlor with other boarders to listen to American records on an old phonograph. The music of Benny Goodman was Chana's favorite. The musician's swing tunes always set her feet tapping.

Though not everything in Vienna was rosy. Stories of crimes across the city traveled fast. As she waited on emigration lines with Mama, she heard of refugees who were robbed of their clothes in broad daylight by black-market dealers. Even worse, women—both gentile and Jew—were attacked and raped by Soviet soldiers just as Meyer had warned them. She kept her guard up. Chana mused she would be a rich woman if she had a groschen for every time she glanced over her shoulder as she walked to and from work.

It eased some of her anxiety to understand how the Allies had divvied up Vienna. Austria was the same as Germany in that way, where the United States, Britain, France, and the Soviet Union each governed a section of the country. Vienna was divided into five sections, a zone for each Ally country and a fifth section—Innere Stadt—the city center, which was overseen by the Allied Control Council, consisting of people from all four powers. The Empress Hotel was in Innere Stadt, while Nachmann's was outside the center, but still in Vienna's first district. A steady presence of American soldiers in both was a relief for Chana, though no city section was wholly safe.

At the hotel, she checked in with Aron every few hours, to ease her worry over him. On most days, her brother worked with the concierge, a young man with a boisterous personality, who sent Aron on errands all over the hotel. He was a good boss.

The same could be said for Chef Heiss. Meyer had promised the chef would be fair, and it was true. The hotel was full of hungry soldiers, and their kitchen work left no time to rest. On days when Chana cleared tables in the dining room or went to the lobby to retrieve a delivery, she barely had a second to take in the hotel's marble floors, textured wallpaper, and gold leaf–covered moldings. She worked hard and efficiently. Chef's instructions were concise. If followed, he doled out praise. If one made a mistake or showed laziness, he yelled. Chana was never lazy, and she was careful not to make a mistake.

Both she and her mother spent most days peeling, chopping, and slicing ingredients for the day's meals. Though the chef worked them hard, he also fed his kitchen staff daily, preparing stews and soups made from vegetable and meat scraps. In the Stutthof concentration camp, the Nazis fed them only once a day, in the morning. A meal of watery soup made from dirty potato peels—sand and grit were part of every mouthful—and a thin slice of bread. SS soldiers, wearing green uniforms, held whips and flanked the door of the barrack. To get to the soup, the prisoners filed out one by one, and the soldiers whipped them as they passed.

Every day began the same: *Whip! Soup!*

Within a month, the soldiers had whipped Chana's back, buttocks, and legs, leaving welts all over. By comparison, Chef Heiss's staff meals in Vienna equaled a joyous feast.

At the end of their second week, Chana fell onto her mattress after another long day. She listened to the rhythmic breathing of her slumbering mother and brother. Her thoughts traveled to Meyer. It had been fourteen days since he'd suggested they have tea. Though the black-market dealer had come by the kitchen once to deliver a slaughtered boar and a crate of plates for Chef Heiss, he hadn't even glanced at Chana.

She rolled onto her side, pulling the blanket to her chin. She stared at the wall's peeling paint illuminated by moonlight slipping through the window. Meyer's lack of attention should be a relief, considering Mama's eagerness to have Chana marry. But his acceptance of her scars, and the boyish look on his face when he'd invited her . . . Well, Meyer Suconick occupied her thoughts like no man ever before. Here in the darkness, curiosity needled under her breastbone. Chana's chutzpah had reminded Meyer of someone. Who? A girlfriend? A wife? His mother?

Mama wanted her to spend time with him. If she and Meyer were to be friends—and nothing more—then the next time Chana ran into him, *she* could invite him to tea. Yes! It was a splendid idea.

She tossed onto her other side. Exhaustion made her limbs feel heavy, yet sleep eluded her.

Elias came to mind. He would be baking again tonight. She'd overheard him asking for Trolfe's permission. She dreamed of baking with him. Work had been so busy that there'd been no chance to talk with Elias again. Yet every so often, she would glance up and their eyes would meet. He'd smile. Then she'd smile. These exchanges made her feel connected to him, and she wondered if he felt it, too. Chana had also noticed how his brows drew together when he concentrated and the way he tapped his fingers during instruction. There was a quiet confidence about him. *I'll get it right next time* was what Elias had said to her that first day. Often, his next attempts were perfect. Like Chana, he was a quick learner.

An idea propelled Chana to sit up. If she couldn't bake with Elias, she could at least watch.

The room was silent except for Mama's light snoring. Her mother could sleep through bombs exploding, and occasionally had. Her brother lay still.

Chana tiptoed to the bureau and gathered some of the left-behind clothes, then her boots, and carefully crept from the room.

In the communal bathroom, a spare space containing a toilet, a sink, a cracked mirror, and a bathtub, she dressed, pulling men's trousers and a shirt over her nightgown. They were big, but would do.

Next, she tucked her hair into a brimmed Tyrolean hat, the kind favored by men in the city. In the cracked mirror, she scrutinized her reflection. Anyone looking would see a teenage boy. Her disguise pleased her.

When she'd helped the Vilna resistance, her only disguise had been her blond hair, a confident attitude, and a good coat; three things that had allowed her to move around the ghetto and the gentile part of Vilna. Of course, on those trips, she wore no yellow patch on her chest and back to mark her as a Jew (an offense punishable by death).

Natan gave her the coat after weeks of successfully smuggling messages in and out of the ghetto. Smuggling, all kinds of things, was an everyday occurrence for the Jews of Vilna. Some, like Chana, carried information. Jewish laborers, Papa included, strapped flour, sugar, eggs, and meat to their bodies as they returned to the ghetto in the evening after working grueling days in Nazi factories. Coffins ferried in hospital supplies. Sympathetic gentiles tossed over sacks of potatoes from rooftops beside the ghetto's barbed-wire fence. At one point, some partisans Chana knew snuck in concert instruments, burying them in a courtyard. Eventually, Jewish musicians retrieved the instruments and organized a secret symphony to raise the spirits of the ghetto's Jews. For an hour, the music had transported Chana beyond their daily hell.

On one mission into the gentile section of Vilna, Chana made it out of the ghetto by scrambling under a sliced section in the barbed wire. She moved quickly to blend in with others on the street. Four blocks and ten minutes later, she found the correct apartment building, climbed the narrow stairs to the second floor, and knocked on the fifth door. A woman answered, and Chana immediately recognized her as a singer who used to frequent her father's bakery. She was a towering woman, a foot taller than Chana. Sonye. That was her name, and she had loved Papa's *Napoleonas Torte,* a custard-filled layer cake. Chana swore recognition dawned in the woman's eyes.

Sonye ushered Chana inside and shut the door. Three men stepped in from another room. Chana recognized the one with a thick beard. He was a high-ranking Vilna partisan who often spoke at meetings. Chana pulled the book from the slit lining inside her coat. "Natan said to give this to you."

He took the book, and gave her a pamphlet that she slipped into the same slit. The men left, climbing out a window at the rear of the hallway. She was about to leave, too, when a pounding hit the door.

"*Aufmachen!*" a man's hard voice shouted.

Chana jumped.

Sonye's eyes widened and she whispered to Chana, "Stand behind me."

Chana did, and this woman grabbed a long cape from the coat stand. "Wrap your arms around my waist."

She hugged the woman from behind. Sonye swept the cape over the two of them, trapping Chana in a fog of strong perfume and stale cigarettes.

"Say nothing," Sonye hissed. "Move as I do and try not to breathe." From Sonye's motions, it was clear she was clasping the garment closed.

This will never work. Sweat dampened Chana's neck. If the Nazis caught her with the pamphlet and the message within, they would take her to Ponary and shoot her. After, they'd likely kill her family and the others in their apartment. Sometimes, the Nazis killed everyone in the building to make a point.

The door opened. "What can I do for you this evening?" Sonye asked.

Footsteps marched in and past, and Sonye adjusted her stance. Thankfully, the cape covered Chana's feet.

Minutes stretched into an eternity as Chana fought to stay perfectly still. Footsteps neared again. "I'm looking for some men," the same German voice said. "You're the only one here?"

"Sadly, yes," she said.

Chana held her breath.

"Are you going out?" the German asked.

Dear God, don't let them make her take off the cape.

"No. I returned a few minutes ago," Sonye said. "It's chilly in here. No one to keep me warm." Her sultry voice vibrated against Chana's chest.

"Hmm," the German said. "You're the one who sang at the concert last week?"

"*Ja*," she said.

"You have a lovely voice."

"Thank you." She giggled.

"Sorry to disturb you."

"Don't be sorry." Her voice had purred.

The men left, and neither Chana nor Sonye moved. For several minutes, they stood with Chana hugging Sonye's soft middle. At last, the woman whipped off the cape, and Chana gulped her next breath as if emerging from a dark, airless cave.

"We need to get you out. They could come back."

"But it's late." Chana was supposed to have turned around immediately and cut through the city before curfew. She didn't know if she could make it now. And what if the soldiers were watching the building?

"Don't worry," Sonye said, clearly reading Chana's concern. "With your hair, we'll waltz you right past the Nazis." She draped her cape over Chana's shoulders and fluffed her hair. "Let the gold in your hair twinkle under the stars. You're too glamorous for the Nazis to stop."

Sonye's courage was contagious; Chana's hands stopped shaking. The singer drew a fur stole over her own shoulders and guided Chana out the same window the men had used before. They climbed down a narrow metal ladder attached to the brick wall and landed in an alley. It seemed Sonye knew where Chana needed to go, and they hurried up the block toward the cut in the barbed-wire fencing.

The woman produced a silver flask from her pocket, drank, then passed it to Chana.

She sipped, finding it filled with water. Sonye stumbled, obviously pretending to be drunk, then began singing softly. Chana joined in. They passed a patrol, a Nazi, who smirked, but didn't stop them. They made it to the fence.

Sonye kissed Chana's cheeks. "I loved your father's cake. I hope he's well."

"He is," she said, the mention of Papa's baking making her voice crack.

"You must go." With gloved hands, the woman heaved the fence up, which gave off a whining creak. Chana slid underneath and hurried away without looking back.

She imagined every swish of Sonye's cape were the wings of a bird, transforming her into her code name, and carrying her to safety. Thankfully, she made it back to the apartment. Two days later, Natan informed her that, later that night, after Chana had escaped, the Gestapo had arrested Sonye and sent her to Lukiškės Prison. No one ever saw her again.

Now, in Nachmann's bathroom, Chana splashed water on her face, then shrugged on the men's jacket. She froze. In the lapel was a Nazi insignia pin. Whoever left these clothes behind had been a member of the party. Chana considered stripping off the garments and ripping them to shreds. *No!* She would not. She swallowed her revulsion. They were a means to an end, a way to stoke her love of baking, even if she only watched from afar. "God, forgive me," she whispered and slipped the pin into her pocket.

She pulled her hands into her sleeves to still their shaking and reminded herself that moving around Vienna as a slight-bodied man was better than walking alone as a woman.

Chapter Ten

Chana

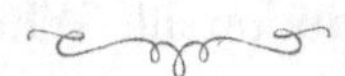

Once Chana landed outside, she moved quickly and with purpose. After two weeks in Vienna, she'd grown familiar with the streets between Nachmann's and the Empress Hotel. If she heard footsteps or loud male voices, she could duck behind mountains of wreckage or dash into abandoned buildings.

A block from the hotel, she arrived at a sewer grate. She took the Nazi pin from her pocket, spit on it, then dropped it between the grids. "Shit rejoins shit," she whispered.

Chana ducked into the familiar alley by the Empress Hotel kitchen, where light poured from the high rectangular windows. Chana quietly scaled a stack of wooden boxes and peeked inside a cracked window. A whiff of sweet dough washed away the putrid stink of the alley, and her mouth watered. Hunger made her feel weak.

Elias stepped into view. A mound of dough rested on the worktable and a pot simmered on the stove.

What was he making? Chana tipped up on her toes to see better.

Elias dipped a spoon in the pot, then tasted a dark liquid. He pulled a face and dropped the spoon in the sink with a clatter.

She inhaled and caught the faint smell of cooked fruit. *Grapes or plums?* She couldn't be sure.

A car horn blasted from the street, startling her, and the boxes shifted. She gripped the windowsill. When she looked back in the kitchen, Elias's eyes were on her.

She leapt from the boxes, ready to flee, when he slammed out of the kitchen and blocked her.

"Who are you, and why are you spying on me?"

She looked up at him.

Recognition dawned on his face. "Chana? Why are you dressed like a man?"

"It's safer this way if I need to move around by myself."

"What are you doing here?"

"I wanted to watch you bake."

Instead of being flattered, his mouth twisted. "You're a spy! Herr Trolfe warned me that other chefs were after his recipes. Who are you working for?"

She pulled back, offended. "I'm working for Herr Heiss in the same kitchen as you! You saw me hired. Meyer Suconick brought us here."

"As if he's trustworthy." His voice had grown rough with contempt.

It was possible she'd misjudged Elias. But she was here now, and her fingers itched for the mound of dough inside the kitchen. An idea came to her. "I told you my father was a baker, and I've missed it. I sensed what's on the stove dissatisfied you."

His eyes narrowed. "How did you know?"

"My father . . . If one of his recipes wasn't perfect, it tortured him until he got it right. I see it here." Her fingertips touched the outer edges of his soft brown eyes. "Maybe I can help you."

He licked his lips. It seemed that her offer tempted him. "How?"

"Let me taste it."

"How do I know you won't sabotage me?"

"You'll have to trust me."

His doubt sat between them. Until he said, "Come inside, but if you give away anything I'm doing, you'll be out on your ear. I'll make sure of it."

"Okay," she said.

Once inside, Chana went straight to the pot. The aroma of plums—*yes, definitely plums!*—reeled her in. She grabbed a spoon and tasted the dark jam. Her lips puckered and her nostrils stung. It was bitter. Tart. "Do you have honey?" She removed her hat and coat, slipping on an apron.

"One jar." He produced the jar from his crate. "Don't use too much. I pay for these supplies."

"We only need a little." She understood his need for frugality and added honey in half-teaspoon increments. After two teaspoons, the plum jam was sufficiently sweet.

Elias took a taste, his mouth forming a surprised O. "It's better."

"I know." Honey was Papa's favorite ingredient for fixing bitterness.

"It's not perfect," he said.

She bit the insides of her cheeks to keep from responding. It was more palatable than his attempt. "Are you making *Buchteln*?" she asked instead.

"Yes, good guess." Elias's eyes twinkled as his suspicion ebbed. "I bought the plums myself in the Karlsplatz. My parents sent me a schilling for my birthday. I turned eighteen last week."

"Happy birthday."

He smiled, and she eyed the dough.

Her father had also made the traditional Viennese sweet rolls, teaching himself the recipe after a brief trip to the city when he was a younger man. "Before your mama or you and Aron were even a dot in my mind," he'd once told Chana. "Can I help you assemble them?" she asked Elias.

He looked between the dough and the pot. "All right."

She couldn't contain the smile that spread across her face. Elias couldn't know how momentous this was for her. It would be her first time baking since the Germans invaded Vilna.

Chana and Elias spent the next hour rolling out dough, cutting three-inch rounds, dolloping jam on each, and molding the dough into balls. Every breath brought a heady mix of flour and sugar to her lungs, and she savored it, wishing she could spend every day this way.

Elias tapped her arm. She looked over to where he'd written *I'm sorry* in a thin film of flour on the counter. His cheeks reddened, the color spreading to the tips of his ears. He pinched dough edges together and avoided looking at her as he said, "I shouldn't have accused you of spying. I didn't want to get in trouble with Herr Trolfe."

She appreciated his apology and wiped the flour smooth. She poked two dots for eyes and drew a smile. "I shouldn't have snuck up on you."

He grinned. "So, our first fight is over?"

She laughed, and so did he. It had been a while since anyone had made her laugh. It was wonderful. She peered up at him. "Are you expecting us to quarrel often?"

"We're both passionate about this." He waved at the dough and jam. "Passionate people can argue, but it doesn't mean they can't be friends."

Of course, there were times even she and Papa had clashed. And she liked Elias.

With that settled, they both grew shy, and focused on filling four pans with rolls. Elias showed her how to use a small greased ladle to create uniform round tops—a lesson from Trolfe. Chana instructed Elias to tighten the dough around the jam so they wouldn't leak. After, they brushed the rolls with melted butter and popped them in the oven. Chana eyed the clock. It was nearing midnight. She wanted to stay until the rolls had finished baking, but she needed to leave. If Mama woke and found her gone, well . . . She didn't want to think of what would happen.

"When do you think they should come out?" he asked.

Chana and the rest of the kitchen staff had witnessed Elias over-cooking baked goods. "Twenty minutes." She hung up her apron and slipped on her jacket and hat. "Keep an eye on the clock."

"Aren't you going to wait?"

"I need to get back." She buttoned her coat. "Do you live near the hotel?"

"No, I billet here, in the basement, along with the other apprentices." He coughed. "Thank you for helping. They'll come out better because of you."

Pride and gratitude twined together in her chest. Her abilities were still part of her, even after these horrible years. "I've learned from you as well." It was true. As Trolfe's apprentice, Elias could teach her plenty. She had a question, and though she knew she should bury it, she couldn't. "If I met you here on another night when you bake, would you let me help?"

His face glowed as if she'd given him wings that would allow him to fly. "I was about to ask you the same thing." His lips lifted into a grin and she didn't need a mirror to know her smile matched his.

"When next?" she asked.

"In four nights. I need to replenish my supplies. Does ten o'clock work?"

She could sneak out again once Mama and Aron were asleep. "Sure." She turned to go, but stopped. "Please, don't tell anyone."

"The same goes for you. If Herr Trolfe found out, he wouldn't like it. I'm surprised he allows me to do this at all."

They shook on their agreement, the burns and scrapes on his knuckles matching her own; scars from Papa's kitchen beside those more recent.

"You're a very talented baker," he said, hanging on to her hand.

"Thank you." The kitchen grew brighter, and a pleasant sensation glided under her skin. Landing in this kitchen with Elias was like being hauled out of a raging sea and into a sailboat. She was alive, and now look at this luck.

He smiled. *Had he read her mind?* The clock seemed to tick inordinately loudly, and reluctantly, she let go of him. "Take the rolls out of the oven in sixteen minutes," she said and tipped her hat in goodbye.

Chana hurried back to Nachmann's, her spirit the lightest it had been in years. Two hours with Elias had passed easily, in part because of the baking, but also because of him. His enthusiasm matched her own, and she found him easy to be around. She stifled a giggle as she recalled his flour-written apology.

Her imagination raced forward. She would bake with Elias, honing her skills, and absorbing the lessons he took from Trolfe. Though

Chana and Elias had agreed to secrecy, she hoped eventually they could tell Trolfe she'd helped Elias. The pastry chef was a tyrant, but if her abilities won him over, then maybe she could become an apprentice, too. But if Trolfe wouldn't accept her, as Meyer had implied, Chana would take what she'd learned with her to America. There she would find work in a bakery, using the skills she'd inherited from her father. Making *Buchteln* tonight had made her feel as though Papa was still with her.

The war and the Nazis had not killed this vital part of her.

In Stutthof, at night, she had made a habit of repeating Papa's recipes in her mind, despite the hunger in her belly—a ritual to stay whole.

Now, as she made her way back to Nachmann's, she recalled the ingredients for her father's *Cremeschnitte* to keep her company on the dark streets. Eggs, milk, sugar, butter, flour, vanilla, and several sheets of his pastry dough would create slices of heavenly thick custard between layers of flaky pastry. "A *bisl* of confectioners' sugar on top makes it pretty," her father would say.

She pulled the collar up on her jacket, grateful to be camouflaged in these men's clothes.

Halfway to the boardinghouse, she spotted a woman walking alone, slowed by the bundle she carried.

A few steps later, Chana heard voices. Her alarm escalated as several soldiers appeared by the corner. Even in the dark, she made out the tall sheepskin hats and sharp-angled uniforms that belonged to the Red Army. Chana took cover in a bombed-out building, crouching behind a broken wall. She'd already crossed out of Innere Stadt, and these soldiers were beyond their zone, not that there was anyone to chase them out.

One soldier yelled, and the only bit Chana made out was "Fräulein."

Ice filled her veins. She peeked out as a Soviet soldier pointed at the woman with the bundle, who had halted like a rabbit facing a hunter.

Crouched in the shadows, Chana wanted to do something. *But what?* She tugged down the brim of her hat. It was dark. If she hurried, she prayed those soldiers would see her as a reedy man.

She sped forward, beating the soldiers to the woman. "*Der Schatz*," Chana said, throwing her voice to its lowest octave and grabbing the lady's arm.

The woman startled at the endearment.

Chana whispered, "Don't be alarmed" as she took the bulky bundle and skirted her arm protectively around the woman's waist. "I mean no harm. But I can't say the same for them." She gestured toward the soldiers closing in.

The woman's gaze darted from Chana to the men, who hesitated.

"*Ja, mein Liebling*," she said with wide, frightened eyes.

"This way." Chana tugged the woman up the block and away from the soldiers. Then they turned left, then right down an alley, before hunkering behind a broken wall. The woman panted, and said, "*Ich—*" but Chana put her finger to her lips.

Footsteps neared, followed by voices speaking Russian. Chana didn't need a translator to know the Soviet soldiers were cursing them. Sweat dampened her armpits.

Silence fell. Chana and the woman didn't move.

Chana silently counted to one hundred, then peeked out from their hiding spot. The soldiers were gone. Her legs shook as she stood.

"*Danke*," the woman said, wiping her eyes.

"You're welcome. You shouldn't walk alone at night." Chana kept her voice deep.

"I had no choice. I had to meet someone to get food and medicine for my parents."

The woman had a narrow face and her tattered coat hung loose on her frame. Chana knew the *someone* she referred to had to be a black-market dealer.

"Where do you live?" Chana asked.

"Three blocks that way." The woman's arm stretched in the direction of Nachmann's boardinghouse.

"Come, I'll walk you." She lifted the bundle higher. It was heavy, but she could manage it more easily than the woman could. It was best for them to hurry.

They fell in step, speaking enough for Chana to learn the woman's name was Louisa, she was Austrian, and her house was the one where she'd grown up, and ridden out the war.

"This is it." Louisa indicated a brooding, dark stone house.

Chana handed back the bundle. Louisa rummaged through the bag and handed Chana a tin of meat. "For your trouble. It's all I have."

"I didn't ask for anything."

"You're a sweet boy," she said. "But your cheekbones tell me you need this meat as much as I do. Don't let pride get in the way."

Chana slipped the can into her pocket. "Thank you."

Louisa looked up the street, where the level of damage varied among the buildings. "It's terrible what the Soviets did to our city when they overtook the Germans." She shifted close enough for Chana to smell her musty breath. "They're almost as bad as the Jews."

Chana froze. What about their interaction would make this woman believe it was all right to share her hatred?

"I should go in." Louisa bounded up the stairs, and the door thudded shut behind her.

Rage flared in Chana's chest. She hurled the can of meat at the door, where it clanged against the wood and ricocheted back, landing by her feet. *Come back out!* her thoughts cried. She wanted nothing more than to announce herself as a Jew. For Louisa to know who had saved her skin that night.

But no one came.

A car sped past, and it was Meyer's face Chana pictured, recalling his intensity and advice as they left the train station.

Build your lives back. That will be your sweet revenge.

Chana put the dented can in her pocket. Food would help her grow stronger.

Chapter Eleven

Chana

Chana woke early on a Sunday morning three weeks after their arrival in Vienna. It was her and Mama's first full day off from the kitchen, and though they only planned to do errands, she was looking forward to their day together. The hotel concierge expected Aron at nine, so first, she and Mama would escort him there.

She rose from her mat, careful not to wake her brother, who liked to sleep as late as possible. Mama snored lightly from the bed, and Chana patted her arm. Her mother's eyes flew open, startled, but calmed once she'd taken in her surroundings. "I'll meet you in the bathroom," Chana whispered.

"Mm." Her mother flipped onto her back.

Chana slipped her coat over her nightgown, using it as a robe, grabbed her rough, thin towel, and went up the hall to the bathroom.

She was brushing her teeth when her mother came in. "I woke Aron. He'll be ready soon," Mama said.

After they'd both finished washing up, Chana and her mother left the bathroom, nearly bumping into Frau Gruber, who lived across the hall.

"I shouldn't have to follow you two," Frau Gruber said. "Be quicker next time."

"We weren't in there but a few minutes," Mama said.

The woman's nose wrinkled in disgust, as if Chana and Mama were nothing but a pair of spiders who'd crawled out from under the washroom door. "You two don't belong here." She snapped her towel at Chana's mother. "Go back to your country."

Mama pushed past the woman. "I pay my rent and I'm not leaving."

Frau Gruber shouted, "How dare you touch me!"

Mama stood her ground. "You don't frighten me."

"Mama, let's go." Chana touched her mother's arm, but she jerked away.

At the end of the hall, Aron stepped out of their room, his hair mussed from sleep. Herr Gruber appeared from his room as well and stormed over. "What's going on here?"

His wife sneered at Mama. "She put her hands on me."

"You're lying," Chana said.

Herr Gruber got in Mama's face. "You keep your filthy paws off my wife, or you'll be sorry."

Danger signs loomed in front of Chana, and she tried to pull her mother away. "Come."

Mama tugged free, then told Herr Gruber, "What do you think you're going to do?"

The man punched Mama in the eye, and she fell back into Chana's arms. Chana staggered, struggling to keep her mother from landing on the ground. "I've got you," she whispered. Though she helped her mother stand, the older woman slumped against Chana's side, her hand to her eye.

"Mama!" Aron screamed and ran to them. He supported their mother from her other side. His cheeks were splotchy.

Herr Nachmann bounded up from the stairwell. "What's going on? I can hear you shouting from the bottom floor."

A murderous rage distorted Mama's features. "That hoodlum hit me!"

Herr Nachmann positioned himself between Mama and the smug-faced Grubers. "I won't have this trouble in my house." His warning look touched all of them. He told Chana and Aron, "Take your mother to your room."

He couldn't blame them for this! "We didn't start it." Chana's voice shook.

"Go," Nachmann ordered.

She and her brother gently guided Mama down the hall and into their room, settling her in a chair.

Aron hugged their mother. "Mama, will you be all right?"

"I'll be fine," she said, patting his back.

Mama's eye was already red and swollen, and Chana wanted to go back to the bathroom and make a cold compress. Only, she didn't dare, fearing more trouble would come in her absence.

A few minutes later, a knock hit their door, and Herr Nachmann came in.

"The Grubers are despicable," he said. "They always have been."

Mama looked vindicated. "Are you kicking them out?"

"No. And I'm not kicking you out, either," their landlord said. "This building benefits by staying in Meyer Suconick's favor. But I won't abide fighting in my house. I'll look the other way this time, but not again."

"Thank you, Herr Nachmann," Chana said, relieved. Then another emotion sloshed around in her chest—she was also grateful to Meyer. Her mother was right; he could be helpful to them.

Herr Nachmann left, and Mama pushed up to stand, using the table for support. "Let's get ready."

"You should rest," Aron said. "I can walk to the hotel on my own."

"*Narishkeit*," Mama said. "It's too dangerous."

"She's right," Chana added.

Aron's eyes hardened. "Why do people still hate us?"

Chana looked to her mother because she didn't have an answer.

Finally, Mama frowned and said, "*Boychik*, I have no idea." Then she turned to Chana. "If only you had a husband, that man wouldn't dare touch me. See what I mean now?"

Chana took in a sharp breath. Of course she understood what her mother meant, and the last thing she wanted was for them to be hurt. She rubbed her mother's back. "We'll find a way out. This week, I'll go to the emigration offices with you again." She and Mama had been making good use of the list of offices from Meyer. Her mother, especially, who went anytime she was off from work.

Mama didn't answer. Instead, she cut three thick slices of bread from the half loaf they'd bought with rations, gave each a slick of butter, and handed them out. "Eat and finish dressing." She touched the skin beneath her eye and winced. "Yes, we'll visit the offices together this week."

Aron slowly pulled on his shoes. Chana ate her bread, grateful to slide marriage off the table for the time being.

After leaving Aron at the hotel, Chana and Mama linked arms and walked for a bit to learn their way around Vienna. It was a clear, crisp Sunday morning, and church bells rang at varying intervals. Chana found something comforting in the clanging echo; it meant people were out attending church, and perhaps there was safety in numbers on the streets.

Their walk took them by Stadtpark, over the Donaukanal, and near the Prater in Leopoldstadt, where they stopped. They could see the ruins of the amusement park, debris and bent metal filling much of the lot, save for the Ferris wheel, which was unscathed. People milled about, staring up at the giant ride.

Chana said, "I read the emperor built the Ferris wheel in 1850."

"You have an astonishing ability to recall facts." Her mother appeared more impressed with her daughter's smarts than the spectacle in front of them.

"It's how I remember Papa's recipes."

"Not that it will do us any good now."

"Someday it will."

"Ah, Chana, your papa was a dreamer, too." For the first time in a long time, her mother didn't make this comparison sound like a curse. Mama seemed transfixed by the ride. "It's as though God himself shielded it."

And us. Chana tilted her face toward the sky, appreciating the sun on her cheeks.

"We should go," Mama said. "Lingering isn't wise."

They stopped first at the Jewish soup kitchen Meyer had mentioned as he'd led them through Vienna, where they devoured large bowls of a hearty chicken stew. It wasn't anything as tasty as what Herr Heiss fed them, but on days off, this kitchen helped fill their bellies and stretch their money and rations.

They stopped on the way back to Nachmann's for Mama to buy thread at one of the few stores open in Innere Stadt. "It was once a fine store," the burly man behind the counter said to another customer as he looked woefully at the sparsely stocked shelves. "Until the Anschluss. Then the Nazis shut it down."

Chana knew the Anschluss had occurred in March 1938 when Germany took power in Austria, and new laws stripped many Austrian Jews of citizenship. They were forced to sell their businesses and land for a pittance to any gentile who wanted it.

The past weighed heavily on her as she inspected a basket of cloth remnants. A few feet away, Mama picked up a can of meat. Chana's eyes drifted to a box of fine yarn, the kind used for needlepoints. Before the war, needlepoint had been her mother's favorite pastime.

She could picture her mother in the evening, settled in their parlor rocking chair, a canvas draped over her lap, and her fingers pinching a needle and deftly stitching flowers. The last time Chana had seen the needlepoint bouquet was in 1941, and it was a memory that broke her heart.

Her father had burst into their apartment out of breath.

"We're leaving," her father said. "Take one bag and only what you can carry." He'd been at a meeting with other Jewish businessmen in the city. There he'd learned that the German army was advancing toward Vilna.

Papa wanted them to head east and cross into the Soviet Union before it was too late.

"Better to take our chances with the Soviet soldiers than the Nazis," her mother mumbled with a shaky voice.

The air in their apartment grew thick with fear as Chana whipped open her drawers and didn't know where to begin. She stuffed clothes, undergarments, and socks in a bag, then stopped. She moved past the dolls she no longer played with and grabbed the notebook where she wrote Papa's recipes. The only other item she took was a book—*Little Women*—her cousin had sent from America. It was in English, but annotated by her uncle in Yiddish, so she could learn the language.

They left in their horse-drawn wagon. Once they were on their way, it appeared as though all the Jews in Vilna were pouring out of the city. Some walked, others pushed handcarts or, like them, rode in wagons. A few drove cars. Later, dozens of abandoned automobiles dotted the road—either broken-down or out of fuel.

On the first night, Chana and her family stopped in a forest. Mama had brought food: bread, water, apples, and a hunk of cheese. They ate a little, then slept close together on a blanket, keeping a firm grip on their belongings to prevent them from being stolen.

Back on the road the next day, Luftwaffe planes streaked overhead, their dark, evil swarm filling the sky. Bombs fell, and explosions followed, first in the distance, then nearer. Their wagon rocked violently as black plumes of earth and smoke mushroomed over empty fields. Another explosion made their horse buck, but Papa held tight to the reins. Chana's teeth chattered. She was certain it was the end of the world.

They continued on their way toward the Soviet border. An hour after the planes disappeared, people trickled by, only they were coming from the direction of the Soviet Union. More followed.

Papa stopped a man pushing a cart. "Where are you going?" he asked.

The fellow shook his head. "The Nazis have blocked the ways to the border. They're marching in this direction. Didn't you see the planes?"

"We did," Papa said.

The man shrugged, as if that answered everything. "We're going back to Vilna. If you keep on that way, you'll greet the Germans."

Papa hopped down from the wagon and stood in the middle of the road.

"Jacob?" Mama asked. "What should we do?"

Her father didn't answer. He stared east as if wishing the man were mistaken. More people passed; women who were hunched over as if the sky had collapsed onto their backs, and grown men sniffling.

Her father hauled himself back into the wagon. He guided the horse to turn their wagon around, and as they followed the road back to Vilna, Chana saw many dead bodies in fields and ditches. She couldn't tell if they'd died from bombs or bullets. She vomited twice and cried for most of the trip.

When, at last, they neared Vilna, they found a Nazi checkpoint manned by rifle-toting soldiers and their dogs. The soldiers made them surrender the wagon and most of their belongings. Mama had taken the bouquet needlepoint with her. A German soldier slammed it against the ground, splitting the wood frame. Mama gasped, and Chana felt something crack in her chest.

Now, in the Vienna store, Chana said, "Look, Mama." She gestured to the basket of yarn.

A smile lifted her mother's lips. She picked up a royal-blue bundle, but quickly dropped it, as if touching it would oblige her to buy it.

"Do you miss it?" Chana asked.

"I miss a lot of things."

"We could buy some yarn and find a canvas for you."

"Not now. Train and ship tickets aren't free." She lingered by the basket, a pale bruise already visible under one eye. "We need to save."

Although Chana understood, it made her sad. "Did you find thread?"

"He wants too much. We'll have to go to the Karlsplatz."

Chana touched a basket of cloth remnants. "I also . . . I need some rags." She looked down, embarrassed. Her menstrual period had started that morning, and she needed supplies.

Mama lifted Chana's chin. "It's wonderful. It means you're growing healthier. Don't be ashamed." She kissed Chana's cheek. "Come."

Chana was grateful that in the past few months her bleeding had returned. When they were in Stutthof, she and many women had lost their periods. Several women believed the cause was that the Nazis had slipped something into their food. A former nurse among them attributed it to starvation. Whatever the reason, in whispered conversations, prisoners sobbed about no longer feeling like women or even human. Chana had been seventeen, and wept as well, though she didn't know when she would want children.

A short walk later, Chana and her mother were near the back of the Empress Hotel, and at the edge of the Karlsplatz, where the black market operated daily. Several hundred people had already gathered in the large open space, bargaining with dealers and farmers for food and paying with whatever items they were able to fit in their pockets. Even a chocolate bar could serve as money. Cigarettes, too. People tried not to draw attention to their dealings, though the Inter-allied police force looked the other way.

It didn't take long for Mama to purchase darning thread and a small bag of rags. They walked through rows of everything from food to furniture and parts of bombed-out buildings—there were doors and shutters for sale, often bought for use as firewood because of the city's ongoing shortage of coal. They found a man selling clothes and selected several dark skirts and white blouses for Chana and her mother to share, as well as two shirts and two pairs of pants for her brother—their work uniforms. Chana was uncomfortable buying from the black market because there was no way to know if this dealer had stolen these clothes off the backs of innocent people. When she protested, Mama said, "I can't darn fabric that is ready to disintegrate. With a few extra items, we won't have to wash as much for work."

She stepped away, letting her mother haggle with the man.

"What are you buying?" asked a voice at her shoulder.

"Nothing," she said, assuming it was another dealer peddling more goods. When she turned, she found Meyer holding a handful of flowers wrapped in crinkled newspaper.

He smirked at her apparent surprise. "Is he giving your mother a fair deal?"

"I think so."

"We'll see." Meyer approached the man and whispered in his ear. The fellow scratched his neck and listened. When Meyer was done, they shook hands.

Chana appreciated Meyer helping her mother and smiled as he returned to her while her mother paid the other dealer. "I have to go," Meyer said, "but here." He handed her the flowers.

Her stomach flipped. "Thank you." The only person who had ever given her a flower was her father. They'd been in the Vilna ghetto, with Papa working in the underground bakery. He'd fashioned a teeny flower from spoiled dough, let it harden, and gave it to her. The Gestapo forbade toys and trinkets in the ghetto, so Chana kept her gift under a floorboard where they lived, taking it out only when she was alone.

"These are lovely," she told Meyer.

"I'm glad you like them." His even tone was hard to read.

She peered up at him. "About your invitation for tea . . ." Her nerves momentarily stopped her, but his wide, curious eyes helped her press on. "How about sometime this week?"

Meyer's brows lifted. She found that she liked surprising him.

"I'm very busy this week," he said.

"Yes, I am as well," she countered with exaggerated importance. "*Very* busy."

He grinned at her teasing. "Ah, Chef Heiss keeps you hopping?"

"I prefer skipping to hopping. Always did."

He laughed, a warm, hearty sound that drew her to laugh along.

Shouting broke out between several men nearby. He looked over, a frown replacing his good humor.

"Excuse me." He moved to leave, but stopped. "We'll go for tea soon." Then he hurried toward the ruckus.

Mama came over wearing a radiant smile. "Meyer gave you flowers. They'll brighten our room." She lifted the clothes in her arms. "He negotiated a good price for us."

Chana glanced to where Meyer spoke with several men, the commotion having died down. She willed him to look at her. After a few seconds, he turned and gave her a dashing smile, before his attention went back to the circle of men.

She left the Karlsplatz alongside her mother, inhaling the fragrant bouquet to dispel a smidge of regret over still having to wait for her outing with Meyer.

Chapter Twelve

Chana

Chana and Shifra left the cinema in high spirits after seeing the American film *State Fair.* It was a balmy afternoon at the end of April, a full month after Chana's arrival in Vienna. The film had been in English, and she was proud of having kept up with the story. She even whispered bits of dialogue to Shifra so she would understand, too.

"Do you want to know my favorite part?" Shifra asked.

Chana had enjoyed all of it—the romances, and the spectacle of a big fair with rides and contests. "Sure."

"That a stranger can sit next to you on a roller coaster and become the love of your life."

Chana smiled. "Should we go to the Prater and the Ferris wheel to find your husband?"

"If only . . ." Shifra sighed. "But we promised your friend from work that we'd meet her at Café Trinken, so my husband will have to wait."

They laughed.

They arrived at the café at the same time as Gita. After a quick introduction, the three found a table in the crowded room. The cramped café with its cracked walls served only tea and lemonade, but drew a steady crowd each day. Gita chattered away about a promising date she'd had two nights earlier with an American soldier staying at the Empress Hotel. Shifra hung on every word.

"Which one?" Chana asked.

"Corporal Nance. His name is Jeb. He's from North Carolina. Is that where your father's family is from?" Gita asked.

"No. New Jersey." Chana filed through the times she'd cleared dishes in the dining room, trying to recall this corporal. She remembered a GI tossing a handkerchief to a fellow who was sneezing over and over. "Blow your nose, Jeb." The GI had smacked the chest of the man beside him. "If this guy has a good meal, he sneezes seven times." The soldiers surrounding Jeb counted as he continued to sneeze.

"Does he have dark curly hair?" Chana asked. "He sneezes after a good meal, right?"

"That's him!" Gita said brightly. "And that's not the only good thing he sneezes after." She winked, and Chana felt herself blush.

"He sounds like a dream," Shifra said.

Gita added, "His family lives on a farm. They grow tobacco."

Shifra propped her elbows on the table. "If you marry him, he'll take you to America."

"Wouldn't that be something?" Gita's face glowed.

During weeks of shared breaks and hastily eaten meals in the Empress kitchen, Chana had learned Gita was from Vienna, her mother was gentile and her father Jewish, which made her what the Nazis had declared a *Mischling* of the first degree. Gita's father had been a professor of medicine at the University of Vienna. When the Anschluss began, the authorities prohibited Gita's father from teaching and subsequently arrested him, sending him to Dachau. Gita, her mother, and two sisters survived the war by moving in with her mother's parents in Linz. They never saw her father again, and only after the war had they learned he'd been on his way to the concentration camp when he was shot and killed while leaping off the train to escape.

"Jeb is meeting me here." Gita glanced toward the door.

"I can't wait to meet him," Shifra said. "Perhaps he has a friend for me, though there are several eligible fellows here already."

"Really? Like who?" Chana asked.

Shifra leaned in with a fetching smile and whispered about others in the café, which was frequented by black-market dealers and soldiers from all four Allies.

Chana found it dizzying to keep up with all the details.

Shifra sipped her tea, her face turning serious. "Of course, we need to be cautious around others." She gestured to two men seated in a corner. "That's Kirill Volkov and his brother, Grigory."

Chana immediately recognized them as the men who'd accosted her in the train station.

Shifra told them, "There are two dealers who run the city, and Kirill's one of them. Volkov is a Soviet, not Jewish. Word is he sells items on loan, but if a customer doesn't pay on time, he'll take a beating so badly that he'll never pay off his debt." She carefully pointed. "See the big gold ring on his finger? I've heard he wears it because it leaves a scar."

"That's awful," Chana said.

"He's dangerous," Shifra said, rather matter-of-fact.

War had given them all far too many encounters with dangerous men.

Shifra touched Chana's arm. "Some say he was in a Soviet gulag before the war, and once fighting began, he enlisted in the Red Army. They say he deserted his troops. Some claim he might have been in one of the concentration camps as a *kapo.* Who knows what's true? But watch out for his brother, Grigory; he's the bald one and the crueler of the two."

Chana shuddered. There had been a particularly savage *kapo* in Stutthof. A prisoner, who when entrusted by the Nazis to enforce the camp's rules, stole the paltry soup and bread of others until they starved to death. Chana and her mother had been lucky he never set his sights on them. Chana asked Shifra, "How do you know all this?"

"The women in the laundry talk. A lot."

"Who's the second dealer?" Gita asked.

"Meyer Suconick, of course." Admiration lifted Shifra's voice. She directed their eyes to a lanky, pale man leaning against a wall at the back of the room. "That's Vlad. He's a Soviet and works with Meyer. Acts as his bodyguard." She craned her neck around. "If Vlad's here, Meyer can't be far."

Shifra indicated several other men who worked with Meyer, then sipped her tea. "Meyer and Kirill buy goods across Europe and cross borders like ghosts." Next, she gestured to a group of American soldiers. "That bunch . . . they sell goods on the black market, too. They come to the laundry selling cigarettes and tins of food. Him . . ." She indicated Sergeant McManus—the same soldier who'd given Chana a candy bar on her first day at the hotel. Now he held court with half a dozen GIs. "He's the ringleader. Or so I'm told."

According to Shifra, the sergeant and some other American soldiers had been selling army canteen goods—bought cheap and resold at a premium—but word of their enterprise had spread to their Congress back home, and the government's disapproval had spurred a crackdown. Most stopped what they were doing, but a few, like Sergeant McManus, carried on, using black-market dealers as middlemen to hawk cases of cigarettes, chocolate bars, hard candy, flashlights, and canned foods.

Gita looked over both her shoulders before whispering, "It's true. Jeb told me so, but he's not involved."

"Jeb sounds like a good man." Chana squeezed her friend's hand.

They drank their tea and digested Shifra's gossip until Meyer stepped in through the café's back door. He looked around and gestured to Vlad, who came to his side. Meyer scanned the room, his gaze landing on Chana. She pictured the flowers sitting in a chipped jar on the table in their room. They locked eyes, and a thrill shot through her. She lifted her hand to wave when a woman called over the din, "Meyer?"

He turned, and Chana dropped her hand. A pretty brunette, sporting a green beret, motioned for him to join her table. She looked about the same age as Chana. Meyer hugged her before settling at her table. Had he given this woman flowers, too? If Meyer looked back at Chana, she didn't see. She engaged with her friends, working to ignore the rock lodging in her chest. She had no desire to watch him have tea with someone else. Was his initial request only a polite way to spare her feelings after she'd revealed her scars? Regret pecked at her for having followed up on his invitation.

Shifra tipped toward Chana. "That's not his girlfriend."

Chana ventured another glance. "How do you know?" The woman threw her head back and laughed at something Meyer had said. She even grabbed her beret, as if it would fall off. It was quite a performance.

"I listen when people talk. Meyer doesn't have a girlfriend, though plenty want the opportunity." Shifra's tone had grown annoyed.

"Are you interested in him?" Chana held her breath. The last thing she wanted was to be at odds with her friend.

"He's a man, isn't he?" She laughed. "But no, not really. I have my eyes on a few other prospects."

"Oh, Shifra." Chana giggled, squeezing her friend's hand. In that moment, she wished for all of Shifra's marriage hopes to come true.

Chana said, "We have better things to do than watch Meyer Suconick." But as she looked again, another woman sauntered over to him. A comely redhead. She put her hand on Meyer's shoulder, and he looked up and smiled. The brunette pouted. Chana peeked one more time, noting how Meyer's expression never matched the boyishness she'd detected when he'd looked at her in Nachmann's.

"I'm glad you're still here," said a voice above her.

Chana looked up and found Elias giving her a crooked smile. Her mood lifted like a balloon caught by the wind. "This is a surprise! What are you doing here?"

"Gita mentioned she was meeting you, and I thought I'd come by before the dinner shift. May I join you?"

"Of course." She slid to one side. Elias pulled over an empty chair, sandwiching it between her and Gita.

Gita jumped up. "He's here! Jeb!"

Shifra said, "Perhaps play a little hard to get."

But Gita had already flown toward the front of the café, where her American beau swept her off her feet and planted a kiss on her lips.

"Never mind." Shifra sipped her tea.

"You're working tonight, right?" Elias asked.

"Yes. Mama and Aron are coming by here so we can walk together."

"Ah . . . good. Perhaps I can join you?"

"Of course."

Chana looked up and found Meyer watching her. Heat gathered in her cheeks. The woman at his table, now the redhead, touched his arm, and he gave her a tight smile.

Gita returned to fetch her coat. "Jeb and I are leaving." Then she floated away again.

Chana checked the wall clock. Mama and Aron would be here any minute. "I need to go as well. Come, Shifra, we'll see you to the laundry."

Chana and Elias stood.

"I'm not going," Shifra said.

"But you shouldn't walk alone."

"Maybe I won't." She pulled her shoulders back, enhancing how her blouse's low neckline flattered her bust. "Don't look so worried. That girl works with me at the laundry"—she raised her chin toward a woman two tables over—"I won't leave alone. I promise."

As Chana and Elias neared the door, she spotted Mama and Aron outside. Mama frowned at the sight of Elias following her. Chana glanced back toward Shifra, who'd walked over to a GI near Meyer's table. She giggled at something the soldier said. Chana looked at Meyer, who met her gaze as yet another woman joined his table. His lips flattened when Elias touched her elbow. As if he had some right to her after his afternoon in the company of so many women. Yet, as she turned away, she smiled.

"What amuses you?" Elias asked.

She drank in his kind brown eyes and sturdy presence, even when her mother refused to greet him. "You do, in a good way." She meant it.

"I'm glad."

They headed toward the hotel, falling in step with each other.

Chapter Thirteen

Chana

Vienna, Austria
May 1946

Chana couldn't believe when the calendar turned from April to May; her time in Vienna was passing so swiftly. That first week of May, after a grueling breakfast and lunch working at the hotel, she shifted from foot to foot while waiting in line beside her mother in the American consulate office. She was used to standing in a queue, but that didn't mean she liked it. This wait was especially depressing. She and Mama were invisible, drowning in a sea of refugees also seeking help from overwhelmed bureaucrats.

She pressed on her lower back, trying to soothe a dull ache. The dining room had been short-staffed, and besides food preparation, Chana had spent a chunk of her time clearing tables and hauling heavy trays of dirty dishes.

So far that week, Chana and her mother had already visited the American Jewish Joint Distribution Committee office, the Hebrew

Immigrant Aid Society, and the Red Cross. At each, they'd met overwhelmed, bloodshot-eyed officials, who with varied degrees of sympathy told them the same thing: *Our condolences for your troubles and your loss. The United States is issuing few visas. There are quotas.*

The underlying message was clear: *America doesn't want you!*

Chana was glad Aron was still at work and spared this task at the consulate.

Now a woman in a neat army jacket and skirt led her and Mama to a counter staffed by a man, who grunted as they neared.

"Frau Rosenzweig . . . Chana . . . last time, I told you both that it would be a while before I had news." The man shuffled a stack of folders, pulling one to the top.

Chana spied *Rosenzweig* on the tab.

"Herr Abernathy, it's already been a week," her mother said.

He adjusted his eyeglasses, making his eyes appear bug-like. "A week was not what I meant."

"You have our paperwork," Chana said. "What more do you need?"

In their room at Nachmann's, Chana had helped her mother fill out a seemingly endless number of forms, requiring variations of the same information: their names, birth dates, country of origin, current employment, and any details beyond names that they possessed about their American relatives.

"Did you find the U.S. address for your family?" Herr Abernathy asked.

"Where would I find it?" Mama said.

"Perhaps on a piece of mail?"

Her mother leaned over the counter. "Do you think when the Nazis herded my daughter and me into a concentration camp, they let me bring letters from my family?"

"Some prisoners received and sent mail." He relayed this as if it were Ruth Rosenzweig's fault the Nazis wouldn't let her have a steady correspondence in their death camp.

"Were these prisoners Jewish?" Mama asked.

"I don't know."

Her mother's face turned the color of beets. "I told you that my husband's family lives in New Jersey."

"New Jersey is a big place. We've found no one named Rosenzweig that is related to you."

"Are you even looking?" Mama's voice shook, her despair easy to see.

Chana caught the disapproving glances from those at nearby desks. One man rolled his eyes. Chana remained stoic. A few looks of derision were nothing compared to Nazis with guns.

Abernathy mopped his shiny forehead with a handkerchief. "I have no reason to lie to you. Why not go back to Vilna and see if your family tries to find you there?"

"I will never live with the neighbors who tried to kill us."

"Surely not every neighbor was out to get you."

"Easy for you to say as you sit here with your forms and folders. You don't care about us."

"Madam, look at that line." He indicated the queue that stretched from near the counter, past a maze of desks, and out the door to the hallway. "I have to help all of them, not only you." He sounded defeated. "If I could do more, I would."

Chana felt a flash of sympathy for Herr Abernathy, recognizing how the visa quotas tied his hands. Taking in the line of refugees, people exactly like Chana and her mother, the idea of reaching the United States seemed as impossible as flying to the moon.

"Do you see *this*?" Mama touched the fading bruise under her eye. In the weeks since the altercation with the Grubers, her injury had transitioned from deep purple to pale yellow. Soon it would be gone, though the memory would linger.

Chana placed a calming hand on her mother's arm. "We told you our neighbor did this to my mother. They're Nazis. Have you done anything about that?"

"We questioned the Grubers." Herr Abernathy cleaned his eyeglasses before returning them to his face. "They've been declared innocent of working with the Nazis. There is nothing else to be done."

Her mother's nostrils flared. "I'll be back."

"I have no doubt." Herr Abernathy moved their folder to the bottom of the stack.

They passed the line of refugees still waiting. Sallow-faced men and women, all carrying tales of loss and desperation. Abernathy was right. Her family's sad story was not unique, but didn't that make the situation even more tragic?

They exited to the street as Meyer approached, with Vlad hovering behind him. Chana noticed Meyer was again handsomely dressed in a well-tailored suit. The black market was clearly lucrative.

Meyer brightened at the sight of them. Chana acknowledged him with a dip of her head, keeping her emotions in check. She decided that if they were ever to go for tea, it would be for him to do the asking now.

"This is a nice surprise," Meyer said. "I have business in the consulate myself."

Her mother scowled. "Herr Suconick, is there any word from Herr Schumacher? Can we go to the ports?"

He looked around before telling Ruth, "You should keep your voice down, unless you want the rest of the Brihah to get arrested."

"I want what we were promised. To go to America."

"Mama," Chana said, "it will happen. We must be patient."

"I've been patient. I want action."

"Listen to your daughter." Meyer waved at the building. "Did you have any luck inside?"

"No, and I've also been to the Joint and HIAS, both who have nothing for us. *Gornischt!* Do you know what one woman told me? She said, at least you're free now. I want to go to America, but they won't let me." Mama paused. "How is that free?"

The consulate door burst open and a tangle of refugees tumbled onto the street. Two policemen ran over and broke up the fracas, hauling two of the men away. Chana had seen this scenario on other days, angry quarrels over visas or rations in front of other Vienna offices. Every time, Chana was reminded of the fathers, husbands, and brothers who'd faced off against each other in the Vilna ghetto on the night of the yellow *Schein*; papers given out by the Nazi commander, allowing those with a trade to keep three family members with them in the ghetto. Men tore each other apart in the courtyard, because people without a *Schein*, and their families, were to be taken away. Everyone knew the Nazis would kill those they expelled.

"I know a fellow inside," Meyer said now. "I'll talk to him and see what I can find out. Wait here."

Chana appreciated his willingness to intervene on their behalf, assuaging her mother in the process.

He palmed the door handle, then turned. "Chana, I've been meaning to come by for our tea. Perhaps we'll go today. I won't be long inside."

Despite the women who had surrounded him the other day, Chana was ready to agree. But before she could answer, her mother said, "She would love to."

He left, and she told Mama, "I can speak for myself."

"I was worried you'd say no."

"I was going to say yes." Her mother smiled. "Mama, don't get excited. If anything, we're only friends. Meyer Suconick keeps company with many women. I saw him at the café. He's not looking to be anyone's boyfriend or husband."

Her mother batted away Chana's assessment. "Other women are not you. They are not Golda-lox," her mother said, butchering the nickname bestowed on Chana by the kind American soldier teaching English at Foehrenwald. Mama smoothed Chana's hair. "*Bubbeleh*, he'll be enchanted by you."

"It's pronounced Goldilocks," Chana said, recalling how the fairy tale ended with bears chasing the girl, ready to eat her. "It's only tea, Mama." Still, she had to admit that she was looking forward to the outing; she was curious to learn who Meyer was under all that bravado.

Chapter Fourteen

Chana

It was Chana's first time at Café Victoria, the Innere Stadt place popular with returning Viennese, refugees, and American soldiers. By day they served weak tea, chicory coffee, lemonade, and *heisstrunk*, a bitter mulled water. By night, the café transformed with singers, comedians, and bands performing on a makeshift stage.

Two waiters greeted Meyer, bowing, and immediately escorted Chana and him to a table centered in the room. The place was far from fancy; its wood floor showed patches of dirt where slats were missing. One wall had a jagged round hole about the size of a wagon wheel, affording a view of the stone building next door.

Meyer followed her gaze. "The café is like the rest of us. Shuffling along with parts missing."

Pain filled his voice. Chana wondered what parts of him the war had taken.

The server brought two cups of tea, steam curling off each. She cradled the cup in her palms, appreciating the warmth, because though the hunger in her belly had eased, she was often chilled to the bone.

Meyer said, "There are better places we could go, but I figured we'd start here."

His presumption made her pause with the cup near her lips. Flowers and tea would not entice Chana to become another woman who circled around him as if playing musical chairs. "We've only arrived, and you presume that I'll go out with you again."

He chuckled until he realized she wasn't joking. "Do you always say exactly what's on your mind?"

"I do now." She'd bitten her tongue plenty during the war. Like on the day in the ghetto when a Nazi soldier clubbed a boy much younger than she. The child collapsed to the ground, spitting up blood. Every *Aktion* in the ghetto when soldiers tore people from their homes. The countless times she'd heard gunshots followed by screams. In Stutthof, when another prisoner tried to sneak an extra bowl of soup in the morning and was whipped to death. Chana didn't dare speak out, not even once. Doing so would only earn her a billy club to her back, a jackboot to her ribs, or a bullet to her head.

Silence took a toll on her, too. Guilt crushed her even now as she sipped weak tea. The hot liquid scorched her tongue.

"Tell me," he said, tilting back in his chair. "Was that Trolfe's apprentice that followed you out of Café Trinken?"

"His name is Elias. And he didn't follow me."

"Is he your boyfriend?" His chair legs landed on the ground with a slight *thud.*

"He's my friend." She lifted her chin. "The way we're friends."

He chuckled. "Is that what we are?"

She shrugged, smiling as she sipped her tea. "I think so."

"All right." He drank, too. "So, you ask your friends to go for tea?"

"I suppose I do. And what about you? Was one of those women with you at the café someone special?" Her palms grew slick, but she locked eyes with him, appreciating the sparkle of amusement she saw there.

"No one special." His tone was light.

At a nearby table, two men shook hands. Meyer watched them, then leaned in to tell her, "When I was a boy and out with my family, my sister and I would play a game where we guessed what was happening at other tables." He cast his attention onto the men who'd shaken hands. "I believe they have agreed to put aside a long-held grudge."

"Do you know them?" she asked.

"What would the fun be in that?" He gestured at those sitting at other tables. "Care to play?"

She glanced around. It had been years since she'd played anything. She watched two men at a different table, one at least ten years older than the other. The elder was better dressed, and his mannerisms were more refined. The younger talked a lot, demonstrating something with his hands. "I think the older fellow has agreed to tutor the younger one."

"Tutor?" Meyer said. "In what?"

The older man lifted his glass, and she claimed the first thing that came to mind. "Astronomy."

Meyer stared. "Interesting. You don't strike me as someone who gazes at the stars."

"Like anyone else, I have dreams." She expected him to question, and when he didn't, she told him, "There were nights in the camp when the stars were out and I'd imagine a different place where those same stars sparkled, only there, I'd witness them from under a thick, warm blanket, in a soft bed, and with a full belly." The frigid winter in Stutthof had been brutal. When they'd arrived, the guards had given each prisoner striped pants and a top, and a thin blanket. To survive the harsh cold, Chana and her mother had torn off pieces of blanket to make shoes, scarves, even hats and gloves, leaving not much blanket.

Meyer's gaze grew concerned. "Should we continue playing?"

"Sure," she said.

For the next few minutes, they took turns discussing others in the café, their predictions growing a bit wilder, including a postman proposing to rebuild the Prater, and a magician attempting to conjure a bird from the purse of the woman beside him.

After that last one, Meyer burst out with a rumbling laugh. It was contagious, and she laughed, too.

Once they'd quieted, he asked, "Tell me, Chana, how is Chef Heiss treating you?"

"We work hard, and he feeds us . . . as you promised. My mother, brother, and I eat better than most in the city."

"And you look well."

"Thank you," she said, pleased.

Meyer's comment hadn't come out awestruck or as a crude assessment. Instead, he sounded appreciative for her good health.

She did indeed feel stronger than she had in years. In the weeks since their arrival in Vienna, Chana had filled out. Her clothes fit better, and Aron's cheekbones no longer looked like they could slice through paper. "I'm used to working in a kitchen, though not one as splendid as in the Empress Hotel."

Her mind traveled to the four nights that she'd baked with Elias. Though the city's ongoing rationing made baking difficult, their ingenuity at stretching and substituting ingredients had allowed them to make croissants, *Vanillekipferl*, cheesy *Topfenstrudel*, and *Linzer Torte*. It was her first time making the torte, and Elias had taught her to use ten identical strips of dough for the lattice top, using a ruler for cutting them, as Trolfe had taught him. While they worked, Elias liked to ask about her life back in Vilna, though he remained tight-lipped about his childhood before the war. But she found other ways to get to know him. Already, she'd learned to recognize how Elias bit his lip when a recipe challenged him. Or how when he solved a problem, he would scratch his cheek, leaving behind smudges of flour or jam. It made her giggle, more so because he didn't even realize. She'd pass him a rag, and he'd give her a half shrug and wipe his face. He was passionate and honest, qualities she admired.

"Ah, yes, your father was a baker," Meyer said now.

She raised an eyebrow at his recalling that detail about her papa.

He told her, "I spoke with Aron the other day. A few American soldiers leave me goods in the hotel alley, and your brother helped me move them to my truck."

"Aron didn't mention it," Chana said tightly. She didn't approve of her brother doing black-market work. It could be dangerous.

He smirked. "Don't worry, I tipped him for his trouble."

"Did you?"

"He told me your mother takes most of your earnings. My advice was he should tuck away what I gave him."

"Our mother gives us an allowance and makes sure we have enough to pay for what we need and to save," Chana said in her mother's defense.

"What do you want to buy?"

She'd eyed red lipsticks in the Karlsplatz the other day. "I'm saving for something."

"And that is . . . ?" He tipped closer.

"My mother used to enjoy needlepoint. I found yarn in a shop, and a man in the market has a canvas. It's expensive, so I'm saving."

"That's thoughtful." His jaw shifted. "Who was the dealer?"

"I didn't get his name, but he's there every Thursday."

He drank some tea. "My mother also made needlepoints. She loved art. She liked to take my sister and me to museums."

"Did you enjoy that?"

His lips quirked into a smile. "As a boy, not much. But I appreciate it now."

It amused her to picture Meyer as a rambunctious little boy with a mother attempting to tame him into being an art lover. Chana found she enjoyed talking to Meyer.

"My sister adored the museums," he said. "She reminds me of your brother in that way."

"How so?" Chana asked.

"Drawn to the arts. Aron told me he loves to read."

"Yes." Her brother's hunger for books had grown in the Vilna ghetto. The Judenrat overseeing the ghetto for the Nazis had required Jewish children to attend an underground school. As Aron's classmates disappeared, the more books he borrowed from the secret library in a shuttered prayer house.

"Your brother's a good sort. I like him. I promised to bring him some new books." Meyer's finger traced the handle of his cup. "He claims that you love to dance."

Chana found it curious that Meyer and her brother had discussed her. "I did for a time." Her chest warmed as she remembered Papa turning on the radio, tuning to a music program, and filling their Vilna apartment with sweet melodies. They would dance—her whole family—until they were sweaty and their legs ached and the room smelled like toasted bread. Her mother would grow playful and tease her father that flour and sugar had baked into his skin, and when he perspired, it perfumed the air.

"There's dancing in the cafés at night," Meyer said. "Perhaps you'll come sometime."

His invitation excited her, until she realized it wasn't really an invitation at all. He didn't say perhaps you'll come sometime *with me.* He obviously invited many women for tea, and Chana had no doubt he invited many to go dancing. Despite this happy outing with him, her pride left her no choice but to stay equally ambivalent. "I'll think about it."

He kept his eyes on his cup. "You're unlike other women I've met."

"I assume the sister who accompanied you to museums was more reserved?"

"No, she was quite outspoken. And I only had one sister."

Had. She softly asked, "What happened to her?"

He raked a hand through his hair as his jaw tightened.

"I'm sorry, I shouldn't have asked."

"No." His voice was ragged. "You should ask. We should talk about those we've lost. The Nazis killed her and my parents after an *Aktion* in the Riga ghetto."

The pain in his voice brought horrific images to mind. "What was she like? Your sister?"

"She was blond." He motioned to Chana's hair. "Only, with green eyes, bright as emeralds. We were close, like you and your brother. And she was headstrong."

Chana recalled Meyer saying her chutzpah reminded him of someone. *His sister.* Her chest ached.

"Dora had a wicked sense of humor." A fond smile erased years from his face. "Our father was stern, and my poor sister spent a good deal of time confined to her room."

It always surprised Chana to hear of harsh fathers. Papa was the kindest man she'd ever known. The waiter refilled her cup, and after he'd gone, Meyer seemed lost in thought. She asked, "How did you become part of Herr Schumacher's network?"

He looked at her as if he'd returned from somewhere far away. "I met him six months ago outside Foehrenwald. I'd been searching for my family . . . hoping they'd somehow escaped the killings."

Chana leaned closer. She understood his feelings. Since their liberation, she'd tried to convince herself that it had been someone else shot in the street in Kovno. Not her beloved papa. With the crowds that day, she could have been mistaken. Doubt or hope was why Chana had searched the face of every newly arrived man to Foehrenwald.

"To answer your question," he said plainly, "Herr Schumacher is a persuasive man."

"I know that well. He and my father were friends."

Meyer drained his tea in two large gulps. "Herr Schumacher convinced me to meet the refugees here in Vienna and escort them to the trucks the next day."

"Not for nothing?" she asked.

"There's always a price." He grinned.

Their eyes locked, and the mischief in his gaze made her laugh.

Loud voices from the front of the café drew her attention. Kirill filled the doorway with his shorter, bald brother, Grigory, at his side. When she faced Meyer again, his gaze was riveted to the doorway. He unbuttoned his jacket, revealing a holstered gun strapped to his side.

"Excuse me," he said. "Last week, Kirill robbed one of my men."

Meyer met Kirill by the door, and their faces quickly changed from tense to contorted. Theirs was not a friendly exchange.

Chana wanted no part of their quarrel. *Leave!* her thoughts shouted. She eyed the back door. She could slip into the alley and be gone. Halfway to her feet, a hand landed on her shoulder. She looked up, expecting Meyer. Instead, Grigory loomed over her.

"Hello, beautiful," he said with a tone that turned *beautiful* into something menacing. He pushed her down into her seat.

She shoved away from the table, and he gripped her wrist. He drew close enough for her to smell his sour breath and read the hatred in his eyes. It wasn't the same hatred she'd seen in the eyes of the Nazi guards, but it was a look that melted her bones all the same.

"Let go of me," she said.

His grin widened. "You're a feisty one."

Though others occupied nearby tables, they all looked away. No one moved to help her.

Grigory sniffed her hair. "Girl with the golden hair, let's see how much you fight when I take you into the alley."

He would have to kill her first. She spit in his face. His eyes rounded, and he smacked her across the cheek. Hard. Her skin burned.

Suddenly, Meyer hauled Grigory back by his shirt, forcing him to release Chana. "Never touch her again," Meyer ordered.

Chana stood and backed up, right into Kirill, who blocked her escape.

"No need for a commotion," Kirill said. "Grigory, this one's not worth it." His eyes cut to Chana. "My brother never could spot a Jew."

Grigory yanked free from Meyer, whose other hand rested on his gun.

"You and your brother should stay in the Soviet zone," Meyer warned.

Kirill sniffed loudly. "Innere Stadt is for everyone. I'll go where I please. And if you want to keep your hands at the ends of your arms, you'll keep them off Grigory."

Once they were gone, Meyer took Chana's hand. "Are you all right?"

She pulled away. "I've known worse."

He eyed her buttoned blouse. "I know."

Did she detect pity in his tone? Or something harsher like Zvi? "You know nothing." She picked up her bag and left.

Once Chana was on the street, she touched her fingers to her tender cheek. Tears filled her eyes, but she refused to cry. Then Meyer stepped outside, and she dropped her hand.

"You can't walk home alone," he said.

"I can take care of myself."

"I have no doubt, but still . . . the streets are dangerous."

"As are the cafés." *And you*, she thought. Her mother believed Meyer could protect them. Now Chana doubted that. She strode away, expecting Meyer to return to the café, where surely another young woman would make room for him at her table.

A block later, she crossed the street and spotted Meyer following a few lengths behind. It was a sweet gesture, and despite what had happened, she couldn't help slowing down and allowing him to catch up. They walked side by side, but didn't speak. She focused on her stinging cheek to remind herself of the danger shadowing this man—something she wanted to steer clear of.

Once they reached the boardinghouse, he touched her sleeve. "You should put a cool rag on your cheek. That's what my mother did when I got into scrapes at school."

She expected he found himself in many scrapes. "I will." About to go, he caught her wrist, but struggled to speak. "What is it?" she asked.

"I'm sorry about what happened." His expression was earnest. "Are we still . . . friends?"

Before she could stop herself, she placed her palm on his warm cheek. Surprise ignited in his eyes, and electricity sparked up her arm.

He stepped back. "Good night, Chana." His eyes were bright, though his voice was hoarse.

"Yes, good night." She ran up the building's stairs, part of her wishing Meyer would call to her. He didn't. Baffled over what she'd felt when she touched him, she didn't dare look back. The heavy wooden door slammed behind her, punctuating her ambivalence over him letting her go.

Chapter Fifteen

Zoe

Vienna, Austria
April 2018

To Zoe's disappointment, Henri Martin's story concluded when the elevator doors dinged and Liam and a handful of others swept in. Everyone came armed with a hundred things needing Henri's attention. Most pressing was the keynote address, starting in minutes.

Henri stood. "Let's talk again tomorrow?"

Zoe scrambled up, wishing she had time to ask questions. "That would be great, sir. When do you have in mind?"

"Breakfast. Meet me at eight thirty in the dining room downstairs." He guided her to the elevators. "And please, call me Henri."

"Yes, sir . . . I mean, Henri."

He held the doors open. "There's a seat saved for you in the front row for my speech."

"Thank you," she said, surprised by this thoughtfulness. "I appreciate it." So many questions spiraled in her thoughts, but one was most pressing: *Who are you really, Henri Martin, and how do you know all of this?*

She opened her mouth to question, but the elevator doors closed, and he was gone.

Zoe followed the tide of conference goers headed toward the grand ballroom for the keynote address. She jammed her clammy hands in her pockets. It was unsettling hearing what her family had endured during and after the war. Chana's hunger. Peril lurking around every corner. The blatant antisemitism. Not that the latter surprised her. Even in North Carolina, when Zoe was in the eighth grade, a kid in gym class had called her a *kike* after she stole the ball during a soccer game. A text pinged her phone. Wes.

How is everything?

Zoe hesitated, unsure of how to answer, considering the NDA. She glanced around at the crowds.

ZOE: All good. I just met with Henri.

WES: Excellent. You recorded, right?

ZOE: He wouldn't let me.

WES: Damn. Call me.

ZOE: Can't. The keynote is starting.

WES: Get a picture as soon as you can, then send me two hundred words on his speech. I'll upload it on the website pronto.

ZOE: Ok.

There was a heaviness in her body as she entered the ballroom. The cavernous space had a stage at the front, and rows of white folding chairs flanked both sides of the room, most of which were taken. She cut up the center aisle, fearing she'd already screwed up the most important assignment of her career. Henri had left her no choice but to sign his agreement. She considered Wes's request for a photo, reasoning that Henri's speech, a photo, or anything else happening in this room couldn't be considered off the record. This was a public event. Though, she had the sinking feeling Henri would feel betrayed.

She stopped by a sign at the front that read: RESERVED: GUESTS OF MARTIN BAKING. One chair had her name on it. She sat and slid her backpack under it.

Liam and Henri chatted by the stairs at the far end of the stage. People milled about, but no one paid Henri any attention. Neither he nor Liam wore name tags.

Zoe straightened. People didn't know Henri Martin was standing right in front of them!

This was the time to snap a picture. She had a clear shot. If she sent Wes a photo now, it would blow Henri's cover by a few minutes at most, because once onstage, everyone in the ballroom would plaster his face all over the internet. A familiar thrum hit her chest; she could scoop everyone. This was too good to pass up. She snapped a picture without Henri noticing.

ZOE: This is Henri Martin.

She attached the photo and sent it to Wes.

WES: Excellent! Posting it now. Good work!

An older man dropped into the seat to her left and she darkened her phone. The name on his chair read: JACQUES SIMON. Neatly cropped silver hair contrasted with his tanned face and caramel eyes. He wore a gray suit with a crisp white shirt. The only jewelry of note was a scuffed gold wedding band.

He held out his hand to Zoe. "Jacques Simon, and you are?"

"Zoe Rosenzweig." She shook his hand.

"Ah," he said with an interested smile.

"Are you with Martin Baking?" she asked.

"No. I'm a friend of the family. And you?" He spoke in German-accented English.

"The same, I think."

"Not a bad thing to be," he whispered, as if the two of them went way back, and it puzzled her.

Zoe reasoned this man might have insights about Henri or Eveline, but before she could ask anything, the president of the Boucher Foundation, a middle-aged, elfin-like woman with spiky red hair, strode to the stage's podium. She welcomed everyone and covered the conference logistics, then her introduction quickly moved to the keynote speaker.

"At this time," the woman said, "I invite Jacques Simon, owner of Wonne Bäckerei, to the stage to introduce this year's keynote speaker and co-recipient of our Lifetime Achievement Award."

The man seated beside Zoe walked to the podium. Phone cameras went off, and the anticipation in the room was palpable, everyone waiting to *see* Henri Martin.

Jacques leaned into the microphone. "It is my honor to talk about my friends, Henri and Eveline Martin. We go way back." He paused. "One thing most don't know about Eveline was, when she focused on cracking a recipe, she'd work day and night. The woman barely slept for days, even weeks." He gave a soft chuckle. "Henri once told me he knew a recipe was ready when he'd find Eveline seated at her worktable sound asleep, her cheeks and hair dusted with flour." Jacques quieted briefly, as the audience laughed. "That was Eveline Martin's level of commitment. Together, Henri and Eveline produced some of the best biscuits in the world . . ." He dipped closer to the microphone. "Even I traveled with a pack of Fudgies in my suitcase." Laughter rang out, and Jacques's white-toothed grin lit his face.

Liam shared a conspiratorial smile with Henri.

Jacques's smile faded. "Sadly, we lost one-half of this culinary duo when Eveline passed away in February. She was remarkable." Affection weighed down his words. He gazed out at the audience. "Now, without further ado, I give you Henri Martin."

Henri climbed to the stage, and the crowd's murmurs grew louder. At the podium, the two men hugged, then Jacques returned to his chair.

Liam slipped into the seat on the other side of Zoe. He gave her a business card. "My contact information, should you need it."

She looked at the card as Henri spoke into the microphone. "It's a pleasure to be here. I am Henri Martin."

Photographers swarmed the stage. She hoped Wes had already posted the picture, and that *Savouries* had scooped everyone. *Please let*

Henri understand and not cut me off. The room grew hot as a sauna. She draped her jacket over her chair.

Henri waited for the commotion to die down and continued. "First, I want to thank my old friend Herr Simon for his warm words. If you aren't familiar with his Wonne Bäckerei in Zurich, well, crikey, you should be."

Zoe glanced back. People held their phones high, recording everything. She itched to do the same, but with Liam beside her, she thought better of it.

Henri forced a smile. "As you all know, I prefer to move around anonymously. Looks as though that ship has sailed."

Chuckles followed.

He dipped toward the microphone. "I'm not used to sharing publicly about myself and my company. I'd appreciate your patience as I get used to the attention." His eyes met Zoe's, and she knew he meant this plea for her.

He kept talking, the crowd hanging on every word as unease flooded through her. The room clapped at something Henri had said.

Zoe fidgeted, uncrossing and recrossing her legs. The weight of Wes's expectations, plus Henri's warning, made it hard to sit still.

After the speech, Henri was swept offstage by Liam and several others. Even Jacques Simon disappeared before she could talk to him.

Zoe left the ballroom and sank into a chair in a quiet corner of the outer lounge. She opened her laptop and quickly cranked out two hundred words for Wes, keeping it brief and focused on events in the ballroom.

An international coterie of fourteen hundred attending this year's Boucher Foundation Conference in Vienna, Austria, were in for a treat when Henri Martin, the reclusive CEO of Martin Baking Company, gave the opening keynote address.

Zoe added details about Henri's speech, then sent it to Wes.

He replied: *There's nothing from your conversation with him?*

Tell him about the NDA! her mind screamed, but imagining doing so made her jumpy. Better to wait until she'd sorted out this situation.

ZOE: Saving it for now. More to come. We're talking again in the morning.

WES: Okay. Keep me in the loop. BTW, Henri Martin is all over Twitter. Your picture beat everyone!

Zoe shut her laptop, knowing that her boss was pleased for now. But if she didn't deliver the article on Henri, everything Wes had promised—the bonus and promotion—would go up in smoke. *Poof!* Meanwhile, Henri had warned, *Don't disappoint me.* He could ghost her or sue her. Her leg bounced up and down. She checked the conference brochure, and headed for the panel on Sustainable Growth for Restaurants, eager for a distraction from how this trip had quickly left her teetering on a tightrope.

Chapter Sixteen

Zoe

The next morning, Zoe was up at sunrise, having crashed soon after she checked into her room. From the second she opened her eyes, her thoughts circled to Henri, and everything she'd learned about her great-aunt and Grandpa Aron.

She opened her laptop and checked her emails, the first of which was from Wes:

> ***Your photo has racked up over a million views on Savouries' website.***

Then she reread the brief notes on Henri's stories that she'd typed up before nodding off; she planned to flesh them out later in the day. She opened a tab for the *Savouries* website and found her photo of Henri on the home page, attributed to her, though Wes hadn't added her copy yet. Various social media also showed her shot trending, along with other videos and photos from Henri's speech. Zoe told herself Henri couldn't be upset. Hers was one picture among many.

She closed her laptop and glanced outside. A cerulean-blue sky beckoned, but she only had an hour before breakfast with Henri, and she desperately needed to wash off the previous day's travel with a hot shower. Exploring Vienna would have to wait.

As they'd planned, Zoe met Henri in the dining room. They exchanged *good mornings* as a hostess seated them and served up steaming espresso in delicate porcelain cups. Zoe took a fortifying swallow of the dark, bitter brew, then twirled her bracelet under the table, fearing a rebuke from Henri over the picture on the *Savouries* website.

Instead, he smiled. "I'm glad my stories didn't scare you off."

It was just the two of them at a table separated from the rest of the room by several yards and tucked behind a wide buffet table. The sunburst lines around his eyes reminded her of Grandpa Aron and calmed her. "No, not at all." She decided to be honest and get the picture issue out of the way. "I want to be upfront—I took a photo of you before your speech yesterday. My editor published it on my magazine's website. Dozens of videos and photos were taken of you. You were in a public place, and . . ." She hesitated. "Your NDA didn't specify public situations." She left unsaid how such a stipulation would never hold up in court. But of course, he would know that. Still, his stiff silence lobbed anxiety into her throat. "Respectfully, sir, I am staying within the bounds of our agreement. *Savouries* paid my way here. This is my job."

"I thought you came to learn about your family." His voice had turned gravelly.

"It is the main reason."

He adjusted his silverware. "I've seen no pictures. Liam handles the company's press and social media." His eyes met hers. "I can live with a photo. Have you revealed any of what we talked about yesterday or when we spoke on the phone?"

"No." She stared into her coffee. She wished she hadn't told Wes any part of her phone call with Henri, but without those details, she might not be sitting here now. That conversation had to remain between her and Wes, and as long as it did, there was no harm. She met Henri's gaze and waited for his next move.

"Come, let's get some food," he said.

Her shoulders inched down from around her ears, and she followed him to the buffet.

With a plate in hand, she realized the giant display was reserved for them. On it was an insane amount of food: platters laden with sliced meats, cheeses, and smoked fish, as well as bowls of fruit nestled beside grilled vegetables, roasted potatoes, and chafing dishes of sausage and bacon. There were baskets of glistening baked goods and a shoebox-sized plaque of honeycomb. A server tended their private smorgasbord.

Once they were seated with plates of food, Henri insisted she smear honeycomb onto her croissant. She did, and her first bite proved crisp on the outside while the tender, interior dough melted in her mouth. Baked-in butter balanced with the sweet honeycomb, and she actually moaned. Embarrassed, she covered her mouth. "So sorry, but this is better than any croissant I've ever tasted."

Henri grinned, pleased, and bit into a croissant, chewing thoughtfully. "It's good, but I should have let the dough proof one more time."

"Wait." She motioned from her plate to him. "Did you—"

"Yes."

The croissant tasted fresh-baked. "When?"

"Early this morning." He sipped coffee. "These past few days, I've been having trouble sleeping. When I can't sleep, I wander. I found myself near the kitchen."

"And the hotel let you cook?"

He shrugged. "For a few hours. I made the dough the night before."

The idea of the Empress Hotel—or any hotel—letting a random guest into its kitchen seemed impossible. However, if the guest was Henri Martin, a person with money and influence, as well as the owner of a renowned baking company, she supposed people made exceptions.

They ate, and then Henri went back to the buffet. "We should try the *Esterházy Torte*. I made that, too." He brought over two slices, placing one in front of her. It was a layer cake, frosted white with distinct chocolate stripes on top.

"I've never had *Esterházy Torte*." When Zoe glanced up, she caught inquisitive looks from others in the main dining room. A camera flash went off, but she hadn't seen who took the picture. She had a feeling they'd aimed the camera at her. Strange, but of course people must be curious. If she had been on the other side of the room, she'd want to know who was eating with Henri Martin. And she'd be jealous as hell.

Henri picked up his fork. "This torte was named after a diplomat who once worked under the nineteenth-century Austrian empire. Buttercream is spread between thin layers of hazelnut-flavored meringue. Some prefer to use almonds. My wife, Eveline, believed hazelnut's mild bitterness tempered the cake's sweetness. The stripes are fondant with"—he pinched his fingers together—"a wee bit of chocolate in a perfect marriage of flavors. A true partnership." He glanced away. Zoe wondered what or *who* he might be thinking about.

She said, "My grandfather liked to joke how he never met a cake he didn't love."

"Aron liked sweets. Belgian chocolates were his weakness."

Zoe could see the boxes of Belvas truffles her grandfather used to hide behind files in his desk. Her eyes filled, and she blinked back tears, fearing she would appear unprofessional.

"Losing your grandfather must be hard for you," Henri said.

Like cutting off a limb. "He and I were always close, but after my parents died, we grew even more so."

"Yes." Sympathy brimmed in Henri's eyes. "You were young when your parents passed."

She was surprised, but then realized he must have checked into her background. "I was eleven."

"I was also young when my parents died."

"I'm sorry."

Henri gave her a knowing nod, then left the table to refill his espresso.

Zoe checked her phone for texts and emails, working to push aside her melancholy.

"Everything all right?" Henri set his cup on the table.

"Fine." She stashed the phone in her bag and dug into her cake. Her first mouthful delivered a rush of creamy flavor, infused as Henri had claimed with a hint of hazelnut. "Wow. My grandfather would have loved this."

"I believe that's true," he said.

She envisioned what an amazing article she could write about Henri. Her familial connection to him would give it a unique angle. And he was so much more than the figurehead of a massive corporation. This whole thing—him baking in the middle of the night and bringing her a slice of homemade cake—would humanize him for readers. If she could only convince him to go on record. Eventually, she would have to try.

"Should we begin? We can nosh while we talk." He gestured to their plates.

She grinned, hearing the infinite times Grandpa Aron had said with his eyes sparkling, "You don't have to be hungry to have a little nosh."

"I'm ready when you are." Zoe slid her cake closer.

Chapter Seventeen

Chana

Vienna, Austria
May 1946

A week after Chana's tea outing with Meyer, she and Shifra walked to the Empress Hotel. The morning was warm, and Chana relished the buttery sunshine on her face as she tightened the soft blue ribbon at the end of her braid. Now that her hair had grown enough to be worn this way, she preferred it for work. When the braid's tail brushed her neck, it reminded her of how far she'd come since the war.

Shifra had been begging Chana to get her a job in the kitchen, and for weeks Chef Heiss had been moaning over the kitchen's lack of staff. Today, she planned to introduce the two. Chana took this bright spring day as a good omen that everything would work out.

The girls were cautious, sticking to the most patrolled streets in the Innere Stadt. Days earlier, someone had robbed a hotel bellman of his pants, shoes, shirt, and coat while he was out for a cigarette break, leaving him on the street in his undergarments. It was no doubt that the thief quickly sold the man's things on the black market.

Shifra filled their walk by recounting her recent flirtations with men she considered husband potential. Chana let the conversation wash over her as she spied tulips blossoming in more than a few window boxes among the broken buildings. Jewels among ruins.

Several blocks from the hotel, they passed mountains of rubble where homes once stood. People milled about, searching the debris for any bit of rubbish that they could use or sell.

"I found a lighter in a similar pile last week," Shifra said. "I traded it for an extra rasher of meat. Should we stop?"

It was tempting. "No, we can't be late."

Shifra gave the heaps a wistful look.

When they neared the edge of the busy Karlsplatz, Shifra craned her neck.

"What are you doing?" Chana asked.

"Seeing who's out."

Chana figured her friend meant Meyer, but said nothing. She hadn't told her about their tea, because in the end there was nothing to tell. She and Meyer had made no plans to see each other again.

They walked in silence, and Chana debated confiding in Shifra about Elias and their late-night baking, eager to tell someone. But before she could speak, Shifra said, "Kirill Volkov asked if I wanted to work for him."

Chana stopped. "Doing what?" She remembered how he'd made her a similar offer in the train station.

"Spending time with some soldiers."

Chana grabbed her friend's arm. "Shifra, do you even know what you're talking about?" Panic filled her voice.

"Ow! You're squeezing my arm."

Chana let go. "I'm sorry."

Shifra smoothed her sleeve. "He arranges for women to earn extra money entertaining some of the Soviet soldiers."

"*Entertaining*? Do you realize what that means?"

Pink circles formed on Shifra's haggard face. "Don't look at me like that. I have to survive."

Chana noted the shadows around her friend's sunken eyes and the way her clothes hung on her bony frame. Shifra managed on a worker's meager day rations—ten ounces of bread, one and a quarter ounces of meat, a bit of cooking oil, two ounces of beans, and a spit of sugar. It wasn't enough. Every week, Chana smuggled leftover hotel scraps to her friend. A soldier's uneaten roll. A half-eaten strip of bacon. A bite of scrambled eggs. Collecting dirty dishes had its benefits.

"Please, don't do this." She gently took Shifra's hand. "Volkov is dangerous. You said so in the café. Surely, you're not thinking—"

"I'm not doing it." Shifra pulled away.

They walked in silence.

Finally, Shifra said, "*I* wasn't the one who got the easy job in the kitchen." She clenched and unclenched her hands, her fingers red and chafed from days spent submerged in soapy water at the laundry. "I'm barely surviving."

Chana linked her arm through her friend's. "Herr Heiss will hire you today," she said. "And remember, we're free, and this work isn't forever."

"We're not getting out so quickly. And I don't have relatives in America or a Ruth Rosenzweig to look after me." Shifra wiped her eyes. "I wish Meyer would look at me the way he looks at you."

Chana felt a blush rise in her cheeks. *Tell her the truth!* her thoughts shouted. "He and I went for tea last week."

Shifra looked at her, surprised. "What happened?"

"It was nice, and then it wasn't." *And then it was again*, she thought.

"Are you seeing him again?" Shifra asked.

For days after their tea, Chana had questioned whether Meyer would seek her out again. One moment she couldn't bear it if he didn't, while the next moment she considered herself lucky he hadn't. The man was a recipe she couldn't crack.

"I don't think so," Chana said.

Shifra *tsk*ed. "Same old Chana. If someone handsome and powerful asked me to tea, I'd hang on and I wouldn't let go." She looked at Chana. "You, my friend, don't see that Meyer is one of the most sought after men in Vienna."

Chana stayed quiet. She saw more, and felt more, than she cared to let on.

Chef Heiss led Shifra to a corner of the kitchen for them to speak. Chana waited and found it hard to breathe, let alone wash and peel the basket of carrots on the counter. Heiss talked, and Shifra responded with a beguiling smile. Chef Heiss laughed. Yes, of course Shifra's infectious good humor would surely win over Chef Heiss. After several minutes, Chana looked over as Heiss gave Shifra a firm nod. Chana's hopes soared, until Shifra turned, her face wet.

Chana met her friend at the alley door. "What happened?"

"His budget won't allow him to hire anyone. He said perhaps in a few months." Shifra used her sleeve to dry her cheeks.

"I'm sorry." Chana hugged her friend tight, blinking back tears of her own.

When Shifra stepped away, she said, "It's fine. I still have the laundry." With one last hungry look at the counters laden with food, Shifra left.

Chana spent much of the morning peeling an endless mountain of carrots and trying not to worry about Shifra. From the corner of her eye, she watched Herr Trolfe and Elias. They were making a plum streusel called *Zwetschgenkuchen*, and it was a welcome distraction. Elias split and pitted the fruit, then Trolfe lined up the halved plums in a sheet pan full of dough. Each precise column looked as though he could have drawn it with a ruler.

"We add cinnamon sugar over the plums to sweeten the fruit," Papa had once instructed her while making this same cake.

With a light sprinkle, Chana knew that Herr Trolfe's *Zwetschgenkuchen* would be divine. Only, Trolfe didn't add any sugar or cinnamon. Oh, how Chana yearned to cross over to their side of the kitchen.

Once the lunch rush ended, and before dinner prep began, Heiss opened his sugar canister and yelled, "*Verdammt!* Chana, get me half a cup of sugar from the baker's pantry."

"*Ja.*" She wiped her hands and hurried to the large pantry on the opposite side of the room. She filled a half cup, careful not to lose a single granule. Sugar, like everything else, was rationed and in short supply.

"What do you think you're doing?" Trolfe shouted, stepping into the pantry.

She jumped, spilling sugar on the floor. "Herr Heiss needs sugar," she said, once she'd found her voice.

"He has his own." He stomped his foot. "Do you think you can come in here and steal my supplies?"

The smell of schnapps clung to him, and she stepped back. "He told me to take it from here. It's the kitchen's sugar, isn't it?"

Trolfe ground granules under his shoe. "You stupid girl, you dropped some."

"You startled me."

"Perhaps you're a thieving Jew, stealing it for yourself."

She pulled her shoulders back. "If you don't believe me, ask Herr Heiss."

"Chef Trolfe." Elias appeared in the doorway, straightening to his full height, and she noticed for the first time that he was a few inches taller than the pastry chef. "I heard Chef Heiss send her over," Elias said in a firm voice.

The pastry chef stared at his apprentice, who didn't budge, then shouted at her, "Get out! And don't come back unless you have *my* permission."

She left, brushing against the man's hulking frame, and despising him as much as he despised her. Chana mouthed *Thank you* to Elias. He gave her a surreptitious wink, turning the air less hostile. She felt a surge of affection for Elias that warmed her skin and made her want to hug him.

Later, Chana took her meal break up on the hotel roof, as had become her habit when she and her mother didn't share shifts. Outside, a cool breeze swept by. She didn't mind the slight nip in the air; it was refreshing after hours in the hot kitchen. She settled on a stack of bricks, enjoying the solitude, and grateful for the steaming bowl of wild boar and vegetable soup in her lap. During the war, she was almost never alone. In the ghettos, they crammed into tight apartments with four to five families, or what was left of families. In Stutthof, she'd been held in barracks filled with triple-stacked hard wooden bunks and crowded with hundreds of women. Only two sinks and two toilets served them all. She almost never had a turn at the sink and often used the weak coffee they were given to wash her face and hands.

Chana dipped her bread into the stew and ate, the crust offering a satisfying crunch as soup dribbled down her chin. Across the roof, she spotted Elias smoking. She quickly wiped her chin with the back of her hand.

As if pulled by her thoughts, he looked over and smiled. It had been a week since they'd last baked together. He was struggling to buy supplies. He walked toward her with an eager expression on his face. She didn't mind if he joined her. Instead, she looked forward to chatting with him.

"I was hoping you'd come up here," he said. "I might have enough to buy sugar and flour. Can you slip away tomorrow night at ten?"

"Yes, my mother and brother should be asleep by then." She had an idea. "Elias, my mother gives me a small allowance. I can't spare much . . ." She'd already bought several spools of needlepoint yarn for her mother in burgundy, green, violet, and gold, and now she finally had saved enough for the canvas. Tomorrow was Thursday, and she planned to find the dealer in the Karlsplatz. "Would it be easier if I contributed?"

"It would." He looked at her for a long time. "Can you manage it?"

"I can . . . a little. I could even go with you to buy the goods."

"Okay. Tomorrow morning before our shifts start. Could you come to the hotel early? I'm to meet the fellow near the Karlsplatz."

"Yes." Chana would have to tell her mother that Heiss needed her earlier and that she could walk to the hotel with Gita, who lived only a few blocks away.

He took a final drag of his cigarette, dropped the butt, and crushed it with his shoe. "Baking is good for the soul, is it not?"

"It is."

"When my hands are on the dough, everything else fades away." He glanced toward St. Stephen's Cathedral. "I sound silly, don't I?"

"Not at all. I think if my father hadn't had Mama and us, he would have worked day and night. He would lose himself in the work."

"Yes, it's like that."

Chana ate more stew. "Did you learn how to bake here in Vienna? Did your mother teach you?"

His expression clouded. "Mama Ursula taught me how to bake. I lived here as a boy in the ninth district. Then we moved to the countryside." He swallowed. "Papa Johan's family owned a farm in Dürnstein. We spent the war there. They're still there."

She found it strange how he referred to his parents with their first names. Perhaps it was an Austrian custom.

He stared at her with a curious expression. "What is it?" She dabbed at her mouth and chin, believing food must have stuck.

"You're the prettiest girl I've ever seen."

"Oh. Thank you." Heat rushed into her cheeks, and confusing emotions swirled within her. Elias had a pleasant face, reminding her not of the dashing, mysterious heroes in the American movies she'd seen in Foehrenwald, but of a softer, clear-eyed supporting character. Like

Paul Henreid versus Humphrey Bogart in *Casablanca.* And Chana and Elias had much in common. She enjoyed the time they spent baking, and in fact, she'd grown fond of him. But Chana didn't want a boyfriend or a husband—not at this point in her life. *Or did she?* Elias was a gentile, a match her mother would forbid. She grew jittery and quickly forced down her last sips of soup. "I should get back."

"Sure." He sat on the pile of bricks. "I'll go in a minute."

She galloped down the stairs with her heart pounding against her ribs.

Chapter Eighteen

Chana

Back in the hotel kitchen, Chana sensed a renewed energy among the staff. The room buzzed with activity, and the women kept eyeing the alley door.

"What's going on?" Chana asked her mother, who'd arrived for her shift while she was on the roof with Elias.

"Herr Heiss said Meyer is coming by with fresh goods," Mama said.

"You'd think they expected a prince."

Her mother scrubbed a beet, her hands stained red by the effort. "Meyer has earned such regard."

Her mother sounded like Shifra. Chana picked up a beet and cleaned it, noticing how the other women had suddenly dolled up, wearing lipstick and pinching their cheeks.

She worked to restrain her emotions along with a peck of jealousy. "The beets are done." Chana swept them into a bowl and set them at the table's edge for the cooks. "The chef needs more onions."

Her mother's jaw jutted forward. She didn't enjoy taking orders from Chana, but Herr Heiss had appointed Chana to direct the other women. It was last week, when at day's end, she had taken it upon herself to refill Chef Heiss's spice bowls. A chore she'd done for Papa. The next morning, Heiss had shouted, "Who did this to my herbs?"

She feared he might dismiss her. Still, she spoke up. "I did."

"Hmm. *Gut.*" He patted her shoulder. "Do it every day."

"*Ja.*" She took a relieved breath.

Her mother hacked into an onion with a cleaver, spraying juice onto the counter. Chana's eyes watered. "Mama, how was everything at the consulate this morning?" she asked tentatively.

"To hell with them," Mama said as a second onion died by her hand. "Quotas. Today, that man, not Abernathy, the other one with the skinny little neck—he had the gall to tell me that if Papa's family wanted to find us, they would have."

Chana glanced over at Aron, who sat on a crate by the alley door. He was helping in the kitchen for the evening and waiting for his next assignment. Her brother frowned at their mother's grousing.

"It will work out," Chana said. "I'll go to the offices on my next day off; you'll rest."

Mama snorted, her mood as foul as rotting cabbage. "That Schumacher sold us nothing but a fairy tale. And he was your father's friend!"

Chana grabbed an onion and caught Elias's eye.

Mama set down her knife. "Why is he looking at you?"

Chana began slicing. "Who?" she asked, even though she knew.

"The baker," her mother spit out.

Before Chana could respond, Trolfe emerged from the pantry with Chef Heiss on his heels. "Don't turn your back on me," Heiss said.

"I won't do it!" Trolfe shouted. "Since when is my *Apfelstrudel* not good enough for the Americans?"

"The soldiers are our customers, and they want apple pie. Sergeant McManus requested it for his men. Give them what they want," Heiss said. "Besides, pie is easier than strudel."

Chana silently agreed. She'd watched Trolfe and Elias prepare strudel, which required two sets of hands to lengthen and stretch the dough until it was paper-thin without rips.

But she kept her opinion to herself. Everyone in the kitchen focused on their tasks. No one wanted to get in the middle of the chefs when they argued.

"Why should I?" Trolfe pointed at Heiss. "At least when the Nazis stayed here, they ate my strudel."

Heiss's eye twitched. "Get your finger out of my face and lower your voice. Do you want the American general to hear you? He's having coffee in the dining room. He'll think you were a collaborator."

Trolfe's hand went to his chest. "That's a lie! The Nazis ruined my beautiful city. The barbarians. They even tried to set fire to St. Stephen's!"

"This is my kitchen!" Heiss thundered. "I'm in charge! Not you!"

"*Ach,*" Trolfe said.

"One last thing. The general wants us to use the yeast from their canteen."

The pastry chef grimaced. "What's wrong with the yeast we get from the brewer?"

"I'm told it's a new formula. The dough will rise quicker and produce bigger loaves."

"Bigger. Quicker." Trolfe frowned. "There's nothing wrong with our Austrian yeast!" But the pastry chef would obey Herr Heiss, and everyone knew that, later today, they'd be using American yeast and the kitchen would serve apple pie instead of *Apfelstrudel.*

A hard knock hit the alley door.

Heiss signaled for Aron to open it. Meyer Suconick swaggered in.

"Look at you, Aron Rosenzweig." Meyer patted his shoulder. "You look good. You've grown taller."

The air in the kitchen shifted. Women smiled. Two cooks glanced over. Chana looked over briefly before bringing her blade down on an onion.

Meyer handed Aron the coat he'd had draped over an arm. "Here. Your mother mentioned your coat had gotten too small. Try this one," he said.

Aron's eyes darted to their mother.

"We have no money," Mama said.

"It was lying around. Consider it a gift."

"All right," Mama said, and Aron happily slipped on the coat. The one he'd brought from Foehrenwald had indeed grown tight and short thanks to steady food from Heiss's kitchen. This new coat hung on his frame, and though Chana was grateful for this kindness toward her brother, it also made her wary. Whose back had this coat been stolen from? And would her brother now owe Meyer a favor?

Heiss said, "Meyer, give me a moment." Then he crossed to Chana and told her, "Leave the onions to your mother. I need you to chop more potatoes. This way . . ." He demonstrated a chopping motion, and she gathered he wanted them cubed.

"*Ja*," she said and retrieved a basket of potatoes from a shelf. Chef Heiss shook Meyer's hand as Chana slid in beside her mother to clean and cut the potatoes.

The black-market dealer moved deeper into the kitchen, standing within arm's length of her. His dark suit and crisp white shirt shone under the overhead lights. Elias watched Meyer, too, his expression a blend of awe and disdain. Even jealousy. Did he envy Meyer's clothes, power, or confidence? Perhaps some combination of all three.

Meyer's man, Vlad, hovered in the doorway. "What do you have for me today?" Chef Heiss asked.

"Everything you've wished for." Meyer motioned to Vlad, who then brought in two wooden crates that he set down.

Meyer pulled a dark bottle of wine from the top box and handed it to the chef.

"Ah, yes." Heiss thumbed dust off the label. "Château Haut-Michel. How many bottles?"

"Three dozen straight from France. Apparently, the Nazis left them behind when they retreated. There's another case in my truck."

"I want them all." Heiss wagged a finger. "Don't sell a single bottle to anyone else. This will make our hotel the talk of Vienna." Herr Heiss handed Meyer a thick envelope.

Meyer's eyes grazed over Chana as he stuffed the envelope in his jacket.

She plunged her knife into a potato.

"He can't keep his eyes off of you," her mother whispered on the way to the sink. "He brought your brother a new coat. Would it kill you to smile at him?"

"Leave me be, Mama," Chana said. "Please." Yet, she couldn't keep from stealing glances at Meyer, too. She recalled the electricity that had pulsed through her when she'd touched his cheek. The surprise in his eyes. Yet, he'd let her go. *Focus!* her thoughts shouted. Now was not the time to parse through her feelings.

Vlad passed Meyer a sack, and he carried it over to Trolfe. "Do you still need chocolate?"

Trolfe's head ticked up. "What do you have?"

Meyer spilled a dark, coin-sized disk into Trolfe's hand. "Try it."

The pastry chef eyed the chocolate with doubt before he smelled it, then placed the piece on his tongue. He looked as though he might swoon.

Meyer smirked at Elias. "Your boss knows good chocolate when he tastes it." He turned back to Trolfe, and Elias made a face as he tossed sliced apples in a mixture of cinnamon and sugar.

"It's the best Belgian chocolate available," Meyer told Trolfe. "Nearly impossible to acquire."

"It's delicious," Trolfe said hoarsely.

Chana couldn't believe the besotted look on the pastry chef's face.

"Are you buying?" Meyer asked.

"No," Trolfe choked out. He went back to kneading his dough.

A muscle in Meyer's jaw twitched. He wasn't used to having his goods spurned.

Herr Heiss called, "It's good to see you, Meyer," then he grabbed a case of wine and motioned for Aron to grab the second case. Together, they trudged toward the wine cellar.

Chana expected Meyer to leave, but instead her mother summoned him over.

"Thank you for Aron's coat," Mama said.

"Glad to help," he said, switching from German to Yiddish.

His nearness made Chana's palm slick, and she tightened her grip on her knife.

He asked, "How is everything? Is there any news from the consulate?"

Mama told him, "Herr Abernathy is trying harder, and the fellow at the Joint is doing his best. Thank you for that."

Meyer asked Chana, "Did you receive the blankets I left for you?"

Gita stirred vegetables in a frying pan and glanced over.

Herr Nachmann had delivered blankets to their room a few days back. "I didn't know they were from you." She met his eyes. "Why didn't you come say hello?"

"I had other business, but Nachmann should have told you." His tone was soft, even apologetic.

On the other side of the room, Elias watched them.

Chana stayed quiet. Meyer's eyes turned expectant in a way that reminded her of Papa after he'd asked her to taste some batter. She'd always felt important in those moments, knowing that her opinion mattered greatly to him. Her pulse quickened.

"Thank you for the blankets and the coat for Aron," she said sincerely. Their eyes held, neither moving until Elias, carrying a bowl of flour, bumped into Meyer. When the dealer turned, the bowl slipped, and flour exploded onto Meyer's suit.

"So sorry," Elias said.

Chana noticed a glint in the young baker's eyes. He had done this on purpose. She handed Meyer a damp rag, and he attempted to dust the mess from his jacket and pants.

"You should watch where you're going," he told Elias.

"Yes, though I belong in this kitchen." Then Elias scooped the bowl off to the sink before Meyer could respond.

Mama told Meyer, "I don't like him."

"Nor do I. Trolfe would have been better off hiring my friend's son." A powdery film coated Meyer's suit no matter how hard he scrubbed at it.

The apprentice had returned with a dustpan, crouching to clean up. He muttered, "But he didn't."

When Elias straightened, the two men glared at each other.

How on earth had she landed in the middle of this face-off? She turned to Meyer. "You should go." She palmed her knife. "I must return to work. Heiss expects it."

"Yes," Meyer said, squinting. "I'll leave you to your potatoes." He left quickly.

She felt a pang of regret at his departure.

Mama grabbed her wrist. "How could you send him away?"

"I'm doing my job, Mama. We need this work. Not a fight."

"I know." Her mother let go as her eyes grew misty. "But don't you realize how well Meyer treats us? He found us these jobs. Last week he brought us extra tins of meat. Today, he gave your brother a coat. We need him."

The fragility in her mother's voice pierced Chana's heart. "I'm sorry. I know he's been helpful." If she'd hurt Meyer's feelings, she hadn't meant to, though not because of any gifts or her job or their desire to go to America.

Her mother patted Chana's arm, then her eyes slowly narrowed. She was looking at Elias, who'd moved to the other side of the kitchen again. "That one better stop looking at you. Meyer is the kind to blind someone for looking at what is his."

Chana went back to chopping potatoes, wanting to meet Elias's eyes, but instead, she channeled her emotions into every *thwack* of the blade. "I belong to myself," she told her mother. "Not to anyone else." She ignored the furtive glances from others in the kitchen, but she couldn't ignore the nagging feeling that something had begun here between Elias and Meyer and her. Something inescapable.

Chapter Nineteen

Chana

As Chana and Elias had arranged, the next morning, they met with a black-market dealer on a side street near the Karlsplatz. They were alone, and mostly out of sight from the plaza. Ripe to be robbed. She took measured breaths to hide her fear. Elias seemed unperturbed as he inspected bags of flour and sugar that the dealer had handed him.

"You're smart to check," the man said. His name was Hershel, and this was Elias's first time buying from him. "These bags could be full of sand." Hershel laughed. He had dark hair and deep lines around his eyes, though overall his demeanor was bright.

But Chana didn't find him funny. People had been swindled before, buying half-empty tins of meat or cartons of cigarettes containing sticks.

"My boss is friends with your chef. I'll give you a good price. Half a kilo of flour and half a kilo of sugar for a schilling."

Elias coughed. "That's too much. I usually pay half that; fifty groschen."

Chana had agreed to chip in twenty groschen. She couldn't spare any more.

Hershel put up his hands. "Then buy from your other man."

"He's not selling," Elias said.

Hershel lifted his eyebrows and looked at Chana.

She stiffened, expecting him to suggest an unsavory alternate payment. She glanced at the Karlsplatz, regretting agreeing to meet on this quiet street. "We'll pay fifty groschen or we're done," she said firmly.

Hershel didn't answer right away, then looked past her. "Let's ask my boss." He waved as footsteps grew louder behind her.

Chana turned, and Meyer joined them.

"These two are offering fifty groschen." Hershel wagged his hand at Elias and Chana.

Meyer's gaze bounced between them as his jaw shifted in the way of one chewing on something unpleasant.

"You work for him?" Elias asked Hershel.

"He does," Meyer answered. "Are you buying for Chef Heiss or Chef Trolfe?"

Elias let out a grim laugh. "We're buying for ourselves."

"To do what?" Meyer asked, a razor-sharp edge in his voice.

"To bake," Chana said.

Meyer fell quiet, until he said, "Like your papa." He looked sullen. "Does Mama Rosenzweig know?"

"Of course," Chana said, forcing a light tone.

His eyes darkened as if he saw her answer for the lie that it was. He didn't approve of her being with Elias. As if what she did in her free time was any of Meyer's business. She folded her arms across her chest, feeling exposed.

Meyer's attention cut to Elias. "You're a fool to bring her for this." Anger had seeped into his voice. "There are dealers who would expect her to pay the difference with her body. And they don't always take no for an answer."

"I would protect her." Elias pulled his shoulders back.

"You?" He stepped closer. The air crackled with tension. "I don't think so."

"Try me." Elias lifted his chin.

Both men fisted their hands at their sides.

Chana had no intention of letting these two throw punches. Not because of her. She put a hand on Elias's arm. "We only came to buy supplies."

Meyer's brooding gaze fell to her hand.

"What do you want me to do, boss?" Hershel asked.

Meyer said, "Cut the price. Fifty groschen."

Chana was about to thank him, when Elias said, "Actually, we can do without."

She shot him a look. "Elias? What—"

"I think we should go." He locked imploring eyes on hers. "We're due at work."

She pressed her lips together, feeling Meyer's scrutiny. It went against her nature to stay quiet, especially because she believed it was out of pride on Elias's part. But she also wouldn't allow Meyer to cause an argument between her and her friend.

"We're not buying," she told Hershel before turning to go.

When they were out of earshot and blended among pedestrians in the Karlsplatz, she said, "We needed those supplies. The price was fair."

"Do you want to be indebted to Meyer Suconick? I don't."

"I don't think we would be."

"I have another contact."

"I . . ." she said, then spotted the fellow who sold the needlepoint canvas she wanted for Mama. "All right"—she pointed—"but I need to talk to him."

"I'll go with you."

Once they reached the man with his overflowing cart, Chana tapped his arm. "Excuse me, a few weeks ago you had a needlepoint canvas of flowers. I want to buy it now."

He scratched his neck. "I remember you. You should have bought it then. It's gone." He started away with his cart.

"Oh, no!" she said. She followed him, stumbling slightly over a crack in the sidewalk. "But surely, I mean there must be—" He kept going. "Please wait!" The man stopped. "Do you have another? It's for my mother."

"Let me see." He dug through the cart, pulling out pots, cups, pieces of wood, a camera, and last, a chipped vase. "Give her this. It's thirty groschen. Cheaper than the canvas."

"No," she said with a shake of her head. "Can you get another canvas?"

"Nah." A couple approached the man, and he turned away from Chana.

She and Elias slowly headed toward the hotel. How she wished she'd had the money to buy the needlepoint sooner.

"I'm sorry," Elias said.

"Thanks." She stared at the ground.

"Listen, I'll have supplies for tomorrow." He took her hand. "I know you're disappointed, and I can't produce a needlepoint canvas, but I can make sure we bake. I hope it helps."

"It does," she said, soothed by his touch and his promise.

Neither let go, and they walked to the hotel hand in hand. She peeked over at his cheerful face, and fondness expanded in her chest. Steps from the hotel, Chana reluctantly let go of him, worried someone would see and tell her mother. He nodded, as if he knew.

They were so similar. The thought made her smile.

The next night, Chana made her way to the hotel. Despite the city's ever-present dangers, Chana relished her late walks to meet Elias. She was again disguised in men's clothes, with her braid tucked into her hat. She basked in the solitude and the ability to choose her route. No armed soldier dictating her life, or Mama scrutinizing her every move.

About to turn into the hotel kitchen's alley, she heard a familiar loud voice speaking Russian, and pulled back. When she peered around the corner, she spotted Elias by the kitchen doorway with Kirill Volkov.

Volkov gave Elias a sack, and Elias dropped coins in his hand.

Chana's stomach lurched. Elias had chosen to do business with Kirill Volkov. Though he didn't know about her run-ins with Kirill, it still hit her as a betrayal. She shrank back, hiding behind a pile of bricks. Footsteps passed, and the black-market dealer headed up the street, his dark coat flapping behind him like bat wings.

When Chana finally entered the kitchen, Elias had the sack on the counter.

"Good, you're here," he said, beaming.

She stormed over. "How could you deal with that animal?" He

stepped back, stiffened, but said nothing. "Kirill Volkov is the worst of the black-market dealers!"

"But he . . . he . . . charges less than anyone else." Elias blinked several times. "We need our money to stretch as far as it can."

"He's brutal and cruel. I never would have agreed to buy from him." She told him about how Kirill's brother had attacked her and about Kirill's offer to Shifra.

Elias crossed his arms. "I have no choice. Trolfe forbids me to deal with men like Meyer Suconick."

"Men like—" Chana had believed they'd walked away from Meyer and Hershel because of jealousy over her. Now she could see one big difference between Meyer and Kirill. Meyer was Jewish. "Why not Meyer?"

Red blotches formed on his neck.

"Tell me!" She was going to make him say it to her face.

His eyes darted around the room. "If Trolfe found out my ingredients came from a Jew, he would never even consider serving what I make."

"Look at me." He did. "You let me bake with you. You acted as though we're friends!" Disgust rattled her body. "Yet you take my ideas and pass them off as your own. The ideas of a Jew!" She pounded her chest. He didn't respond. "I'm leaving."

"No!" He caught her arm. "Please, let me explain."

She pulled free. "There's nothing to explain. You're as awful as the rest."

"I'm not. You see . . ." His voice faltered. "I . . . I am a Jew."

She stared at him, her thoughts struggling to catch up with what he said. "I don't understand."

"I'm like you," he whispered, "Jewish." In a rush, he told her, "Johan and Ursula were my parents' close friends. My father owned a violin store and as the Nazis came to power, he wouldn't leave his shop. The Bohms, Mama Ursula and Papa Johan . . . they weren't Jewish, but they saw what was coming and moved to a small farm in Dürnstein to wait out the war." Elias licked his lips and glanced around as if the bowls and pots had ears. "They begged my family to join them. My father refused, but my mother insisted I go. On the day we arrived on the farm, Mama Ursula told me I had to change my name to Elias and take their surname. I had to pretend to be Christian. There were weeks when I had to hide in a bunker behind the barn for fear someone had found out the truth about me."

His confession landed heavily in her gut. All this time and she'd had no inkling that Elias was Jewish. No wonder he barely talked about his past, consuming hers instead. Chana had assumed he'd coasted through the war out in the Austrian countryside.

Now she was both relieved and a little put off. A friend in the Vilna resistance had once suggested that Chana move in with sympathetic gentiles. She declined. Staying with her family was most important to her. Nor did she want to be anyone other than herself. At the time, Elias had been a boy. She wouldn't judge him or his parents for the choice that had saved him.

"What was your name, and your parents' names?" she asked.

"Chaim Lieb," he said. "And they were Dov and Rivka Lieb."

Elias recounted how before the war the Liebs and Bohms had lived in the same building in the ninth district, in the Alsergrund. "Johan was a music teacher at the university. My father was a violinist and ran our family's string-instrument shop. My father and Johan were friends since they were boys." Elias swallowed, his Adam's apple bobbing up and down. "My father said he was Jewish but also Austrian. Not religious. He told my mother the Nazis wouldn't bother with him."

Chana learned how before Elias left with the Bohms, his mother promised him the trouble wouldn't last forever, and they'd be together soon.

"What happened to them . . . your parents?"

"In 1938, my father was forced to sell his store." He repeatedly rubbed the back of one hand. "Like many others, the Nazis forced my father to scrub the sidewalk in front of the store using a toothbrush. Other merchants jeered and spit on him." Elias told her that, after, Dov Lieb went home and hanged himself. Rivka was murdered in a concentration camp.

Chana clamped a hand over her mouth.

"You're crying," he said.

She touched her cheek. So she was. And he was surprisingly dry-eyed. She wiped her face on a rag. "I'm so sorry about your parents."

"Thank you." He glanced away.

She struggled to find the words for what she wanted to say. Gently, she took his hand, drawing his gaze, too. "The war is over. I know it won't bring your parents back"—she paused, sensing he was holding his breath—"but don't you see? You can reclaim your old name."

"No. I can't." He slipped from her grasp. "Trolfe is the brother of one of Mama Ursula's friends. It's how I came to work here. Apprentice to Chef Trolfe is a good job for Elias Bohm." He looked to the floor. "It is impossible for Chaim Lieb."

It was true, of course—if Trolfe knew Elias was Jewish, the pastry chef would fire him.

"You don't approve," he said, reading into her silence.

"It's not that. I understand what you're telling me. I just don't think I could do it."

Alarm magnified his eyes. "Please, Chana . . ." Now he clasped her hands. "If you care for me at all, I beg you to keep my secret."

She took in the worry on his face. "I care for you a great deal. I won't tell."

His next breath shook his body, and he leaned toward her as if he were about to kiss her. Her heart sped up. Instead, he asked, "Will you still bake with me tonight? Please?"

She struggled to find her voice. "Yes," she finally said.

"Thank you." He offered her a smile, one that somehow accentuated his cheekbones, and she imagined how he might look when he was older; he would be quite handsome.

Elias had asked if she cared for him. Had he meant only as a friend? He let go of her, and she quickly turned toward the ingredients, flustered by her thoughts. "We're making *Sachertorte.*"

"Yes," he said. "That's right."

She relaxed a bit. "Show me what else you bought."

He emptied the sack of goods. "What do you think?"

She arranged the ingredients, grateful for the diversion. "Our eggs are most important. You have six, but they're small. Two more would be magic." In her mind's eye, she saw her father nodding.

Elias produced two more eggs from the sack, proud as if he had laid them himself. "I guess I won't save them."

"They'll help the cake's texture." She lifted an egg, enjoying the feel of the cool, dimpled shell in her hand. "Our goal is moistness."

"Ah," he said. "Trolfe beats the butter before adding the sugar. Do you agree?"

"I do." She tapped her lips. "Some mix rum into the apricot jam, but my father liked to brush the cake with rum instead."

"We can't afford liquor, but a syrup of water, sugar, and a drop of vanilla will do the trick."

"Good idea."

He scratched his cheek, as if he'd figured something out. Perhaps it was that they could trust each other.

She and Elias went to work.

Chapter Twenty

Chana

The next morning, Chana couldn't wait to get to the kitchen, eager to see Trolfe's reaction to the *Sachertorte.*

When she arrived at her workstation, she found a note from Chef Heiss, instructing her to direct the staff—both kitchen women and commis chefs!—on their morning tasks. A responsibility Heiss had been doing himself. The chef listed the day's meals, and added that if she did well, this would continue, and she would receive extra pay for the added work.

Mama read over her shoulder. "Extra money will help us. You did good. I'm proud of you." Her mother kissed her cheek.

Chana took in a deep satisfying breath. "Thank you, Mama."

"At least we won't starve while we wait to go to America. I'll work on preparing the potatoes."

Chana let her mother take the task, reminding her, "Portion them. It makes it easier for the cooks."

Mama grabbed a knife. "I know what to do. I once managed our home and was quite capable."

Her mother's words wormed into Chana's bones. War had degraded them all, and though liberation had been sweet, it hadn't restored Ruth Rosenzweig back to the place she'd once held in their Vilna community. Chana's mother had been a respected, and sometimes feared, woman among the other Jewish wives. They often turned to Mama for advice, and because of her sharp tongue, no one dared cross her. "I remember, Mama," Chana said, briefly hugging her mother's shoulder.

Mama smiled as she sliced into a potato.

Chana smiled, too, and as others arrived, she assigned their tasks. No one questioned her, though two of the cooks eyed her with suspicion, as if she might take their jobs. *No.* She snuck a glance at the pastry side of the kitchen. Their jobs were not what she was after.

She reminded all the kitchen women to portion their ingredients and asked Gita to check the supplies and spices in the kitchen and pantry.

Trolfe and Elias emerged from the baker's pantry. The pastry chef looked happier than Chana had ever seen him.

Gita returned from the spice cupboard. "We're low on rosemary."

Chana assumed Heiss would send her to the Karlsplatz in the next day or so to buy more. "Anything else?"

"Several cheeses." Then Gita eyed the pastry side of the kitchen. "Can you believe those two? Trolfe is certainly pleased with his apprentice today."

"Is he?" Chana bit the insides of her cheeks to hold back a grin, absorbing the compliment as her own.

She sliced their bacon wafer-thin for the morning's meals as Trolfe said, "Elias, my boy, you're a genius!" The pastry chef filled a platter with slices of *Sachertorte.*

Heiss appeared, surveying the calm order of the kitchen, and nodding approval to Chana.

"What are you going on about?" Heiss asked Trolfe.

"My apprentice. You must taste his cake!"

Standing in the shower of his mentor's compliments, Elias glowed brighter than the kitchen lights.

"Must I, now?" Heiss accepted a piece from Trolfe. "What's so special about it?"

"He used eight eggs—the texture is remarkable. My pupil will do great things and they will say he learned from Chef Trolfe of the Empress Hotel! And I'll have you know his eggs came from Kirill Volkov, not Suconick, who sells you subpar goods. We need to switch our supplier."

Heiss ate a few bites of cake. "Good, but I'm not switching suppliers."

Chana let out a relieved breath, knowing deep inside that she would be in danger with Kirill parading through their kitchen.

Trolfe handed the cake off to a waiter. At first, Chana was full of pride at having her and Elias's cake served in the dining room of the Empress Hotel. But those feelings quickly faded. Trolfe had crowed over a *Sachertorte* created from many of *her* ideas. Yet, Elias happily accepted praise without so much as a conspiratorial nod or a wink.

Don't be a fool! Elias couldn't risk acknowledging her. Trolfe would fire him. Heiss would likely fire her. Still, being ignored smarted. Chana finished slicing the bacon and moved on to chopping a mountain of onions. Tears slicked her face. *From the onion, only from the onion.*

Hours later, Chana was scrubbing a soup pot when shouting erupted in the alley. She shut off the faucet.

"You're a thief! You're stealing from the wrong person," shouted a man in awkward German. It sounded like Sergeant McManus.

"*Nein, aber ich bin es nicht!*"

Aron. His voice was strangled.

What was happening? And why was the sergeant yelling at him? Chana dropped the pot with a clang and dashed for the door. Only, Elias stepped around her, beating her into the alley. The sergeant had Aron up against the wall, an arm against his throat and a metal pipe in his hand.

"Liar," McManus said. "I caught you helping yourself to those boxes."

"No!" Chana called.

McManus narrowed his eyes at her, but didn't release Aron.

Elias said, "He runs errands for Meyer Suconick. That's who you left the boxes for, right?"

McManus's eyes raked over Elias. "What's it to you?"

"We're shorthanded in the kitchen and the hotel." Elias put his hands up. "We need every worker we have."

"Why didn't he tell me that?"

Chana stepped forward. "His German isn't so good. Nor his English."

The sergeant dropped the pipe, then asked Aron, "You work with Meyer?"

Aron gave a vigorous nod.

The sergeant let go of her brother, who stumbled to Chana. She hugged him, but after a second, he pulled away, straightening.

"I tried to tell him," he said, frustrated.

McManus gave them a withering look before turning to clap Elias on the shoulder. "What's for dessert today, kid?"

"Come, I'll show you." Elias stayed a step behind McManus and gave Chana a reassuring nod.

She mouthed, *Thank you.*

When they'd gone, she grasped Aron's arms. "You cannot work for Meyer Suconick!"

Aron pulled free. "What's the harm in moving a few boxes? I'm earning extra money that we need."

"Why does Meyer want them moved?"

He pursed his lips, likely sensing she wouldn't like his answer. "He's worried one of the other dealers will steal them."

Did that mean Kirill Volkov? Aron's run-in with the sergeant was bad enough, but if it was the Soviet black-market dealer in this alley . . . She shuddered at what could have happened to her brother.

"Where were you taking the boxes?" she asked.

"A truck parked in front of the hotel."

She eyed the street. "I'll help you, but you can never agree to this again. Meyer's world is dangerous." She lifted his chin. "*Farshteyn?*"

"I understand." Aron rolled his eyes, but didn't argue. He lifted a box. "Oh, I almost forgot." He took a small package from the box. "Meyer left this for you."

Chana unwrapped the bundle and gasped. It was the needlepoint canvas she'd intended to buy from the dealer in the Karlsplatz. Her finger traced over the stiff fabric depicting flowers in the thread colors she'd already purchased.

"It was what you'd wanted for Mama, right?" Aron said.

"Yes." She'd mentioned it to Meyer at Café Victoria, but never imagined he would seek the man out for her. Unless . . . "How much does he want for it?" The parcel felt heavier in her hand.

"No, he told me to just give it to you."

It was kind, and she knew Meyer could be kind. Yet, she didn't know what to make of this gift or what it signified between them.

She rolled up the foot-long canvas, rewrapped it, and tucked the package in her apron pocket. "Come, let's move the boxes. We both need to get back to work."

That evening, Chana wrapped the yarn and canvas together in the parcel paper Meyer had used. Mama was working later than she and Aron, and since a dining room waiter also lived at Nachmann's and was working late, he had promised to escort their mother home. Once wrapped, Chana and Aron left the gift on Mama's bed, turned out the lights, and tucked themselves in, wanting to surprise her.

"Meyer asks me things about you," Aron said as they lay in the dark, side by side, on their mats.

She rolled toward him. "What kinds of things?"

He leaned on an elbow. "About things you like. Who are your friends?"

"What do you tell him?"

"The truth. You love to bake. You used to love to dance. American movies and big band music puts you in a good mood. And Shifra and Gita are your friends. But, of course, I'm your best friend."

"You are that." A strange energy filled her body at the news Meyer had asked about her. "Hmm." She glanced at the parcel on Mama's bed. It was such a thoughtful thing for him to do. Though he'd put Aron in danger with the sergeant, Chana found it hard to stay angry at Meyer.

Keys jingled in the hallway, and Chana and Aron lay flat, pretending to sleep.

Mama stepped in quietly, and soon she left for the bathroom. When she returned, she changed into her nightgown.

The parcel paper crinkled. "What is this?" their mother asked.

Chana couldn't take the suspense anymore, and popped up, turning on the lamp. Her mother had the package in her hands. Aron sat up and laughed.

"It's for you, Mama," Chana said.

"Chana got it for you," Aron said.

They joined their mother on the small bed, the mattress sinking under their weight. Mama's hands shook as she carefully pulled away the paper and unfurled the canvas. She looked at Chana. "You did this for me?"

"Yes." Chana's eyes filled. "I know how much you loved it. You can make this one, and we'll hang it here." She glanced around the dingy room. "And when we go, we'll take it with us to America."

Tears dampened her mother's cheeks. Mama gathered Chana and Aron to her. "This is the best gift I've ever received."

When Chana was in the concentration camp, she would daydream of moments like the one she was living now. Of seeing joy on her mother's face. Of knowing her brother was safe and fed. Sometimes dreams of better times weren't enough, and Chana had to order herself, *You will not die today.* There were days that obstinance alone had kept her from throwing herself against the electrified fence.

Now Chana's tears wet her mother's nightgown.

"My children." Mama kissed Chana, then Aron.

That night, before sleep overtook her, Chana vowed to do whatever she could to find her family a way out of Europe.

Chapter Twenty-One

Chana

The next afternoon, Chana strode into the Karlsplatz with a basket over one arm and her mother at her side, set to replenish supplies for Chef Heiss. Herr Heiss never sent the women out on a task alone, and she appreciated his concern for their safety.

Chana had been glad to escape the kitchen, and Trolfe's endless fawning over Elias. It was too hard to watch, even though she knew she shouldn't take it personally.

"What do you want me to get?" her mother asked.

The market was packed. Heiss's list included cheeses, plums, and apricots, along with several spices. Chana touched her pocket, where she'd tucked the kitchen money. Today's trip would have them dealing strictly with farmers. Even when Chana had no choice but to buy from the black-market dealers, she sought out smaller operators, and had grown comfortable with a few.

"Go to the spice man," Chana told her mother, carefully slipping her some money. "We can meet by that corner in about thirty minutes." She didn't worry as much about their safety in the crowded market.

Chana walked through the rows and stopped at Goran's fruit baskets, purchasing plums and apricots. Heiss had said if Goran had berries, she should select a few for him to taste. Blackberries, though puny, filled several bowls, and she bought a handful. Otto's cheese cart was next. She tasted slivers of four hard cheeses, with Otto extolling the virtues of each. He was a portly man, balding on top with black hair circling his head from one ear to the other. He claimed it was a miracle that he'd kept his cow during the war. Now Otto charged exorbitant prices. Chana purchased only two cheeses, reminding him, "Herr Heiss likes a bargain," while knowing they would do this same dance on her next trip.

With the cheese tucked into her basket, she was about to leave when, across two rows, she spotted her mother talking to Meyer, whose arm rested in a black sling.

Chana shouldered through the crowds until she was near enough and ducked behind a curtain that separated two merchant wagons. She crept closer until she made out her mother's voice.

"No one can find them. Please, I need you to do something," Mama begged. "You said you know people."

Meyer said, "Perhaps I could do more. Though there'd be no guarantee that they'd find these relatives of yours."

"Are you calling me a liar? As if my husband's family doesn't exist!" Her mother scoffed. "If not for a birthmark on my husband's iris, the emigration doctor would have approved our leaving long before the war. That doctor looked for any excuse to deny visas. We would be in America now, and my husband would have lived."

In her head, Chana could see the white mark cutting through her father's brown iris.

"I didn't mean to offend you," Meyer said, "but you must understand, the U.S. and New Jersey are vast places. Finding your family will be incredibly difficult. Goods will have to trade hands."

"We don't have much; we barely earn enough to survive."

"I'm not sure what I can do for you." He sounded apologetic.

Chana sensed Meyer attempting to leave. Tension eased from her chest.

Her mother said, "I have something else you might want."

"What is that?"

"I see your interest in my daughter. You're drawn to her as if she's your *beshert.* I see it. Any man would be lucky to have my daughter as his wife."

Chana's breath grew shallow, and if not for the bustle of the market, she was sure they would hear her. Mama desperately wanted to get their family to America, and Chana wanted the same. But how much must she sacrifice to land in the arms of Papa's family? Some would see a mother trading her only daughter like a carton of cigarettes as gruesome. Chana wished her mother had at least discussed this with her, especially after what had happened with Aron in the alley.

"I'm not like other men." Meyer's voice had turned into a growl. "And is that what you're offering? Your daughter?"

"Who are you to judge me? I'm no different from other mothers in this city. I'm doing what I must for myself and my children. Vienna is dangerous. Two women in Nachmann's were attacked last week. Defiled. A Soviet soldier left another woman pregnant. Her family has shunned her, and the soldier has gone back to his country." Chana didn't need to see her mother to know she was shaking with rage. "We are two women and a teenage boy all alone. We need help."

"There are other mothers who've pushed their daughters at me. It hasn't worked."

As Chana had witnessed, Meyer had his pick of women.

"My Chana is special," Mama said. "Other men can't take their eyes off her. The Nazis liked to look at her, too. If not for her golden hair and eyes, I'd be dead."

"What are you talking about?"

Chana stiffened. *No, Mama, don't.* She didn't want Meyer Suconick's pity.

Her mother cleared her throat. "When we were in Stutthof, no one knew she and I were mother and daughter. She'd worked with the resistance in Vilna, and they told her that if we were ever caught and sent to a camp to go in under different last names."

"Wise advice," he said. "I've heard similar instructions from others who were in the forest. The few who'd escaped the camps told of German soldiers separating families, or worse—they'd kill one in front of the other."

"And there was jealousy among the prisoners," Mama said. "Those who would resent a mother and daughter having survived together. Too much loss to go around. By chance, the Nazis put Chana and me in the same labor group to dig trenches for their soldiers. We were near a battlefront and heard bombs and shooting not far off. There were days we wished a bomb would fall on us, killing us. It would be a better way to die than being beaten or sent to the gas chamber."

Chana's legs shook and she could still feel the weekly horror of standing in line as the Nazis weeded through prisoners, sending them either to work or to death, depending on how strong or weak they appeared. She'd slap her cheeks attempting to look healthy, while beset by terror that one day either she or Mama would be sent to the execution line. Over months, growing piles of discarded shoes and eyeglasses beside the crematorium doors tallied lost lives.

Now, in the Karlsplatz, Mama continued, "Day after day, we dug trenches. One soldier didn't think I was digging fast enough. '*Macht schnell*,' he yelled." She coughed. "'*Macht schnell*.' I'll hear those words in my dreams until the day I die. He beat me with his rifle. That's why I have this scar on my eyebrow. I'm fortunate I can still see."

"I'm sorry."

"*Ech*." Her mother had no use for anyone's sympathy. "He would have killed me. Only his superior, a captain, had taken a shine to Chana. He called her 'Adela.'"

Chana could picture the captain, his pale complexion, thin nose, and hair the same color as the straw that littered the floor of their barrack. Adela had been his daughter's name; she'd died at twelve from pneumonia. She'd been blond with amber eyes.

"My daughter accepted his compliments. She's not stupid," Mama said firmly. "For months, the captain snuck his lunch to her. It was a gift to all of us, though he didn't know." She chuckled. "The Nazis gave their dogs more to eat than they gave us. Chana shared the extra food with me and some of the other women in the camp."

The captain always made sure none of the other soldiers were watching before giving Chana his meal. He'd often brush his hand over her cropped hair. She didn't mind because she would close her eyes and imagine it was Papa's hand. Chana had no illusions about this Nazi captain. He was far from innocent. In their labor detail, if a prisoner was too weak to dig, he either ordered them shot, or sent them without hesitation or emotion to the gas chamber or the hospital. They never returned.

Mama went on. "That day, when the guard beat me, my daughter wept. The captain asked her, 'Who is this woman to you? Why are you crying?'"

Chana didn't want to listen to her mother recount the rest of the story. She could see and feel it—the tightness in her chest as her mother screamed and blood sprayed the ground. "She's my mother," Chana had told the captain.

Anger contorted the captain's face, and Chana braced for a beating like her mother was getting. The captain whipped out a pistol. Her heart raced. He would shoot her for lying. She would die doing what Papa had asked—looking after Mama. Instead, he hauled the soldier off her mother. He pressed the pistol against the man's forehead and told him, "If you ever lay a hand on that woman again, I'll kill you."

A backfiring truck jarred Chana back to the Karlsplatz, and to her mother saying, "I lived because of my daughter. I went back to work because the captain said I had better meet my quota. My girl dug enough for two people that day. That's my Chana. She is a rare jewel."

Her mother ended the story there. She left out the part about how the threatened Nazi soldier had carried Chana from the barracks a few nights later, dropping her on the cold dirt behind the building. He'd hauled her to her feet, his beer-filled breath on her face as he shoved her against the wall, where rough wood scraped her back through the thin striped sack she wore.

"Frau Rosenzweig," Meyer said now. "I'm very sorry for what you and your family have been through." He sounded sincere. "Chana is indeed different. She's beautiful. Incredibly so." His tone had deepened, as if her beauty vexed him.

"Any man would be lucky to have her as his wife," Mama said.

"And that lucky man would go with you to America?" Meyer asked.

"Of course, he'd be family."

"I had an older sister," Meyer said slowly. "She was beautiful, like Chana. She wanted more than anything to be a teacher. Our father didn't approve. For him, she only had to make a good wife. My father's friend wanted my sister to marry his boy . . . asked about her skills in the kitchen. He wanted to know if Dora would be willing to have at least six children because he wanted a big family for his son."

"I see nothing wrong with that."

"No, I suppose you wouldn't," he said. "My sister wept when our father told her she would have to marry that boy. You're correct that this city grows more dangerous by the day. I've paid steep fines, been arrested twice, and others have been arrested even more. The time is coming for me to get out. But . . ." His tone had grown dark. "I lost my entire family and will not insult my sister's memory. You would make me no better than my father . . . may he rest in peace . . . if I agreed. I would never marry your daughter as a bribe."

Two lorries full of American GIs rumbled past the market and Meyer walked away from Chana's mother.

Mama called after him, "You will change your mind."

Chana stumbled away, unseen by either of them. She should feel relieved. Only, her eyes filled, and the market grew blurry. She took a few breaths to regain her composure. It was time to return to the hotel; Heiss would be expecting her. Chana wiped her eyes and turned, running straight into a man's chest. When she looked up, his head blotted out the sun.

"They're pretty, don't you think?" he asked in smooth German, gesturing to a nearby crate of scarves.

Kirill Volkov.

Chana clutched her basket to her body. "Let me through, I'm expected back at work."

He didn't move. "You should try one on. If you don't have the money, my friend and I can work something out for you." He looked to the moonfaced man beside the crate, whose grin made his eyes disappear into his fat cheeks.

"I don't want a scarf." She stepped to the right, and Kirill blocked her.

He held a blue scarf near her face. "This color is nice. Payment would be easy for one so pretty."

She wanted to shove him away, but he was much bigger than she. Chana caught sight of Meyer several yards away. His eyes widened when he spotted her. As Meyer started toward her, she shook her head, then told Kirill, "I need to get back to the hotel. Herr Heiss is waiting for me."

She pushed past him, and though she could feel Kirill's eyes on her, she didn't chance looking back. When she reached the other side of the market, she was trembling.

"What did Kirill want with you?"

Chana turned to find Meyer. "Nothing." She pulled her shoulders back, grateful her steady voice didn't give away her knotted feelings regarding what she'd overheard.

He moved closer. "Are you sure you're all right?"

"Of course." She had been hoping her next encounter with Meyer would allow her to thank him for her mother's needlepoint. Also to tell him that Aron couldn't run his errands anymore. But she was too drained and confused. "I should find my mother and head to the hotel."

Meyer didn't stop her from leaving.

She went straight to the man who sold knives, buying a small knife with her allowance. With her purchase in her pocket, she kept her fingers wrapped around the hilt as she went to find her mother.

Chapter Twenty-Two

Chana

Surprise," Shifra called as she hurried into the hotel alley.

Chana had stepped out of the kitchen, ready to head home after a taxing dinner shift. It was several days after her trip to the Karlsplatz, and her mother's attempt at a *shidduch* with Meyer.

Shifra fluffed her hair. "Do you like it?"

Her friend's hair was now red, an unnatural shade between a beet and a carrot. Chana didn't like it at all, but Shifra's eyes shone brighter than they had in a while. She forced a smile. "It's lovely."

"What's wrong?" Shifra asked.

"It's been a long day." Actually, a few long days, during which Chana had barely spoken to her mother. The kitchen had been busier than ever, and Chana cited fatigue when Mama asked about her silence.

Chana knew her mother loved her and only wanted to get them to America, as she did, too. Mama's motivation came from her heart—for Mama, Aron, and Chana, Papa's family equaled safety. But for her mother to have pressed forward with an engagement to Meyer without consulting Chana . . . Even days later, it hurt.

Shifra nudged her. "Wake up, my friend. I'm walking you home so you can change. We're going to Café Zweite tonight."

Chana tied her scarf over her head. "Shifra, my only plan tonight is to put my feet up."

She smoothed her hair. "My name is Sophie now."

"Since when?"

"This week. It suits me." She tugged on Chana's arm. "Come tonight, please."

Mama stepped outside, and Chana spotted Elias hovering by the door. They'd spoken little since the morning Trolfe had praised the apprentice's talents to the heavens. She'd been avoiding him, even though she missed their time together. Missed him.

"Aron will be ready to go in a minute," Mama told Chana as she buttoned her coat. "Shifra, what kind of trouble are you trying to get my daughter into?"

"My name is Sophie now, Frau Rosenzweig. It makes me sophisticated."

"It makes you *meshuga*," Mama said. "And what did you do to your hair? You had perfectly fine brown hair."

"A girl at the laundry colored it for me. And I'm not *crazy*. Perfectly *fine* wasn't getting me a husband." She tossed her hair back. "I want Chana to come to Café Zweite tonight."

"No," Mama said, to Chana's relief.

"There, Shifra, it's settled," Chana said.

"So-phie." Her friend gave her a challenging look. "It's not that hard to remember."

"Sorry. It's just—"

"What?"

"I don't understand it."

She stared at Chana, her chin quivering. "Horrible things happened to Shifra. She lost her parents . . . her sisters." Her voice was scratchy. "Shifra has nothing. It's too hard. I'm Sophie. I want a new life. *Farshteyn?*"

Chana squeezed Sophie's hand, regretting questioning her. "I understand."

Sophie sniffled. Then she turned sober eyes to Chana's mother. "Frau Rosenzweig, the American soldiers are going to the café tonight. Lots of them. There will be a band and dancing." Once again, giddiness trickled into her friend's voice. "Gita's going, too; she's meeting her GI boyfriend."

Chana watched her mother's mind working, and before she could object, Mama said, "Okay, she'll go."

"I'm tired," Chana said. "Aron and I are practicing our English tonight."

"You can practice with the American soldiers. It'll be good for you."

Sophie said, "See, even your mother wants you to go. It'll be fun."

Chana glanced between the eager faces of Sophie and her mother, and her irritation abated. "Fine. I'll go, but only to keep you out of trouble."

Music was the first thing to greet Chana as she walked into Café Zweite. Young men and women filled the room, and conversations created a hum beneath the music as she followed behind Sophie and Gita. The three girls nudged past groups and couples to claim a table near the dance floor, where musicians played on a stage built from wood planks. She glanced up to where the ceiling should have been. The roof had been half bombed out, and the moon doused the dance floor in cool light.

Shifra . . . *Sophie*, Chana corrected in her thoughts, smoothed her red hair. The two had gotten ready together at Nachmann's, Sophie styling Chana's hair in waves using a lavender-scented cream. She told Chana, "Tonight, you're a Hollywood girl."

When Chana caught her reflection in the broken bathroom mirror, it was indeed like looking at those starlets in the magazines the GIs left in the dining room. Her friend had also loaned her a navy, jewel-necked dress, plain compared to Sophie's dress that showed off her cleavage in a rich shade of purple. Even when pressed, Sophie refused to tell Chana how she came by this garment or her own. None of what they wore was new, but their dresses were in decent condition overall.

Couples crammed the dance floor and American soldiers filled the café, just as Sophie said they would. Chana recognized a few from the hotel. The private who asked for his tea to be served at room temperature and with as much sugar as the kitchen could spare. The hefty soldier who, after a full meal, then devoured all of his friends' leftovers. The GI who lingered over his food, chewing at a glacial rate, and was often the last to leave the dining room.

Chana scanned the crowd, noticing Elias at a table across the floor. He was with two men who also worked at the hotel: a handyman, and the concierge. The men tossed back drinks, and she looked away.

"I'll be back in a minute," Sophie said.

It was clear her friend was no stranger to the café's nightlife as she bounced through the crowd, openly flirting with any man who glanced her way. Even Kirill Volkov. She stroked his lapel as she passed and offered a bold smile.

Chana grimaced. Why couldn't he stick to the Soviet-run section of Vienna?

Sophie veered toward the back of the room, where Meyer huddled at a table with Sergeant McManus. She touched Meyer's shoulder, and he whispered something to her. Her laughter rang out, and she tossed her hair back. Chana looked away, shifting on her hard wooden chair.

Gita passed a flask to Chana. "Drink up."

Chana had only ever had a few sips of wine at Sabbath dinners. But she drank, and the liquid burned as it slid down her throat. She coughed.

Gita giggled, then patted Chana's arm. "You get used to the taste."

With cheeks as flushed as her new red hair, Sophie returned to the table and took the flask. "The sergeant was asking many questions about our Chana. Mama Rosenzweig will be thrilled."

Chana might have to compromise her future to enter America, but it would not be on the arm of Sergeant McManus. "I have no interest."

Sophie took out cigarettes and gave one to Chana, though she hadn't asked. "Here he comes."

Chana looked up into the sergeant's face. "You are the prettiest table of ladies in this place," he said in German.

The others laughed, and Chana eyed the cigarette. She had never smoked. The sergeant drew out his lighter.

"*Danke*," she said, leaning her cigarette toward the flame as she'd seen women do in films.

"Ah, Austrian." He gave her an appraising look.

She took a tug off the cigarette and nearly choked. Meyer watched from his table, his expression unreadable.

"You look familiar," Sergeant McManus said.

"I work in the Empress Hotel kitchen." She took another puff. The second one wasn't so bad.

He snapped his fingers. "Blondie. You clean up nice." He ran his tongue over his lips.

Like a wolf.

"I'll be back," she whispered to the women and excused herself to get away from the sergeant's gaze.

On the dance floor, women shimmied and flirted, and Chana tried to discern any genuine emotion behind their actions. The café's forced gaiety weighed on her, and she leaned against the wall, feeling the cool bricks through her dress.

The musicians laid down their instruments, taking a break. Across the room, a tawny-haired woman slid into the seat opposite Meyer, grabbing his hand while flashing a pearly smile, her mouth ringed with vivid red lipstick. So many women vying for his attention. Chana wondered how this one could afford both lipstick and her boldness. Meyer gave this lady a wide grin, and he looked so wickedly handsome, like a matinee idol, it stole her breath.

"I'm glad to see you," said a voice to her right.

Chana turned to find Elias.

"I heard your friend inviting you to the café," he said, keeping a shoulder to the wall, and from his drooping eyelids, she could tell he'd had a lot to drink. "It's the whole reason I came. I've barely seen you. Have you noticed how impressed Trolfe has been? He called me a genius."

"It's hard to miss."

Elias smiled broadly, oblivious to how his comment wounded her.

He straightened for a second, before propping against the wall again. "Our plan is working."

"Was that our plan?" she asked, confused.

"Of course. You offered to help me."

He was right. She had made that offer on their first night. They'd been in the alley with him accusing her of spying. She focused on the trumpet player, who'd returned to the stage. His fingers tickled the shiny valves, sending out a blast of song. Her eyes burned. She'd entered their arrangement so she and Elias could learn from each other. She hadn't entertained the idea of gaining recognition until Trolfe had showered it on him.

"Are you angry with me?" he asked. "Chana, baking with you is the highlight of my days. You're incredibly talented."

His compliment touched her. "Do you think so?"

"Of course! You make me a better baker. We're quite a team."

Elias viewed them as a team. The way she and Papa had been a team. Her despair eased. "I'm not angry." She took a puff of the cigarette.

"Trolfe told me the next time that I bake, he'll cover the cost of the ingredients. You'll bake with me again, won't you?"

"Of course," she said, and he lurched slightly, as if to keep himself upright. "How much have you had to drink?"

"A bit." He pinched his fingers together. "Can I tell you a secret?"

"Okay."

He put his lips to her ear. She caught a whiff of alcohol, but also something sugary, and wholly him. After a deep inhale, her pulse beat faster. "You're my best friend," he whispered.

Chana relaxed, because being with Elias was always easy. She turned her head, and she thought Elias might kiss her. She tipped toward him, feeling both ready, yet uncertain. He wobbled, and she grabbed his elbow to steady him.

"I think I need to sit," Elias said.

The intimate moment was gone. Disappointed, she said, "I'll help you back to your friends." She guided him toward his table, unsure of what that moment between them had meant. She'd leaned toward him. Had she wanted him to kiss her?

Elias thumped down in his chair. For the time being, Chana tucked away her confusion. She squashed her cigarette in an ashtray and turned to the other two men, one who filled Elias's cup with clear liquid. "See that he makes it back to the hotel," she said to the men, then she whispered to Elias, "Be careful." He lifted his head, his damp brown hair falling into his soulful eyes.

A lively song began, and she was on her way back to her table, prepared to tell the girls she wanted to leave, when someone caught her wrist. She turned.

Meyer.

His warm hand felt pleasing against her skin, and she didn't pull away. "No sling?" she asked. He appeared confused. "You were wearing one when we saw each other in the Karlsplatz."

"I'm better." Meyer moved his arm to demonstrate. "Will you dance with me?"

The floor was full. She told herself to decline. But even so, she said, "All right."

His hand stayed on her wrist as he guided her to the dance floor, holding on to her the way a boy might cling to a string tethering a balloon, fearful it might fly away if he dared let go.

She wondered if Elias was watching her, and felt a flicker of worry that dancing with Meyer might hurt his feelings.

Couples swayed on the packed floor. A flutter of nerves brushed Chana's belly. She'd danced with Papa and her family on those long-ago afternoons, but she didn't know how to do any of the steps displayed around them. "I'm afraid I don't know how to dance like that."

He opened his arms. "I'll show you."

She stepped forward, and he took her hand, placing his other around her back. She glanced at the surrounding couples and rested her other hand on his shoulder, feeling his muscles tense beneath his shirt.

"Pretend there's a box between us," he said.

Chana's gaze fell to her feet, and they moved together as if around a small square. Her foot landed on his toes. "I'm sorry." She bit her lip.

"It's all right," he said kindly.

She did it again, but he didn't seem to mind. "Where did you learn to dance like this?" she asked over the music.

"I had a friend at school who'd spent time in England. She taught me."

"She?" Chana looked up to meet his eyes.

"We were in school together before the war. Her father was a university teacher and for a while they'd lived in London. They should have stayed there."

The bitterness in his voice let her know what had happened to that friend.

"I wish there was something I could have done for them," he said.

They moved in silence, and he gradually shifted her closer, their imaginary box shrinking and their bodies nearly touching. She could feel the heat of him and found she didn't mind.

"Are you and your family managing?" Meyer asked. "Do you have enough food?"

"We do." She smiled, thinking of the basket of eggs and box of candy bars he had left for them at Nachmann's the other day.

His hand rested against her back. Her body tingled, and suddenly she yearned to know more about Meyer Suconick than the things people whispered about him.

"I believe you're more caring than you let on," she said.

The apples of his cheeks turned pink. "Let's not talk that up around town," he teased.

The music swelled, and she felt light enough to fly up and touch the moonlit sky. "I'm serious. You are. And I feel bad now."

"Why?"

"I've been meaning to thank you for the needlepoint." Chana thought of Mama's hug after opening the present. "My mother loved it. It was so thoughtful of you."

"I'm glad she liked it." He tilted closer. "And Aron told me about the misunderstanding with Sergeant McManus. Trust me, it won't happen again."

Chana had to make Meyer understand Aron had no place working in the black market. She hadn't survived two ghettos and a concentration camp for her brother to end up injured or worse here in Vienna. "Meyer, my brother can't work for you. If Elias hadn't stepped out—"

"Elias . . ." His eyes narrowed. "I would never let anything happen to Aron."

"Really?" She fixed him with a stare. "A few days ago, you were wearing a sling. What happened then?"

"I had a run-in with Kirill."

She recalled her tea with Meyer, and how after he'd threatened Grigory, Kirill had delivered a warning to Meyer. "Because of me?" she asked.

"It was business." Yet, he held her gaze.

You're drawn to her, Mama had said.

They swayed slowly in a circle. "Tell me, Chana, what do you want to do when you get to America?"

She smiled, pleased because no one since Papa had ever asked her what she wanted. "I want to be free."

His lips twitched to one side. "I could've posed that question to every other woman in this café and easily have predicted what they'd say."

"And what would that be . . . ?"

"They would tell me they wanted to meet a man like me . . . and that they wanted to marry, have children, and take care of their family."

"Yes, I suppose that's true."

He smiled as if amused, but coolness darkened his eyes. "You don't see a husband and children in your future?"

"Perhaps someday."

"Then what do you want to do with all your freedom?"

"My father wanted us to bake together. That's what I want. I want to become a baker."

His cheeks sank the way they would when holding back a response. Meyer had admired that his sister wanted to be a teacher, yet Chana's answer clearly bothered him. What did he expect? Even with her growing affection for him, she wasn't ready to fall into his arms shouting, *Marry me, Meyer?* He'd turned down her mother because his sister had wanted the same thing as Chana—to be more than some man's wife.

"Honest Chana," he said in a heavy voice.

"You once said you admired my chutzpah."

"Did I?"

The saxophone player screeched out a long note that made her cringe.

"I saw you talking to *Elias*." Meyer drew out his name, *E-li-as*. "What exactly is your relationship?"

"I've told you, he's my friend."

"And you *bake* together?" He made *bake* sound wrong.

"We do." She kept her head high.

"Perhaps you'd prefer to dance with the baker. Or the sergeant. He was at your table, and I hear you have a way with soldiers."

"You've been talking to my mother. I saw the two of you at the Karlsplatz." Chana no longer cared if he knew she'd eavesdropped.

"Your mother wants my help. She believes I can deliver you all into the bosom of your family."

"I know." To her surprise—and despite all she'd claimed about freedom—his earlier refusal to marry her made tears prick the backs of her eyes. "Meyer, why did you ask me to dance? There's no shortage of partners for you."

"Aren't friends allowed to ask friends to dance?"

Friends.

"I should go." She pulled away, bumping against the couple dancing behind her. Instantly, she missed Meyer's arms around her. She'd been the one to claim their relationship was platonic. Now it had blown up in her face as he held to that view, while her feelings had expanded. She wondered if using the same description—*a friend*—about Elias had been unfair to him as well. Oh, what a mess!

The song ended, and Chana took a step back. "I appreciate the help you've given my family"—she kept her voice even—"but unless you hear from Brihah, I don't think we have much more to say to each other. And please"—she paused—"please leave Aron alone."

Chapter Twenty-Three

Chana

Chana broke through the crowd of dancers in Café Zweite, desperate to get to the table, where Sophie was flirting with yet another man. She needed to protect her heart and get as far away as possible from Meyer. Chana grabbed her coat. "I'm leaving."

"Wait," Sophie said.

Meyer watched them from the dance floor. "No, now. If you're not coming, I'm going by myself."

Her friend frowned. "I promised your mother we'd stick together." She kissed the man's cheek. "I have to go," she said in a frisky voice. "I'll see you on another night."

"Where's Gita?" Chana searched the crowd.

"She left with Jeb."

Outside, they pulled on their coats. Chana was glad for the bracing wind, which beat away the memory of Meyer's warm breath on her cheek.

Sophie tripped. "I don't see why we have to leave! My night was getting good."

Chana steadied the girl. "All the more reason to go."

It was an eight-block walk to Nachmann's. Chana touched the knife in her pocket. When they arrived at the boardinghouse, she and Aron would walk Sophie the extra block to the laundry.

They strode through the streets without event until they were a block from Nachmann's. Several men stumbled out from an alley; when Chana tried to cut past, they circled around the two girls.

"Let us through," she said in German. Her eyes darted up the street, but found the blocks deserted. She and Sophie faced three men, all dressed in dark clothes. The two taller men flanked a shorter fellow.

Grigory.

"We meet again," Grigory said, stepping forward.

The hair on her neck rose.

Sophie hiccuped, and the men laughed, a menacing sound.

Chana gripped her friend's arm as someone yelled, "Leave my sister alone!"

The sound of someone running cut through the night. Then Aron rammed into the man to the right of Grigory, knocking him off balance. Though not for long. He and the other man threw Aron to the ground.

"Stop it!" Chana shouted. If they hurt Aron, she would never forgive herself.

"Why? What does this little pup mean to you?" Moonlight reflected off Grigory's shiny head. The two men hauled Aron to his feet. "Tell me, what will you do to save him?"

Panicked, Chana froze. She would do anything to keep Aron safe. She had the knife in her pocket, but could she take all three of them?

"She won't do anything," Aron said. "Don't touch her."

Grigory grumbled and punched her brother in the face. Though

Aron equaled Grigory in height, he was much thinner, the blow causing his head to snap back, and his legs to buckle. If the other two hadn't been holding him, he would have hit the ground.

"No!" Chana yelled, brandishing her knife.

"What do you have there?" Grigory sneered.

Suddenly, a car came screeching to a halt at the curb. Four men jumped out of the vehicle. One of them was Meyer. Another was Hershel, the dealer she and Elias had met to buy sugar and flour.

"What's going on?" Meyer asked.

"We're only having some fun," said Grigory.

Meyer stepped closer, spotted the knife in Chana's hand, and turned his attention back to Grigory. "Not with these women or that young fellow."

"Oh, no? Says who?"

Vlad leveled a shotgun at Grigory.

Chana tightened her grip on her knife.

"Let go of him," Meyer said.

Grigory slid a hand over his scalp. "I don't have to listen to you."

"Because of Kirill?" Meyer said. "I don't give a shit if your brother is Joseph Stalin. Let him go."

Vlad cocked the gun.

Grigory swore in Russian, but gestured to the others, who released Aron. Aron moved to Chana, and she wrapped her arm around him. His shirt was damp with sweat. He leaned against her, allowing her to support him.

"Come on." Grigory faced off with Meyer. "What do you care about a couple of whores?"

Meyer punched him in the stomach, and he doubled over, groaning. One of Grigory's cronies pulled a gun, aiming it at Meyer.

Chana clung to Aron. Sophie whimpered.

Vlad *tsk*ed. "Put down your gun."

"You first," the other man said.

Vlad grinned. "You had better be an excellent marksman, my friend, because if you're not, I'll shoot your ear off before you can pull the trigger. Then I'll kill you." His voice was silky. He seemed to be enjoying this. "After, I'll hang your ear from my wall."

Grigory barked, "Put it away."

His friend lowered his gun.

"Now leave," Meyer said.

Grigory waved to the alley, and they ran.

Relief rippled through Chana as she tightened her hold on Aron. She was so grateful Meyer had shown up. *Had he followed her?* Perhaps he cared after all. "Thank you," she said. "I don't know what would have happened if you hadn't . . ."

Meyer's eyes blazed. "I can tell you exactly what would have happened. Do you always act this reckless?"

"No!" Chana's voice shook at having her gratitude thrown back in her face.

"Without me you'd—" Meyer's words cut off, and he glanced away. When he looked at her again all she could read on his face was scorn. "And what were you going to do with that little knife? The man would have shot you."

Meyer's friends snickered.

"Not before I stabbed him," Chana said. And she would have, before the man could reach for his gun. She would have fought like the devil to save her brother. "I said thank you, and I meant it," she said through a clenched jaw.

He pointed. "You, Chana Rosenzweig, are trouble."

His fury sliced through her, and she tightened her arm around Aron. "Let's go." Her brother staggered beside her, with Sophie trailing along.

From behind her, Hershel said, "Meyer, never anger a lady who carries a knife. Lucky for you, she didn't give you a second bris."

Another man chuckled.

"Shut up," Meyer said. "You can all go. Follow them in the car and make sure they get to Nachmann's."

"Meyer's not a bad sort," Aron whispered. "Not at heart."

"*Shhh,* don't worry about him," she said. "Let's get you home." Chana suspected Meyer's rescue tonight meant he did indeed care for her more than he let on. The idea thrilled and frightened her, turning her legs weak. After seeing Sophie to the laundry, Chana and her brother hobbled back to the boardinghouse. As they climbed the steps, she wasn't sure if she was holding up Aron or if it was the other way around.

A few days later, soldiers raided the Karlsplatz, taking dozens of black-market dealers into custody. Since the location was in the Inter-allied zone, American, French, British, and Soviet soldiers aided in the operation. The Allied forces believed the black market undercut their authority. Most men weren't held long. Those like Meyer and Kirill were let out quickly, with whispers of interventions by certain officers, both American and Soviet. At least that was what Herr Heiss claimed; he was grateful to keep his access to superb wine and hearty livestock.

Chana viewed the crackdown as both good and bad. On the one hand, she wanted safe streets, free from the threat of robbery, and worse. But safety would come at another cost. Many would starve without the food peddled by the dealers.

A week after Chana's altercation with Grigory on the street, Meyer made a delivery to Herr Heiss. He gave her a curt nod, but didn't stop to talk. This saddened Chana, though she didn't let it show. It entirely soured her mother's mood. After Meyer finished his kitchen business, he joined Sergeant McManus in the dining room. The two men drank plum brandy and spoke in hushed tones as Chana cleared tables, hardly looking at them. He'd called her *trouble*. How ironic!

One thing was certain, she'd misread him having any feelings for her other than as a friend. If he even considered her that.

That evening, she was in the alley tying her kerchief when Elias came out after her.

"If you're heading home, can I walk you?" he asked.

Chana smiled. "Yes, I'd enjoy the company." Aron was working late, and she was eager to go home. She'd planned to brave the walk on her own with her knife in her pocket.

Once they'd reached the sidewalk, he said, "I wanted to talk to you."

"What about?" For a second, she worried he might tell her they could no longer bake together.

"I wanted to make sure that you were all right."

"What do you mean?"

"I looked for you again at Café Zweite, but you were gone." He kicked a rock, sending it skittering into a pile of rubbish. "I drank too much, and I heard what happened to you . . . and your brother."

She hated how talk spread in the kitchen.

He said, "I wish I could have escorted you home."

"You might have gotten hurt."

"I would risk it for you." He squinted and stared up the block. "You can rely on me, Chana."

"I know." And she meant it. It occurred to her that Elias might also have learned of Meyer's intervention or seen them dancing at the café. Before she could ask, he went rigid.

"I didn't realize you lived out this way." His voice was thick.

"Out which way?"

He pointed across the street, toward a perpendicular road with several abandoned shops. "Can we hurry?" he said.

"All right."

They sped along several blocks until she grabbed his arm. "What's going on?" she asked. He bent over and placed his hands on his knees. "Are you sick?"

When he glanced up, his sweaty hair was plastered to his forehead. "That street was where my father's violin shop had been. Since being back, I've avoided it."

"Oh." She recalled the terrible story he'd told about his father losing his store and then taking his life. She laid a hand on his back. "If you need to return to the hotel, I'll be all right. It's only two blocks to my boardinghouse."

He gulped some air. "No. I'll take you the rest of the way."

"Do you want to talk about your parents?" she asked as they crossed the street.

He was quiet. The only sound was their footsteps on the pavement. Then he said, "Rivka, my mother, used to make challah on Fridays. Her hair . . . damp curls were always in her eyes when she cooked. It was hot in our apartment even in winter." He looked at Chana expectantly.

"It can be like that," she said, her heart twisting at the anguish in his voice.

"On Friday evenings, when my father came home, he'd hang his hat in the foyer and take a deep breath. He liked to say he could smell my mother's challah from the sidewalk. Then he'd kiss my mother." Elias smiled. "I would try on his hat when he wasn't looking. It had a long gray feather, soft as velvet."

"That's a lovely memory. You must miss them."

His gaze dropped to the ground. "I try not to think about them."

Chana wondered when, if ever, Elias would talk openly about his parents again. It was like that for some. They couldn't face the pain of their losses, so they stuffed their grief away. Chana differed from him. She couldn't help but think and talk about Papa.

A few steps later, they arrived at Nachmann's. Chana fidgeted with her scarf. "I should go in." If her mother saw her with Elias, she'd never hear the end of it.

"Thank you for letting me walk you." He lifted his hand to her cheek, and she pressed into his palm. "You are brilliant in every way." His compliment lifted her spirits, and their eyes met and held, until he suddenly dropped his hand, kissed her cheek, and said, "Good night."

He walked away. His kiss had been so quick it could have been a dream. She brought her fingers to her face and felt the slight dampness from his lips. No, she hadn't dreamed it at all. Happiness spread through her, and she giggled. It was her first kiss from a boy. And it was from Elias.

Chana climbed the stairs inside the boardinghouse and wrinkled her nose at the sulfur smell of boiled cabbage wafting out from the communal kitchen. When she reached the third floor and neared their door, she heard a deep voice coming from inside.

"I think it's a good idea now," the man said.

It was Meyer. She stepped closer to listen.

"Why have you reconsidered?" Mama asked.

"Have you gotten a better offer?"

"No. Whatever you may think, I love my daughter. I want us to reach our family, but I also want a good match for her."

They were discussing her marrying Meyer. Chana knew she should burst in, but instead, she became rooted outside the door.

Meyer said, "She and Aron were almost hurt the other night."

"I know. I'd sent him to watch for her." Her mother's tone was grim. "We need to get out."

"Things are more dangerous for me, too," he said. "Last week's raid on the market won't be the last. It's time for me to go, and America is as good a place as any."

"What about the ports?"

"Not an option. I've had no contact with anyone in the Brihah since Schumacher's arrest."

"You lied to us!" Chana heard a thump and imagined her mother pounding her fist on the table.

"Your quarrel isn't with me. I'm nothing but a middleman. If I talk to the fellow I know at the consulate, will your family sponsor me?"

"Yes, if you marry my daughter."

"That's good." Heavy footsteps sounded from inside as if Meyer were pacing. "There's an American soldier . . ." He paused. "He wants to help, but I'd be indebted to him. And if he does step in, I'll work for his civilian associates in America. I've been told they prefer I be a married man." Silence fell until Meyer said, "I don't want to see anything happen to any of you. I'll treat Chana well and be a good husband. I'm sure we can learn to respect each other."

What about love? Chana had hoped that when the time came for her to wed, it would also be for love.

"There are marriages built on less," her mother said.

No! Chana rushed into the room. Mama and Meyer stood by the table as if they'd finished an innocent meal instead of scheming about her future. A fresh bouquet of six yellow roses bloomed from a large jar. She assumed they were a gift from Meyer.

"What's going on here?" Chana was sweating, her shirt tacked against her back.

Her mother stepped forward. "Herr Suconick—"

"Call me Meyer, please."

"Yes . . . Meyer has agreed to help us get to America using his connections."

Chana met her mother's begging eyes. She'd been a dutiful daughter, fulfilling her promise to Papa to look out for her mother and brother. She'd spent countless hours at emigration offices, filling out form after form. But was this how it all ended? "What does he want in return?"

Meyer told her mother, "Please, leave us alone for a moment."

Mama did as asked, but not before whispering to Chana, "This is our chance."

Once they were alone, Meyer said, "We're to be married." He drew a velvet pouch from his pocket. "We'll get to know each other better, and you'll see . . . I'll treat you well." His tone was matter-of-fact as he handed her the small package. "For you."

It had some weight, and her fingers shook as she loosened the string and removed a hair comb adorned with a jeweled bird.

"Aron had mentioned that your partisan code name was Wren. When I saw it, I thought of you."

The overhead light made the comb's amber, green, and topaz gems shimmer as if it were alive and could fly out the window. Off to find freedom. Chana dreamed of following its lead.

"What did you do for the resistance?" Meyer asked.

"I passed messages."

"Why Wren?"

She looked over to find him watching her. "My contact said it was because of their amazing ability to survive and their hopeful song, but I liked the idea of having wings."

"Fitting. They also symbolize determination and joy." He stepped closer. "They're a small yet beautiful bird with a powerful voice."

Her spirit soared at his comparison, despite her struggle to fully make sense of what was happening here and between them.

"Were you afraid?" he asked.

"Always." Her thoughts turned to her last errand for the partisans, when few people were left in the Vilna ghetto, and a final *Aktion* to remove the remaining Jews was imminent.

It was summer of 1943, and terror weighed on the few Jews still left. The partisans would soon move to the Rudnicki Forest, having determined a battle with the Germans from within the ghetto would likely end in a massacre of the remaining population. Her parents, along with three other families, had built a *malina*, a hiding spot in an abandoned building's attic. When the final *Aktion* came, they would go there. For months, the adults had been stocking food in the *malina*: wheat, potatoes, oil, and anything else that wouldn't spoil.

The last message Chana delivered took her to the gentile part of the city. Only then, she traveled through Vilna's sewers, hunching in tight tunnels, and guided by the beam of an unreliable flashlight. On her return, she navigated through knee-deep sludge, gagging, when suddenly her light hit something sticking out from the wall stones. She shouldn't have stopped, but couldn't help herself. It was a note that read:

To whoever finds this message, my name is Ivan and I escaped the Ponary Forest. My family did not. On the transport, the Nazis tortured us in unspeakable ways. Killing us isn't enough for them. I leave this in the hope of spreading the truth to the world. These are the names of my family.

Five names were listed.

Chana committed each to memory and left the message for others to find. On the slog forward, in rising dreck that threatened to drown her, she wept and whispered the Mourner's Kaddish for Ivan's family.

Meyer studied her face. "I've upset you."

"My memories upset me. I worked with the partisans because I had to do something, anything, to help. Were you afraid when you rescued Jews from Bialystok?"

"Always." His tone was somber.

Perhaps this arrangement between them could work. He studied her for a long moment, then stepped back, his face going blank. "I hope you like the comb. I believe it was meant for you," he said evenly.

"It's beautiful." She was touched at the thought behind his present, yet miffed at his coolness. As if all of this was nothing but a business transaction. She traced her fingers over the jewels, anger rising within her. Chana imagined another woman's head, a brunette or redhead, wearing this comb. Perhaps even someone Meyer had taken to tea—a woman who'd traded it for lipstick or cigarettes. She didn't know who it had once belonged to and feared its original owner would haunt her forever.

Before she could stop herself, she said, "It was meant for whoever owned it before me. I don't have to guess how you came by it. Someone needed eggs, a bottle of milk, or a pair of shoes. And now it's mine." In Vilna, Jews who'd hidden jewelry traded outside the ghetto for any bit of food. Mama had sold a gold and pearl pin that had once belonged to her mother in exchange for three potatoes.

"I bought it for a chicken, two loaves of bread, and a carton of Lucky Strikes. But what does it matter?" His voice was rough. "I only want what's best for you and your family."

Good. She'd wanted to provoke emotion from him. "Why? Because you need a wife for some business arrangement? Are you using me?"

He flinched as if she'd slapped him, and she worried she'd pushed him too far as he charged closer. They faced off in silence, standing only a breath away. She should have been repelled. Instead, her heart lifted at the challenge in his dark eyes and the nearness of him. "I'm helping because I care for you," he said.

She opened her mouth, but nothing came out.

"Don't tell me honest Chana has nothing to say?"

Now she thought of Elias's lips on her cheek. "I . . . I'm surprised." The intensity on Meyer's face left her breathless. Confusion shook her, and in a rush, she asked, "Do you love me?"

"I said I care for you."

"Care, but not love?"

"I can't love anyone," he said.

His declaration rocked her. "It's not enough for me," she told him. "When we danced, you asked what I wanted"—she took in the room as if her future were drawn on the walls—"I want to go to America, but if I marry, I want a man like my father." In her mind's eye she saw Papa happily greeting customers, dancing as he baked, and even juggling rolls to make her smile. "I want someone who loves with his whole being. Someone with passion."

He bowed his head. "I will be a good husband, but I am not a man such as you describe."

"Why?" She heard the plea in her voice.

"My sister and my parents died at the Rumbula Forest massacre, along with thousands of others." His tone was bitter. "I was fighting with the Soviet army, off saving others when I should have been saving my family." Meyer looked at her. "My heart will never be whole."

"Meyer, I'm so sorry." Emotion clogged Chana's throat. Loss had hallowed her out for a time, too. She moved to comfort him, wanting to hug him and to be hugged back, because surely they could work toward loving each other.

But he put up a hand. His hard look stopped her in her tracks.

"I have a way out of Europe for us. It will take some time, but it *will* happen. Do you want to take your family away from here?"

"I do." There was nothing she wanted more. *But not like this.*

"Then we're agreed," he said.

She straightened her spine. "I don't want to marry this way," she said.

He pinned her with his eyes, his gaze seeming to sift through her soul, hunting for something. "You are the most stubborn woman I've ever met." He backed away, then left.

Her mother came back in. "How did it go?"

"There must be another option, Mama," Chana said. "Meyer will never love me."

Her mother stood in front of her, tears glossing her eyes. Mama shuddered; her misery was palpable. Several nights ago, Chana had overheard her mother crying in the bathroom. She was about to go in when Mama had said, "Tell me what to do, Jacob."

Jacob. Her papa. Chana had pressed her ear to the door.

Inside the bathroom, Mama continued, "We're trapped here. I tried to make a *shidduch* for Chana. To help us." Her mother sobbed. "God, forgive me. I don't know what else to do. I've lost you and I'm trying to save our children. To give them a good life." If her mother said anything else it was consumed by her weeping. Her confession broke Chana apart. She left, allowing her mother her privacy. By the time Mama entered their room, the only evidence of her sorrow was a bit of redness around her eyes.

Now her mother said, "If there was another way, I'd have found it. Do you want to stay here and be taken by a soldier or a man on the street?"

Of course not. She had survived it once in Stutthof. But she couldn't live through it happening again.

Mama gathered Chana's hands in her own. "He has seen your burns. He doesn't mind." Her voice had lowered. "He'll get us to Papa's family, and we'll build new lives."

"We don't love each other." Admitting this made her feel empty, and it was only partly true. Chana had strong feelings for Meyer. She couldn't deny it to herself. Moving forward, she would have to hold those emotions in as an act of self-preservation.

"You want to know about love?" Mama asked. "Aron and I love you, Chana, and you'll have children, and *they'll* love you. It'll be enough. Not every man is built like your papa." Mama kissed Chana's knuckles. "Please, you must do this. If not for yourself or me, do it for Aron. They could have killed him the other night."

Chana saw a flash of her brother being dragged to his feet by those awful men. Grigory punching him. She pulled away from Mama and hugged herself. Chana loved her brother more than anything. She couldn't lose Aron.

Chana moaned as if she'd suddenly fallen ill. Mama rubbed her back, intending to soothe her. Yet Mama's desperation seeped through her hand and into Chana's skin. Her mother wholly believed that this was the best route for them. That she was doing something right for their family. Chana didn't want her mother to have to cry alone at night anymore. And it was done. Mama had made the match. Chana would honor the promise she'd made to Papa to take care of Mama and Aron. But at what cost to herself?

Chapter Twenty-Four

Zoe

Vienna, Austria
April 2018

Most of Zoe's cake had gone uneaten, her appetite abating as her family's story progressed. Zoe and Henri were still in the hotel dining room, though the far side of the room had emptied.

"I want you to know that I greatly appreciate your willingness to talk to me," Zoe said. Did her grandfather withhold these stories to protect her from the horrors, or to protect himself from reliving it?

Henri stared at her, finally saying, "These are things you deserve to know." He stood. "I have to meet Liam. Let's get together again tomorrow. Meet me at Steirereck at noon. It's in Stadtpark."

"I'm familiar with it." The fine-dining establishment was consistently listed as one of the top fifty restaurants in the world, and she'd wanted to eat there since first reading about it two years ago.

"Tomorrow, then," he said.

Henri left, his stories swirling in Zoe's thoughts, and adding to her jitteriness from the four cups of espresso she'd downed during breakfast.

The following twenty-four hours crawled by. Zoe attended conference panels, counting the minutes until her lunch with Henri, while knowing she should check in with Wes and let him know about the NDA. She couldn't bring herself to make the call, hoping that she would find a way to convince Henri to go on record. Then Wes would never have to know.

At a few minutes before noon, Zoe stood in Stadtpark in front of Steirereck. The connected modern buildings constructed from mirrored glass were pure architectural eye candy.

A text landed on her phone.

WES: How was your meeting with Henri Martin yesterday?

ZOE: Good. We're about to have lunch.

WES: Great. You should check Savouries before you do.

She tapped the *Savouries* website into her phone, when someone said, "You're here."

She looked over her shoulder as Liam approached. Alone. "Are you joining Henri and me?"

"No. I'm here instead of him. My grandfather had urgent business." He motioned toward the restaurant, and Zoe tucked her phone in her purse, promising herself to check the *Savouries* website as soon as lunch concluded.

Liam led the way inside to an inviting decor of honey-colored wood, white linens, and fresh-cut flowers. Zoe inhaled the yeasty scent of baked bread mixed with floral notes and tried to quell her disappointment over Henri's absence.

"Reservation for Henri Martin," Liam told a model-pretty maître d' dressed in a cream monochrome suit, her inky hair shellacked into a sleek bun at her nape.

Once they were seated, Zoe said, "I've been wanting to eat here for years."

"Hm." Liam checked the wine list.

They perused menus, and after they'd each ordered the five-course meal, Zoe said, "I had a lovely walk through the park to get here."

"Did you? I drove."

"You must have passed some of the same sights."

He sighed. "Like what?"

Henri must have forced Liam to meet her. The only other way to explain his attitude, bordering on rudeness, would be that he'd disliked her from the moment they'd met.

Zoe told him about the statues and gardens she'd passed on her walk to the restaurant, which led to her describing her European teen tour. In between her nervous ramblings, courses of artfully plated food arrived, each with a wine pairing that she sipped judiciously. She needed to keep her wits about her with Liam. The food was spectacular, especially the char. This delicate filleted fish was prepared table-side in hot beeswax, which was meal preparation as performance art. Though every time she looked up at her stony companion, she found the food hard to swallow.

"Did you have a pleasant talk with my grandfather yesterday?" Liam finally asked after she'd eaten her last bite of fish. It was the longest string of words he'd uttered the entire meal.

"I did. He's telling me about my family."

"Mm-hm." He toyed with the stem of his wineglass. "Your grandfather?"

"And my great-aunt. Do you know much about Henri's time in Vienna after the war?"

"I see you're digging wherever you can."

"I'm not—" She shook her head. "I'm making conversation."

"Are you?" His lips became a thin line as he handed her his phone. The screen showed an article posted on the *Savouries* website before their lunch.

The byline jumped out at Zoe:

> By Wes Donnelly, reported by Zoe Rosenzweig

The piece started with the paragraph Zoe had sent after Henri's speech. Only, that's not where it ended. She kept reading.

> Now there's new intrigue surrounding Henri Martin. Various social media and foodie sites have exploded with theories regarding a woman he's been seen with at the conference. *Savouries* can confirm she is Zoe Rosenzweig, a staff writer at our magazine. Rosenzweig had contacted Martin prior to the conference regarding a family connection going back to World War II. Martin confirmed that he once knew Rosenzweig's family and agreed to meet with her in Vienna to discuss their shared history, stories including a beautiful woman, postwar black-market dealers, an apprentice baker, and an organization dedicated to smuggling Jewish refugees out of Europe. How this pertains to Henri Martin's past remains a mystery, but not

> for long. It appears Rosenzweig has penetrated Martin's protective shell. Is a future biography in the works? After losing his wife earlier this year, is Henri Martin concerned about his legacy and how it will be told? The culinary and literary worlds will have to wait and see.

She had only told Wes about her phone call with Henri so he would send her to Vienna. Not to be ambushed! *How could he run this without asking her?* And what was this stuff about a biography? She'd claimed no such thing.

She felt Liam's eyes on her. By legal standards, Zoe was in the clear. Her first conversation with Henri wasn't off the record. How she wished she'd told him about sharing pieces of his earliest story with Wes. Henri's ominous tone at breakfast over the photograph made her insides churn.

Zoe scrolled below the story to the comments section. She stopped on a remark with a photo taken yesterday of her in the dining room with Henri serving her cake.

Panic raced through her. Zoe needed to talk to Henri. "Is this why Henri didn't join me for lunch?" She handed back Liam's phone.

"I told him I would handle it."

Handle it? Zoe had to make Liam understand this wasn't intentional on her part. "Wes Donnelly is my boss, and he wrote this without my consent." She decided to tell him the whole truth, praying he would explain it to Henri. "I'd confided in him before I came to Vienna." He glowered, but she kept explaining. "I shared bits of the story Henri had told me, but only broad strokes. No details. It was *before* I signed Henri's NDA. Before I met him. And sure, I would love to write an article about your grandfather. My boss promised me a bonus and a promotion, and I could use the money. But I didn't." She pointed at his phone. "It's clickbait. You're a communications director, you know how this works. Wes is driving traffic to the magazine. As for the comments . . . I don't know why anyone would have taken a picture of Henri and me."

"I took the picture in the dining room and leaked it," Liam said briskly, signaling their server for the check.

She stared at him, incredulous. "Why would you do that?"

"From the start, I had a hunch you were an opportunist, and this article proves me right."

That confirmed Liam's dislike at first sight. "That's not who I am."

He resettled his napkin on his lap. "These rumors regarding a biography about his life, it's never going to happen. I won't allow you to use him to further your career."

Zoe opened her mouth to protest, then shut it. Liam wasn't all wrong. A potential article partly motivated her trip to Vienna. She told him, "I came here to learn about my family. Henri's the only one who can give me those stories."

"Right." The server brought the check, and Liam gave it a quick glance before handing over a credit card. When they were alone again, he said, "I forgot Zoe Rosenzweig is the poor little orphan girl."

"What?" The word came out as a croak.

"Your parents passed away when you were young and you have my sympathies, but don't for a second think I'll let you con my grandfather."

"Don't bring my parents into this."

"Fine. But now your grandparents are gone, too, and you're scraping by on a journalist's wages."

"I'm doing fine." Though she wasn't exactly fine, she wouldn't admit it to him.

"Do you know I spent my ride over here fielding calls from literary agents and journalists all over the world?" He glanced at his phone. "I've missed twenty calls in the time we've been in this restaurant. Understand something, if my grandfather was entertaining the idea of a biography—and he is not—it would not be with someone like you."

Liam's hurtful words set off an echo in her head of Wes saying he didn't want to regret sending her for *Savouries*. As though she couldn't play in the big leagues.

Zoe blinked rapidly. She would prove Wes wrong. "Says you, or Henri?"

The server brought the receipt and retreated. Liam signed with an aggressive flourish. "I'm in charge of communications for the company *and* for him. My grandfather trusts me. You won't stand a chance."

Henri was *his* grandfather, and despite her brief bravado, she had the sinking feeling Liam was right. She'd messed up. Big time. She doubted she'd ever get near Henri again.

"Thank you for lunch," she said, and hastened from the room before tears spilled down her cheeks. Outside, she hurried deeper into the park and away from what was the best-tasting meal of her life, experienced with the absolute worst company.

Chapter Twenty-Five

Zoe

About half a mile from the restaurant, Zoe collapsed on a park bench. Her tears rendered the nearby gardens and playground into nothing but a green and brown swirling mess. How dare Liam bring up her parents. And the way he'd called her an orphan, as if she'd trotted it out like some merit badge, like she had a choice in the matter.

Liam's cruelty made her furious, a wave of emotion that carried her back to the days surrounding her parents' deaths.

It was June, the summer before sixth grade, when Zoe's parents traveled to the Blue Ridge Mountains of North Carolina for a long weekend to celebrate their wedding anniversary. Zoe stayed with her grandparents.

It was a regular weekend for Zoe. Saturday morning, Grandpa Aron drove her to soccer practice, and in the afternoon, she attended a session of Young Scribes Camp, for kids who liked to write. Early the next day, Zoe set out with a notebook to roam her grandparents' Westfield, New Jersey, neighborhood. She planned to write about how surroundings influenced her weekend; it was the following week's camp assignment.

When she returned, it was late afternoon, sunny and hot, and her skin was tacky with sweat. She headed to the kitchen for some cream soda, but when she neared, she saw the phone on the kitchen floor. Then she spotted her grandparents. They were on the floor, too. On their knees. Grandma sobbed into Grandpa's shirt. His eyes were also wet. They raised their heads when they realized she'd come back.

Zoe never could recall the exact words Grandpa Aron used to tell her about how her parents' rental car had crashed on a mountain road while they were heading to hike among waterfalls. But she remembered falling into her grandparents' arms, wailing. Her eyes fixed on a sticky spot on one of the kitchen drawers, where she'd spilled orange juice and done a sloppy job of wiping up. At one point, she took off out the back door. Heat from the late-day sun pressed down on her shoulders.

In the weeks after the accident, Zoe was miserable, angry, and tired all the time. During the last week of August, her grandfather decided they should relocate to North Carolina. He'd found a better job at a bigger food distribution company. "Instead of being a salesman, I'll be a manager," he said. "Less travel means I'll be home more, and a fresh start *vill* help us all."

They moved two weeks later. In time, Grandpa Aron's words came true—living in their cozy bungalow in a new place did help.

Now on the park bench, Zoe dried her eyes and gulped a few deep breaths. Then she took out her phone. There was a text from the real estate agent.

LINDA HICKS: **Have you read the brochure and decided? I have an interested buyer.**

Zoe had done neither, so she didn't respond. Instead, she called Wes.

"It's about time," Wes said, picking up. "Ready to go over your notes?"

"I can't believe you printed information about my conversation with Henri." He might be her boss, but he'd also crossed a line. "That was personal."

"*You* never said it was off the record. You used it to pitch attending the conference."

She opened her mouth to argue, but couldn't. He was right. It was time to tell Wes what she had done. "I signed a nondisclosure agreement."

"You what?"

"If I didn't sign, Henri would've thrown me out. He's been sharing my family's history with me, and I want those stories."

"I sent you to Vienna because you promised to write about him."

"At the time, I meant that promise." She paused, considering the bonus and promotion, and her dream of being able to *really* afford her grandfather's house. Then Henri walked into her thoughts, along with the stories he'd told her. Zoe didn't want to betray the trust they'd built. "But now . . . I couldn't write a story even if I wanted to. And no one ever mentioned a biography. Did you make that up?"

"I wanted to plant the idea in Martin's head."

From what Zoe could tell, no one planted anything in Henri's head. "Listen, I'm spending a lot of time with Henri Martin and he's ungettable. *Savouries* won't lose out to another publication. I've also been attending panel sessions, and what about a story on the conference?" She was spitballing. "Something about the Lifetime Achievement

Award? I know the bonus and promotion will be off the table, but I swear, I'll turn in a great article." *Please let Wes agree and cover these trip expenses.*

Wes stayed quiet until he said, "I knew you'd be in over your head."

She winced.

He told her, "Let me explain this. If you don't deliver on Henri Martin, you won't be writing for *Savouries* anymore. In fact, I doubt you'll be writing anywhere."

"You're going to fire me? On what grounds?"

"You're in Vienna on *Savouries*' dime. You should have checked with me before signing."

Zoe hadn't called him because she'd been thinking of her family.

Wes said, "And I'll remind you that you're on staff and your notes belong to the magazine."

"Henri wouldn't let me record or take notes."

"I'm sure you wrote something after." Tapping sounded on his end. "Martin is shrewd, but there's a way to maneuver around his NDA."

She pinched the bridge of her nose. "How?"

"We'll find others to verify your information on Henri, and you'll be a deep background source."

Zoe had learned about deep background in J-school. They were sources who remained in the shadows of an investigation, anonymously guiding the reporter to information. "My notes are sketchy. And Henri hasn't told me how he knows my family. I doubt there's anyone else who has that kind of information."

"What about the guy who introduced him before the keynote?"

"Jacques Simon?" Jacques had vanished after Henri's speech. "I haven't seen him."

"Reach out to his bakery in Switzerland."

A friend of the family. "It'll get back to Henri," Zoe said. The peeling laughter of children rang out from the playground—at odds with what was happening to her.

"Fine. I'll reach out. But we're writing an article on Henri Martin. He was unreasonable to ask a journalist to sign a nondisclosure."

"Henri will sue me," she said. "And since when do you run articles without an interviewee's permission?"

"Henri Martin is a public figure; we don't need permission. We're going to tell the truth. We won't libel him." He paused. "You asked for a serious assignment; this is it. Plus, you'll still get your bonus and promotion. I'm doing you a favor." Wes hung up.

By the time Zoe returned to the hotel, it was past five. She made a beeline for the elevator, desperate to get to her room and figure out what to do. A text lit her phone.

HENRI: I'm waiting for you in the second-floor gallery.

Zoe took the lobby's grand marble stairs two at a time and landed in an art gallery—the first time she'd seen such a thing in a hotel. The large rectangular room was lined on both sides with display cases and paintings, and a series of backless, tufted sofas ran down the middle. Henri sat on a sofa, and she headed toward him.

"I hated canceling on you," Henri said as she neared. "And I'm also apologizing for my grandson."

So, he already knew about her dismal lunch with Liam. "I didn't think I'd hear from you again."

"Is that what you want?"

"Not at all."

He looked at her. "I want *you* to tell me how this article happened."

She drew in a steadying breath. "Wes Donnelly is my boss at *Savouries.* I told him that you knew my grandfather and great-aunt, but that was before I came here. I had to tell him something to convince him to send me to the conference."

"Because . . . ?"

"Because I wanted you to tell me about my family"—her fingers worried along the links of her bracelet—"and I promised to write about you."

"Are you still working for him?"

"I am."

His jaw tensed. "Do you still plan on writing about me?"

"I'm honoring my agreement with you." Zoe meant it, too. Despite everything she had on the line, she didn't want to sell out Henri. She was grateful for what he had shared so far and she kind of liked him. "So, the answer is no." If she ever planned on writing about Henri Martin or his company, she would only do so with his cooperation.

Zoe dreaded breaking this news to Wes. And her after-the-fact notes, even if he forced her to hand them over, wouldn't be enough to produce a story. No other magazine was going to interview Henri, so Wes would have to understand and keep her on. After all, she'd scooped everyone regarding Henri's photo. That had to count for something.

Henri remained perfectly still, looking at a royal portrait on the nearest wall. Had he accepted her explanation? She couldn't tell.

"I suppose I can forgive this," he finally said.

She stared at the painting, and her anxiety dialed down. "Thank you, sir."

He looked at her. "Do you know why I'm talking to you?"

"Not really."

"Because it's time." He grew pensive. "I don't think you'll betray me. Not anymore."

"I won't," she said.

An unspoken acceptance passed between them.

He indicated for Zoe to follow him as he crossed to a nearby display case. There, under the glass, rested a bejeweled decorative comb on a velvet cloth; the kind of comb women wore in their hair. An amber, emerald, and topaz–encrusted wren decorated the top. She gasped and cut him a look. "Is that . . . ?"

"Chana's comb, yes." Henri's reverent tone and misty, soft brown eyes made her recall the description of Elias Bohm, the apprentice baker.

Was that who Henri was? Had he taken her great-aunt's baking instruction and built an empire?

The gems seemed to wink at her. Or perhaps the light was playing tricks. "It's even more beautiful than I imagined. But how did it get here?"

"We'll get to that eventually," Henri said. "Come, let's walk. Evening in Vienna is a fine time to hear a story."

Chapter Twenty-Six

Chana

Vienna, Austria
June 1946

It was dusk in mid-June, and Heiss had kept Chana later than expected, discussing the next day's menu and how he wanted her to divvy up the tasks. She didn't mind staying late. Work was a welcome distraction from her situation with Meyer.

She'd had to assure Mama and Aron when they left work that they needn't return for her.

"I'll be fine," Chana told her mother. "I carry my knife with me everywhere."

Mama said, "If only Meyer were here, then he could walk you."

But Meyer was away. Since their arrangement, he had mostly been traveling to Linz and Salzburg, picking up goods. He'd stopped by the boardinghouse once, and their conversation was polite. Far from the closeness Chana had envisioned with her future husband.

Dressed in trousers and a thin overcoat with her braid tucked up in her hat, Chana sidestepped bricks and debris. Chana had told Mama that she would also disguise herself as a man for the walk home, and that seemed to placate her worry. Alert as always, she listened for unexpected noises and quickened her pace. She had hoped Elias would offer to walk with her again, but as she left, Trolfe had ordered him to clean their pantry.

She and Elias had baked only once since her engagement. It was a few nights ago; they'd made *Krapfen*, fried apricot-filled dough balls, with Trolfe having paid for the ingredients. Elias had repeatedly praised Chana as they worked, affectionately patting her arm, and taking her hand at one point. Conflicted emotions had whisked about her chest. She couldn't bring herself to tell Elias about Meyer, but after leaving, she'd promised herself the next time they were alone, she would. She had to.

Now, a few blocks from Nachmann's, she spotted Meyer cutting down a side street without noticing her. He'd returned earlier than expected.

Instead of heading straight home, Chana followed him, staying a suitable distance behind. Mama expected her to marry this man, and it was time to find out more about his life and his work.

Over the past week, Chana and her mother had gone back and forth over her engagement to Meyer, with Chana lamenting the dangers in his world.

Mama had set down her needlepoint and pulled Chana into her arms. "*Bubbeleh*, others fear him, and because of it, he'll keep us safe. You'll have a comfortable life. We all will."

She thought of what Meyer had claimed when she'd spoken of love and passion. *I am not a man such as you describe.*

"You and Papa loved each other, didn't you?" she asked her mother.

"Very much." The words reverberated in Chana's chest. Mama stroked her hair and continued. "In time, who knows what will grow? Someday, you'll have children, and they'll love you more than anything."

"And what about my baking?"

"You'll bake for your family, if nothing else."

"Oh, Mama, I want more," Chana had said, resting her head on her mother's shoulder.

"We are women and we don't always get what we want, *maidel.*"

Chana couldn't accept that as a way to live.

Now she followed Meyer, weaving through streets until reaching a block with buildings heavily damaged by the war. Walls resembled ragged teeth. Roofs were blown away. Ruined stairs tilted off-kilter. But one house on the corner—a small, bruised building—though neglected, remained intact. Meyer went inside.

She crept closer, aware of every pebble scraping beneath her boots. When the front door opened, she ducked behind the broken wall of the building next door, fearing what Meyer would do if he discovered she'd followed him.

You are the most stubborn woman I've ever met. He'd meant it as an insult, but Chana saw her stubbornness as a strength. She was not someone who gave up easily. Ever.

Meyer went around the back, and she snuck toward the side of his house, inching slowly toward the back. A quick peek around the corner showed a door open to an underground bunker. She listened for footsteps as Meyer emerged from the space carrying boxes. She inched back while he went around to the opposite side of the house. Next, the front door slammed shut.

Chana told herself to go back to Nachmann's. This was dangerous.

Even so, she decided to take the risk. She had a right to know what he kept hidden under his house.

She tiptoed to the nearest side window. The glass was filthy, but she made out a parlor, furnished only with a table and a few chairs. There were no adornments. Meyer appeared in the room and rummaged through a box. She pulled back as the wind whistled through the narrow yard, rattling the leaves on the trees.

She went around back and found the bunker door unlocked, carefully opening it. No one came, and she headed down the steep stairs. As her foot touched the bottom step, a gun cocked behind her, the sound reverberating in her body.

Meyer said, "You picked the wrong house to rob again. Your luck's run out. Turn around."

She put her hands up, and with her legs shaking, she faced a flashlight, momentarily blinding her.

"Chana?" The beam shifted to the ground, and she blinked a few times for her eyes to readjust. "What are you doing here? And why are you dressed as a man? I almost shot you!" Meyer's confusion turned to fury.

"I wanted to see where you lived."

He lowered the gun. "No, that's not all you wanted to see."

She would tell him the truth. "I'm supposed to marry you, and I have the right to know what you're doing."

"Do you, now?" He barreled down the stairs, anger twisting his mouth.

She braced. Let him strike her. She wouldn't break, and it wouldn't be the worst of what she'd endured.

He motioned for her to continue into the bunker. "Go on."

She kept a hand on the dirt wall as she negotiated the last step into the dark, dank space. Meyer joined her, tucking the gun into his waistband. He could easily shoot her, and no one would know what had happened to her. She quashed an urge to dash for the stairs.

Meyer scrubbed a hand through his hair and sighed, his anger seeming to ebb into resignation. He gave her the flashlight. "Have a good look."

She cast the light around the room, focusing on the stacks of boxes against one wall—their contents printed on the sides. Cigarettes, chocolate bars, and canned foods: meats, beans, fish. There were crates of wine, and another of vodka. There were also bundles of clothes and other unmarked boxes.

"When did you know I was here?" she asked.

"I sensed someone when I came up the stairs. My time in the forest taught me to be observant. To listen." His eyes ran over her. "When did you learn to move like a ghost?"

"In the ghetto. What did you mean when you said you were being robbed again?"

"Someone broke into my house last week; they stole cameras and watches."

She aimed the cone of light on the food boxes. "Why don't you sell it all?"

"I will in time."

"You could give it away. People are hungry."

"Would you believe me if I told you I sometimes give a great deal away?"

She didn't know, so she didn't answer, but instead asked, "How did you get started in all this?"

He scanned the crates as if his history had been scrawled there. "At first, by accident. When the war ended, several of us from the forest wandered into a town and into abandoned homes. We took food, eating whatever was left behind. Then we took other things. Clothes. Shoes. I left one house with silver cutlery. For months, I moved between DP camps in the futile hope of finding my family. I traded a crate of shoes to a German for an American hundred-dollar bill. A week later, I traded the bill for a ruby ring. The ring bought twenty coats. It went on from there, and I saved most of what I made." He lifted his eyes to hers. "I didn't wake up one day and decide to be a black-market dealer." He shrugged. "I was continuing the business of staying alive."

Chana knew the lengths one would go to for survival. Sometimes at Stutthof, she would make herself small and hide behind other women to avoid the whips when exiting the barrack. Others absorbed blows meant for her.

She swallowed. "I understand."

Outside, tires ground against rocks, and a horn beeped.

"Come." He held out his hand to help her up the stairs.

She placed her hand in his, and as they ascended, he gave her a crooked smile.

He let go of her once they were outside. Chana slipped her hand into her pocket to quell her sudden longing. A truck waited in front of the house, and several men stood around it. She recognized all but one as the same men who'd been with Meyer after Café Zweite. They looked as surprised to see her as she was to see them.

Meyer made the introductions: they were Oscar, Isaac, and she already recognized Hershel and Vlad, the latter who scowled when Meyer said his name. She guessed the men were several years older than her. Meyer told them, "Chana is riding with us tonight."

"Am I?" she asked.

"You want to know what I do, right?" His tone held a challenge.

This was unexpected, but she didn't beg off. Where she should have been apprehensive, she was curious. Her exhaustion melted away and her senses heightened the way they had when she'd carried messages in Vilna. A chorus of chirping frogs grew louder, and outlines of the house, truck, and trees sharpened despite the waning light. But it was late, and Mama would be worried. "My mother is expecting me home."

"We'll stop by, and one of my men will run a message up that you're with me. Mama Rosenzweig will be fine," Meyer said.

A short while later, she sat up front in the truck, Meyer between her and Vlad. The others rode in the back bed. She was acutely aware of Meyer's muscled thigh beside hers, close but not touching.

In the day's dying light, they drove past the city's Soviet zone, a place Chana avoided. Stone-faced soldiers in tall fur caps patrolled the streets. Up ahead, on some official-looking building, hung bright-colored banners depicting Lenin and Stalin. The vivid palette failed to soften the leaders' stony expressions.

Once the truck hit a country road, Chana asked Meyer, "How long have you all been working together?"

"It varies. I met Isaac a few months ago in the Karlsplatz. I met Hershel and Oscar last year on the road between displaced persons camps. They'd been searching for family members, as I had." The road grew bumpy, tossing them around. She clung to the door handle.

"As for this one"—Meyer's head ticked toward Vlad—"we met in the Białowieża Forest."

"*Da*," Vlad said. "Meyer saved my life."

"I was already with the partisans, on patrol around our camp's perimeter, when I found him shot through the leg." In the dim cab, she watched Meyer as he told her how Vlad had been a Soviet soldier and not a Jew, and their forest partisan leader had been suspicious at first.

Meyer patted Vlad's arm. "He's saved my life many times, too." He looked at Chana. "Vlad watches my back." He paused. "Though sometimes he takes things too far," he said with reproach.

"If people wrong Meyer, or me, they deserve what they get," Vlad said.

Vlad's menacing tone sucked the air from the truck. Chana's nails bit into her palms.

They then rode in silence until Meyer pointed out the window. "We're heading to farms east of the city. We'll stop at two or three before daylight."

"And what are you doing there?" she asked.

Vlad said, "We're taking. Chickens, goats, rabbits, and as many eggs and vegetables as we can grab. Several cafés are counting on us, as well as your Chef Heiss. Meyer has promised him a fat goat."

She thought of Elias. He'd been hidden by the Bohms out in the countryside. In Dürnstein. Was that family's farm in danger, too? "What about the people who own the farms? What happens to them if you rob them of their animals and raid their gardens?"

Meyer stared into the darkness. "You'll understand once we're done."

She recognized thousands were starving in Vienna and across Austria, and the black market allowed many to eat a little more. But some dealers made a hefty profit, which rankled her, and in the end, this was stealing, and it was wrong.

The truck hit a crater, tossing Chana into the door. A fist pounded on the cab's divider. Hershel called, "Come on, Vlad. Enough. After last week's trip, I couldn't sit for days."

Vlad smiled wryly.

"Enough," Meyer said. "They're no good to me if they're injured."

Vlad didn't respond, but the rest of the ride was smoother until the truck jerked to a stop behind a tree. It was chilly when they all got out of the truck, cooler than it had been in the city, and Chana was grateful for her overcoat.

Hershel said, "Vlad, my dead mother, may her memory be for a blessing, could drive better than you."

Meyer moved beside Chana.

"Next time, I'll toss you out," Vlad said, crossing to the tree with a limp she hadn't noticed before.

"It was a joke," Hershel said. "How come you never laugh?"

"You're not funny," Vlad called back.

"Everyone ready?" Meyer asked.

"Yes," they said in unison.

Chana glanced at the sky's speckling of stars and its half-moon. Papa used to compare the shape to his *Kifli* rolls, though they were slightly crescent-shaped. Chana could picture the rolls now. Shimmering, thanks to a generous egg wash, and freckled with poppy seeds. Papa would say, "The night is sweet." Now Chana shivered and turned up the collar on her coat.

Meyer handed flashlights and sacks to all the men but Vlad, who would stay with the truck.

Hershel nudged Isaac. "This one eats too much cabbage. He stunk up the back of the truck."

Isaac buttoned his coat. "My sister likes to cook with it."

"But do we all have to smell it?" Hershel pinched his nose.

They all chuckled except Vlad.

It was heartening to hear these men joke about something as witless as passing gas. Though she knew little about Meyer's men, she knew they had lost loved ones and endured injustices. Yet, they acted like boys in a schoolyard in the face of tonight's danger. Chana appreciated it, though she couldn't fully relate. She kept her guard up for every second spent outside of their room at Nachmann's.

Meyer gulped liquor from a flask and passed it around, each man drinking, until Hershel handed it to her. Chana took Meyer's cheeky grin as a dare, and she drank, the fiery liquid tasting smoky and bitter. She handed it back to Meyer.

"Let's go." Meyer told Chana, "You stay next to me."

It was an order, and she didn't argue. Danger waited in the shadows, though it wasn't Meyer she feared now. It was farmers armed with clubs or pitchforks. And surely there must be soldiers on patrol. She kept her hand in her pocket and the knife in her palm.

Meyer told them, "Use your flashlights only if absolutely necessary. We have thirty minutes."

They cut into a field toward a farmhouse in the distance. Oscar and Hershel headed for the barn. Isaac went toward a patch of crops. Only Meyer and she headed toward the house. Her heart pounded.

They crept around back, and Meyer whispered, "This family bought this farm during the Anschluss." He practically spit the last word. "It had been owned by a man named Volf Chesler, a Jew. He sold it for next to nothing. Only, that wasn't enough. The man who bought it beat Chesler with a shovel, in front of his wife and children. Left him with two broken legs."

She shuddered, and hatred flared in her.

Meyer cut away from the house toward a full clothesline. "Look at this. The farmer's idiot wife has started leaving her washing out overnight." Meyer pulled out a sack. "Her loss." He tugged down two dresses and a pair of overalls. "Chesler died in Mauthausen. His wife and children, too. I suffer no guilt driving off with the chickens, goats, and vegetables from men such as this."

She glanced over her shoulder, nervous about being overheard. They were a suitable distance from the house and, clearly, Meyer thought it safe to have this quiet conversation.

He tore down bedspreads and sheets, and Chana recalled the blankets he had given her. It likely came from a similar clothesline.

A woman's dress went into the sack. "My mother and sister loved buying new clothes," he said. "Mother always bought new dresses for Rosh Hashanah. My sister told Father how she and Mother couldn't greet the new year in old dresses." His frown was barely visible in the dark. "Foolish to think of now."

"No, not foolish at all."

Meyer said, "My sister was a force to be reckoned with."

"She sounds like someone I would have liked to meet."

"You two would have gotten on famously. I'm sure of it." He stared at her. "I find you easy to talk to."

The stars seemed to twinkle brighter. "I'm glad." When Meyer spoke of his family, he became a softer, more thoughtful version of himself. Perhaps the man he'd once been before the war. It occurred to Chana how much she would enjoy knowing that man.

He grabbed more garments. "Being out here reminds me of my time with the partisans in the forest. We lived off what we could catch or kill . . . deer and rabbits, mostly. Fish and a few wild boars if we were lucky. I built temporary shelters in the woods, labor that helped me stay strong." He put the bulging sack down and wiped his forehead. "I didn't deserve it. Why me, when my mother and sister were gunned down?"

"It's not your fault. Blaming yourself is a terrible trap. You survived! I'm sure your family would be glad."

"Did I survive? Because when they died—" His voice faltered. "Part of me died, too."

It was clear, Meyer had built thick armor around his heart. Chana wondered if she'd ever manage to penetrate it. She told him, "In the train station that first day, you said that building back our lives would be our sweetest revenge."

"Not for me." He looked at her with tired eyes. "Do you think your dream of becoming a baker will bring your father back?" he asked sadly.

His question, at first a shock, landed like salt in an open wound. But Chana wasn't really angry. Instead, she recognized that he was hurting. "Maybe not," she said. "But I can honor him in that way."

"Yes. Perhaps that's right," Meyer said. He turned his attention to the children's clothes on the line—short pants, small shirts, and girls' dresses. Part of Chana agreed with this retribution. Yet another part of her did not. Yes, she hated the farmer. But did she hate his children? Would they only learn to hate her and those like her? She thought of the soldier who'd shot Papa, and fury whipped through her. Must she hate the soldier's children, too? His grandchildren? If she did, the world would never find peace. It would be a place where the horrors of the past six years could happen again.

"Enough," she said as Meyer reached for the last of the little dresses.

He stopped. A breeze caught the ends of a blanket, making it flap in a way that made Chana think of an angel's wings. "Okay." He slung the sack over his shoulder. "No need for their children to go naked." He checked his watch. "Let's go."

They left the line, and in the distance, the other men approached, full bags in hand. Hershel pulled two goats on a rope.

"Keep the animals quiet," Meyer said as they walked.

They repeated the routine at another farm, its owner having also benefited from the Anschluss. Was this all true? Or was it a tale told to appease Chana's sense of right and wrong? She knew enough of how the Nazis stole Jewish property and businesses to suspect it was likely true.

On the drive back to Vienna, they stopped midway at a convent. With its stone walls, it could easily be mistaken for a fortress. Meyer climbed out, bringing several sacks and a crate to the door. He spoke briefly to a nun and handed her the goods.

"What's he doing?" Chana asked Vlad.

Vlad said, "This convent took in Jewish children during the war. Hid them among their Catholic students. Some are still there, their parents having been killed in the camps. Every month, Meyer brings clothes and food for the children."

"Oh." Chana recalled what Meyer had said in the bunker: *Would you believe me if I told you I sometimes give a great deal away?*

Meyer slid past her into the seat beside Vlad.

"That's generous of you," she said, aching to take his hand.

He shrugged, but said nothing.

The truck pulled away from the convent. Guilt washed over Chana. In some ways, she'd been wrong about Meyer. He was a better man than she'd initially believed. Perhaps Meyer's heart could open again.

Mama had said, *In time, who knows what will grow?*

Yes! That would be her plan going forward. It was possible that love could blossom from friendship. If Chana was being honest, for her, love had already taken seed.

Chapter Twenty-Seven

Chana

Chana stepped into Café Bruner along with Meyer and her family. A week had passed since their nighttime raid on the farms, and she'd been looking forward to this evening out. She'd been delighted when Meyer suggested it, hoping it reflected greater affection for her and a desire to truly be a part of her life and her family.

She, her mother, and Aron wore finer clothes than they had since before the war, all gifts from Meyer. Chana's blue dress featured white polka dots and draped nicely over her figure, with the neckline cut from gossamer that fluttered over her chest. She ran a hand over the delicate fabric, appreciating its silky feel. Meyer had claimed the garment came from a tailor in Vienna, a German Jew, who'd once owned a dress factory in Berlin.

"Not a clothesline," he'd said proudly.

Mama wore a gray dress with pearl buttons down the front, and Aron looked like a man, with his new trousers and an ivory dress shirt.

A maître d' led their foursome to a cozy table in the corner. Meyer clearly enjoyed the admiring looks of the other diners, walking head high and shoulders back; he cut a dashing figure in his navy pinstriped suit.

Chana had heard Chef Heiss fret about Café Bruner. It was owned by one Herr Grimmell, who was an esteemed chef in her boss's view.

When Mama had bragged about their upcoming plans to dine there, Heiss had pulled Chana aside. "You'll tell me everything you eat and what you see. I want a description of it all."

A waiter brought to their table a bottle of Château de Eisel, describing it as a white wine made from Sémillon grapes. Not that Chana knew one vineyard grape from another. The server poured them each a glass and left. Meyer lifted his wine. "My father used to begin dinners out with the same toast. And so I'll follow in his footsteps. To family, and *l'chaim.*"

They echoed the sentiment. Chana's eyes prickled, thinking of how Papa would have enjoyed a night such as this. Meyer's eyes glistened as if he also thought about those he'd lost.

"Did your family dine out often?" Mama asked.

"Occasionally." Meyer drank. "My father owned an optometry store. We dined at his customers' restaurants."

"Were you planning to join him in his business?"

Meyer swirled his glass and frowned. "He wanted me to, but I had set my sights on becoming a doctor. Now we're here and no one is anything." He drank. "Did your family dine out much before the war?"

Mama scoffed. "Hardly. My husband poured every penny he made into his bakery."

Chana snapped open her napkin and said, "It was more than a

bakery. Papa had ideas. He was saving for a truck. Papa wanted to deliver bread and desserts to restaurants all over Vilna. He said it was the future."

"He did." Mama looked weary. "But what a shame we didn't live a little. Our future turned out differently, didn't it?"

Aron placed a comforting hand on their mother's arm.

"Tell me, Chana, what was your father's favorite thing to bake?" Meyer asked.

The intensity of Meyer's gaze made Chana shift in her seat. "Challah."

"Ah, yes," Aron said, leaning in.

"Such a simple recipe, but he loved everything about it." Chana smiled, glad for the change to a lighter topic. "From mixing the dough to letting it rise and braiding. He used six strands of dough and would sing as he wove them together. And his challah was beautiful. I could hardly wait until it came out of the oven." In her mind's eye, she could see the glistening loaves releasing steam into the air.

"My mouth is watering," Meyer said.

"Once we're in America, Chana will make it for you," Mama said. Her mother's eyes sought Chana's, telling her, *See, you will bake.*

Their meal came out in courses. It was clear Meyer did business with the café's chef, and the staff treated them like royalty. First, they ate a *Pichelsteiner* stew, a dish Herr Heiss often made, using lamb along with beef scraps and vegetables. Tonight, it came with a steaming loaf of bread. Their server tore off hunks at the table, and the yeasty scent rose above all the others.

Next, their waiter presented them with *Tafelspitz*, boiled beef in dill sauce, *Käsespätzle*, egg noodles, cheese, and onions, and potato goulash.

The beef was so tender it melted on her tongue. Two bottles of red wine added to their table's convivial mood. The café's abundance was remarkable, considering the hunger still pervading the city.

Eventually, Chana sat back from eating, her stomach near bursting, as Meyer told a story about an ornery cook named Mikhail, who owned a restaurant in the second district.

"A customer sent a steak back to the kitchen, complaining it was too tough," Meyer said. "Only, when the waiter brought it to Mikhail, he threw a fit. He tossed the meat on the floor and stamped on it with his boot." To illustrate, Meyer pounded the table, causing the plates and cutlery to clink. "Mikhail slapped the steak back on the plate and made the waiter serve it."

"What did the customer do?" Aron asked.

Meyer grinned. "He ate it. He mopped up every bit of juice with a *shtikle* of bread. The man told the waiter to let the cook know it was the most tender meat he'd ever eaten in his life."

Chana laughed, as they all did, and Meyer's eyes sought hers. It was a wonderful night, everything she had hoped for, and she smiled at him, hoping to convey it.

A man tentatively approached their table. "Meyer Suconick?" he asked.

Meyer looked up, recognition lighting his face. "Levi!" He stood, and the two men embraced. "When did you arrive in Vienna?" Meyer asked.

"Last week."

Meyer quickly introduced Levi, referring to Chana as his fiancée, which pleased her. Levi smiled wide and shook her hand with vigor. Then Meyer and the man stepped away for a moment of hushed conversation that she strained to hear, but could not. They parted with a hearty handshake, before Levi joined a woman seated across the room.

When Meyer returned to their table, Chana asked, "Is that an old friend from Riga?"

"A friend, but not from Riga." Meyer glanced over at the man. "I haven't seen him since the war ended. I helped him escape the Bialystok ghetto. He joined us in the forest. Levi is a good man."

Her mother's fork scraped against her plate. "Tell me, Meyer, how many people did you save from Bialystok?"

He cut into a piece of meat. "I didn't keep count."

"Chana saved me," Aron said.

"Did she?" Meyer's eyes went to her.

"It was when we were in Vilna," Aron said.

"Yes, it was," Chana said.

"What happened?" Meyer asked.

Aron leaned into the table. "Everyone was talking about another order coming. The Gestapo was about to round up children and take them away."

Mama speared a carrot with her fork. "They would have had to kill me first."

Aron smiled fondly at their mother and continued. "I was twelve. Chana's contacts in the resistance warned us. We were ready when they arrived." He paused. "The soldiers came, pounding on every apartment door on the floor below. Then their boots stampeded up the stairs."

The staccato hammering of their heels against the stair boards would haunt Chana's dreams forever. She twisted her napkin as fear punched her in the gut and threatened to bring up the fine food she'd just eaten.

"I know the sound well." Meyer set down his knife and fork. "In

Bialystok, Nazi boots would echo against the sidewalk at night. We hid in the alleys and shadows of buildings until the sound faded. Men and women from our camp died, with that sound being one of the last things they heard."

Chana let the café's din of conversation wash over her, anything to drown out the memory of those stampeding boots.

"Should I stop?" Aron asked with worry in his eyes.

Meyer came out of his revery and grabbed his fork. "No, continue."

Aron went on. "They reached our floor. Papa was frantic. But Chana was brilliant. She opened Mama's pickling barrel and helped me climb in." He wrinkled his nose as if he could still smell the vinegar.

Mama said, "I brined whatever vegetables I could get my hands on. We lived on them."

"Did they discover your hiding place?" Meyer asked.

"No, and the vinegar was up to here." Aron cut a hand to his neck. "I had just enough room to breathe."

"The night before, I poked holes in the lid," Chana said.

"Papa sat on top of the barrel while the Nazis searched," Aron said.

"What about you, Chana?" Meyer asked. "They could have taken you as well."

Her face grew hot. "I was almost sixteen, but already looked like a woman."

Mama drained her wine and stifled a burp. "My husband told the soldiers she was our only child, and that she was eighteen. One of them stared at her for a long time." Mama scowled. "'She's yours?' he asked with his lip snarled like a dog's. He pulled a chunk of her hair, shocked it was as light as his own."

Chana would never forget the rough way his fingers had wound into her hair, and the painful yank.

"They left and didn't come back." Aron took her hand. "I smelled like vinegar for a week."

Her brother's smile calmed her.

"Meyer, you've grown quiet." Mama ate a bite of potato.

"Visiting with ghosts." He poured himself more wine and gestured to Chana and Aron. "The two of you remind me of my sister and me." He put the bottle down, then looked to her brother. "Tell me, Aron, what did you enjoy doing before the war?"

Her brother pondered the question. "I've told you; reading is something I've always loved. But especially about football. Papa and I followed some teams. Tottenham and Chelsea in England . . . and Juventus in Italy."

"Did you ever play?"

"No. Though I wish I had."

Meyer drank more wine. "And what did you think of tonight's meal?"

"It's the best dinner I've ever eaten," her brother said. "But a meal really isn't done without dessert, is it?"

Aron's comment mimicked something Papa had often said. Chana squeezed his hand, amazed at how at fifteen he sounded so much like him.

Meyer slapped the table and laughed. "Of course!" He flagged down the waiter. "What does Herr Grimmell have for dessert?"

Their server's pleased grin revealed a wide gap between his front teeth. "Tonight, our chef has prepared *Cremeschnitte* and *Esterházy Torte*."

Meyer told him, "Bring us a taste of each."

"Yes, sir." The waiter cleared the supper plates, which, despite all they'd ordered, they'd eaten clean.

Meyer pulled a pack of Chesterfields from his jacket and offered them to the women. Chana accepted one, though her mother's lips flattened in disapproval. Meyer lit her cigarette, her hand touching his lightly, shocking her fingertips. Her heart lifted. She searched his face to see if he felt it, too, but his eyes were on the flame. She pulled back, inhaling and exhaling deeply.

When the waiter delivered their desserts, Aron reached for a plate, but Mama stopped him. "I'll make it for you. Which do you want?"

"Mama, I can cut my own cake," Aron said.

Meyer smirked. "Let your mother do the honors."

Aron hesitated, then sat back.

The exchange made Chana realize that her brother admired Meyer, listened to him, and she was unsure how she felt about that.

Mama doled out plates of cake to each of them. Once they were served, Meyer stubbed out his cigarette. "After dinner, I want Chana to come with me to the Empress Hotel. I have a meeting with a few of the soldiers, and they're bringing their girlfriends."

Chana had planned to bake with Elias later. "I can't. I have to work in the morning." There was no way she would miss baking with Elias, not after what he'd gone through yesterday to replenish their supplies.

Elias had been returning to the hotel from the Karlsplatz when three men demanded his clothes, even his shoes. At first, he'd stood his ground, and they'd given him a split lip and bloody nose before he relented. She'd been in the kitchen boiling eggs when Elias returned, bleeding, and wearing only his undergarments. She'd moved to help, but Trolfe got to his apprentice first. The grumpy old pastry chef wrapped Elias in his own coat and led him to his apprentice quarters. Elias skipped work that day.

On her break, Chana had snuck to the basement and knocked on Elias's door.

"Chana," he said when he answered, wearing a robe. "What are you doing here?"

"I wanted to check on you."

He smiled, winced, and touched his lip. "I tried to hold out, but they gave me this for fighting back."

"Is there anything I can do?"

"Meet me tomorrow night to bake."

"Are you sure you still want to?"

He smiled carefully. "Baking with you will be the best medicine."

Now Meyer picked up his fork. "I'm sure Herr Heiss will understand if you come a little late tomorrow morning."

"I don't want to be late." She extinguished her cigarette in the ashtray, hoping he would see her point.

Her mother ate a mouthful of cake, then said, "Chana will go, but you'll see her home again. And not too late. She will go to work on time."

It was as though Chana hadn't spoken at all.

Meyer stood, then grabbed a bottle of port and filled their glasses. Droplets of red wine spilled and seeped into the white tablecloth. "I admire your dedication to Herr Heiss." Meyer brought his lips near her ear, his breath teasing her skin. She inhaled something earthy, slightly sweet, and distinctly him. "But you must come," he said. "I promise I won't keep you out late. I know your work is important to you."

Attraction and affection tugged on her. She appreciated Meyer's attempt at taking her wishes into account.

"All right," she said, "I'll go." She pictured Elias pacing the kitchen while he waited for her, and she hated herself for disappointing him. But Meyer was her fiancé, and she needed to see her plan through.

His grin transformed his face, as if her agreement were a special present. She ate a forkful of *Esterházy Torte*, and smiled, too, from the cake, which was sublime, but also at the possibility that this family dinner had brought her and Meyer closer.

Chapter Twenty-Eight

Chana

After dropping Mama and Aron off at Nachmann's, Meyer and Chana drove over to the Empress Hotel. He parked a few car lengths away from the entrance and fidgeted with the keys. Chana sat with her hands clasped in her lap, unsure if she was supposed to get out or wait.

"Do you still carry your knife?" he asked.

"Of course," she said.

"It'll get you in trouble. A man could disarm you in seconds." A passing car splashed light on his face, illuminating his worry. "I'm to be your husband. I'll protect you."

She faced him, encouraged by what she perceived as his deepening fondness for her. "I appreciate that," she said gently. "But if the war taught me anything, it's that if harm wants to find you, it will. I did my best to protect my family, and Papa did his best to protect all of us. I know you believe what you say. And as I told you before, I can take care of myself." She ached to know—to hear—how Meyer truly felt about her. "You said you can't love me, but I don't believe that you're marrying me solely to get to America."

He slid closer, and despite the dark, she saw his brows draw together. "It's true the men who want me to work with them want a married man. They want someone with a weakness. *You* would be my weakness because I care about what happens to you. I told you that I can't love anyone. Not even you. But it doesn't mean I won't be good to you." He paused. "As you said, we're friends. Not a bad thing to be."

She had lost nearly as much as he had. But her heart still beat in her chest, and she was grateful for it. Even now, his nearness cued up a rhapsody within her. *Did that mean she was in love with Meyer?* And if so, where did that leave her? He'd plainly stated his feelings. The night they'd driven away from the farms, Chana had believed she could open Meyer's heart. Oh, how utterly that hope was failing.

He stared at her, and she looked back at him. He showed such kindness to her, Mama, and Aron. *Aron.* Meyer listened to her brother, and Aron's confidence grew under his encouragement. At dinner, Aron had soaked up Meyer's attention and had hung on his every word.

She told him, "You've been good to Aron, and he looks up to you."

He caught the edge in her tone and said, "You don't approve?"

Meyer's men all did his bidding. The idea of Aron becoming one of them was out of the question. Chana wouldn't allow it.

Her fingers worried along the buttons on her sweater. "You're fearless, and Aron needs a strong man to guide him. Papa would have been that had he lived." Her voice broke on *lived*, but for her brother's sake, she continued. "My brother can't take part in your dangerous world. He will not work with you again. I forbid it."

Meyer said nothing as he slid from the car, opened her door, and offered her his hand. She placed her palm in his and a hum went straight to her bones. It carried her back to dancing in his arms at Café Zweite and took her breath away.

"Aron will be my brother, too," he said as she joined him on the sidewalk, "and you will forbid nothing."

She dropped his hand. If Meyer expected her to hold her tongue or that she would allow him to do whatever he wanted with Aron, he would be sorely disappointed.

For the next hour, Meyer drank and talked with the soldiers in the lounge adjoining the hotel dining room, one being Sergeant McManus. From a nearby banquette, where she sat with the other girlfriends, Chana listened to the men talk about an American reporter and photographer. They also discussed the black market, and she came away with the impression that the sergeant planned on increasing the goods Meyer sold for him.

The other women at her table, all Austrians, drank and chatted, while Chana kept glancing at the large grandfather clock looming nearby. She was twenty minutes late for meeting Elias in the kitchen, and drummed her fingers on her leg, eager for an excuse to get away.

The women at her table laughed at a joke Chana had missed.

Thanks to Meyer, Chana was as well-dressed as the others, and several women shot admiring, if not jealous, glances at the jeweled comb in her hair.

"There she is, my favorite photographer," Sergeant McManus called as a woman strode into the lounge. Dressed in a burgundy bell-shaped skirt with a matching short jacket, her auburn hair cascaded in curls around her shoulders and bounced as she hurried to join the sergeant and the other men. "Gentlemen, this is Peggy York-Black," McManus said. "She takes pictures for *Life* magazine."

"Hello, fellas," Peggy said with a confident smile and not a hint of flirtation.

In short order, the woman told them how she was in Austria to take photos of the Allies' efforts to help Europe's recovery. She had a loud voice and a bold manner, holding her own among the men. "I want to explore the city from the perspective of a refugee," Peggy said. "Especially one acquainted with the black market."

"This man here is your refugee." The sergeant slapped Meyer's back.

Meyer glanced away, his expression tight. Despite Meyer's reputation in Vienna, Sergeant McManus was the one in charge. The one with the goods, and the power to throw Meyer in jail and toss away the key. Chana could tell Meyer didn't appreciate McManus treating him as a subordinate.

The sergeant gave the group a satisfied grin and continued. "If he ever goes to America, I have friends waiting to welcome him."

Sergeant McManus must be the soldier Meyer had mentioned to Mama. The idea of Meyer relying on Sergeant McManus and being indebted to him once they were in America made Chana more anxious than ever.

She excused herself from the table and tapped Meyer's shoulder. "I want to go outside to smoke."

"You don't have to go outside for that," Meyer said.

"I need some air."

He handed her a pack of cigarettes and his lighter. "We'll leave soon, don't be long." When she headed toward the dining room, he called, "You're going the wrong way."

"I prefer to smoke on the roof." She felt his eyes on her as she left.

Chana's cigarette was a glowing dot against the spotty lights of the city. She stood close to the roof's ledge, peering over the edge. Wind whipped by. She wrapped one arm around herself.

"Chana, what are you doing up here?" Elias's voice came from behind her, so soft at first that she thought it could be the wind playing tricks.

She turned to be sure. There he stood. He sounded concerned. "I was in the lounge and came up here to smoke." She looked back at the city. "I'm sorry I missed our baking tonight. What did you make?"

"I haven't started yet. I planned to make apricot *Marillenkuchen*."

A rumbling truck and a few shouts from the street punctured the quiet night. A loud honk followed, and Chana wobbled. In a quick step, Elias caught her arm and guided her away from the ledge.

"I was afraid you might fall," he said.

She eyed his hand on her arm, waiting for the same electricity she felt when Meyer had touched her. It wasn't there, but she didn't want Elias to let go, either. Surely, that meant more than a few fleeting seconds of whatever it was she felt with Meyer.

Elias dropped his hand. "I'm sorry."

"It's all right." Her cigarette trembled. Chana stepped farther back from the roof's edge. "Why are you up here?" she asked Elias.

"I saw you in the lounge . . . and I followed you."

She looked at him then, and in the dim light, she saw his swollen eye and split lip. "Does it still hurt?"

"Some." He touched his lip. "Can you bake with me tonight?"

She desperately wanted to. Violin music drifted up from somewhere down below, a sound both sluggish and sad. "I can't." She worried about Meyer looking for her and starting a fight with Elias. He looked crestfallen, and she hated herself for disappointing him. "But I've seen you and Trolfe make *Marillenkuchen.* I have thoughts on the recipe."

Elias smiled, flinching from the pain, then pulled a pen and paper from his pocket. "Tell me."

She relaxed into the easiness that existed between them. "Trolfe likes to push the sliced apricots into the dough. Don't. Instead, lay them on top and let the cake rise around them so they aren't covered. Place them cut side up to allow their juices to stay within the fruit. That way they won't dry out. And use an extra half teaspoon of lemon zest to brighten the cake's flavor." Thinking through the recipe helped quiet her roiling emotions.

"How can you tell all that from the other side of the kitchen?"

Papa had said she was a quick learner. She'd proven so with baking, and languages, too.

"You're special," her father had said. "You blend what's in here"—he touched his heart—"with what's up here." He tapped his head.

"The mechanics of things interest me," Chana told Elias. "The only way to describe it is I *see* it come together."

"What do you mean?"

She thought of the cinema and how last week's film had momentarily slowed, making each frame visible on the screen. "Like a picture show," she said. "Before I bake, I have the ingredients in my mind. In quick succession, they come together in various measurements, until I know in here"—she tapped her breastbone—"that I have the correct recipe before I begin."

Elias scratched his head. "Are you always right?"

"Mostly." She didn't understand how. Nor did Papa, though they'd both quickly learned to trust her instincts.

"That's amazing." He regarded her with wonder, and she felt her face redden.

"One more thing," she told him. "Sprinkle on a bit of icing sugar after it's cooled. Only a little."

He wrote this down. "I'll do one cake your way, and the other Trolfe's way." His eyes traveled from her face to the jeweled comb in her hair. He pulled back his shoulders. "I won't be an apprentice forever. I plan to move to Switzerland for a time, then on to Paris. Herr Trolfe has taught me a lot, but there are others I want to learn from."

"It must be nice to be a man."

"Why do you say that?" Concern bracketed his eyes.

"You can do as you choose."

"And you?"

"I'm expected to marry." A gust swept across the roof, blowing strands of hair in her face. She pushed them back.

"Marry Meyer, right?" His voice was raspy.

So Elias knew. "Yes," she said. Chana took a final tug on her cigarette. "He's helping my family get to America." She dropped the cigarette, grinding it under her heel.

"Is that what you want?"

Chana didn't know how to explain her complicated feelings. Mama's words echoed in her mind: *We are women and we don't always get what we want, maidel.*

"I need to do what's best for my family." She inhaled, and the air tasted bitter. She was a bird in a cage. A fish tossed onto a dock. No matter how much she squawked or flopped, she remained caught.

Elias rested his hand on her wrist. "But what's best for you?"

She didn't pull away. "My mother made an arrangement with Meyer."

"And did you agree?"

"It will help my family." She looked at him. "But I'm like you in that I want to live my life my way. I want to bake." A new future bubbled up in her thoughts, one where she went to Switzerland and Paris with Elias. They would find jobs in a bakery, and together they would perfect their recipes. As a woman alone, and a Jewish one, becoming a pastry chef could be difficult, but with Elias as a partner, it might be possible. They could be partners and help each other in the way she and Papa had planned. They could even be more than partners.

"The war is over." Intensity sharpened Elias's features. "You can do what you want."

"If only that were true."

"Chana, on Sunday, I'm traveling to Dürnstein to visit the Bohms. I noticed you're off as well . . ." He appeared to be holding his breath, then said, "Would you come with me?"

The invitation pleased her. "How would we get there?"

"There's an unofficial bus that goes back and forth. We could leave in the morning and be back by evening."

She considered this. Meyer had told her he would leave for Belgium on Sunday. He would never know she'd gone. "Yes. I'll join you."

Elias put his hands in his pockets. "Excellent. Sunday, then."

She smiled. "I need to get back to the lounge." She hurried down the stairs, and when she reached the archway between the dining room and lounge, she came face-to-face with Meyer.

"Where were you?" he asked, not angrily, but instead, he wore his worry in the deep groove between his brows.

"I went to the roof to smoke, as I told you."

He glanced past her, and she stayed still, praying Elias didn't suddenly emerge from the stairwell.

Meyer took her hand in his, and despite her misgivings, she tilted toward him. He stared directly into her eyes. "I'm sorry for what I said earlier about Aron." His words were deliberate; apology didn't come easy for this man. "You were only looking out for your brother. Family is so important; I know that now more than ever. I would never let harm come to you or anyone in your family."

His sincerity hit her first, followed by a twinge of guilt over her lying about her time on the roof. Meyer was tough and stubborn, but also filled with so much good.

"I appreciate your apology," Chana said, brimming with tenderness toward him and again wondering if, despite his protests, he felt more for her than he claimed.

He placed her hand in the crook of his arm. "We should go. You have work in the morning."

"Yes, I do." Chana's hand rested against Meyer's muscled forearm, giving her a sense of peace. She fell in step with him. Then she worried Elias could be watching. Her torn feelings made her temples throb. She leaned on Meyer, grateful for his solidness because she was utterly depleted. There was nothing she wanted more than to collapse on her mat back at Nachmann's.

Chapter Twenty-Nine

Chana

A few days later, Chana left Nachmann's hoping to prompt a miracle by determinedly visiting the different emigration offices. This time she carried letters she'd penned to Jewish organizations and synagogues in New Jersey, driven to reach anyone who might know Papa's relatives. Despite her closeness with Elias, Chana decided it was best to keep the promise she'd made to her mother and go through with marrying Meyer. But with a caveat—she would extricate him from Sergeant McManus's clutches. If Chana connected with her family, surely, she, Mama, Aron, and Meyer could leave on their own terms.

Her last stop was the office for the Joint, where she handed half a dozen letters to Herr Krauss, the kind, gray-haired, and bearded employee, who would address and post them for her.

She readied to leave when Herr Krauss said, "Before you go, let me recheck our new correspondence."

Chana offered him a grateful smile. "I appreciate that."

He sifted through several folders until he told her, "I'm sorry.

There's nothing related to your family." He smoothed a hand over his beard. "Chana, to be frank, U.S. authorities may not grant you entry even *if* we find your relatives."

"Why not?" Anxiety strangled her insides.

"There are limited visas. We have over a thousand people who've already found sponsors, and there simply aren't enough visas for everyone. This is a plight for refugees across Europe." She blinked several times, struggling to absorb this news. "Now, if you have someone guaranteeing your entry, your papers . . . say a government official, well, that's a pot of gold."

Meyer was well-connected throughout the city, and she surmised the *guarantee* he referred to was Meyer's connection to Sergeant McManus. "You know of my engagement?"

"Yes." He gave her a broad smile. "Congratulations, my dear. Meyer is a fine young man."

She clutched her handbag. "Thank you for your candor, Herr Krauss. I'll check back next week." Chana left the office with a headache.

The next day, dark clouds hung over the city. The overcast sky kept the temperature moderate but humid, a fine match for Chana's sticky mood regarding Meyer and their emigration.

She and Aron were on their way to meet Meyer at Pejsach's tailor shop, an abandoned shoemaker's store that now did double duty as a sewing workroom and a makeshift shul for the Sabbath. It was Saturday, and *Shabbos* services would end soon. Meyer claimed to have a surprise for her brother. As they strolled, Chana was grateful for this time alone with Aron. It was rare, as they were usually either surrounded by others in the hotel or accompanied by Mama anywhere else.

Aron unwrapped a small parcel from his pocket, producing a square of apricot *Marillenkuchen*. Chana instantly recognized the cake as the one Elias had made with Trolfe's method. The dough had covered most of the orange stone fruit, as she had predicted.

"Feed that one to the staff, or the pigeons for all I care. The fruit is dry and the flavor is dull," Trolfe had said when Elias asked what to do with that cake. The second *Marillenkuchen* had resembled a checkerboard of glistening apricots and dough. Sweet and perfect, as Chana knew it would be. Elias had carried out her instructions well.

"Where did you get that?" she asked her brother.

"I saved it from our meal the other day." He bit off a piece, chewing thoughtfully before saying, "I bet Papa could make this better."

"Yes, he could."

The way Herr Trolfe had fawned over Elias, and the second *Marillenkuchen*, reinforced Chana's confidence. The pastry chef had extolled her ideas.

"Do you remember much about Papa's bakery?" she asked Aron, who had been only ten when it shut down.

"Not enough. I remember the rolls he made with raisins."

"You ate yours so slowly."

"I ate the bread and saved the raisins. I always wanted my last bite to be sweet." Aron finished the cake and licked crumbs off his fingers. It seemed the more he ate, the hungrier he got. And he'd grown—standing taller than Chana now. "This is so good, but I bet the other one was even better. The one we weren't allowed to eat."

She longed to tell her brother the truth.

"Papa would be proud of the other cake," he said, "and of you."

She stared at him. "Aron—"

"I don't sleep as soundly as Mama." He smiled and bumped her shoulder. "I've heard when you leave our room at night. And then, in a matter of weeks, the apprentice's baking skills improve."

Of course her brother would know. "You can't tell a soul."

"I would never. But what's going on?"

"Elias and I are helping each other. I've learned from him as well." She thought of her efficiency with croissants and their *Cremeschnitte* with its custard that melted on the tongue, owing both to her friend's tutelage. "And I'm baking. It's what I do. What Papa wanted."

"You're alone with Elias? But what about Meyer?"

She didn't know what to tell her brother. Chana swallowed past the hard ball of uncertainty in her throat, but didn't answer.

Chana and Aron entered the tailor shop as *Shabbos* services broke up. It was the first time Chana had seen Meyer in a yarmulke, and something about it touched her. A vision of Papa came to her, him wearing a skullcap and wrapped in a tallit, Chana braiding his shawl's fringe as he prayed.

"You'll use that skill to braid challah," Papa would tell her.

Meyer broke away from a clutch of men and smiled at her. He introduced her to the rabbi, an older bearded man from Germany who'd survived the Treblinka concentration camp.

"I look forward to performing your wedding," the rabbi said. "In these times, there is no greater mitzvah than joining two people in love."

"Yes, I suppose that's true," Meyer said.

Chana looked at Meyer and found his gaze on her, his eyes warming to the color of deep, velvety sienna. Was he putting on a show for the rabbi? She wanted to believe it was real.

Once out on the street, Meyer pulled the yarmulke off his head and stuffed it in his pocket.

"Where are you taking us?" Aron asked.

"It's a surprise." Meyer offered Chana his arm.

She looped her arm through his, feeling a pleasant heat rise in her at the firmness of his muscled bicep. She imagined that to anyone passing, they looked like a contented couple. They walked for several blocks, until Meyer led them to an empty lot where a building once stood, near to Nachmann's. Meyer peered up the street. "There she is," he said, pointing.

Peggy York-Black, the photographer who'd been at the hotel lounge, rode toward them in a GI-driven jeep. She hopped out and waved. She wore army-green trousers and a matching button-down top, her camera strapped around her neck and a large brown bag under one arm. The driver sat back, but didn't get out.

Chana knew Meyer had met with this woman and a reporter several times over the last week. They'd driven around Vienna as he took them to the Karlsplatz and a handful of smaller open-air markets. He'd told Chana how the pair had been amazed by the lists papered to abandoned storefronts and filled with goods people sought. These lists were so abundant, Chana barely noticed them anymore. Meyer claimed Peggy and the reporter were interested in Vienna's black market after spending weeks in Berlin, where underground deals were also rampant.

Meyer introduced Chana and Aron to Peggy.

"You're right, Meyer, she's a beauty," Peggy said in German.

"*Danke*," Chana said.

"You speak German?"

"I do. And Yiddish, English, and Polish. Though my English still needs work."

"Sometimes so does mine," the woman said with a sunny smile.

Chana had never met a woman who traveled alone and earned a living taking pictures. It was a wonder.

"Here you go." Peggy handed Meyer her bag.

Meyer pulled out a scuffed white football and gave it to Aron.

"This is amazing," Aron said. "But I'm afraid, I'm not very good."

"Come, I'll show you a few things," Meyer said.

Chana couldn't believe he had remembered such a detail about Aron. Meyer winked at her now, and she couldn't hold back a smile or ignore the butterflies in her belly.

"Drop the ball," Meyer said.

Aron did, and despite Meyer's wearing a suit and good shoes, he worked the ball halfway up the lot by tapping it between the insides of his feet.

"Where did you get that?" Chana asked Peggy when he stopped, his cheeks ruddy and forehead gleaming with sweat.

"Meyer asked me, and I told him I would get one even if I had to have my editor ship it from the States. It's the least I could do for his squiring us around the city. I took some fabulous pictures." Peggy stroked her camera lovingly.

"Try it." Meyer kicked the ball to Aron. It skidded past her brother and bounced against the wall of the neighboring building.

Aron approached the ball as if it were a sewer rat about to bite.

"Use the insides of your feet, and don't be afraid of it," Meyer said. He told them how he'd played some football before the war, on a club team in Riga.

Aron mimicked the footwork he'd seen, his first kick sending the ball into the wall. "Come, let's do it together," Chana said.

They kicked the ball back and forth several times while Peggy and Meyer watched.

Meyer cut into the game, and Chana joined Peggy at the edge of the lot, wiping sweat from her forehead.

The photographer said, "I appreciate Meyer's showing us around. Casper and I are compiling one hell of a story. He's the reporter I'm working with on this trip."

"Where do you go next?" Chana asked.

"Italy. Then we'll head home." She tucked her hair behind her ears. "What're your plans?"

Chana didn't know how to answer. "I work in a hotel kitchen."

"I meant for your future." She looked on with genuine interest.

"I want to be a baker like my father was." Chana left unsaid the idea of her own bakery, though she bet Peggy would understand.

"Great!" Peggy said. "Meyer told me you have family in America, and you're planning to go."

"My mother and I have been working with the authorities, the consulate, and the Joint, but we don't remember exactly where they live. They were my father's family. And without them sponsoring us, we can't go."

"Damn quotas." Peggy *tsk*ed. "You'd think they'd open the doors and roll out the red carpet after everything your people have been through." She took out a pad and pencil. "What's your family's last name?"

"Rosenzweig. They live in a place called New Jersey."

Peggy wrote everything down. "That's where I was born, but I live in New York City now." The photographer ran a hand through her glossy auburn hair. “Maybe I can do something. When a magazine gets involved, it can grease the gears. We career gals have to stick together.” She put a hand on her camera. “Hey, can I get a picture of you three?”

“I suppose.”

“Meyer,” Peggy called. “Let me get a picture.”

Chana, Aron, and Meyer clustered together, Aron between them as if they were already a family. The fleeting thought surprised her, and she looked over at Meyer, who smiled back.

“Face the camera,” Peggy called.

Chana focused on the photographer as she snapped a few pictures. “Got it. I’ll develop them soon. If I have an extra, I’ll send it to you. Deal?” she said to Meyer.

“Yes, good,” he said.

“*Arrivederci*,” she called. “That’s goodbye in Italian.”

Chana watched the jeep drive away, imagining what life would be if she were like Peggy. She would find a job in a bakery, her skills paving the way to success. If only she could find an easy road to that life. Though she doubted Peggy’s path had been easy. Surely, the woman had to claw and fight for everything she’d achieved.

The rest of the afternoon went by this way, playing football in the lot, laughing, and telling stories. It was Chana’s happiest day in years.

As daylight waned, Meyer checked his watch. “Aron, take the ball and head home. I want to talk with your sister before it gets dark.”

Aron picked up the ball, but stayed.

“What’s wrong?” Meyer asked.

“Mama told me not to leave Chana alone with you for too long.”

She laughed. “Don’t worry, Aron. I’m fine.”

Meyer held up a hand. “Can I talk to him?” His eyes shifted to Aron.

"Okay," she said.

He led Aron to a corner of the lot, and she had no idea what they were discussing, only what struck her was how her brother's bearing reminded her of their father.

"What are you two whispering about?" she called.

"Be patient," Meyer called back.

She crossed her arms. The two looked chummy. Her breath caught. Meyer was so kind to Aron, it always softened her toward him.

Aron shook Meyer's hand.

What on earth?

Her brother called to her, "I'll see you in a bit."

Watching Aron carry the ball off toward Nachmann's made Chana's heart swell—what a fun afternoon the three of them had shared! Chana smiled at Meyer. She was eager to hear what he might want to discuss. A little nervous, too.

Chapter Thirty

Chana

After Aron left them, Meyer led Chana several blocks over to a small park. The fading day had warmed, and the evening air smelled grassy and sweet like honey.

Meyer took off his jacket and rolled up his sleeves, exposing his strong forearms. She imagined him wrapping her in those arms; the thought warmed her cheeks.

"Can we sit?" He stopped at a bench.

"All right." Once they were seated, she said, "I'm curious, what were you and Aron whispering about?"

His eyes held hers. "I told him that he could trust me. I would never take advantage of you." He brushed a lock of hair from her eyes, and she drank in the affection on his face. "Tell me, did you enjoy our day?"

"I did," she said without hesitation.

"And what did you think of Peggy?"

"I loved meeting her."

"I knew you would. You're alike, I think." He rubbed his jaw, and she saw him struggling with what to say next. "Baking is important to you, isn't it?"

She sat back, surprised. "Yes, and I've made no secret of it."

"I once told your mother that teaching meant the world to my sister." Chana knew he was referring to the conversation she'd overheard in the Karlsplatz. Meyer stared out at the flak tower in the distance, a cement structure built by the Nazis to shoot at enemy aircraft. One need not look far for reminders of the war and its toll. Meyer squinted as if in pain. "Spending time with Peggy over these past days allowed me to imagine who my sister might have become had she survived."

He sounded so sad. Chana waited for him to say more, but he didn't. She slid nearer. It seemed the more he revealed this thoughtful side, the more she wanted to know about him and the closer she wanted to be. Yet, something worried her.

"Meyer, can I ask you a question?"

"Of course."

"You examine items in the market, separating them based on what they can get you. I'm no different; I'm a smashed carton of cigarettes or the watch that doesn't tick. How can you look"—she touched her chest—"at this and not turn away? Other men have."

"You're not any of those things," he said, his serious gaze meeting hers. "Don't you see how special you are?"

She searched his face and found only tenderness. He meant what he'd said.

He took hold of her hands, his touch sending heat straight to her center. She recalled dancing with him. His palm on her back. His breath brushing her cheek. He made her feel electric.

"I want to know what happened to you in the camp," he said.

"I don't like to talk about it."

"Please, Chana." His thumbs stroked the back of her hands. "I won't judge . . . I promise."

She believed him. A few seconds ticked by before she started. It was the same story Mama had told him, only now Chana would tell the rest. She repeated how, when the Nazi soldier had beaten her mother, she'd confessed their relation to the captain.

Now the hairs stood on the back of her neck. "It was a few days after . . . in the night . . . he found me in the barracks and dragged me outside."

"The captain?" Meyer asked quietly.

"No." She needed to get it out. "The other, the one who'd beaten Mama." She told of how he'd carried her outside, forced himself on her, and after, he lit a cigarette, stripped her, and branded circles into her flesh, cursing her the whole time.

"If not for the captain favoring me, he would have marked my face. Instead, he scarred me where his superior wouldn't see. If I told anyone, he promised he would kill Mama and me." Nausea rolled over her, and she ran for the bushes, where she bent over and vomited.

Meyer came to her side, holding her hair and rubbing her back.

She stayed hunched over, clutching her stomach. "I worked as hard the next day, and the day after, and the day after." She retched again. "To do otherwise would've brought certain death, though there were times I wished for it."

"Oh, my dear Chana. My darling." As he cooed endearments, his hand glided in soothing circles over her back. "I'm so grateful you didn't die."

When she straightened, Meyer wiped her mouth with his handkerchief, then passed her his flask. She drank, welcoming the fire in her throat. Meyer took her in his arms. Her head told her, *He doesn't love you*, but the way his heart vibrated against her chest, she thought, *Yes, he does.* She let her body mold into his.

"My sister . . . Dora," he said into her ear. "She was shot and killed in the Rumbula Forest with thousands of others. With my parents." His voice halted. "And every neighbor we knew. After the war, I found someone who'd witnessed the shootings. He told me that the soldiers tortured my sister before they killed her." Tears spilled down his cheeks.

"I'm so sorry, Meyer. Truly." Chana wiped away his tears. For each of them, the war had stolen the person they'd cherished most. But their shared pain wasn't the only way they were alike. They were both stubborn. Proud. Only, Meyer wore his grief like armor, keeping off anyone who attempted to make him feel again. But here they were, two wounded people who had found each other despite everything. Pressed together now, years peeled away, transporting her to a time when she was once whole. *Yes, this is what love feels like!*

His mouth was mere inches away. He leaned toward her. She wanted nothing more than to kiss him, and stood on her toes, allowing their lips to meet. He tasted slightly sweet, yet salty, an intoxicating combination. He whispered into her mouth, "I love you, Chana. I tried not to. I fought it . . . day after day . . . and then I fought even more. But I can't deny it any longer." He kissed her harder, and she matched his hunger. He tightened his arms around her, and she did the same, her body catching flame, a sensation like nothing she'd ever known.

"I love you, too," she whispered as his lips trailed to her neck.

His mouth found hers again, and nothing else mattered than the urgency of his lips pressed to hers. Yearning thrummed through every inch of her.

Meyer slowly pulled back. Chana smiled, shaken by her desire. He took her hand and led her back to the bench.

They were silent, though not uncomfortably so.

His lips brushed the back of her hand. "Since the war, I've considered happiness a fool's errand, like chasing the wind." He held out his palm. "Now I feel like the wind is resting in my hand."

She thought of their encounters since her arrival in Vienna. His intervention with Kirill at the train station. Steering her family toward better jobs and a room at Nachmann's. Following her home from the café to ensure her safety. His kindness toward Aron. Her flowers, the sweet wren comb, and the needlepoint for Mama. Meyer had done these things not to toy with her or because of his black-market ambitions toward her brother, as she'd cynically assumed, but instead out of his growing affection for her. And for her family.

After the war, Chana had seen the newspapers and magazines filled with photographs of joyous celebrations taken in the Allied countries. People filled the streets, crying and hugging. The closest feeling to joy Chana had felt was when she and Mama had reunited with Aron. Any happiness she found came tinged with loss. But that was before this moment with Meyer.

He said, "I'm going away tomorrow afternoon, and I'll be gone a week. I hate to leave you."

"I'll be all right." And for the first time, it seemed true.

"What are your plans for while I'm away?"

"Mostly, I'll be working at the hotel, but Elias is going to Dürnstein tomorrow. I'm off, too, and he's invited me to go along."

Meyer studied her face. "Elias," he said. "Yes, I know you still sneak off to meet him late at night."

She stiffened. "I don't sneak off."

"Whatever you want to call it"—his expression softened—"do you really believe that you slip through the streets unharmed on your own? I love you, Chana, and I won't let anything happen to you. I've had people watching out for you, your mother, and your brother." He touched the comb in her hair. "We'll be family soon."

"You're following me?"

"I'm protecting you, as I said I would. You know what happens to people who go out alone at night. I haven't forbidden you from going, have I?"

She pulled away. "Forbidden me? As if you could stop me!"

He shook his head. "You are the most—"

"Stubborn," she said. "I know."

"Fine. But tell me exactly what you're doing with *him*?"

Meyer was clearly jealous, and she bit the insides of her cheeks, recalling the times Elias had held her hand or touched her arm. How he kissed her cheek. "I told you, we *bake*."

"Okay." He sniffed. "And I'm making sure you're safe when you do. Unlike your baker *friend*, who lost his clothes the other day."

In her mind, she saw Elias's bloody nose and split lip. What if . . . "You did that to him!" She shot to her feet.

"I had nothing to do with it. Some men stole his clothes."

"Your men. They beat him! Give back his things."

"I don't have them, because they weren't my men."

"I don't believe you. Who was following me? Was it Vlad?"

Meyer's jaw clenched.

Anger pulsed through her. "You claimed Vlad can get carried away. He could have attacked Elias of his own accord, but still because of you!" She pulled the jeweled comb from her hair and held it out. "Is this enough to buy back his clothes?"

Meyer took off his shoes, clutching them in a bundle with his jacket, and shoved it at her. "If he matters so much to you, give him these. The comb was my gift to you."

"Don't be ridiculous." She pointed to his stockinged feet. "There's rubble everywhere."

"I'll manage."

Had she overreacted? Was Meyer telling her the truth? His gesture was heartbreakingly boyish, and absurd, and she wanted to laugh, and for him to laugh with her.

Until he said, "Enjoy your day in Dürnstein." Adding sourly, "Remember to wear a kerchief over your head. The baker won't be able to protect you."

"I'll manage," she said, echoing his words and unable to admit she might have misjudged the situation. She slipped the comb in her pocket and tore away, aching to go back to him and end their quarrel.

"Don't leave this way," Meyer called.

She cradled his jacket and shoes, turning to hear what he had to say. But as he opened his mouth, a truck barreled onto the sidewalk, revving its engine, and four men jumped out.

One was Kirill Volkov.

She reached for the knife in her pocket, but Meyer quickly latched onto her arm and pulled her behind him. "Let me handle this," he said.

Spying Meyer's pistol tucked in the back of his pants waistband, she whispered, "Okay."

Kirill stepped forward. "Meyer, my friend, I've been told you had another run-in with Grigory." He noticed Meyer's stockinged feet and chuckled.

"Don't believe everything you hear," Meyer said, letting go of her arm and slowly reaching for his gun.

"Put your hands where I can see them," Kirill snapped, opening his coat to reveal a gun holstered to his side.

Meyer tensed, then put his arms in front of him.

"Good." Kirill stepped closer. "Is it true you sold several watches to our komdiv? And you have more?"

Meyer had told her to let him handle this. But his gun was within her reach. Chana kept her body still as she inched her hand out from under the bundle of Meyer's shoes and jacket, stretching her fingers toward the weapon. Sweat trickled down her back.

"What of it?" Meyer said. "You sold livestock to Chef Heiss. Didn't you?"

"You'll stop doing business with our Soviet soldiers."

"All because your brother is an animal?" Meyer asked.

Kirill sneered at Chana. "She started all of this."

Her pulse thundered in her ears. She couldn't just stand by doing nothing. She wrapped her palm around Meyer's gun handle. His back stiffened. The weapon's cold metal was a shock to her skin.

"Leave her out of it," Meyer said, keeping his arms in front of him.

Two of the men edged closer, and Chana reacted, aiming the gun over Meyer's shoulder.

"Oh, I don't think you want to do that," Kirill said.

"Leave us alone," she said. In all those years of war, she had never held a gun. It was heavier than she'd imagined. She didn't know if she could hit any of them if forced to pull the trigger. Meyer shielding her was a relief; at least the others couldn't see her shaking legs.

Kirill seemed to calculate his next move.

"Hey!" came a yell from up the block. Vlad rushed toward them, his gun in hand, and quickly positioned himself in front of Kirill. "What's going on here?"

Meyer eased his pistol from Chana.

Kirill's hand rested on his holster. "Nothing but a friendly conversation between two businessmen."

"I doubt that," Vlad said.

Meyer said, "I'll deliver the watches to you, but you'll pay me what I laid out."

Kirill considered this, then said, "Done." He ordered his men back to the truck, and they scurried away like ants back to their hill.

"Have him make the delivery." Kirill pointed at Vlad and gunned the engine.

"I'll send who I can," Meyer said.

Kirill kept his eyes on Vlad. "You're working for the wrong king."

Vlad spit on the ground.

"In case you refused, I took something for insurance." Kirill signaled to his men in the back. "You probably want this." Two men rolled a person off from the back of the truck, who hit the ground with a groan.

Aron!

Her brother shifted to his side. They'd gagged him and bound his hands and feet with rope. They tossed the football out next.

Chana ran to Aron as the truck sped away. Her hands shook as she removed the gag. "Are you hurt?"

"No." He gulped in a big breath. "I don't think so." She tore off the ropes and helped him up, leaving Meyer's shoes and jacket on the ground.

Meyer joined them. "Aron, I'm so sorry. Kirill will pay for this."

Despair flooded through Chana. Meyer's life was more dangerous than she'd imagined. It was no place for her and her family. "No," she told Meyer, her tone harsh. "We want no part of any of this." She ached all over as if she'd suddenly caught a fever. To Aron, she said, "Come, let's get you home." They headed toward Nachmann's.

"Chana, where are you going?" Meyer called.

She didn't turn around and didn't answer.

Behind her Vlad told Meyer, "She's made you vulnerable and she's not worth it. That friend of hers, Sophie, she's helping Kirill find women willing to sell their bodies to the soldiers. This one's probably a whore, same as the rest."

Chana's steps faltered, and she glanced back as Meyer grabbed Vlad by his shirt. "Don't you ever call her that."

"Let go of me," he said coolly.

Meyer let go.

"Chana?" Aron said.

She guided her brother away. "Come."

Chana's thoughts spun as she and Aron walked the few blocks toward Nachmann's. The news about Sophie rang in her ears. It had been a few weeks since she'd seen her friend. *How could she do this?* Though disappointed, Chana knew she had no right to judge. Sophie's desperation had led to changing her hair, her name, and straight into Kirill's arms to survive. If Chana had been left without Mama and Aron—and Meyer's protection—who was to say she wouldn't make her own deal with the devil?

She glanced behind to see Meyer following them, but she didn't stop.

When she and Aron reached Nachmann's, Meyer called, "Chana, talk to me. Please."

He stood with his shoes and jacket in his arms. His face was ashen after his argument with Vlad, his most trusted protector.

"I don't blame him," Aron told her.

"Go inside," she said.

"But—"

"I said go inside!"

Aron glared, but slowly climbed the steps. Once the door had closed behind him, it took all her strength to stand tall. "Tell me, Meyer, what will you do in America?"

"What do you mean?"

"Is this it? These men. This life"—she paused—"I know you're working with Sergeant McManus. In the lounge, he told you men were waiting to welcome you to America. Are they like this?" He didn't answer, and she told him, "You must see the danger you're putting us in. They could have killed Aron."

"But they didn't. And your brother's right . . . it's not my fault."

Thunder rumbled in the distance. "I want you to walk away from this life. Can you do that?"

"You have to understand that my ability to strike back at Kirill is what protected Aron today."

She took that as a no. This wasn't about protection. This was about power. "If you believe that, then you're a fool." She inched back.

"I love you."

She loved him, too—a realization that filled her with joy, then hammering sadness, because there was more at stake than her heart.

He stepped forward.

"Don't." Chana put up a hand. "I don't want the life you're offering."

The wind picked up and droplets pelted the sidewalk.

"It's too late," he said. "Do you want to go to America? Your mother is desperate to go. And it will be better for all of us."

"So, you'll make me your prisoner."

"No," Meyer whispered. "You'll be my wife."

"Same thing." Chana shook her head. "I will not marry you. We're done," she said, and ran into Nachmann's, her heart splintering as the rain came down in punishing sheets.

Chapter Thirty-One

Chana

Early the next morning, while her brother used the washroom, Chana told her mother the full extent of what had happened with Meyer. Though Mama already knew about Aron's abduction, Chana had been too heartsick and too exhausted to broach the rest. Now she said, "I broke off my engagement with Meyer."

Mama looked aghast. "You did not!"

"Kirill Volkov kidnapped my brother; I had to. We'll find another way to America."

"It wasn't Meyer's fault."

"You sound like Aron."

Mama held Chana's hands. "Don't you see, this is all the more reason for us to leave as quickly as possible. Meyer is our way out." She kissed Chana's cheek. "I'll speak with him and smooth things over."

"But Mama—"

"Not another word." Her mother grabbed her coat and left for work.

But in Chana's mind, her engagement was over. It had to be. She readied for her trip to Dürnstein with Elias, though Meyer's warning weighed on her mind.

Wear a kerchief over your head. The baker won't be able to protect you.

Elias was braver and sturdier than Meyer could ever know. Still, she opted for a sweater, trousers, and boots, and a black kerchief hiding her unbraided hair. A short while later, Chana and Aron left to meet Elias. At their mother's insistence, Aron was coming with her to Dürnstein. The sunny sky coupled with her brother by her side helped push Meyer's dire warning from her mind.

When they turned onto the block where they were to meet the bus, Elias waved, loosening the last knot of anxiety in her chest.

"You're here," he said, flashing a wide smile.

"I am." It was so good to see him.

"Hello, Aron," Elias said.

Aron flipped up a hand in greeting, then looked up the street. "Where's the bus?"

"It'll be here soon. The arrivals are dodgy, though this one, Sundays at eight, has run consistently for several months."

"We've been looking forward to this," Chana said.

"We?" Elias asked.

"Our mother insisted I come," Aron said firmly, daring Elias to protest.

"Our chaperone," Elias said, amused.

His use of the word *chaperone* hinted at an intimacy between them. Chana smiled, genuinely pleased, but memories of Meyer and their kiss in the park lingered in the back of her mind.

Others gathered as a dilapidated gray bus lurched to a stop in front of them. The door was missing, as were all the windows, and a scraggy-bearded man sat behind the wheel. "The only stop is Dürnstein," he called. "Ten groschen there and ten groschen back. Pickup is at five o'clock. Pay both ways now."

Chana looked between the bus and the far end of the block, where she spotted Vlad leaning against a building. He didn't move despite her noticing him; his behavior was that of a cat toying with a mouse. Had Meyer sent him to spy on her? Or had he come on his own? She could feel his contempt for her in his brooding stare, even at this distance. Meyer was the one with the connections across Europe, and Vlad had a lot to lose if Meyer left for America *with her.*

She looked to Aron, then Elias. "Let's find seats."

They settled in the bus's last row.

After two hours traveling on crater-marked country roads, the bus stopped at the edge of town. When they disembarked, Soviet soldiers descended on them, demanding everyone's Inter-allied identity cards.

Chana held her breath as a soldier examined her papers, then gave them back with a wave toward a cobblestone walkway lined with shops. Aron and Elias followed.

She took a few hearty steps and relaxed, listening to Elias point out the things he missed most about the village. He directed their gaze to the top of a hill and a medieval castle. "It's been here for centuries. It's said King Richard was the first person imprisoned there by an Austrian duke."

Aron noted the cutouts in the stone walls and talked of books he'd read about battles between kings and knights. Yes, they were meant to be here with Elias today. Cocooned in his sunny outlook. Out of harm's way.

He led them to a country road, where they walked until a tidy wood house came into view along with a sloped forest behind it. Elias broke into a run, passing through the front gate as a tall man carried wood to the house.

"Elias!" The man's eyes widened. He had white hair incongruent with his youthful face.

"Papa," Elias called.

Papa Johan, as Elias had often called him, dropped the wood and wrapped Elias in a tight hug.

The noise brought a woman out of the house. She wore a brown dress and an apron over her pillowy figure, her dark hair woven into a long braid. She quickly embraced the two men. Of course, this was Mama Ursula.

When they untangled, Elias brought Chana and Aron forward, smiling broadly as he introduced them in German. The Bohms were as warm and welcoming as Elias had described them.

Once inside, Ursula got busy preparing food. "You'll eat with us," she said.

Their parlor was furnished with a sofa and several wooden chairs. A green-tiled stove dominated the kitchen, along with an icebox, and a wood table and chairs. A narrow hallway off the main room looked to lead to bedrooms.

Soon after, Mama Ursula gathered them around the table, serving rabbit stew along with rosemary bread she had baked that morning.

Elias ripped off a hunk of the loaf and chewed thoughtfully.

Chana could see the wheels turning in his mind, judging the bread the way Trolfe would. She ate a piece and found it crisp on the outside and soft, herbaceous, and slightly sweet inside.

Chana and her brother ate as Elias chattered on about the hotel, the kitchen, and Herr Trolfe. Her eyes cut to Johan when he asked

Elias if he was still planning to leave for Switzerland by the end of the summer. Elias answered with a lifted shoulder. Chana knew Switzerland, then Paris, were Elias's goals, but she didn't know he meant to leave in mere months. It was a wise plan. News articles referenced how Switzerland's wartime neutrality helped the country remain mostly intact. Their resources weren't as ravaged as the rest of Europe. France was self-governing now, and she believed also less dangerous than Germany and Austria. Of course, by the time Elias left, she'd likely be heading to America. Her body grew heavy, thinking of how terribly she would miss him.

Johan asked Aron, "When we're done with the meal, would you like to join me with the animals? The goats need feeding, and it'll be time to check the chickens for their late-afternoon eggs."

Aron smiled. "Sure. I'm not so familiar with farming, but I bet I can help."

"Do you have enough of what you need here on the farm?" Elias asked Johan.

"We're getting by." He patted Elias's shoulder. "We've lost a few chickens, but the thefts aren't so bad here."

Once they'd finished eating, Chana joined Ursula in clearing the table. Johan turned to Aron. "Ready for the barn, my fine fellow?"

"Lead the way." Aron followed Johan, and Chana dried the dish Mama Ursula handed her.

The three of them chatted for a short while, until Elias asked, "Mama, would you mind if I steal Chana and show her around the farm?"

"Of course, I can handle these dishes on my own." She smiled warmly at Chana and winked at him.

What a kind woman to have as a substitute mother.

Outside, he said, "Let's go toward the woods." He headed off in the barn's direction. "We'll walk by the river. It's nice this time of year."

She followed Elias onto a dirt path that led through woods to the shore of the Danube River. Sunshine feathered across the water's green surface, intensifying the colors of the river and the forest lining the opposite bank.

"I didn't know you were heading to Switzerland so soon." She matched her stride to his, a breeze pushing her kerchief back until it hung around her neck.

"I've been saving for it. Chef Trolfe has contacts in a bakery where he apprenticed. He's promised to put in a word for me." He said, "And does it matter? You'll likely be in America . . . with Meyer."

She chose her words carefully. "I told him I was coming here with you today."

Elias stuffed his hands in his pockets. "Did he mind?"

"Yes."

"Well, I would, too, if I were him."

She pondered his comment. "Why?"

"I wouldn't want anyone else to turn your head." He took her hand. "Or your heart."

A swooshing noise filled her ears as blood rushed to her head.

"Do you want to marry Meyer?"

Chana struggled to answer. Finally, she told him, "Yesterday, I broke off our engagement, though my mother hasn't accepted it." She wondered if Meyer would respect her decision. She slipped from Elias's grasp. "What does it matter? You're leaving." She walked ahead.

He caught up. "Come with me to Switzerland."

It was an idea that had been simmering within her since the first time Elias had mentioned his plan. "What about my mother and brother?" she asked, as much of him as of herself.

"Your mother is forcing you into a marriage with a criminal."

"Meyer isn't all bad. He can be incredibly generous." And other things she left unsaid, like kind and loving.

Elias said, "You're defending him? He steals from farmers like Mama Ursula and Papa Johan."

"You've bought goods, too," she countered. "From Kirill. You're not innocent."

"No, I'm not, but I'm not the one stealing. Meyer Suconick steals and sells everything, thieving again in the barter. Is that the life you want? Is that who you are?"

"You want to know who I am?" She gripped the neckline of her sweater. Elias cared for her, and she cared for him. It was time for her to learn whether he could accept everything that she had endured. She leveled her eyes at him and yanked down the collar of her sweater. Cool air brushed over her clavicles.

His eyes widened. "Who did that to you?"

"A Nazi soldier in the camp," she said. "Much worse could have happened. Did happen."

Elias averted his eyes, which contained only pity. Well, it was better than the disgust she'd encountered with Zvi. She adjusted her sweater and her breath hitched. Only one man had seen her scars and not looked away: *Meyer.*

Her ears filled with the lone morose warble of a nearby bird.

Was she falling in love with Elias? She wasn't sure, but if the answer was yes, of course love would enable her to overlook this. After all, Elias had protected her and Aron from Sergeant McManus. If not for him, she never would have been able to bake over these past months. She told him, "You asked who I am. I am a Jew who is still standing." She brought her fist to her chest. "I am like you. I'm a baker."

"Then come with me to Switzerland"—he straightened—"as *my* wife."

"You're offering me the same thing as Meyer."

His head jerked back. "How so?"

She walked along the river. "Elias, I want to be an equal." Chana had seen too many marriages where wives were made to curtail their lives—their ambitions—after standing under the chuppah. Once married, they were to run the household and care for children. She needed to know Elias's view of their future, because those things alone weren't what she wanted.

"Aren't we already equals when we bake?" he asked.

"No. You claim my work as your own."

"I have to! Chef Trolfe would have us both fired if he knew." He paused. "Frankly, a woman as a pastry chef in a grand bakery or hotel will take time. But someday, we'll open our own place."

"As partners?" She stood firm, with her feet planted apart.

"Of course. We're perfect together. It's what I dream." He stepped closer. "Chana, my heart is about to fly out of my chest because I love you. I want to marry you, and I want you to come with me."

Partners in a bakery. It would be her dream come true, but there were others to consider. "I don't know. My mother will never stay here in Europe, and I won't abandon Aron or her."

"I understand your concern, but if you leave them in Vienna, your mother will take care of your brother. Tell me yes, and I'll find us a way out."

"I need to think." She headed back toward the farm, uncertain. She believed Elias would keep his word about their partnership. But what about her family? She realized now that ending her engagement didn't mean she and her family were out of danger. Vlad's menacing glare that morning had made that evident. Without Meyer's protection, Kirill and Grigory were also threats. Pieces of a plan came together: if contact was made with Papa's family in America, and they were granted visas, Chana could steal away with Elias. First, she would have to make safe travel arrangements for Mama and Aron—arrangements without Meyer. They'd have to hide until it was time for them to leave.

Meyer had promised: *I would never let harm come to you or anyone in your family.*

But one of his men could come after her or Mama and Aron, taking matters into their own hands. Vlad had said, *If people wrong Meyer, or me, they deserve what they get.* Chana couldn't count on Meyer's protection then. A fresh idea lit through her, and she pictured the one person she could appeal to for help. Herr Heiss. The chef was tough, but kind. And he liked Chana. Would he agree to hide Mama and Aron until they left for America?

If this plan worked, she could in one stroke free herself and her family from the daily dangers they faced in Vienna, and those she foresaw with Meyer. Chana's separation from her family didn't have to be forever. Eventually, she and Elias could follow Aron and Mama to America. This single belief kept her legs from buckling.

Even though she'd ended her engagement with Meyer, her spirit dimmed as she imagined herself fading from his memory.

They emerged from the path with the Bohms' barn in view, and Elias scooped her hands to his chest. "I meant what I said, Chana. We'll be partners. I'll find a way for us to escape. Say you'll come with me. It's all I want."

Life with Elias was the one that made sense. He was solid, thoughtful, and good. He would make a wonderful, loving husband. They already shared so much. They would bake together the way she and Papa had intended.

She held tight to his hands, willing her desire to awaken.

He dipped his head closer, and Chana tipped hers up, ready for his kiss. Desperate to know if what she felt for Elias could match her love for Meyer. She kissed him, and he gave a sharp inhale, surprised by her boldness, but then he leaned in. His lips were soft, and he tasted sweet, and she begged for this kiss to expunge Meyer from her head and her heart. To banish the yearning that tugged at her soul. Elias pulled her closer, his arms winding around her back. She wrapped her arms around his neck. Birds serenaded them as she waited for something to ignite within her. Kissing Elias was nice, but that was it. Chana loosened her grip on him. She didn't want Elias in the way she wanted Meyer.

Chana pulled back. Elias was her friend. But she wasn't in love with him. Her heart hurt as if a dark future had dropped an anvil on her chest. Elias loved her, but she couldn't return his feelings. She truly loved Meyer. He was her *beshert.* The realization made her body vibrate. But she'd called off their arrangement because she couldn't stay with Meyer, not after what had happened to Aron. Who knew what the men in America would do to his family to keep him in line? Tears wet her face.

Mistaking her emotion, Elias hugged her. "Don't cry, darling. I'll find a way for us to be together." Before she could speak, he kissed her again.

"Chana," came a voice from a few feet away.

She pulled back.

Aron was in the field.

"What are you doing here?" She wiped her cheeks.

"I came looking for you." He stared at her accusingly.

"And you found me."

Her brother shot a sharp look at Elias. Chana took her brother's arm. "You can't tell anyone what you saw. Do you understand?"

Aron glanced over his shoulder. "I understand." His dark tone made it clear he didn't like it.

"Good." She pecked his cheek. Turning to Elias, she said, "I agree with what we discussed." Feeling sick to her stomach, she paused, until dawning showed in his eyes. She'd agreed to go with him to Switzerland. "We should walk to town and wait for the bus," she said. "We don't want to miss it."

"No, we don't," Elias said with a fresh bounce in his step.

She wrestled with her guilty feelings as the three of them went back to the Bohms' house, said goodbye to Ursula and Johan, then returned to town. She didn't want to mislead Elias. He was her dear friend, but that was all he was. Yet, she believed as bakers, they could make a formidable team. She would have to make her feelings clear if she was going to act on her plan.

When they arrived in Vienna, Elias walked them back to Nachmann's. As Aron headed up the stairs, Chana hung back.

"Aren't you coming?" Aron asked protectively.

"In a minute." She tapped two fingers against her chest twice.

Aron hesitated, then mimicked the motion and slowly went inside. She glanced up and down the block. The street was empty. "Did you mean it when you asked me to come with you?" she asked, facing Elias.

He took her hands. "With all my heart."

She squeezed his hands and met his eyes. "Elias, I'm not going from one man to another. You're dear to me. But know this: I'm going as my own person. I'm not going to marry you. Do you understand?"

"Of course. You need more time."

She let go of him. If only he was right. "I don't think so."

He bit his lip. "We can see what happens," he said with too much optimism.

Chana's aim wasn't to deceive him, but his shining eyes let her know she wouldn't be able to convince him otherwise. Not tonight. Still, she opened her mouth to protest. "Elias, I shouldn't have kissed you. Please, you must understand—"

"I want you to come with me," he said firmly. "There's nothing you can say that would make me change my mind."

She had to let it go for now. "I have to make sure my mother and brother will be safe."

"Do you want them to come with us?"

"More than anything, but Mama would never agree." She thought of Zvi and his plans for Belgium. "If any of Meyer's men come after me, Mama or Aron could be hurt." Meyer's name on her lips made her stomach drop. "I have to go in, but once our visas are arranged, and I leave, hopefully those men will forget about us, and we'll all be out of danger."

And eventually, Meyer will forget about me. The thought hollowed her out as she left Elias on the sidewalk.

Chapter Thirty-Two

Zoe

Vienna, Austria
April 2018

Zoe woke on Thursday morning—the fourth day of the conference—a little hungover. She and Henri had walked around the city center for two hours, taking in landmark buildings such as the Hofburg Palace and Vienna State Opera. Only a few minutes away from the opera house, they stopped at Albertinaplatz in front of the Monument Against War and Fascism. The exhibit had deeply moved her, especially the bronze statue of a man kneeling to clean the street with a brush. Chains were roped across his back, and the statue wore a yarmulke. She thought of Elias's father and how he'd suffered this same humiliation. Heaviness slowed her gait as they walked away.

At dusk she and Henri had arrived at Karlotta, a traditional Austrian restaurant in a residential area of the city.

She had been starving and ordered what was the best Wiener

schnitzel of her life. Their conversation stayed light as they drank their way through two bottles of Riesling. There were times her mind wandered through gloomy scenarios involving Wes's threats.

If she did nothing, Wes would fire her.

If she asked Henri to let her write about him, he would surely shut her out.

And if she'd seemed distracted, Henri didn't comment. He kept up a steady conversation as if he could read her distress and was giving her space. The way Grandpa Aron would. She shook away the comparison. It wasn't possible for Henri to be that intuitive; they barely knew each other.

Henri's chauffeured sedan dropped her back at the hotel a little after ten o'clock, and they set plans to meet the following afternoon to talk and go for dinner.

Now, in her room, she opened her blinds and gazed at a graffiti hummingbird for a long minute. The morning was overcast, and she didn't mind. It suited her worried mood.

As if on cue, a text arrived from Wes: Has Henri told you how he knew your family?

She thought carefully about her response.

ZOE: No. We talk only about my family and Vienna.

WES: Because he's hiding something. His NDA is not going to stop me.

ZOE: This is wrong. We should respect my agreement with him.

WES: Compile your notes and let me be the judge.

Judge or executioner? Zoe sank onto the bed, feeling cornered.

> ZOE: I can't send anything today.
>
> WES: Why?
>
> ZOE: Meeting with Henri at 3.
>
> WES: Great. Meet me in the hotel lounge at 2:15 to hash out our plans.

Her gut lurched as an ellipsis in a bubble showed he was still typing.

> WES: I land at 1.

She marked his text with a thumbs-up.

~

That afternoon, Zoe stood opposite Wes at a cocktail table tucked in a back corner of the hotel's lounge. Zoe kept checking the room's entrance, fearing Liam or Henri walking in.

"I'll crack this with or without you," Wes said. "Without you means you can say goodbye to *Savouries* and your writing career." He sipped his double espresso. "When it comes to a story, I'm no one's friend. And neither should you be."

"Henri told me everything was off the record. I'm trying to do the right thing and stand by the ethics of what we do."

He was unmoved. "If we find another source, then you're just confirming information. I spoke with someone at Jacques Simon's bakery, and according to her, he's still in Vienna."

"I haven't seen him."

He gave her an ironic half smile. "How hard have you been looking?"

Her gaze fell to a steel-gray swirl in the marble table, and she made no reply.

"That's what I thought." He downed the rest of his coffee. "My coming here might throw good money after bad, but not if this story gives the magazine the subscription boost we need. Your scoop on Martin's picture helped, as did my article. Website traffic has shot up. Now *Savouries* is where readers are following this story."

Everything about this felt wrong. "I have to go. It's almost three o'clock." She gathered her purse.

Wes threw down a few euros. "Lead the way."

"What?"

"You're meeting Henri Martin? I want you to introduce me."

She blinked a few times, but there was no point in arguing, so instead, she trudged through the lobby. Outside, Henri waited beside a black sedan.

Wes cut past her. "Mr. Martin," he said, extending his hand. "I'm Wes Donnelly. It's an honor to meet you."

Henri hesitated before accepting Wes's greeting, briefly shaking his hand. "Thank you." His questioning eyes flicked to Zoe.

She knew she should say something, but Wes flashed a high-watt smile and continued. "Zoe and I work together. She knows what a fan I am of you and your company, and graciously offered to introduce us."

"Ah," Henri responded.

Zoe quickly added, "He flew in today."

"Yes, and I was sorry to miss your keynote." Wes let out a fake chuckle. He pointed to the sedan. "Where are you two off to this afternoon?"

Henri eyed Wes and after a long pause said, "Nowhere special. If you'll excuse us, Zoe and I have matters to discuss."

Wes's smile slipped. He was unaccustomed to being dismissed, but he was in Henri Martin's world now, and Zoe freaking loved it.

"Of course. Forgive my intrusion." He turned to Zoe. "We'll talk later."

Once Wes disappeared through the hotel's revolving door, Henri asked, "Your boss?"

"That's right."

"He's a slippery one, isn't he? Has the eyes of a snake."

The tips of her ears grew hot. "I don't know what you mean." Though warranted, she prayed Henri wasn't suspicious of her.

"When you've lived as long as I have, you recognize traits in people."

Henri's driver opened the back door of the sedan for them. Henri slid in beside her and raised the privacy glass between them and the front of the car.

"Is he pressuring you?" Henri asked.

"He still wants me to write about you."

"Even though I would sue you?" He gave her a sharp look.

"He doesn't care. I won't do it. I meant my promise to you." God, she hoped she could keep it. "But there's something else."

"Go on."

"Wes wants my notes. I typed up a few things after we spoke the first few times. But he's planning on contacting Jacques Simon. If Jacques has information that you don't want out, get in touch with him right away."

Henri scoffed. "He'll get nowhere with Jacques." He settled back in his seat. "How detailed are your notes?"

"They're sketchy at best," she said, glad it was the truth.

A sly smile lifted one side of his mouth. He'd foreseen her being put in this position.

"So . . . where exactly are we going?" she asked.

"Dürnstein. We're having dinner at a winery."

"Dürnstein is where Elias took Chana."

"That's right. I thought you'd enjoy seeing it."

"I would."

For their outing, Henri had worn a light gray suit, matched with a pale blue dress shirt. Zoe was pleased to have dressed in the nicest item she'd packed, a black sleeveless jumpsuit paired with low-heeled black pumps.

Once they reached the highway outside the city, the landscape changed to what one would expect from the Austrian countryside. Forests of silver birch trees dotted the terrain, along with clusters of homes resembling gingerbread villages. Henri pointed out rows of flowering apricot trees.

She sank deeper into the car's leather seat, grateful for a brief reprieve from her troubles.

An hour later, the sedan crept along a cobblestone road, where a long walkway ascended into the village of Dürnstein. Zoe gazed out the window, transfixed by the pale-colored buildings filled with stores and restaurants. Her eyes went to the castle above the village and the backdrop of lush green mountains touching puffy white clouds in an azure sky. She imagined the village that had greeted Chana, Elias, and her grandfather. Boarded-up shops. Rifle-toting Soviet soldiers on patrol. She clasped her hands tightly in her lap.

"Are you okay?" Henri asked.

"Driving through here . . . it's as though I can feel the past bleeding through the cobblestones." Zoe turned toward him, unable to hold back from asking, "How do you know my family, Henri?"

He pulled on the cuff of his shirt. "We'll get to it soon." He was putting her off, and before she could press, he added, "What do you hope to get from these stories?"

Years of her pent-up curiosity about her grandfather's life sprang to mind. "I suppose this is my way of knowing my family and keeping them with me. I've lost them all, and I miss them." She focused outside, blinking away the stinging in her eyes, and oddly enough, she thought of Meyer and his losses.

Henri said, "Grief is always hard. But particularly difficult for one so young. How did you get through it?"

Grandpa Aron's smiling face filled her mind. "My grandfather helped me."

"Ah, yes," Henri said, as if his knowledge about Grandpa Aron made Zoe's response easy to believe.

Fifteen minutes later, they arrived at a winery with rows of vines carved into the mountainous landscape. The setting sun painted the vineyard in a graded palette of green, orange, and yellow. A white stone house stood in the forefront with a brown pitched roof and scalloped wood molding. Flowers overflowed from blue window boxes.

"It's like landing in a fable," Zoe said, stepping out of the car. She turned around, and Henri was already at the front door. The sign above him read:

LA MONASTERY VINEYARD AND RESTAURANT

She followed him inside, through a front lounge sporting cream walls and a long bleached-wood bar that was the perfect blend of airy and welcoming.

"Henri," a middle-aged man called, rushing up from the dining room behind the lounge. The man hugged Henri. "Welcome! The others are already here."

Others? Zoe looked to Henri. He didn't explain, but instead said, "Rolf Simon, I'd like you to meet my friend Zoe Rosenzweig. She's a food writer. Rolf is the restaurant's owner and chef. The vineyard property has been in his family for generations."

Rolf was gray at the temples and dressed casually in dark jeans and an untucked black button-down shirt. He said, "It's nice to meet you" with a German accent. To Zoe's surprise, he deposited air kisses by both of her cheeks.

"Wait a second," she said. "Your last name is Simon?" It was the same surname as the Swiss baker.

"Yes." Rolf smiled. "Come, this way."

Henri avoided looking at her as Rolf led them to the dining room, where four people, including Liam, were seated at a table set for six. The rest of the room was empty, and it wouldn't have surprised Zoe if the restaurant had been closed to host this private meal.

The dining room was as inviting as the lounge. Their large round table was draped with a pristine white tablecloth, and the chairs were covered in ethereal white fabric. Flickering candles in varying heights created the centerpiece.

Liam pulled out a chair for her, the one between him and Henri. As she sat and hung her bag over the chair back, he said, "Good to see you again."

She searched his face for irony, but found none. "You too." She half expected him to whip the chair away so she'd land on the floor.

Henri went around the table with the introductions. First was a middle-aged couple, Rose and Jack Martin-Eastman. Rose Martin-Eastman was Henri's daughter and Martin Baking's chief operating officer. Zoe found her classically beautiful with a patrician nose, pronounced cheekbones, and full lips, yet the resemblance between her and Henri was clear in her dark wavy hair and the angled shape of her face. Rose greeted her warmly, a maternal shine in her eyes that made Zoe's breath catch. Jack Eastman headed up the company's international sales division. He had dirty-blond hair and an athletic build, and she had no doubt he was Liam's father.

On the other side of Liam was his fiancé, Oliver. It was easy to pick up that the two men were yin and yang: Oliver's shaggy jet-black hair and porcelain skin were the opposite of Liam's tanned, beach-boy vibes. And she quickly learned Oliver was a metal sculptor of rising esteem, compared to Liam's life in the business world. Despite their differences, it was clear they were smitten with each other, laughing easily and finishing each other's sentences.

Zoe rather liked this version of Liam.

Rolf circled the table, delivering charcuterie and filling wineglasses. Everyone helped themselves to pâtés, sliced meats, cheeses, fruit, and slices of warm bread. The restaurant owner seemed to know the family's food preferences—providing no menu—and the experience was like dining in someone's home rather than in a restaurant.

Oliver said, "This is my first time in Austria. It's beautiful. And this village is charming as hell. I have to get a souvenir before we head home."

"Snow globes are my souvenir of choice," Zoe said.

"So kitschy," Liam said approvingly.

"I just love all the little farms out here," Oliver told her. "Reminds me of a movie."

Henri joined their conversation, saying, "Agriculture has long been part of life here. Centuries ago, much of the land was owned by monasteries that made their own wine. In more recent years, the land was family owned, and people worked on their small farms. It was how I came to know it."

Zoe slathered a piece of bread with pâté. "Have you known Rolf for a long time?"

"By the time you reach my age, the definition of *long* is elastic."

The others laughed, while Zoe noted how deftly Henri had sidestepped her question.

Zoe's phone rang, and she pulled it from her purse. It was an unfamiliar New York number. She sent it to voicemail. An Instagram direct message alert followed. She was about to ignore it when she recognized the name.

"Excuse me," she said quietly to Henri. "I need to check on a message."

"Of course," he said.

Zoe stepped into the lounge and opened the message.

> Hi Zoe,
>
> I've been following your situation in Vienna and your connection with Henri Martin. Are the rumors true? Is

> he shopping for a ghostwriter? Or is it a cowriter or biographer? Either way, I would love to be the one to help you navigate a book deal. Do you already have representation? If not, please reach out. I left you a phone message, too. My contact information is listed below.
>
> Cheers,
> Trudy Tuffin
>
> President, Tuffin and Keller Literary

What? Zoe hadn't landed in Austria this week; she'd landed on some other planet.

Trudy Tuffin was one of the biggest nonfiction agents in publishing. She represented ex-presidents, major Hollywood stars, and music-industry legends. And she would love to help Zoe navigate a book deal? She played the agent's voicemail, reiterating the same information.

If only Henri had agreed to a book. The advance could be a ton; possibly enough money for her to pay off her grandfather's mortgage. But her hands were tied. Now even contemplating a book deal felt like double-dealing.

Zoe closed the agent's message without replying, though with searing disappointment.

Back at the table, Rolf was serving their meal—garlicky pasta, chicken in an herb sauce, and whole braised fish. As the evening progressed the Martins treated Zoe like she was one of them, even Liam. This family was wealthy beyond compare, yet there was nothing off-putting or showy about them. She laughed harder than she had in months.

As dessert was served, a text pinged Zoe's phone. She fished it from her purse.

> WES: I'm talking to Jacques Simon in an hour. Meet me tomorrow at 6:30 a.m. at Bäckerei Lyra—away from the hotel—no prying eyes or ears.

Zoe angled herself so neither Liam nor Henri could see her phone. Damn! Jacques Simon had agreed to talk to Wes, and Henri had been so sure of his friend.

Zoe replied: I'll see you tomorrow morning.

She didn't want to spoil this wonderful dinner, so she planned to talk to Henri on the drive back to Vienna.

Oliver asked, "Zoe, have you ever been to Australia?"

"No." She put away her phone. "I don't know if I could handle the flight. It's so long."

"It's not so bad," Oliver said. "Watch movies or sleep, and in no time you'd be there."

Zoe enjoyed Oliver's accent, which was more pronounced than Liam's, his rising inflections making statements sound like questions.

Liam dug into a slice of cake. "If you ever come to Australia, Oliver and I can be your tour guides. We'll take you to all the sights. Some will be a first for me, too. Though I've lived in Sydney all my life, I've never climbed the Harbour Bridge."

It was an odd invitation in a most odd evening.

Henri excused himself and met Rolf by the kitchen door. She moved a little more toward Liam. "Not that I mind, but why are you being so nice to me?"

"My grandfather and I had a long talk this morning. He made me see how you've proven yourself. Since the unfortunate article, you've remained silent. Bravo." He kept his voice low. "We're careful about the people we engage with. Especially him." His eyes flicked to Henri.

Oliver had turned away and was chatting with Jack on his other side.

"I want to . . ." Liam shifted in his seat. "I'm sorry for what I said to you at lunch." A blush crept up his face. "About your parents."

She could tell he meant it. "I appreciate that."

"You should know, you've earned my grandfather's confidence."

Zoe recognized something now. Over the past few days, the pace of Henri's stories, the days and hours separating their meetings, had served a purpose for him. It had allowed him to get comfortable with her.

Liam reached into his jacket pocket. "You've earned mine, too." He placed a white envelope in her hand.

Inside, Zoe found a torn-up document. "I don't understand."

"It's the nondisclosure agreement. It was our only copy. My grandfather ripped it up himself before picking you up this afternoon."

Henri came back to the table.

This was the answer to Zoe's prayers. *Or was it?* Liam had handed Zoe the knife she could use to stab Henri in the back. Henri trusted she wouldn't. Tomorrow morning, she was supposed to meet with Wes, and now she no longer had the NDA to shield her. Would she tell him? This, combined with what she knew and whatever information Wes pulled out of Jacques Simon, could make her career. Henri still needed to tell her about his connection to her family, but she sensed it was coming.

"So . . . what happens now?" Zoe asked Liam. "Can I write about him if I want to?"

Liam studied her, then chuckled. "Nice one. Good poker face."

He had no idea how good. Zoe would bet her poker face in that moment could win an Oscar. In her heart, she didn't want to betray Henri, or any of the Martins. But might a five-thousand-dollar bonus, a promotion, and the ability to keep her grandparents' house for the foreseeable future win out over sentiment?

In a weird way, Zoe felt like a modern-day Cinderella, and this vineyard visit was her enchanted ball, giving her not a prince, but something she wanted far more.

Family.

But this wasn't her family, and this magical evening would end. When it did, Zoe would go back to being what Liam had called her: *the poor little orphan girl.*

She tucked the envelope in her purse and choked down a mouthful of cake.

Chapter Thirty-Three

Zoe

After her evening in Dürnstein, Zoe barely slept, tortured by her impending meeting with Wes. She debated not going, but ultimately decided that taking the meeting might buy time to figure out her endgame.

She never had a chance to tell Henri about Jacques's agreeing to talk to Wes. When she and the Martins had left La Monastery, Henri had directed her to ride back with Liam and Oliver, though he promised to be in touch the next day. Maybe it was for the best that she hadn't told him about his friend spilling the tea to her boss, delaying the pain of such a betrayal. The thought made her feel guilty by association.

At six thirty that morning, Zoe sat opposite Wes at a banquette table in Bäckerei Lyra, where the interior vibe was more speakeasy than bakery. A lengthy bar displayed baked goods under cloches, and on the opposite wall was a long, pink-velvet banquette.

Zoe ignored her Americano coffee, while Wes dug into his espresso and *pain au chocolat.*

"This is the best croissant in Vienna," he said.

Zoe wrapped her hands around her cup, glad for something to hold on to. Bäckerei Lyra was near empty, and just being there felt like she was betraying Henri. There wasn't enough soap in Austria to wash away how grimy she felt.

Wes wiped crumbs from his lips. "Tell me again how he gave you back the agreement?"

"Liam slipped it to me at dinner." She'd only told Wes out of fear of being sued by the magazine.

"Fantastic, especially because Jacques Simon was a bust."

Her heart beat faster. "He was?"

"The guy deflected every question with stories about his bakery, his wife, or his kids. His son owns a winery outside of Vienna."

Bingo! Rolf must be Jacques's son.

He slid his plate to one side. "So, show me your notes, and we can draw up some scenarios. We'll speculate on who Henri Martin might have been based on his knowledge regarding your family. From there, I'm sure we'll find some sources. I'll whip this story into something special."

She stared at him, his true motivation becoming clear. She'd been so naive. "You never intended to let me have the byline, did you?"

He smirked. "As we'd discussed, you'll be in the background. Try and look at it this way: if it's good for me, it's good for you. Under thirty and you'll be a senior editor. It doesn't matter whose name is on the byline. Let's get on with it."

Zoe hauled her backpack onto her lap. Inside were her notes. They were flimsy, only a few typed sheets, because after Wes's threats, she'd purposely avoided fleshing them out. She knew his next move would be to question her for the details.

Wes devoured the last of his pastry, and all Zoe saw was a wild animal ripping apart its prey. *Was she going to feed Henri to this man?* Her fingers froze on the bag's zipper. "I can't do this."

"Don't be ridiculous."

Zoe swung the bag onto her shoulder and stood. "I'd rather suffer the consequences."

"Sit," he hissed. "I meant everything I said. I'll fire you, and good luck getting hired anywhere else. The magazine will sue you for those notes."

She envisioned Chana's life, outwitting Nazis with the resistance, standing up to black-market dealers, and facing down assailants. Zoe straightened. "You won't have to sue me." She rooted in her bag and dropped a folder on the table; inside were the few papers she'd typed up about her conversations with Henri. "Here."

Wes flipped through the pages inside. "There's barely anything here."

"I told you; Henri wouldn't let me take notes." She tapped the folder. "That's what I remember. It's all about my family."

"This is bullshit."

"No, what's bullshit is your threat to fire me." Zoe paused. "I quit." She lifted her backpack, which felt surprisingly light. "Be careful about attempting to blackball me. I have our texts—trying to force me to break a signed NDA and an off-the-record interview wouldn't be a good look for you. And if I ever find out you're doing this to someone else, I'll go public." She leaned over the table. "On the record, when *I* look in the mirror, I'll respect the person staring back."

She left, and he called after her, but she didn't stop.

Out on the sidewalk, the only person she wanted to talk to was Henri. She couldn't wait to hear from him.

But by five o'clock, she'd left Henri several messages, which went unanswered. Panic set in. Could he be ghosting her now? If so, why? Desperate, she called Liam, who told her Henri had been slammed with meetings and would be in touch. His tone was apologetic.

The next day, Saturday, the second to last day of the conference, she attended panels, hoping to spot Henri so they could talk. He wasn't anywhere to be found.

Time frittered away, and she grew more anxious. She had learned a lot about her family, but she needed to know the rest. Had Chana stayed with Meyer? Or did she run off with Elias? How had Chana ended up perishing in the fire?

By Saturday night, two whole days since Dürnstein, Zoe was ready to crawl out of her skin. Sleep would have been great, but she was too wired. Sunday was the Boucher Conference's last day. The awards dinner would take place that evening in the grand ballroom. It was when restaurants around the world would learn their standing in that year's Boucher rankings, and it was when the Martins would receive the Lifetime Achievement Award. Monday, everyone would fly out, with Henri going back to Australia and out of Zoe's life.

She checked the time. It was after eleven at night. She sent Henri a text anyway.

> Forgive me, I know it's late, but is there any chance you can talk now?

Three dots appeared in a bubble. The dots disappeared. She waited. No response.

Pacing did little to soothe her; the room was too small to release any real energy. Zoe slipped into a T-shirt and sweatpants, clicked through television channels, then turned it off. Devoid of options, she called Liam again.

"Hello," Oliver said, answering Liam's phone.

"Oliver—hi, it's Zoe. Is Liam there?"

"Hang on." Silence followed. He must have muted the phone. She waited for at least a minute before Liam came on the line. "It's late, Zoe." His voice was quiet.

"I'm sorry. I know." She paused. "I think Henri is shutting me out." When Liam didn't respond, she knew she was right.

Finally, he said, "My grandfather does things in his own time."

"But the conference is almost over." She put her forehead against the cold windowpane, her breath fogging the glass. There was only one way forward, and it was through Liam. She took a deep breath, then told him, "I quit my job."

"Why did you do that?"

Zoe fought back tears and calmly confided in Liam about Wes's demands, their meeting Friday morning, and how that led to her quitting. "Wes threatened to blackball me, and now Henri is ghosting me."

"That's a lot to handle," Liam said with genuine sympathy.

"I need to know the rest of what happened to my family."

Silence stretched between them. "Listen, I can't tell you exactly where he is." A lump grew in Zoe's throat. Liam added, "But I'm pretty sure he's where he always goes when the past haunts him."

Zoe gasped. "Of course." She knew exactly where to look. "Thank you."

"I didn't do anything."

She smiled. "I believe what you've done is called plausible deniability."

He chuckled. "Good luck, Zoe."

She grabbed her room key and hurried to the lounge, striding past the few people sharing drinks. The dining room was dark when she entered, but there, to the left, were the kitchen doors with light seeping out from the round windows and across the threshold. She crossed the room and heard jazz music. She cracked the door enough to see Henri alone at a worktable, pressing his palms into a mound of dough.

"In or out," Henri said without looking up. "It's what my father used to say if I hesitated at his study door."

The door *shushed* as it swung closed behind her. "Why have you been avoiding me?"

He slapped the dough onto the counter. Hard. She jumped. "Damn the past," he said.

"I want you to know your stories are safe with me." His head snapped toward her. "I quit my job."

His shoulders drooped as if he'd been beaten down, showing no sign of relief from what she'd told him. "You are strong, Zoe Rosenzweig. Not that I'm surprised. It's in your blood."

A sickly feeling grew from deep in her core. Something else was going on. "How did you know my family? Who are you in those stories, Henri?"

He touched his phone, stopping the music. "Some parts of a tale are harder to tell." He stared at her, and a range of emotions washed over his face—disgust, anger, and finally, sorrow. "Are you sure you want to hear the rest?"

"Tell me."

"Come." He waved her forward, and on unsteady legs, she joined him at the worktable. "Have you ever made croissants?"

"I've written about them, but no, I've never made them."

He slid her a large square of dough. "Follow what I do." He rapidly used the heels of his hands to flatten a second large square, before employing a rolling pin to shape it into a long rectangle. "You try."

The dough was cold and firm when she pressed into it, and after, she worked slowly with the rolling pin compared to him.

"There's no rush," Henri said. "You're doing a fine job."

"Thank you." They stood beside each other, and when he folded the dough, so did she, and when he pushed his palms against the mound, she did that, too. As they worked, Henri told his story.

Chapter Thirty-Four

Chana

Vienna, Austria
July 1946

At the end of the first week in July, and a few days after Chana's trip to Dürnstein, she went to the laundry looking for Sophie. She'd been tense since visiting the countryside, in part because as soon as she and Aron had returned to Nachmann's, Mama had gathered Chana into her arms.

"All is well," her mother said. "I spoke with Meyer. He still wants to marry you."

"Mama, I told you not to."

She placed a gentle hand on Chana's cheek. "We need to leave and this is how."

It was useless to argue—her mother's mind was set. Part of Chana was glad to know Meyer still wanted her, because she still wanted him. Not that it would matter; she planned to leave with Elias.

Now she hurried down the steps to the laundry basement, determined to talk to Sophie about Vlad's accusation. Only, Sophie wasn't there. A woman told Chana her friend had quit weeks ago and had found other lodging. No one knew where.

Fright overwhelmed her as she left. Chana wiped her eyes and scanned the block, willing Sophie to appear.

On her way to the hotel, she passed hordes of people pouring out of the train station. The harried-looking crowd hauled valises and satchels. Some had bruised faces and bandaged limbs. She passed a group huddled together, speaking a mix of Yiddish and Polish. One word stood out.

Pogrom.

It landed like a punch in her gut.

At work, Chana learned more. While she served and cleared meals in the dining room, she overheard the American officers discussing a pogrom on July 4 in Kielce, Poland. Details were sketchy. Polish soldiers and police had been investigating the possible kidnapping of a child by a man some falsely claimed was Jewish. But during the police search, they ended up shooting innocent Jewish residents in an apartment building. Dozens of Jews were dead. More injured. Jewish refugees, who'd returned to Poland after the war, were now fleeing to other parts of Europe.

Soon after the carnage, it was determined that the kidnapping itself was false.

Plates clattered as she stacked them on a tray. *A pogrom.* Sure, she'd overheard stories of harassment while waiting in emigration lines. One Jewish man had talked about returning to his home in Poland and having hostile neighbors tell him he should never have come back. They chased him off with sticks.

Would this hatred escalate again? Would it spread?

Sergeant McManus came into the dining room, parking at a table of officers. Chana heard them discuss plans to increase patrols in the Jewish-populated districts of Vienna to ward off a similar event happening here. Several soldiers grumbled with disgust at the violent details of this recent pogrom.

"How could this happen after what we found in the camps?" one soldier said, pressing his fingers to his eyes. There were many who had fought to defeat Germany that were now forever changed in body and soul by what they had witnessed.

These reactions eased Chana's anxiety some, but not entirely. A hateful, murderous mob could wreak havoc and harm before even the most well-intentioned police or military could stop them.

For the next two days, when they weren't at work, Chana and her mother and brother kept to Nachmann's. Mama spent the evenings pacing their small room. Even her needlepoint couldn't calm her nerves. In the middle of the week, Meyer stopped by.

"I can't stay." There were deep circles under his eyes, and his usually slick hair was a mess. "I wanted to check that the three of you were all right."

"How can we be?" Mama asked, clasping her hands together. "There was a pogrom in Poland. What are we to do? We must leave."

"We will." Meyer forked fingers through his hair and turned to face Chana. "Your mother says you didn't mean to break our engagement." His voice was gentle. "I want to believe her."

Mama drew in a quick breath. Tension gathered on Meyer's face. Silence hung over the room as they all waited for Chana to reply. She couldn't bring herself to add to her mother's distress, so she nodded, signaling Mama was correct.

Meyer gave her a relieved smile, and though a flutter hit her chest, guilt over her plans with Elias made her look down.

"Aron, how are you?" Meyer asked, shifting his attention to her brother.

"I'm okay," Aron said. "I told you; Kirill didn't hurt me."

"Good." He fell quiet, then said to them, "There's a meeting in two nights. In the basement of an abandoned building on Anagasse. Look for a pair of lion's head doorknockers. Several of the survivors from Kielce will discuss what happened. Come if you can." He paused. "I have to go. The rabbi has asked me to help people get settled. The three of you be careful."

The door opened and closed, and Meyer left without another word.

Two nights later, Chana and her mother entered the basement of the abandoned building. Dozens had gathered in the sour-smelling space, reminding Chana of similar clandestine meetings in Vilna, when partisans snuck into the ghetto to warn the Jews of what was happening in the outside world.

Chana spotted the rabbi and Meyer standing with a couple—a man with a bandage around his head, and a woman with a badly bruised face and her arm in a sling. The rabbi and the couple listened with rapt attention to whatever Meyer was telling them. He was strong and confident and . . . she missed him.

The rabbi raised his hands. "Quiet," he said. "Listen to what happened."

People kept talking. Chana spotted Sophie across the crowd; her eyes were red as she brought a handkerchief to her nose. Oh, thank goodness! Relief flooded through Chana. She was about to rush over to her friend when the rabbi's voice rose over the gathering. "Everybody, settle down!"

Everyone quieted.

The bandaged man held the injured woman's hand and said loudly, "Polish police and soldiers came to our building on Planty Street. Someone claimed a Jew living there had kidnapped a young boy. It was a lie, made up, and we believed they'd arrived to protect us." His fist went to his mouth, and he couldn't continue.

The woman stepped forward, and told them, "Officials came into our building. Someone fired a gun. We were attacked. Though there were many of us, we had no weapons. Our Polish neighbors joined in, beating us, and throwing rocks. I was hit on the head by who, I didn't see. A woman stomped on my arm." Her eyes went to her injured limb as if she still couldn't believe what had happened. "Like we haven't been through enough. The Poles saw what happened to us during the war. They still did this. I saw a woman killed with a bayonet. Another, pregnant, was beaten to death with a club. And a baby—" She choked and couldn't go on.

Chana could imagine what horrible fate met that harmless child. Anger circulated through her.

The man hugged the woman, and they sobbed, letting the rabbi tell of how, over the next two days, a mob grew and joined the bloodbath. The attackers robbed, beat, killed, and threw Jews into the river. "Anywhere from thirty to forty Jews died," the rabbi said. "More were injured."

Chana felt crushing sadness. All around her, people wept.

When the rabbi finished, the gathering slowly dispersed, people leaving with their heads bowed.

Sophie came over to Chana and her mother. "You were right, Frau Rosenzweig. Leaving Europe is a smart idea."

"I need to talk to Meyer," Mama said, and barreled over to where Meyer spoke with the rabbi and the couple.

Chana turned to her friend. "I went looking for you at the laundry. They told me you quit."

"I found something better."

"Sophie, are you working with Kirill Volkov?"

Her friend's jaw jutted forward. "What if I am?"

Sophie had to realize what she was getting involved with. "He kidnapped my brother. He's despicable. You know what he does."

"He's a man."

"Do you hear yourself?" Sophie didn't answer. "You're better than this."

"Do you hear *yourself*?" she asked. "It's easy to judge me when you're safely tucked under Meyer's arm. I've been fighting for scraps."

Chana took in Sophie's anger, recognizing the fear crouching behind it. She should have been more supportive of Sophie; she should have pushed harder for Chef Heiss to hire her. "I'm sorry, Sophie. Really, I am. Let me help you now. I'm leaving soon, so maybe you can take my job in the kitchen. Or maybe Meyer knows someone who can hire you in a better place."

"I'm not going from one meager job to another." Her eyes raked over Chana from head to toe. "Look at you. Nice dress. New shoes. You found a good provider. Now so have I."

Chana shook her head. "Kirill and Meyer are not the same."

"I know that." Sophie covered her mouth for a moment. "But didn't you hear what we were told tonight? A pogrom happened in Poland. I need protection. Kirill offers me that." Her eyes bore into Chana. "He likes to talk in bed. I know a lot about what goes on in this city." Sophie's voice dipped lower. "Your fiancé better be careful. You too."

She walked away quickly, as if she didn't want anyone to see her with Chana.

Chana was left speechless, unsure of what to make of Sophie's last comment. Was it a warning? Or a threat?

Her mother came back, shaking her head. "They say I have to wait my turn to speak to my future son-in-law."

When Meyer finally joined them, his face was ashen.

"We have to get out of here," her mother demanded.

"I'm working on it," Meyer said, keeping his voice quiet.

"Work faster. What if a pogrom happens here? I will not wait to be dragged into the street yet again."

Chana understood her mother's fear. She recalled the sight of her father lying in the road with blood pooling under his head. Her body quaked. *Not again.* She thought through her plan to remain in Europe by heading to Switzerland. Everything she'd read in the past months, in newspapers and magazines, suggested Switzerland was *not* like Poland. She should be safe there.

Mama wagged her finger under Meyer's nose. "If you are a man, get us to America now."

"I will." Worry clouded his eyes.

"Good." Mama tugged Chana away.

Chana's decision to go with Elias over Meyer was tearing her up inside. But soon, she, Aron, and Mama would get to a safer place, though not in the way her mother intended.

Two days later, after work, Meyer came to them at the boardinghouse. Aron greeted him with a warm smile and a handshake.

Chana forced herself to stay seated. Despite everything, she had the urge to hug him.

Meyer smiled. "You look good, Aron. Have you been playing football?"

"Yes, I played with those fellows you told me about. I wasn't very good, but I'll get better."

Meyer clapped Aron's back. "Of course you will." He looked first to Mama, who was wringing her hands near the table, then at Chana.

Mama stepped between them. "What news do you have?"

"Tomorrow morning, you'll meet with Mr. Rumson at the Red Cross office. He'll be expecting you. Your husband's brother has been found." He looked at Chana. "Sergeant McManus used his influence after I told him if he didn't act now, I wouldn't help him anymore." He let that sink in for a moment. "Your husband's brother is sponsoring all of us to come over and will wire money to pay for our travel to the ticket agency near St. Stephen's—it's the only one operating. He also left letters with the visa office in New York, taking responsibility for us. The U.S. is giving out few visas, but the sergeant is making sure ours come through. Once you meet with Mr. Rumson, Abernathy will arrange our certificate of identity papers and visas at the consulate." His eyes went to Chana. "We'll need to marry soon and make our travel arrangements."

Chana took a sharp breath. "When do we leave?"

"A week."

"Good." Her mother's voice cracked. Then Mama broke down, her shoulders heaving. "Thank God, thank God, thank God." It was a chant to her mother's answered prayers. Mama pulled Chana into a crushing hug. "You've done this for us, *maideleh.* Soon we'll be with Papa's family." Now her mother's tears mingled with her own. Mama let go and hugged Aron. Chana wiped her eyes and prayed her plan would work.

After the emotion of the moment had settled, Meyer asked Chana, "Can we walk?"

"Sure," she said. She picked up her handbag, and they left.

Outside, the summer evening was still light enough to see. The street was empty as she walked beside him, his closeness stirring longing in her.

"I never had the chance to ask if you enjoyed your trip with the baker," he said.

"It was a nice day. Aron came with us."

"I'm glad you made it back unharmed." Meyer stopped and took her hands. "Chana . . ."

He looked as though he'd stopped breathing. She peered into his earnest eyes. "What is it?"

His thumb stroked the back of her hand, sending heat thrumming under her skin. "Chana, I love you. I want to go to America with you."

She loved him, too. Every part of her came alive in his presence. She saw his kind and caring nature, despite his trying to hide it. But all of that couldn't erase the dark areas of his life, which she couldn't accept.

"I acquired this from a friend in Belgium." He produced a ring from his pocket. An emerald stone set in a simple gold band glinted in the waning light.

Her hand flew to her mouth. It was the most beautiful piece of jewelry she'd ever seen.

"The stone's color reminded me of the flecks in your eyes when you're fond of something." Tenderness filled his voice. "I know we didn't start off in the best way. Your mother wanted someone good for you, and I think that's me. We'll go to America, and I'll do everything in my power to see you want for nothing . . . even baking."

Meyer's declaration was everything a woman would want to hear—everything Chana wanted to hear from him. But if he planned to work for Sergeant McManus's friends, danger would greet them in America.

He leaned in. "I want to marry you. I—" He was on the verge of saying more, but stopped, reading the dismay on her face. "What is it?"

"You're going to work for Sergeant McManus's associates in America, aren't you?" She needed him to confirm it.

"Yes. It was the condition for his help. Chana, with these men, quitting isn't an option."

Their eyes locked, and Meyer's jaw tensed, clearly expecting her to put up a fight. She didn't.

Meyer had told her the men in America wanted a married man with a weakness, meaning someone they could control. Frightening scenarios played in her mind. If Meyer did something these men didn't like, then Mama or Aron could end up in the line of fire. They could kidnap Aron the way Kirill had done. Or worse. But if she and Meyer never married, then Sergeant McManus's friends in America should have no interest in Mama or Aron. If she'd harbored any doubts about escaping with Elias, she no longer did.

"I can go to the ticket agent and make our travel arrangements while you tie up your business," she offered in a steady voice. "If it would help."

He studied her for a long moment. "It would."

Chana held in her relief. The only way her idea would work was if she booked Mama and Aron on an earlier train and ship than Meyer. With Papa's family as sponsors, their travel expenses covered, and visas legally issued, nothing would stop Mama and Aron from leaving for the United States. Nor would they be financially beholden to Meyer or the sergeant. If these men in America canceled their arrangement with Meyer because he was unwed, well, perhaps her plan would have the added benefit of freeing him, too.

Meyer held up the ring. "Chana, will you marry me and go to America?"

She put out her hand.

He slipped the ring on her finger. "It fits." His face shone with hope.

"It does." Her voice had grown thick. What a shame that the universe hadn't brought them together in a different time and place. It pained her to look at him. Yet, she couldn't hold back from cupping his face and bringing her lips to his one more time, emptying every bit of her heart into kissing him.

When she stepped back, he asked, "Was that for the ring?"

"No, it was for everything. Good night, Meyer." She left him without confessing that their kiss would have to sustain her for a lifetime.

Chapter Thirty-Five

Chana

Did you run here?" Elias asked when he opened the alley's kitchen door.

She imagined what she must look like, all sweaty and disheveled. "I walked as fast as I could." She pressed her hand to her side, fighting a cramp. After she'd left Meyer on the sidewalk, she'd waited until Mama and Aron were asleep before slipping out.

"What's happened?" Elias asked.

Beyond him, croissant dough rested on the counter. How she wished she'd come to simply escape into the night's task.

"We must leave soon." She eyed the dough again. Time was not on their side. "We should get to work on the croissants. I need to tell you more and I can't stay. I have one more stop to make tonight."

"All right."

They worked the dough as Chana told Elias that the pogrom in Poland had so terrified her mother that she gave Meyer an ultimatum to find her father's family. In a matter of days, he had done so, and they would leave for America in a week. "In two days, we'll have our papers and visas. I'll be the one going to the ticket agent. I have to make sure Mama and Aron are on a different train and boat than Meyer." She flipped over a mound of dough. "If you want me to go with you to Switzerland, we must leave soon."

He took this in silently, his rolling pin shifting back and forth over a slab of dough. Chana couldn't tell what was going on in his mind until at last he said, "We'll go in three days."

"You'll have to arrange it—Meyer can't know. We'll need traveling papers with new names. He has connections all over Europe." Elias braced against the counter, but she pressed on. "I've saved money, and Aron told me the hotel concierge once arranged papers for a friend. He has contacts."

Elias nodded as if this were not news to him. "I have money tucked away, too, and the concierge is my friend." He drew up to his full height and took her flour-dusted hands in his. "I can take care of this . . . the papers, and whatever we need."

"Okay." She blinked several times.

"What is it?"

"My mother and Aron." *And Meyer,* she thought wistfully.

"Your mother promised you to a barbarian."

She flinched. Meyer wasn't like that. As for Mama, she told Elias, "My mother is trying to save her family. She doesn't understand that my idea of freedom differs from hers, and that her way isn't safe for us."

He said, "They say even a beaten dog licks the hand of its owner from time to time."

His description was a punch in the stomach. She had to admit that sometimes it was true. But not always. Elias didn't know that after the attack by the Nazi soldier, Chana had returned to the barrack, and Mama had crawled in beside her, holding her all night, and whispering a lullaby from when she was a little girl. Mama did the same night after night until Chana's chest had scabbed over.

Chana turned back to the dough. "I have a plan to hide Mama and Aron for a few days, until their train leaves Austria." She blinked a few times. "Someday, I'll contact Aron and Mama in America. Let them know where I am."

"You will," Elias agreed.

She looked at him, and he gave her a reassuring smile. She pressed a rolling pin into the dough, choosing to believe her time away from her mother and brother wouldn't be long at all. It was the only way she could stand it.

Chana had never been to Herr Heiss's home, though she knew he lived in a small, brick terrace house several blocks from the hotel. She left Elias and hurried there. After she knocked, Herr Heiss quickly ushered her inside.

She sat on a stool in his tidy kitchen holding a calming mug of tea, while the chef, clad in his nightclothes and a robe, waited to hear the reason she'd come pounding on his door at this late hour.

"Speak," he ordered with his usual directness.

She met his keen eyes. "I'm leaving Vienna."

"Yes, I've heard that your family is going to America. I'll miss your attention to detail in my kitchen."

"I'll miss working for you as well. You've been kind to us."

"Well . . ." He scratched his head. "You make me sound like a softy. I'm not." He sat on another stool. "You aren't visiting this late to thank me?"

In her desperation, Chana hadn't realized what a gamble it was to have come. She set down her mug and prayed her intuition about Herr Heiss was correct. "I'm not leaving Vienna in the way you think." She told him about her plan with Elias to avoid marrying Meyer, leaving out the details surrounding Sergeant McManus, but intimating that danger would follow them to America if she didn't act. "I can't bring Aron and my mother with me. If Meyer sends any of his men after me, they could hurt my family. Would you be willing to hide them here? They'd come to you once I'm gone, and they'd only stay a few days. They'll have traveling papers and train tickets and will be of no bother. Will you agree to keep them safe for me?"

He didn't answer.

Oh, no! Panic revved through her veins. He could tell Meyer or her mother everything. Ruin her escape before it began. She pushed back from the table. "I shouldn't have come."

"Sit," he said.

She did.

He ran a hand over his stubbled chin. "It's bold of you to ask, but I recognized from the start that you were a bold girl. I liked that. Do you know why?"

She shook her head, praying he was leading toward agreement.

"During the war, I watched the Nazis arrest friends of mine. Jews, and some non-Jews. Many died." He looked at the floor. "I wish I had been bold like you. Like them." The chef's tone had grown soft. "I kept my head down and am left with nothing but guilt." When Herr Heiss lifted his head, he was pale and looked as though he'd aged ten years.

Chana sat still, not knowing what to say.

He wiped his bulbous nose with the back of his hand. "Yes, Chana," he said, his voice husky, "I'll help you. I'll make sure your mother and brother are safe. They can hide here, and I will put them on the train myself."

She launched up and hugged him. "You're a good man."

"Let's keep that our secret as well," he said.

Chapter Thirty-Six

Chana

On a Tuesday, two days after her meeting with Chef Heiss, Chana waited in the ticket agent's office, crossing and then uncrossing her arms, while the fellow behind the desk searched the list of ships departing from Bremerhaven in Germany. The money for their travel had already arrived by Western Union from her uncle. In an hour, Chana was to meet her mother and the rabbi to discuss the wedding, which was scheduled to take place Friday afternoon, before *Shabbos.* If anything went wrong with these tickets, Chana's escape would implode. If anyone suspected—her mother or Meyer—it would all be for nought.

She crossed her arms again.

"Everything looks in order." The ticket agent flipped through papers on a clipboard. "You'll travel to Germany by train, and once there, you'll still need to pass a physical and disinfection before boarding." He looked at her with bloodshot eyes that matched his ruddy nose and cheeks. "So, stay healthy."

She agreed, as if such a thing were in anyone's control.

"I can arrange four tickets leaving Südbahnhof next Friday. You'll have three weeks in Bremerhaven before you board the *Wayfarer*."

"Is there anything sooner?"

He consulted the clipboard again. "There is a train leaving Saturday from Linz. You'd arrive in Bremerhaven on Sunday . . . and could board a ship on Thursday. If I call ahead, there would be time for your physicals and disinfections."

She wanted to leap from her chair. "Excellent," she said calmly. "But I need you to book the earlier arrangements for my mother, brother, and myself. My future husband has business to finish and will meet us later. Buy him a ticket for next Friday's train and the later ship." She couldn't believe how easily these lies left her lips.

The man didn't blink. "All right. No rest or honeymoon, I suppose."

Chana smiled politely, and he swiftly executed her instructions. She hated to waste money on tickets for herself and vowed to repay her uncle someday. She prayed, not for the first time, for her plan to hold water. Herr Heiss had sworn he would see her mother and brother onto the train, including driving them, if needed. Linz was only two hours from Vienna.

When Chana met her mother in the shul at the back of the cobbler's shop, she was twitchy with nerves.

"Did you take care of the travel arrangements?" was the first thing Mama asked.

"I did."

Her mother grinned wider than she had in years.

To Chana's surprise, the rabbi walked in with Meyer.

"You're here?" she said.

"You're surprised?" he asked.

"I thought you'd be busy, what with our leaving."

"It's been a long week, but this is my wedding, too." He settled in a seat beside her. "Did everything go well with the ticket agent?"

"It did."

"Good. Thank you for taking care of that." He patted her hand.

"Sure." She shook out her hair, damp strands sticking to the back of her neck.

The rabbi took a seat with them and talked about the wedding service, what the rabbi would say, what they would respond, and how Chana, as the bride, would circle Meyer seven times—a Jewish ritual meant to create a wall of protection around the groom.

"The ceremony will take less than an hour," the rabbi said.

Pride emanated from her mother, and Chana sank lower in her chair. If only she could beg Mama to come to Switzerland, but she would never agree. Not with America within her grasp. *In time*, Chana repeated to herself. In time, they would reunite. And as for Meyer . . . if only the wedding ritual could build a real wall of protection.

"Chana?" the rabbi said.

She'd been lost in thought, and now three pairs of eyes stared at her. "I'm sorry. What did you say?"

"Will your brother be part of the ceremony?"

She sat straighter. "Aron will walk in with me and Mama."

The rabbi's lips curled, signaling approval. "Ah, yes. Like the papa."

Their meeting lasted only a few more minutes, none of which penetrated Chana's thoughts. She was consumed with worry over how in the world she would explain her plans to her brother.

The following evening, on Wednesday, Chana and Aron walked back to the boardinghouse alone after work. Mama had left the hotel earlier to meet with a seamstress before the wedding in two days' time. Chana had picked up their tickets, their traveling papers, and visas, all of which she'd hidden in a drawer in their room at Nachmann's.

Aron chatted about their trip, while Chana waited for the perfect moment to tell him about her plans. It would be up to her brother to take their mother to Herr Heiss's house. Chana couldn't risk her mother learning of their escape until it was too late for her to do anything but go along with it.

"Do you think we'll live with Papa's parents or his brother's family?" Aron asked.

"I'm not sure."

When they were in their room at Nachmann's, Aron tossed the football up and down. "I'm bringing this. Hopefully, I'll find some fellows to play with in America."

His optimism made her hesitate to confess her plan. It devastated her to leave him.

Elias had kept his word, and because of his friendship with the hotel concierge, everything was in place for them to leave tomorrow night. From her time in the DP camp, it still astonished Chana how many people were peddling forged documents. The papers Elias acquired had new names and blurry photos showing a resemblance. They weren't perfect, but they should work.

Their plan was to meet tomorrow night in the kitchen, as if they were baking. Chana sneaking out to the kitchen had worked for months, and they counted on it working one more time. She'd worried about the location, especially since Aron's altercation with Sergeant McManus, and the soldier sometimes leaving black-market goods in the alley for Meyer. But Elias had heard from the concierge that since the authorities cracked down on the black market, these arrangements were no more. Elias also feared Trolfe suspecting his leaving, and so he wanted everything to appear normal. Their escape meant Elias would forgo recommendations from the pastry chef. He would be starting over, yet he eased any guilt Chana expressed by telling her, "My skills will quickly set me apart. I'm not worried, nor should you be." Johan Bohm would meet them with a truck in the alley, and from there, he would drive them to the Swiss border to where a friend had agreed to take them in. Neither of them wanted to risk someone associated with Meyer seeing them in a train station.

Aron picked up a book. "I have something for you." He slipped an envelope from between the pages. Inside was a photo and a note. It was the picture Peggy had taken of her, Aron, and Meyer.

Chana read the note:

> *Chana,*
>
> *It was an honor to meet you. I hope our paths cross again, either in New Jersey or wherever our travels take us. Follow your passion as I follow mine, and who knows where we'll land?*
>
> *Your friend,*
> *Peggy York-Black*

It was kind of Peggy to leave this for her. Chana was glad to have met this woman, who had shown her it was possible to follow her dreams.

"Where did you get this?" she asked.

"From Meyer. The photographer sent it to him."

"When did you see Meyer?"

He shrugged, as if her question were silly. "At his house today. I had an errand out that way for the hotel manager, and Meyer told me if I was ever around, I should stop in. Some men he works with were there. He's leaving his business to Hershel. He's a funny one."

Chana remembered when she and Elias had met with Hershel, and how he liked to joke. She also recalled the tension between him and Vlad that night they'd raided farms. If Meyer was passing everything to Hershel, she doubted Vlad would be happy taking orders from him.

Aron tapped the picture. "We look like brothers, don't you think? Maybe once we're settled in America, I can work for Meyer."

Chana grabbed Aron and despite his being bigger than her, she shook him roughly. "No! Never! You will never work with him."

Aron pulled away. "What's gotten into you?"

"Listen to me. Meyer Suconick is not your brother."

"Enough, Chana." He rolled his eyes.

The time had come when she had to tell him everything.

"Aron, I know you don't blame Meyer for what Kirill did to you, but I do. And if I marry him, and we go to America together, this danger *will* follow us." She grasped her brother's hands. "But I have a plan. I've arranged for you and Mama to leave a few days early. Chef Heiss will drive you to Linz, where you'll catch a train to Bremerhaven, and once there, you'll leave on the first ship out. Meyer's train will be a week later, so he'll arrive in Germany after you've gone. No one knows I've done this."

"Mama and I?" Aron pulled away from her. "What about you?"

She bit her lip. "I'm leaving tomorrow night with Elias. We're going to Switzerland. You heard him talk about it when we were in the country. Johan has a friend who will take us in. Eventually, we'll go to Paris to bake. Once I leave, you'll have to tell Mama and take her to Chef Heiss's house. I'll leave you the address."

"I know the address. I've run errands for him, too." Her brother's tone was bitter, and he wouldn't look at her.

"It has to be this way."

"You can't leave us." Aron's cheeks grew blotchy.

"I have to." Sergeant McManus had trapped Meyer, but he would not trap her brother. "Not only for me, but for you. The men Meyer works with are dangerous. I won't allow our lives to be caught up with them. If I'm gone, you and Mama are free. Papa's family is expecting you. I have all your papers and your tickets. There's nothing to stop you."

"But you said we would stay together. Mama and I can come with you and Elias."

His pleading scraped her heart raw. "No. If Meyer sends men after me, it would be risky for the two of you. Vlad can be particularly vengeful. I won't see either of you hurt again. When it's safe, I'll find you in America. I promise."

He considered this for a long time. "What if Mama refuses to go to Chef Heiss's house?"

"Mama will see the danger and she'll go. You'll make her go." She smoothed his hair. "There are two envelopes in the bottom drawer. One has our papers and tickets. The other is Meyer's. Leave his on the table. I'm sure Nachmann will give it to him."

Aron nodded, and she knew he would get it done. He lifted the photo. "Do you want it?"

She did, but she would let him hold on to it, hoping it would soften the blow of their parting. "You keep it for now." She hugged him, wishing things could be different. "You can't tell anyone, Aron."

"I know," he said, his voice breaking.

She let go and looked at him, memorizing every detail about her beloved brother. His kind and curious brown eyes that darkened whenever he concentrated particularly hard. How even a hint of a smile brightened his face. The tiny scar on his left cheek from the time he'd fallen on the sidewalk when they were children. Chana's reassuring coos had stopped his crying even before Mama had swept him up in her arms.

Though Chana was leaving to keep Aron from harm, doing so would take every ounce of strength she had. Tears filled her eyes as she tapped two fingers on her chest, and Aron did the same in return. They didn't speak another word.

When Mama returned, they were both quiet. Not that Mama noticed. She chattered about the seamstress, their dresses for the wedding, and how many in the local Jewish community planned to attend.

Chana imagined Meyer discovering she was gone, and she sank into a chair, unable to stand a moment longer. He would despise her. She only hoped in time Meyer would understand.

Chapter Thirty-Seven

Chana

The next night, Thursday, Chana waited until her mother's steady snoring filled the room before daring to rise from her mat. Nerves crackled within her. Aron rolled over and looked at her, then turned away again. She had to hope that though she'd hurt him, he would follow her instructions.

Her packed satchel was in the bureau, but instead of retrieving it, she knelt beside her slumbering mother. She didn't dare do anything to wake her, yet she couldn't leave without saying goodbye. "I love you," she whispered. "Try to understand." Tears dripped onto her mother's blanket, and she hoped her plea had penetrated Ruth's dreams.

Chana slipped from the room with one more thing to do before she met Elias. In the bathroom, she locked the door and faced her reflection. *Get on with it*, her thoughts chided.

With shears she'd bought on the black market, Chana lifted a chunk of hair and cut. She dropped the strands in the sink, paused, and kept cutting until her hair fringed her forehead and face, and hung no longer than her nape. She thought of Samson's story in the Bible, and how once shorn, he'd lost his strength. The Nazi guard at Stutthof had razored off her hair, stealing her last shreds of power. Of personhood.

This was different.

Chana ran her fingers through her hair, which would attract less attention as she traveled. After cleaning up, she stashed the scissors in her bag and donned her hat.

A short while later, Chana tapped on the alley door, clutching her satchel handle. She waited and worried. What if Elias had changed his mind? She tightened her grip on the bag, packed only with a few clothes and her savings. That morning, Meyer had collected the jeweled-wren comb and the emerald ring for safekeeping while they traveled. "I'll give them back to you in America," he'd said.

At last, Elias opened the door, and she fell inside, dropping her satchel by the door.

"I had to be sure my mother was asleep." In a few hours, Aron would wake Mama, and they would go to Herr Heiss's house. She prayed her mother wouldn't protest too much. "When will Johan be here?"

"In about twenty minutes," Elias said.

The room was lit by a single candle. She whipped off her hat.

Elias stepped back. "What have you done? You look like the refugees who first came to the city."

She touched the hair fringing her forehead. "My hair draws attention. This is much easier." His obvious disappointment stung a little.

"Won't you miss it?" he asked.

She was about to tell him no when shouting came from the alley. "What the hell are you two doing here?" a man yelled.

Meyer.

Another man answered, "Putting you out of business for good."

Kirill.

Chana whispered to Elias, "You said there were no more deals in the alley."

"I was told there weren't," Elias whispered back.

Her heartbeat quickened, and the kitchen felt as airless as the cattle car that had carried her to Stutthof. They needed to get out. They would have to cut through the hotel to the front and ward off Johan before he turned into the alley. "Where are your things?" she asked Elias.

"By the basement stairs."

"Get them and hurry. We need to leave."

He disappeared into the hall. She grabbed her bag from near the door.

More shouts sounded outside until one voice stood out. *Meyer.* "How did you know where to look?" Meyer asked.

"I told him," another man answered, and Chana didn't need to peek outside to recognize the voice belonged to Vlad.

Vlad had betrayed Meyer.

"How could you do this?" Meyer asked.

Chana heard the hurt in Meyer's voice.

She heard the grunts of a scuffle, then Kirill yelled, "No guns! Do you want the whole American army to pour out of the hotel?" Footsteps crunched across gravel. Kirill asked, "Why do you keep looking toward the street? Expecting someone? Perhaps the idiot named Hershel?"

Elias returned to the kitchen with a small suitcase.

The alley was quiet until Kirill said, "Let me tell you what happened to him." Chana went numb. She and Elias needed to run, but she couldn't bring herself to leave while Meyer was in danger.

Kirill continued, "He's not coming. I killed him at your house. He was as useless as this one you brought tonight. Recognize this?"

Hershel was dead. Saliva filled Chana's mouth. She fought back the nausea.

"My ledger," Meyer said, his voice tight.

Aron had told her Hershel would take over for Meyer. And now Kirill had taken Hershel's record of Meyer's dealings.

"You bastard," Meyer hissed.

"Consider it payback for your last fight with my brother. Grigory, get some knives."

Footsteps from outside grew closer, but before Chana or Elias could move, Grigory threw the door open. A nasty grin spread across his face, and Chana felt as though she'd been plunged into an icy lake.

"What do we have here?" he said.

She dashed toward the dining room. Grigory caught her arm and yanked her back. Pain shot through her shoulder. She cried out and dropped her satchel.

Elias came at them, but Grigory swung a pan with his free hand, clipping Elias in the jaw and sending him collapsing to the ground. He twisted Chana's arm behind her back, making her scream again. She was sure her arm would snap.

Grigory's mouth dropped to her ear. "I told you I'd have you in an alley."

She glimpsed Meyer outside with his arms caught behind his back by Vlad.

This couldn't be happening. She grabbed the knife from her pocket, whipped around, and slashed Grigory's thigh. He cursed and let go.

She ran toward the alley door. She couldn't let Meyer die at the hands of these men. A few feet away from Meyer lay one of the men—Isaac?—who'd been with them that night at the farms. An object protruded from his chest, and he didn't move.

"Meyer!" she shouted.

He turned his head, and his eyes widened at the sight of her. Her shout caused Vlad to look over, too, his grip on Meyer seeming to loosen. The distraction allowed Meyer to thrust his head back against Vlad's chest with such force that the Soviet struggled to breathe and lost hold of him.

Grigory caught Chana's wrist as her feet hit the alley, wresting the knife away and raising it high.

He would kill her right here. Her next thought was *At least Aron and Mama are safe*. Papa would be proud of her.

Meyer screamed, "No!" and launched himself at Grigory, throwing the bald man off balance as Elias swung the alley door wide. The bottom corner clipped the side of Grigory's temple. He fell, smacking into the wall. On the ground, blood flowed from his head, and he didn't move.

Meyer rushed to Chana. "Are you all right? What were you doing here?"

Her mouth opened and closed, but no words came out. Meyer's eyes darted from her to the doorway, to Elias, then to where she'd dropped her satchel.

He looked confused, but she could see his mind spinning to make sense of it. Once he did, his eyes narrowed.

Kirill put his fingers on Grigory's neck. "He's dead."

Chana and Meyer stepped back.

Kirill stood. "I said my brother is dead!"

"It was an accident," Meyer said, shifting to shield Chana. "He was hurting her."

Kirill faced Vlad, who'd recovered from the blow to his chest. "You were supposed to hold Meyer," Kirill said accusingly. "Now my brother is dead!"

"I'll get a hold of him now." Vlad moved toward them; his gun ready.

Chana spotted her knife in Kirill's hand. In his rage over his brother's death, Kirill rushed forward and stabbed Vlad in the stomach, tugging the hilt upward, inflicting maximum pain before pulling it out. "You're useless." He spit at Vlad.

Vlad wheezed and gurgled as he stumbled a few feet, then fell.

Chana's hand flew to her mouth. She wanted to scream, but she had no power to do so. Kirill gathered up Vlad's gun before turning on them. "Get in the kitchen. No need to announce our quarrel to all of Vienna."

"Let her go," Meyer said.

"Not a chance." Kirill waved the gun.

Chana's brain snapped back to life, and she searched for an escape. If she ran toward the street, Kirill would surely shoot her in the back. She felt weak, surprised that her legs could still hold her up. The only option was to go inside. It would buy time. Maybe they would get out of this alive.

In the kitchen, Elias inched back, blood trickling from a cut on his chin. The candle flickered, casting their shadows onto the wall. The door shut, followed by the telltale click of a gun being cocked—a sound that echoed in her ears.

"Turn around," Kirill ordered.

They did.

Kirill had his gun pointed at Meyer. Kirill grabbed a towel and wrapped it around the muzzle.

"What are you doing?" Meyer demanded.

"Letting the army sleep while I get revenge for my brother," Kirill said.

Think! Chana's mind screamed. There had to be a way out.

"It was an accident," Meyer said. "I didn't mean for him to die. He was attacking a woman."

The Soviet gestured to Chana's satchel. "Why would you care when it appears she was running away with someone else?" He shifted the gun toward Chana, and she held her breath. "Before I kill you, should I take care of her?"

"No." Meyer put his hands up. "Let them go."

Elias spoke up then. "He's right. Your quarrel isn't with us. Let us go."

"I don't think so," Kirill said.

Chana let out a small squeak. She had stood at the precipice of freedom, and now she was about to die.

Elias stayed frozen by the worktable, but Meyer stepped right, shielding her again.

Kirill grunted. "Meyer Suconick, you've been nothing but shit on my shoe. I should have squashed you like a bug months ago. Stopped you from selling your goods to my soldiers. Invading my territory and blocking my expansion. Fighting with my brother."

"You nearly broke my arm after my last fight with Grigory. You've taken your pound of flesh."

"I haven't even begun to take my revenge!" Kirill said.

Meyer locked his hand around Chana's wrist. He was willing to sacrifice himself for her. Tears sprang to her eyes and for a second the kitchen blurred into a muddy swirl of beige and white.

"Leave her out of this," Meyer said.

"She's a pretty one, isn't she?" Kirill licked his lips. "There were pretty ones in the camp. As a *kapo,* I kept them in line."

The rumors were true. Kirill had worked for the Nazis. Her knees buckled slightly. Meyer's hand tightened around her wrist.

Kirill stepped closer. "A blond Jew. Aren't you rare? Too bad you cut your hair off." He sneered like a vampire thirsting for blood.

The same evil as on the face of the soldier who had haunted Chana's nightmares.

He came closer and Meyer charged, getting one hand on the gun and the other on Kirill's wrist.

"I'm going to kill you, and then I'm going to have her," Kirill said.

"The hell you will," Meyer said.

The two men wrestled, and she lunged for a pan. Anything to use as a weapon. Fear seemed to have turned Elias to stone.

The gun went off; the towel muffling the noise. Meyer staggered back, dropping to his knees before toppling over with his hands to his side.

She ran to him. "No! No, no, no." Meyer couldn't die here.

"I'm sorry," Meyer said, wincing in pain.

"Don't move. We'll get you out of here."

Kirill closed in on Elias, the gun aimed at his head.

Elias put up his hands. "I didn't . . . Please, don't."

Kirill struck Elias in the face, sending him staggering to the floor, and as he fell, his hand caught the candle. It landed on a cardboard box, igniting the wall behind it. The first flames were small, but they grew, and within seconds, the room billowed with smoke.

Chana reached for Chef Heiss's cleaver, her fingers inches from the handle, until Kirill caught the back collar of her coat, hauling her toward him. "Come with me."

She punched at him, and he twisted her arm behind her back, causing her to yelp in pain. Elias struggled to his feet and ran toward them, only to have Kirill smack him in the temple with the gun. He fell back.

She screamed as Kirill dragged her toward the alley door. Meyer lifted partway up, his shirt soaked with blood, only to collapse again. "Go, help her," he said to Elias.

Kirill yanked her into the alley and punched her in the face, his hulking gold ring smashing into her cheek. She hit the ground. When she touched her cheek, her fingers came away bloody. Kirill's heavy black boots landed beside her. He held the gun in one hand and her knife in the other.

"You bitch." He kicked her in the side, knocking the wind out of her. Then he kicked her again, harder, sending her body several feet over. Stabbing pain shot through her chest, and she struggled to breathe. She rolled to her side and warm blood trickled down her face. Kirill wasn't going to shoot or stab her. He was going to stomp her to death.

In Vilna, Chana had witnessed a Nazi stomp a woman outside the ghetto gate; her only crime was smuggling in a stem of lily of the valley. Chana had locked her eyes on tiny bell-shaped white flowers as the soldier's boots ground them into the mud.

She lifted her head. *Dear God, where was Elias?* And Johan should be here by now. Her eyes landed on a metal pipe only inches away.

Elias appeared in the doorway. The fire had taken over the worktable behind him, and the kitchen walls beyond that. Elias screamed, "Stop!"

Kirill turned his head.

It was a split second, but long enough for Chana to grab the pipe, hoist herself up, and smash it into Kirill's face as he looked back at her.

He dropped the knife and clutched his face. Blood spilled onto his fingers. He stumbled, and as he attempted to lift the gun, she struck him again. He fell, and the gun slipped from his grasp.

Blood dripped from her face to the ground, and her chest heaved with pain as she lifted the pipe high, ready to strike again. Kirill didn't move.

Elias scooped up the gun. "You're bleeding."

"He hit me." Her voice trembled. "Is he dead?"

"I'll check." Elias held the gun out and slowly knelt by Kirill's face. "He's breathing. We need to go."

Chana dropped the pipe and searched the ground until she found her knife. Then she bent over Kirill.

"What're you doing?" Elias asked, breathless. "We need to leave."

Her shaking stopped as she raised the knife over his chest, and a crash from the kitchen made her turn. Flames licked the doorway. The room was on fire. Meyer was in there.

She looked back at Kirill's bleeding face.

Shouts rose from the street. People gathered on the sidewalk, but wouldn't be able to see them so far down the alley. A second later, Chana stood and called to Elias, "Watch him," as she ran toward the fire, waves of heat trying to force her back.

"You can't go in there," Elias said.

"I have to get Meyer."

He grabbed her arm. "Leave him."

"I can't." She tore free and dove into the smoke-filled room. Her eyes stung, and she kept an arm over her nose and mouth, while pain spread through her rib cage.

Meyer was close, having crawled nearer the door. He coughed.

Thank God, he was alive! The fire had partially eaten away the right sleeve of his coat, mangling the skin on his forearm. He gasped for air as Elias arrived behind her.

They each took a side and lifted Meyer as best they could, half carrying and half dragging him to the alley just as Johan drove in. Fire trucks shrieked in the distance.

"What's going on?" Johan was out of the truck and running toward them.

"We need your help," Elias said. "We have to go."

Johan's eyes were round and frightened, but he took in the scene and said, "Whatever you need me to do."

Chana clung to Meyer. "He's coming with us."

Elias looked at her. "Why on earth would we do that?"

"If we leave him, Kirill will kill him, or he'll die from his wound." Chana's heart wouldn't let her turn her back on Meyer now. Even if they couldn't be together, she needed to know he was alive.

More people had gathered near the alley's edge, onlookers and hotel guests, some in bedclothes and robes, who'd fled the fire.

"Lift him," she said. "We have to get out of here."

They hoisted Meyer up, and he moaned.

"If you can walk at all," she said through gritted teeth, "you have to help us."

They mostly dragged Meyer to the truck, and with Johan, they lifted him into the back bed.

Chana gave one last look at Kirill to make sure he was still down and spotted the ledger poking out of his pocket. With an arm clutched to her side, she hurried over and grabbed the book. He didn't stir. She scanned the entries in Meyer's handwriting, then hurled the ledger into the fiery kitchen.

When she returned to the truck, Elias told her to ride inside the cab, but she refused. She climbed into the back with Meyer, covering him with a blanket.

Johan passed her his jacket. "Press this on the wound. And keep that burned arm under the blanket and away from the wind."

Johan and Elias got in the cab, and as they pulled onto the street and drove away, fire trucks rounded the corner.

From the direction they took out of the city, she knew they were headed for the farm in Dürnstein. They had nowhere else to go. A hospital would involve the authorities, and she didn't trust it. Also, she feared Kirill would easily find them if they went to a hospital—they'd let Kirill live, and she had a feeling that choice would haunt them.

They traveled under an inky sky, lit only by a few stars. Meyer's skin grew ghostly white. She kept pressure on his wound and called his name repeatedly. "Don't leave me," she said, praying her words got through to him. Elias looked back from the cab. Chana couldn't tell if Elias had heard her. Not that it mattered.

When they hit a bump, she winced, and Meyer didn't react. She bent her face to his and felt his faint breath on her cheek. Blood from her face dripped onto his blanket as she clamped down on his wound.

"Stay with me, Meyer." She told him, "I love you. I do, and I always will," because if he died, she needed those words to be the last he heard. Otherwise, she would never forgive herself.

Johan tended to Meyer as soon as they carried him into the house, placing him on the same table where she'd eaten dinner with the family.

"He's lucky," Johan said.

She couldn't understand. He'd been unconscious for the entire ride. Cold and pale. He must be dying.

Johan inspected Meyer's abdomen. "The bullet went straight through. We'll clean it, sew him up, and pray."

What happened over the next two days were mere fragments in Chana's mind. They forced Meyer to swallow a few mouthfuls of vodka to handle the pain, then Chana and Elias held him down while Ursula gently cleaned the wound and Johan stitched him up. He jerked some, but mostly remained unconscious. Johan treated the burns by slathering on a layer of Vaseline.

"There's not much else we can do without a doctor." Johan wiped his hands on a towel.

Summoning a doctor could bring the attention of the authorities. Chana recalled the couple who spoke about the Kielce pogrom. They'd believed the officials, police, and soldiers, had arrived to help them. They'd been wrong.

Together, they decided to wait and see how Meyer was in the morning.

Johan and Elias moved Meyer to a bedroom. At some point, Ursula insisted on washing Chana's battered cheek, stitching the gash, and applying a bandage. She also chipped off a chunk of ice from the ice-box, wrapped it in a rag, and applied it to Chana's ribs, where the skin was tender and bruised.

Chana and Elias barely spoke. He cleaned up and fell asleep for the better part of a day and night. When he woke, it was with deep circles under his eyes and cuts and bruises on his face.

She stayed by Meyer's side, settled in an armchair in his room. There were moments when he was overcome with fever and shouted for Dora, his sister. A few times he called for Chana, and she'd never heard her name spoken with such pain. Per Johan's instruction, for a few minutes each day, she placed a cold, wet towel on his burns. Johan claimed it would help his healing.

On their second night in Dürnstein, Meyer opened his eyes. She was in the chair, almost asleep. A candle flickered on the small table beside him, and he tried to lift his head.

"Chana," he called.

She came to him. "Don't move."

"How?" He sounded like he'd swallowed rocks.

"We got you into a truck."

He worked to speak. "No. You? Cheek?"

"Kirill." She touched the bandage and thought of the gash she'd landed on Kirill's face with the pipe. "You're in Dürnstein. We're with Elias's parents. Kirill shot you."

He tried to sit, but only ended up gasping in agony.

"You mustn't move. Elias's parents tended to your wound and to the burns on your arm. The bullet went through your side. If it doesn't get infected, you'll be all right."

"It's impossible."

"Yes." She smiled despite the throbbing in her cheek.

His head shifted in tiny increments as he took in the room, spare with only a night table, the bed, and her chair. "How long have I slept?"

"Two days."

His hand searched under the quilt, eyes widening as he found the large bandage over his abdomen, and the second one covering his forearm. Those bandages were all he was wearing; Johan and Elias had undressed him.

"I'm sorry," he said. Tears leaked from his eyes.

She dried his face and helped him sip some water. "You should sleep."

"Where's my coat?"

"In the corner. The sleeve was burned off. I was going to get rid of it."

"Don't." Panic filled his eyes.

She picked up his coat and pinched around the seams, detecting pebble-sized bumps in the hem. When the Nazis were headed for Vilna, people had buried large valuables in their yards and sewn jewelry into the linings of their clothes. No wonder Meyer was worried about the coat. "Here it is." She spread the coat at the foot of the bed. Relief washed over his face.

His eyes sought hers. "Were you leaving me for him? Are you in love with Elias?"

"No." She regretted the times she'd wished she could love Elias. "I'm not."

His next breath made his body shudder, and he winced. "I saw my sister."

She took his hand. "You did?"

"I thought I must have died."

It must have been when he was delirious. "Tell me about it."

"I told her I was sorry I hadn't been able to save her, and how hard it was to be alive when they were all gone. Dora smiled at me; she had the most beautiful smile. She told me not to apologize, but to live a good life. To do so for both of us." He fell silent, depleted.

"When you fought Kirill for that gun, you saved my life," Chana said, not daring to say more. She recalled telling Meyer that she'd wanted a man like her father, someone who loved with everything he had. This was what Papa would have done for her. She smoothed his blanket.

"I would do it again," he whispered, "and a million times. I would never let anyone hurt you. It would be impossible for me to go on living in a world without you in it."

Those were the most beautiful words anyone had ever said to her.

His eyelids drooped, then sleep came for him.

She wiped her face and watched his chest rise and fall. Her thoughts turned to her family, and she prayed Mama and Aron were safely on their way to Bremerhaven. She kissed Meyer's cheek and went back to the chair, staying close in case he needed anything. Chana wouldn't allow anyone to hurt him, either.

Chapter Thirty-Eight

Chana

Dürnstein, Austria
July 1946

A week later, Meyer was doing better, though still healing, and Elias wanted to leave for Switzerland as soon as possible and grew impatient with Chana's resistance. All week, the one thing that helped Chana keep her sanity was imagining Mama and Aron boarding a train in Linz, arriving in Bremerhaven, and within days, climbing onto a great ship that would carry them to America.

It was evening now, and Johan had just returned from Vienna. He gathered them all together in the bedroom where Meyer was recuperating to tell them what he'd learned. Chana hugged herself, wincing from her tender ribs, and praying her plans for her family had worked.

"The fire ruined the Empress Hotel kitchen, dining room, and most of the first floor," Johan said. "The hotel is closed. Luckily, the guests escaped with few injuries. A soldier broke his leg jumping from a second-floor balcony." He wiped his brow. "Kirill is alive. The authorities are acting on the assumption that Elias and Chana are dead, as they pulled unidentifiable remains from the wreckage."

Chana gasped, surprised that the authorities even knew she had been there.

Meyer whispered, "Grigory, Vlad, and Isaac." His face turned chalky.

Chana covered her mouth, fighting nausea as the horrors of that night flashed before her. "Have they arrested Kirill?"

Johan shook his head. "The authorities are looking for Meyer. Kirill told the police that Meyer had gone there to confront his fiancée, and in a jealous rage, he'd killed you both, setting the fire to cover it up."

"How did he know I was alive?" Meyer asked.

Johan said, "Someone on the street saw an injured man being lifted into a truck. Lucky for us, it was dark, and they didn't see who owned the truck."

"Good." Meyer rubbed the back of his neck.

"Why would Kirill concoct such a story?" Elias asked.

"Though he's set the authorities on me, I'm sure he hopes to hunt us down himself," Meyer said.

Johan turned to Chana. "I went to see Herr Heiss." He paused. "He said your mother and brother were inconsolable. Still, he put them on the train in Linz himself. They were safely on their way."

"They should be on the ship now, heading to America." A sob broke from Chana's throat. One day, she would send word to Aron and Mama that she was alive. She comforted herself by imagining their reunion, seeing her brother's face, hugging him close, and kissing her mother's velvety cheek. For now, it seemed Kirill was only interested in her, Meyer, and Elias—leaving her family alone. She prayed for this to be true.

They decided Meyer should move to the hidden bunker behind the barn. There were Soviet patrols in the area, and if he was a wanted man, it would be safest for all of them.

Elias said, "What if Chana and I come forward and go to the authorities? We've done nothing wrong."

"No," Chana said. "It's too dangerous."

"She's right," Meyer said. "We don't know who Kirill is working with, and I'm sure he wants to finish what he started. We'll all be dead."

A few mornings later, as had become her ritual, Chana brought Meyer breakfast in the bunker and stayed to talk. He ate scrambled eggs on toast while propped up on a pallet filled with straw. She perched on a stool nearby, quieter than usual and rubbing her hands together.

"What's worrying you?" he asked.

She sighed at how quickly he'd come to be able to read her. "I'm thinking about my mother and brother. What if Sergeant McManus has them detained in America? Or worse, what if he has them sent back?"

Meyer set aside his plate and locked eyes with her. "With us gone—me gone—the sergeant would have no interest in your family and no reason to disrupt their immigration. I didn't double-cross him, and their papers are legal and in order. Your uncle paid for their voyage. I'm sure when they arrive in America everything will be fine."

His unwavering confidence unwound the knot in her chest. "You have an amazing way of easing my nerves."

"I'm glad." He sipped some tea. "Shall we talk of something brighter?"

"Like what?"

He thought for a moment. "Tell me something new about your life before the war. In Vilna. Something happy."

Chana pondered his request and told him about how when she was very young, she often rose early, before everyone in her family. A stray cat used to wander their building. Her mother hated the creature and would shoo it away. But in those early hours, Chana would seek it out.

"I would feed the cat a dish of milk," she told Meyer.

"How old were you?" Meyer asked.

"Seven, I think." Chana sat on the ground beside the pallet and tore off a bite of crust from Meyer's plate. "I drew a picture of it for a contest at school."

"What happened?"

She smiled, recalling the pencil sketch with its slightly misshapen head, triangled ears, and overly large eyes. "Teacher placed a blue ribbon on it. I'd never won anything before, or since."

"Unforgettable." His gaze lingered on her face before he set down his tea.

She ate the bread, then dusted the crumbs from her fingers. "Mama said at least the cat had done something to earn all that milk I'd been sneaking from her kitchen."

"She knew all along. Mama Rosenzweig was shrewd even then." He laughed. "And what became of the cat?"

"He tired of my stories and set out to prowl another building."

"Foolish animal."

It was strange this connection between her and Meyer. They'd known each other for months in Vienna, yet here in Dürnstein they were truly getting to know one another.

"Your turn," she said.

He put a finger to his lips. "There is a day that I recall when we were all of us together. It wasn't long before the war. My father surprised us by closing his store during the week . . . something he never did. He drove us to the country for a picnic. Also something we never did. My mother packed us a feast. Eggs, sandwiches, pickled vegetables, and a cake. We ate in a field by the side of the road. We even played a game of tag. All of us." He smiled. "Dora had a part-time job at a school. It was a job my father detested, because it meant she wasn't settled with a husband and children of her own. Usually, he cut her off when she tried to tell us about it. That day he listened."

"It sounds wonderful." She could picture them all, piled on a blanket, eating, or running around the field. She imagined his sister, the girl who'd wanted to be a teacher, talking to her family as the sun highlighted the gold in her blond hair.

Meyer faced Chana. "It was wonderful. Thinking back on it, my father must have sensed our lives were about to change. Dora lost her job, and my father lost his shop. It wasn't long after, my family was forced into the ghetto. By then, I'd already left for the army."

She placed her palm on his cheek. "Thank you for sharing that story with me."

They held each other's gaze, until he cleared his throat, struggling to speak, but finally he whispered, "Chana?"

"Hmm?"

"You're the most beautiful and amazing woman I've ever known."

Her heart expanded and she smiled slyly, peering at him through her lashes. "Stubborn, too, I hope?"

He smirked. "Yes, of course that."

Later, in the afternoon, Chana was in the back bedroom tending to the wound on her face when Elias came in.

"It will take only two days to get new papers for you," he said, getting right to his point.

Her traveling papers had been lost in the fire, while Elias had kept his papers in his pocket.

He squared his shoulders. "We're strong enough to travel and we should leave for Switzerland this week."

"Not yet," she said. Standing before the dresser mirror, she removed her bandage, revealing an angry two-inch scab below her eye from where Kirill's ring had cut her.

"When, Chana? When can we go?"

"Not until Meyer is well, too."

"Papa Johan and Mama Ursula have agreed Meyer can stay until he can travel."

Chana dipped a washcloth into a bowl of water and patted the cut, which stung and made her eyes water.

He told her, "It isn't safe here. If we're found, it will be bad for Papa Johan and Mama Ursula."

"I know." She dreaded harm coming to the Bohms.

"We should leave."

Unsteady footsteps came down the hall, and Meyer appeared in the doorway. "Elias is right. It's not safe."

It upset Chana to see Meyer this way, a man who had been as imposing as a forest pine, now battered, and bowed.

"See," Elias said, "we agree."

"Once I'm well, I'll take care of Kirill. He won't hurt anyone ever again."

Chana folded the damp rag. "Don't do it for me." Meyer's desire for payback would only bring more trouble. He had to see that.

Meyer gave her a strained smile. "If you want to leave, I won't stand in your way." He slowly shuffled back into the hall, a sight that pained her. Oh, how she loved him.

She looked at Elias, and his stunned expression let her know he had read her thoughts. "I heard you and Meyer talking this morning," he said. "In the bunker."

Chana squeezed water from the cloth. She couldn't bring herself to look at Elias. "Were you eavesdropping?" she asked, busying herself by running the washcloth over the cut again before reaching for a fresh bandage and pressing it to her cheek.

"I might have been. Your tender exchange surprised me." He pressed his fingers to his eyes for a moment. "What's going on?"

"Meyer and I . . ." She didn't know how to describe their relationship. They were in love. At least she hoped he still loved her. He hadn't said exactly that since coming to the farm.

"Oh." Elias bit his lip. "I see."

Guilt pressed on her, reducing her to the size of an ant. "I'm sorry, Elias. I never wanted or meant to hurt you."

"I should have believed you when you told me you weren't going to marry me." He swallowed. "It's all right."

She dabbed her eyes. "Is it?"

He met her gaze. "Chana, I never wanted to be your second choice. When I marry I want to be someone's first—loved the way I love, with a full heart. Do you understand?"

Tears blurred her vision. "You deserve that and so much more." She had expressed almost the same thing to Meyer on the night they got engaged. "I'm truly sorry. You've been my great friend and given me so much."

Though Elias's eyes were damp, he didn't appear angry. "Do you regret our plans?"

"No. If not for you, I would be on a boat with my mother, and she would dictate the rest of my life. If not Meyer, she would find some other man for me to marry, regardless of whether I wanted to. If I ever marry, Meyer or anyone else, it will by *my* choice and in my own time." Chana also believed that had she not shouted and distracted Vlad in the alley, Kirill would have killed Meyer that night.

He stood tall. "I'm going to leave for Switzerland tomorrow. You can still come with me."

She touched his cheek. "Thank you. I'm going to wait for him."

He glanced away and sniffled, his chest slowly rising and falling. "Of course." His voice was tight. "I'm going to miss you." He grasped her hand and lightly kissed her knuckles. "Promise me you'll continue baking."

"Always." Mama had told Chana she would bake for her husband and children. *We are women and we don't always get what we want, maidel.* No. That would not be Chana's lot in life. She would pursue her dream—a dream that had grown bigger, thanks to Elias. She vowed to fight for what she wanted, and when she broke through, she planned to pull other women up with her.

"We would have been brilliant partners," he said.

"I know." Fondness filled her voice.

He left her then.

Elias was right. They would have been wonderful together in all ways, except one—the place where her heart ruled. Because it belonged to Meyer.

*

By sunrise the next morning, Elias was gone, and Chana prepared toast and tea for Meyer and carried it to the bunker.

He was curled up at the far end of the room, on the pallet, clutching a blanket, his coat beside him.

Her footsteps startled him awake. "It's only me," she said. He leaned back and grimaced. "You mustn't move so fast." She placed her tray on a table.

"Where's Elias?"

"Heading to Switzerland. He left before dawn."

"You didn't go with him."

"No." She lit a candle on the table.

"Why not?"

"Because I'm my own person, and what I do with my life is my choice."

"How long will you stay?"

She perched on the stool. "Johan agreed to keep us until you're fully healed."

His eyes widened at her use of *us*. "Elias visited me last night. He told me he was going and you weren't, but I didn't believe him."

Chana was curious to hear about their conversation. "Did he say anything else?"

"He wanted me to know the whole truth before he left. He told me about his parents and how they'd sent him here with Johan and Ursula before the war. This war has stolen so many lives."

"Yes, it has."

"I'm glad Elias told me. We shook hands before he left. He told me to take care of you."

"Did he, now?" She noted the amusement in Meyer's eyes.

"Then we both agreed that you're very good at taking care of yourself." Slowly, Meyer's expression grew troubled. He ran a hand through his hair, and she could tell something was bothering him.

"What is it? What are you not saying?" she asked.

"Grigory is dead," he said. "Kirill will never stop hunting for us."

Terror marched up her spine. "That might be true, and I'll do what I have to for safety. But I want a life without this violence, Meyer. I won't look for it, and I won't live with it." She sat on the pallet and placed a hand on the blanket. If this man wanted to have a future with her, he would have to take up an honest profession and give up working outside the boundaries of the law.

He laced his fingers with hers. "Everything is different now," he said to their hands. "I'm no longer beholden to Sergeant McManus or anyone else. I'm free from that world."

When he lifted his eyes, she found relief that matched her own.

Chapter Thirty-Nine

Chana

Dürnstein, Austria
August 1946

The weeks following Elias's departure were quiet. August arrived and Chana's ribs had healed, as had the cut on her face, the latter leaving her with a two-inch red mark below her eye. She didn't mind as much as she thought she would. The Bohms and Meyer had expected her to let her hair grow out, detracting from the injury. Instead, two weeks after their arrival, she trimmed her hair to keep it short. It was easier, plus it marked the moment she'd taken control of her future.

Meyer healed and grew stronger, and as he did, he insisted on helping Johan around the farm. Chana assisted Ursula with gathering vegetables from the garden and tending the house. One morning when Chana was up before everyone else, she made *Varškės Spurgos*, a simple fried ball of dough using pot cheese Ursula had made by mixing milk with vinegar.

Ursula had been delighted. "They're delicious! Good enough to sell."

"Then perhaps we should," Chana had said.

Over the following weeks, the two women acted, baking every morning, and in the afternoon, Ursula sold their goods in town, their venture bringing in good money. As they worked, Chana shared more about her life before the war, and Ursula told stories about Elias's parents.

"It feels good to speak of them," Ursula said one morning. "I believe when I talk about Rivka that I'm honoring her memory."

"I feel the same when I talk about my father." Chana scattered flour on the table so her dough wouldn't stick. "I think those we've lost left their stories etched on our souls so we retell them and keep their memories alive."

On a morning in late August, five weeks after their arrival at the farm, Meyer sat at the table to watch as Chana and Ursula prepared *Pain Viennois*. Chana brought a mound of dough to him and said, "Watch me." She showed him her kneading technique, and after, she patted his shoulder. "It's all yours."

"What? You want *me* to do it?" From his rounded eyes, one would think she'd asked him to perform surgery on a conscious patient.

"Yes. This isn't a free show." Chana rejoined Ursula at the counter, thoroughly enjoying his befuddled smile. She hummed as she cracked an egg.

Meyer went to work, kneading the dough as she'd instructed, and did a decent job, at that. "What do you think of it?" she'd asked after she checked on him.

"I see why you enjoy it. And you're brilliant at it."

She beamed at his praise. "Ursula and I both do the work."

"Don't be modest. They're your recipes, you're in charge . . . As it should be." Their eyes met, sincerity coming off him in waves.

His compliment sent a buzzing through every part of her body. "Thank you." She smoothed his hair away from his eyes. "Now, back to work you go. We have bread to make." She winked, and he laughed.

For his part, Meyer also spent his time in Dürnstein schooling Johan on how to guard his crops and livestock against the black-market dealers still raiding the countryside. Meyer still slept in the bunker, though they all moved around more openly during the day, lulled by a sense that maybe the worst had passed.

Until an afternoon during the last days of August, when Ursula returned from town. She told Chana and Johan that men had been asking around about Meyer Suconick.

"Meyer went for a walk by the river. We need to tell him," Johan said.

He was right. Chana feared it might be Kirill and his men, having made the connection from Meyer to the Bohms. They needed to be ready, no matter what.

"I'll find him," Chana said.

Chana caught up with Meyer walking by the Danube. On guard, she listened for foreign noises and surreptitiously glanced about. "I have news."

His smile faded once he saw her concern. "What is it?"

"Ursula overheard men asking about you in the village today. I'm worried it might be Kirill. I told her what he looked like, but Ursula wasn't sure any of the men matched my description."

Meyer stopped. "And she's sure it was my name?"

"Positive." They walked in silence. Even in profile, she noted the tension on his face, and anger tightening his jaw. "We need to be careful."

He glanced around, then took her hand. "You're right. But right now, all I want is to walk with you. Can we do that?" They were utterly alone on a path by the river, wind whipping up whitecaps on the water. He added, "Just for a short bit. After, we'll talk to Johan and Ursula and plan what we need to do."

He was asking for a few stolen moments away from their reality. She could give him that. "All right, but not for long."

They carried on, walking along the river in silence, listening to the birds in the nearby trees and the water lapping along the bank. It wasn't but a few minutes until they reached the forest path leading back to the farm. They looked at each other and turned onto it.

Chana's toe caught on a twig, and Meyer gripped her arm to steady her, grimacing.

"Are you in pain?" she asked.

He kneaded his side. "Still a little sore."

"Let me help you." She went to skirt an arm around him in the way she'd done in the weeks after he'd been shot.

"I have a better idea." He held out his arm. "Let's help each other."

She looped her hand through his arm, relishing their closeness.

"We're like onions," he said.

"How so?"

"We've spent our time here in Dürnstein peeling back layers."

"And no one has cried," she said.

He laughed, and she realized she loved the low rumbling sound. Despite the foreboding of impending danger, she couldn't help but laugh, too.

He squeezed her hand, and she squeezed back. They climbed the path toward a break in the trees bordering the farm. This would likely be their last walk for a while; they'd need to be more careful around the farm and not take any chances at being discovered.

A car door slammed in the distance, alarming her. Cars never visited the Bohms, not since the three of them had arrived.

"Stop," she whispered.

Still hidden among the trees, they had a decent view of the barn and house. A car sat between both structures. A black-haired man in a suit came out of the barn, with Johan beside him.

Kirill. She would know him anywhere, and she was certain her frantic heart would break out of her chest.

"My car," Meyer said under his breath. "Bastard." He hunched forward, ready to charge.

Two more men left the barn.

Chana grabbed his arm. "No. If you go out there, they'll kill you. Johan and Ursula will die, too."

Meyer looked from her to the farm, his eyes narrowing. "I know you're right, but it feels wrong to let him leave." His fists clenched. A vein pulsed in his temple.

Kirill and the others walked to the car. The engine started. They were leaving without bloodshed. *Thank God!* But a nagging voice told Chana they'd be back.

Tires crunched against dirt and rocks. Meyer pivoted toward her. "We need to talk to Johan and Ursula."

"Yes."

They hurried as best they could to the farmhouse. Upon reaching the door, Chana took Meyer's hand. "Before we go in, I want you to know I'm proud of you for standing down."

"Why do you care, if you're not engaged to me anymore?"

"Oh, Meyer." Gently, she touched his cheek. "I've glimpsed the man you can be, and I love *that* man with all my heart."

He searched her face. "I was different before the war. I want to be that man again."

"Then don't let Kirill or your hate for him turn you into a monster." She envisioned the moment in the alley when she'd been poised to kill him but chose instead to go after Meyer. "Hate has created enough monsters already."

"I'm trying. But I'm not perfect."

She put a finger to his lips. "Nor am I." She pulled him in for a kiss. Their first since the evening he'd given her the emerald ring. His warm mouth tasted like the *Apfelstrudel* he'd eaten earlier. His fingers wove into her hair, and if she could have melted into him completely, she would have. In between kisses, they promised themselves to each other.

Once they were inside the house, Johan and Ursula said Kirill had asked when they'd last heard from Elias. The Bohms hadn't fallen for his trick. According to Johan, Ursula burst into tears, and they told him of how their son had died in a fire at the Empress Hotel. Kirill didn't refute Elias's death, but still insisted on searching the farm. He'd left them with a warning. "If a man named Meyer Suconick shows up here, you'd better be in touch. I'd hate for your wife to weep because she lost her husband, too." He left them with the name of a man to contact in the village.

Dinner was solemn. After their meal, Chana and Meyer informed the Bohms they would leave for Switzerland by the end of the week. Johan took on securing traveling papers for them. Speed would be costly, but Meyer assured him he could pay, and directed him to a forger in nearby Spitz.

When it came time to go to sleep, they all agreed it would be prudent for both Chana and Meyer to stay in the bunker, in case Kirill or his men returned.

Johan went to get an extra mat for Chana, but she told him it wouldn't be necessary. No one questioned the comment, though she caught a glint in Meyer's eye.

Alone together underground, she stretched out beside him on the pallet, and he told her what she'd already guessed—he'd sewn diamonds and gemstones into the hem of his coat. "On my last trip to Belgium, I met with a friend who sells diamonds. I traded all my cash for stones. Insurance for a new life."

"Is my ring in there?"

He grinned. "It's in the lining under the breast pocket, along with the wren."

By the flickering of a single candle, they kissed, and a tug of desire spread low in her belly. They were in each other's arms when she went to pull off his shirt, but he moved her hand.

"What's wrong?" she asked.

"We don't have to," he said.

"I want to." No words had felt truer.

His cheeks grew pink, and he lifted the arm that had been burned in the fire. "It's hideous. This can't be what you wanted."

"I'm the same, but we survived." Her voice was firm. "You're everything I want." Gently, she lifted his shirt over his head and feathered her fingers over the rough skin. "There's nothing you have to hide from me. Ever."

He kissed her hungrily, his lips traveling along her neck and heating her skin. His touch was nothing she'd ever experienced before. They were starving for each other, and in that bunker, they came together, two war-torn, scarred souls discovering and healing in each other.

Chapter Forty
Chana

September 1946 to 1956

Two days later, Johan had the papers they needed. They were to be Michel and Clair Girard—a married couple.

That they weren't actually married didn't matter. It was something they planned to remedy as soon as possible. Now marrying Meyer was what *she* wanted. She loved him, had faith in his ability to change, and couldn't imagine a future without him. As was true in the plan for Elias and Chana back in July, Johan would drive them to the border of Switzerland, where they would cross on foot.

They took little with them, a sack with clothes, two loaves of bread, a hunk of cheese, apples, and water. Chana carried the money she'd saved from selling baked goods with Ursula. Meyer folded his coat with the damaged sleeve mended and the gems sewn inside, and packed it in a sack, which he slung tight across his body.

Hugging Ursula goodbye was a teary affair. "I owe you so much," Chana said.

Ursula dabbed Chana's face the way a mother would. "Follow your passion, my girl. Promise me."

It was as though Papa were speaking through this tender woman. "I promise."

Later, when Johan let them out at a point with the Swiss border check in sight, they hugged.

"I can never repay you," Chana said.

"Take care of each other," Johan said, and shook Meyer's hand.

Together, they crossed the border and became Clair and Michel, never to use their real names again. She paused and took in the lush greenery of a distant meadow and a range of snowcapped mountains behind it. With a glance back, she saw the small wooden hut serving as a checkpoint, a few soldiers, and a road. Their past. Taking Meyer's hand, they ventured forward, the day's fading light bathing the nearest mountain in a magical pink hue. So beautiful it almost didn't seem real.

Of course, Chana couldn't help imagining Johan Bohm arriving back at the farm.

He would check on the goats and chickens, as was his habit. After, he would sit for a late supper with Ursula. Perhaps she'd heat a stew, something comforting for a day filled with goodbyes. After the meal, he would sit by the fire and pick up the book he had been reading for weeks. In the spot where he'd left his leather marker, Johan would find the small pouch she and Meyer had left for him. Tucked inside were three diamonds. She doubted Johan would make a fuss. It wasn't his way. He'd simply slip them in his pocket and continue with his reading, as dear Ursula sat nearby knitting. It was a quiet life and one worth emulating.

A week after arriving in Switzerland, Chana, as the newly named Clair, along with her fake husband, Michel, boarded a train for France. They arrived in Paris by nightfall. Within days, Clair found work as an assistant in a bakery on the Left Bank, run by a Jewish man, Philippe, who'd survived Dachau. Philippe also gave Michel a job; he was to handle deliveries, picking up supplies, and working the front counter.

The three of them became fast friends.

A month after their arrival, on October 8, she and Michel were quietly married by a rabbi under a pergola serving as a chuppah in a courtyard behind a half-bombed-out library. Claire circled Michel seven times, and in her mind, the ritual created a wall of protection around both of them.

A few nights after their wedding, they were in bed in their tiny apartment, exhausted after a long day at the bakery. Clair lay in Michel's arms, mumbling into his chest about changes she wanted to make to a pie recipe. She could barely keep her eyes open. Work at the bakery was hectic, and the rationing of oil and sugar affected their daily work, but she adored every minute.

Michel must have thought she'd fallen asleep, because he kissed her hair and said, "I love you and I'll never stand in the way of your freedom again."

He'd apologized to her many times for their earlier forced engagement. "I know," she whispered.

"You're awake?"

"I never want to miss hearing you say, *I love you.*" She nuzzled closer, knowing in her soul that her beloved husband would keep his promise for the rest of her days.

The next eight months in Paris were happy, despite ongoing rationing, and as long as Clair didn't think too hard about Aron and Mama. She and Michel spent their days in Philippe's bakery, working hard to provide bread to those in a queue that often stretched from the counter to the sidewalk outside. Evenings, they explored the City of Lights. They marveled at the Eiffel Tower and the Arc de Triomphe. They drank cheap, watered-down wine with artists and writers who'd newly returned to the Left Bank. They took long walks along the Seine, and when they returned to their apartment, they made love.

Those months were the first in years that Clair felt safe. In 1947, when she walked to work during her first spring in Paris, she passed gardens and drank in the sight of daffodils, tulips, and cherry trees bursting with pink and cream blooms. She'd stepped over sidewalks carpeted with fallen petals, dodged around bright orange butterflies, and daydreamed about opening her own bakery. She imagined contacting Aron and her mother, because surely that time would soon be at hand.

In May 1947, Clair was in the middle of her day at the bakery. She missed Michel, who had stayed home, having woken with a fever that morning. She was about to remove a tray of bread from the oven, while Philippe manned the front counter.

Clair opened the oven and hot air blasted her cheeks as the front bakery door jingled.

Philippe offered his usual singing greeting, "*Bonjour, monsieur.*"

She slipped the tray onto the cooling rack. It was unusual that the customer hadn't responded. Philippe's singing made even the grumpiest person smile.

Finally, a man said, "I'm looking for an old friend."

The hair rose on Clair's arms. The voice belonged to *Kirill.*

She inched toward the door that separated the kitchen from the shop front and peered through a crack. Kirill's back was to her, but it was him. Her legs were like jelly as she slipped into the back alley, still wearing her oven gloves and apron. She ran home and burst in on Michel making tea.

"I'm fine," he said, obviously assuming her worry was over his health. "Feeling much better."

"No." She struggled to catch her breath.

He looked at her and his smile faded. "What is it?"

"He's found us. Kirill. He came into the bakery, and I left out the back. I didn't even say goodbye to Philippe."

"I worried this would happen." Michel didn't sound surprised.

"Why?"

He paced. "A few weeks earlier I made a delivery to a wine merchant." He tugged his hair, and the color drained from his face. "I realized I had dealings with him before, as Meyer. I hoped he wouldn't recognize me. But word must have gotten to Kirill."

Chana's stomach sank as Michel glanced around their apartment. She knew what was coming before he uttered a word.

"We have to leave." He strode toward their bedroom. "Now!"

They grabbed clothes, including Michel's coat with the gems still in the lining and their meager savings hidden in socks, and stuffed everything into two sacks. Clair fumbled as she took her notebook, dropping it and retrieving it. It was where she'd been recording recipes—her gems.

They left through a back alley, and when she glanced around the building toward the street, she spied Kirill crossing, heading for their building with two other men. They hurried to the train station on foot, constantly looking over their shoulders. Their ten-minute walk felt like a week.

Three days later, they boarded a ship from Belgium to Australia.

Postwar, the Australian government had relaxed their immigration rules to draw British and European workers in an effort to grow their economy. Their voyage, on a former Australian naval ship, would take fifty-one days. Under their new names, Henri and Eveline Martin, they might finally be safe.

Within weeks of arriving in Sydney, Henri found a job in a coat factory, and Eveline was hired in a bakery kitchen. They rented a cheap room near the harbor, where mice were rampant.

Six months into living in Sydney, Eveline found it to be like no place she'd ever known. There was a bird—the king parrot—that dazzled her with its bright red body and vivid green wings; she thought her first sighting was a mirage. Eveline's favorite outings were her visits to Bondi Beach. She loved watching the surfers, marveling at their daring. But the vast and wild turquoise water intimidated her, and she would only dip in up to her calves. One afternoon, Henri coaxed her beyond the shallows, holding her tight. On the advice of a doctor, he always wore long-sleeved shirts to the beach to protect his scarred arm from the sun. Together, they dove under a wave, and Eveline emerged laughing and safe within her husband's muscled arms. They kissed, their passion tasting like salt, sunshine, and pure joy. She wiped water from her face as her husband tossed his hair back, and she thought, *I'm living in paradise.*

Two years later, in April 1950, Eveline and Henri opened their first bakery. To realize this dream, their first Martin Bakery took all their savings and their last gemstones. They operated with just the two of them during that first year. Eveline manned the kitchen, and Henri the storefront.

In this first bakery, Eveline perfected the recipes she'd learned from Papa, Elias, and Philippe. Business grew steadily. Henri enrolled in night school at Sydney Uni, studying business, and three years later, in 1953, they had a half dozen employees and plans for a second bakery.

Eveline's and Henri's lives were expanding in every way, save one. They were eager to start a family, but struggled. Eveline worried that her years in the Vilna ghetto, or her time at Stutthof, had broken her in this way. Doctors assured her that there was nothing physically wrong, and in due course, she would likely conceive. Henri saw a specialist as well, and was told the same. They focused on the bakeries, and in spring 1955, as they began work on a third store, Eveline and Henri found out that she was pregnant. They were overjoyed.

Henri carefully asked, "Do you think we should postpone the third bakery? You'd have more time to rest."

"Absolutely not." Eveline was twenty-eight years old and healthy. "If the doctor orders me to cut back, I will. But he says I should be fine nurturing our unborn child and our new bakery."

"All right," Henri said.

When she was in labor at the hospital, Henri's blustering reached her from out in the waiting room.

"What do you mean I can't go in there?" he yelled. "That's my wife! She's having my child!" Anger and defiance filled his voice, a sound belonging to a different time and place.

It was the only time she'd heard Meyer's fury since they'd left the continent, and what she detected under all his shouting was fear. Fear that he could lose another person whom he loved.

Later, in her hospital room, a nurse placed her baby, a warm pink-blanketed bundle, in Eveline's arms as Henri stood beside the bed. The nurse left them alone as Eveline gazed into her infant daughter's face. There she met Papa's inquisitive eyes, Aron's bow-shaped mouth, and Mama's full cheeks before the war had hollowed them. She looked at her husband and imagined he saw his family as well, his parents or sister, Dora.

"Rosenzweig," she whispered. "Rose."

Henri grinned. They had discussed names, but hadn't settled on one. She locked eyes with him. "I think we should name her Rose Dora Martin."

Tears clung to his lashes. "Yes," he said, and rubbed his nose. His chin quivered. "I never—" He brought a fist to his mouth as he struggled to compose himself. "I never thought I deserved this happiness. This love. This joy. *Her. You.*" He gazed at Eveline. "Thank you for saving me."

"We saved each other, my love." They kissed tenderly.

Eveline also thought back to what Meyer had said on that long-ago day in Vienna's train station.

Build your lives back. That will be your sweet revenge.

It was indeed.

In ten years, she and Henri had worked hard to build this life and family. They'd grown comfortable and were better off than many. "I think it's time I find Mama and Aron."

Worry deepened the new lines around Henri's eyes. "I know. But let's be careful. Just in case."

Blood whooshed into her ears as Kirill rose in her mind. She hadn't considered him in ages, but Henri was right. She kissed the sweet folds on Rose's neck and delighted in the softness of her skin. There was more at stake now than ever.

Chapter Forty-One

Zoe

Vienna, Austria
April 2018

Early sunlight slipped through the kitchen windows. Morning. Zoe and Henri had finished the croissants hours ago. They sat perched on stools, facing each other. Her muscles ached from tension and from sitting for so long. She stood.

Henri unbuttoned the cuff of his right sleeve, and after a moment's hesitation, he folded it back. Scar tissue covered the skin above his wrist. Zoe lifted her eyes and found he was staring at her. With deliberate movement, he rolled the sleeve up to his elbow. Waxy raised marks, from pink to deep purple, roped around his forearm. The type of scars one would have from surviving a fire.

"In 1956, Eveline hired a private detective to find Aron," Henri said. "We learned he was in New Jersey and was engaged. We secretly sent word to Aron through Peggy York-Black."

"Peggy gave Grandpa Aron the soccer ball." Zoe locked eyes with Henri. "Did my grandfather ever see his sister?"

"Not right away. Because Kirill Volkov had left Europe, too. He went to New York and changed his name. He became very powerful and very dirty. A leader in organized crime. We were certain he was watching Aron. After a few more years, in 1961, she and Aron finally met. He'd married your grandmother by then. Unfortunately, Ruth had already passed away." Henri asked, "By chance, do you remember your grandfather's Grocers Association conferences?"

In her mind's eye, she saw all the keychains he'd bought her. "I remember."

"She would meet him in those conference cities. Aron would skip out of meetings and carefully find his way to her hotel, where they would catch up. They'd share family photos and stories from their lives." He smiled. "Despite time and distance, they were as close as ever."

She pictured Grandpa Aron and his sister in a nondescript hotel room in Cleveland or Pittsburgh, huddled together and trying to make up for years spent apart. How awful for her grandfather to have had to keep everything about Chana a secret from Grandma Tess, Zoe's father, and herself.

"Did you go, too?"

He shook his head. "Those meetings were for them. And we worried if we both went it would be too dangerous. We had our daughter to think about in case anything happened. We wanted to protect all of you."

"Protect us." She braced against the counter, and her thoughts suddenly careened into the stuff of Hollywood thrillers. She considered the accident that had killed her parents. It had never occurred to her—not once—it might have been intentional. "What about my parents? Did Kirill have something to do with their . . ." She couldn't bring herself to finish the sentence.

"No. He didn't. We hired an investigator after their accident. He was thorough."

"If only Chana had gone with you to America to begin with," Zoe said.

"She and I talked about that many times over the years. But she and I always came around to this being the way it had to be. If we'd gone to America with Ruth and Aron, I might have ended up a criminal, an organized crime thug . . . or dead. And as for Aron . . ." He slid off his stool. "She had reason to be concerned for her brother's future. It was possible he would have followed my lead. As Meyer Suconick, there was no way out for me, or for her if we'd married then."

Love for his late wife was clear on his face and in every word. Henri said, "When your parents died, we got word quickly, and she decided to attend the funeral. She hoped that Kirill had given up the hunt for us. It had been years, after all. I had concerns. Grigory had been the only person who meant anything to Kirill Volkov. But she wouldn't listen. Later, she told me she couldn't get over seeing you."

"Me?" Zoe could barely get the word past the emotion blocking her throat.

"You took her breath away. Aron had shown her pictures over the years, but looking at you in real life was like looking at her younger self. You resemble her so much."

Zoe's thoughts turned to her parents' funeral, the awful day coming to her in flashes. She'd been grieving, but she would have noticed the resurrection of a dead great-aunt. "She wasn't at the funeral or the cemetery. Grandpa Aron would have recognized her."

He nodded. "She drove to the cemetery from the airport. You were all at the graveside. Her plan was to wait until after the service to approach your grandfather, but when everyone lined up to toss dirt onto the caskets, she saw Kirill. We didn't know how he found out about the funeral." Henri clenched his fists. "The bastard's dead now. He can't harm anyone ever again." He paused. "Every year on the anniversary of your parents' funeral, he sent Aron a card printed in Russian. We all believed they were warnings."

Her body buzzed as she remembered the postcards she'd discovered written in Russian. "I found four of them in a box after my grandfather died."

"After the first card, Aron refused to meet Eveline. He was afraid Kirill would strike out at you and your grandmother. Every few months, Eveline sent your grandfather a case of Fudgies with a letter hidden inside. She tried to convince him to move to Australia with you and your grandmother. He refused. Aron didn't think a move across the world would be best for either of you. It took two years before they met again."

"What was Kirill's new name?" Zoe asked.

"Andrei Lenkov."

She didn't recognize it. "When did he die?"

"Your grandfather and Eveline died only days apart in February. Kirill died the week before they passed."

"How can you be positive he had nothing to do with my parents' accident?"

Henri hesitated before telling her, "Because Eveline confronted him."

"When?"

"Are you sure you want to hear it?"

Zoe's only answer was a pointed look.

Chapter Forty-Two

Eveline Martin

Vienna, Austria
February 2018

Eveline Martin stepped off the train in the Wien Mitte, Vienna's station near the city center. She was tired, having flown in from Australia on a private jet along with Lucy, her hired nurse. Instead of taking a chauffeured sedan, Eveline had insisted they take the City Airport Train, much like the way she'd arrived those many decades ago.

Being in Vienna now was different for Eveline. She wasn't fighting anymore. The end of her life was coming, and soon. She knew it not only because she was ninety-one years old but because of her diagnosis: inoperable lung cancer. Her bones were brittle, and it was harder for her to move and breathe. Her doctor had allowed this trip if her nurse accompanied her. But he'd warned, "I doubt you'll travel again." Lucy wheeled their bags through the train station and carried a portable oxygen tank in case Eveline needed it.

Outside, the years seemed to peel away, and once again she was a nineteen-year-old girl desperate for a future after so much loss. The spirit of Chana Rosenzweig came to roost in her body.

Her breath became labored, and she told Lucy, "Perhaps we should find a taxi."

"Good idea," Lucy said with a reassuring smile.

"The Empress Hotel," Eveline told the taxi driver. The vehicle smelled of menthol, not a bad scent, considering her breathing difficulties.

"You have an interesting accent," the taxi driver said, his ears sticking out from a knit cap.

"I'm from Australia," she said, leaving out it was by way of Lithuania, Poland, Germany, Austria, France, and Belgium.

"What brings you to Vienna? Business? Pleasure?"

Lucy took in the view as they wound through the city.

Eveline met the driver's gaze in the rearview mirror. "Business."

At the hotel, Eveline settled into the penthouse and Lucy went to her room on the floor below. The oxygen tank rested on the living room coffee table. The luxuries she and Henri could afford never ceased to amaze her. She'd once occupied a space in Nachmann's boardinghouse smaller than the penthouse's main bathroom, and she'd shared it with her mother and Aron. Thinking of her brother brought a familiar tenderness to her heart, while memories of Mama stirred more painful emotions.

The year after learning of her mother's death, grief had overwhelmed her. Guilt and regret, too. There were days she couldn't get out of bed, and at one point, she hadn't stepped into any of their bakery kitchens in weeks. It was after a month of this, in the middle of the night, that Henri had bundled her, still in her pajamas, into the car and driven her to their first bakery. He prepared a mound of dough, and told her, "You do the rest."

"I can't."

"It will help you."

"Nothing will help." She propped against the counter, exhausted.

"Try." He guided her hands onto the cold, firm dough. It gave her a shock, after which muscle memory must have kicked in, because she began to press down, finding comfort from the dough against her palms. Henri massaged her back and hummed a soft tune while she worked.

"Papa had a melody he would sing while he baked," she said.

"I don't think you've ever told me that. Can you sing it for me?"

She hummed as if Papa had sung it to her only yesterday. Henri joined in. Eveline wished she'd contacted her mother and brother sooner. But anytime she said as much to Henri, he reminded her they'd done everything to keep Aron and Ruth safe.

Now she opened her suitcase and took out the red, shoulder-length wig. Time to get on with it. She changed from her cream slacks and silk blouse into a pair of stretchy black pants and a loose cobalt-blue tunic. The wig was next. She pinned up her shoulder-length gray hair. Her blond had been gone for years. Heavy makeup followed, much heavier than she usually wore; today it had to conceal the scar under her eye. She'd never covered it, and over the years the mark had faded a little. Wrinkles obscured it even more.

When done, she assessed the results in the mirror. She had been many women over her life. Chana, Clair, and now Eveline. She met her amber eyes in the reflection, the unchanged part of her, where she still saw Chana Rosenzweig, a girl who before the war had been her father's favorite. A young woman with an innate ability for baking.

Eveline called Lucy's room and told her she planned to nap for the next few hours and wasn't to be disturbed. Then she left the suite, leaving her oxygen tank behind. She could manage for a short time without it.

At the hospital, Eveline gave the woman at the welcome desk her fake identification, and she received a sticker with a photo for her to put on her shirt. For this trip, she was Sophie Deleon, formerly her old friend Shifra.

Though fear of Kirill had kept her from getting in touch with Sophie, Eveline knew her friend had stayed in Vienna for a few years after the fire and eventually made her way to Portugal.

The woman at the desk told Eveline to go to room 314.

At the door to that room, Chana listened to a loud rattling breath from within, and the beeps and whines of machines. Her investigator had told her Kirill Volkov, aka Andrei Lenkov, had moved back to Vienna in the fall, something about evading U.S. prosecution on some old crime. He'd been in a nursing home, but a few weeks ago, they'd moved him to the hospital. He was nearing the end, this monster who'd plagued her nightmares and her days.

The deaths of Aron's son and daughter-in-law had haunted Eveline. Her investigator assured her the car crash was an accident. *But could he be sure?* People like Kirill Volkov got away with heinous crimes all the time.

She couldn't go to her grave without the truth.

Kirill had grown richer, more powerful and dangerous with each passing year, first in Europe, and then in New York. She and Henri felt some security being on the opposite side of the world in Australia. But their privacy was essential to their safety. They went to great lengths to make sure their photos were never published. And nondisclosure agreements became a standard part of their hiring process. They never spoke the names Meyer and Chana, not even to each other.

She received word of her nephew's accident within a day of it happening, giving her enough time to fly to the U.S. on their corporate jet. When she spotted Kirill shaking her brother's hand and touching her great-niece's hair, the shock had almost knocked her over. In the girl's face, Eveline saw her own. Her childhood self. The girl she'd been before the war.

She crossed into his hospital room.

He lay propped up in bed, a man reduced to skin over bones. His oblong head had seemed oddly large years ago and was even more so now, with most of his hair gone. An oxygen cannula was under his nose and his eyes were closed. According to the investigator, he was blind and had a failing heart—not that he ever had one—and his death was imminent. Days, maybe a week.

"Who are you?" he asked in accented English, his voice raspy. "Are you another nurse?"

He must have heard her enter. She forced a smile even as her temples throbbed. "Kirill, don't you recognize your old friend Sophie?" she said, using his old name.

"I don't recognize anyone. I'm blind."

She sank into the chair a few feet from the bed. His eyes were filmy and unfocused. He had a scar on his cheek as well, pink and ugly, and she wondered if it was from the pipe she'd used to strike him.

"How'd you know I was here?" he asked.

"My niece is a nurse in this hospital. A strange coincidence," she said, using her practiced script. "I'm here for a visit."

Silence stretched between them, leaving her to wonder if he'd fallen asleep. Eveline grew tired. She wanted to get to the point of her trip. Finally, she said, "I drove by the old marketplace yesterday. It's a lovely open square now."

He grunted. "I made a lot of money there."

"Yes." She hoped to guide the conversation toward herself and Meyer. "I also visited the Empress Hotel. It's amazing how they rebuilt it."

"The fire." Kirill's tone had turned guttural. "Do you remember my brother?"

"I do," she said, stifling a shudder.

"I lost him that night." He shifted. "Because of Meyer."

Eveline waited, not daring to speak.

"That son of a bitch. Meyer Suconick thought he was so much better than all the other dealers."

"You're right," she said to encourage him.

"I know I'm right." His eyes became slits. "He and that whore of his. They stole Meyer's ledger of contacts. I had to build from nothing." He fell quiet, then said ominously, "They're still alive."

She gripped the armrests. "How do you know?"

"I feel it." He adjusted the cannula under his nose. "I saw Chana's brother years ago. A funeral for his son and daughter-in-law. He looked at me as if I'd killed them."

She was desperate to ask the question she'd come for. "Did you?" Her voice was low and steady, though her insides were breaking apart.

He faced her with the same dead eyes as the first time he'd grabbed her all those years ago in the Vienna train station. "My tasty red cherry." He licked his lips. "You always kept my secrets." He motioned her closer, and she slid nearer.

He gave her a familiar menacing grin. "I went to the funeral believing that bitch would show up. Meyer, too. But they didn't." He coughed again. "No, I had nothing to do with their accident. I read their obituary in the newspaper. They ran Aron's name along with the couple's photo."

Relief washed over her. She had gotten her answer, and now all she wanted to do was leave.

His cheeks reddened. "I should have killed them all." He coughed, and it quickly changed to choking. His hand clutched the gown over his chest, and it was clear he was in distress. The call button was on the bed railing, and her hand got to it first. She had a split second to decide whether to call for help.

Hate has created enough monsters, she'd told Meyer all those years ago on the Bohms' farm. She would not be responsible for Kirill's death. She was not a monster.

Her finger smashed down hard on the button, and she stood, leaning near his face. She grabbed his finger and rubbed it across her scar. "From your gold ring on the night of the fire."

Recognition, rage, and hatred unfurled across his face. "You whore," he said in barely a croak. She let go of him as a nurse hurried in.

"He needs help," Eveline said.

Nurses and doctors converged on the room and Eveline moved into the hall, then over to the nurses' station. She waited. She didn't know if it was ten minutes, twenty, or longer until a nurse came over and told her, "I'm sorry, but your friend didn't make it."

Eveline bent forward as relief coursed through her, though the nurse surely read her reaction as grief, and patted her arm.

After, back in her hotel room, Eveline gulped oxygen until she had calmed. Then she picked up the hotel phone and called her brother. The sound of Aron's voice soothed her. She told him, "Kirill is dead. We're finally safe."

He wept.

"I can't wait to meet your family," Aron said.

"And I can't wait to meet Zoe."

"And Tess."

Aron's wife had been gone for a year, and it pained her to hear his confusion. But she sensed he'd absorbed most of what she'd told him. She said, "I love you . . . I'm grateful for every moment we had together." They spoke a few minutes longer and they were both crying when they said goodbye.

Eveline called her nurse next, and they headed back to the airport.

That night, Aron died in his sleep.

Eveline didn't find out until she'd landed back in Australia and Henri broke the news. Once home, her illness worsened. Bedridden, the oxygen tank became a necessity. She wanted to reach out to Zoe, but was too weak. Her family stayed with her around the clock, and while she still had the strength, she told Rose and Liam about the past, about her brother, and about Zoe.

Eveline's days and nights blended, and when light shone into her room, she gazed out the window at the blue heeler flowers in her garden.

"I wish I could go with you, my love," Henri said one evening, stretched out beside her on the bed.

She was too tired to speak, but ached to tell him it wasn't his time. When she had returned from Vienna, she'd made him promise to tell Zoe the truth.

"Can we trust her?" he'd asked.

"Kirill is dead. The danger is gone. Zoe is Aron's granddaughter. Trust her, please." She added, "It's time for you to come out of hiding."

Now, as the light in her room grew hazy, he kissed her lips. "I don't want you to be alone," he said.

Twice, she tapped two fingers on her chest. Tears ran down his face, and he nodded, understanding someone was waiting for her. *Aron.*

"I love you, Eveline. I have always loved you." He bent close and whispered, "Chana."

She believed she answered, "Meyer" when he pressed his cheek to hers. But Eveline was already surrounded by those she hadn't seen in years—Mama, Aron, and at last, Papa. Love and joy filled her. And there were others gathering. Those she only knew from stories. A girl with her arms held wide—beautiful, blond, and smiling. *Dora.*

It was time for Eveline to join them, and she took what she sensed was her last breath, knowing that eventually, when her husband's time came, they would all be there to welcome him.

Chapter Forty-Three

Zoe

Vienna, Austria
April 2018

"This is a lot to take in." Zoe had found Henri last night to tell him she'd quit her job rather than betray him. But these stories were beyond anything she'd ever imagined finding out. Only, now that she had, she couldn't wrap her mind around it, and felt as though the walls were boxing her in. "I have to go."

"Can we talk later?" he asked.

"I think so." She hurried out of the hotel kitchen and broke into a run until she locked herself in her room. She dropped onto the bed, not bothering to turn on any lights.

It was impossible to process all of this.

As Zoe looked back now, she guessed their move to North Carolina such a short time after the funeral was Grandpa Aron's response to seeing Kirill, the man who'd kidnapped him in Vienna. Her grandfather had framed their relocation as a fresh start for all of them.

In reality, they'd run away. Putting distance between themselves and Kirill. Zoe had lived in danger her entire life, only she hadn't known.

A text came in from Henri.

HENRI: **I need to know that you're all right. Are you?**

ZOE: **I will be, I think.**

HENRI: **Will I see you tonight? I saved you a spot at our table.**

The awards dinner. Henri wanted her to sit with his family. They were *her* family, too.

Zoe thought of Grandpa Aron's envelope. She had gone on this quest because her grandfather had marked it as important for her future. He'd wanted her to know that she had family. She wasn't alone.

ZOE: **I'm going to sleep now, but yes, I'll be at the awards dinner.**

HENRI: **I'm glad. I'll see you later.**

But before sleeping, and in an act of pure chutzpah, she wrote to Trudy Tuffin. She let Trudy know if she was still interested in working with Zoe that she had a different idea for a book that they could discuss, only if she got Henri's approval.

After hitting send, she slid into bed, pulling the covers to her chin. Physically and emotionally drained, she turned to her side and drifted off.

When Zoe woke, sunlight slanted across the bed. A *ping* on her phone drew her attention. It was from Trudy Tuffin.

> Zoe,
>
> I appreciate your note and am very interested in hearing more about your idea. If you get Henri Martin's blessing, let me know and we'll schedule a call. No promises, but I'm intrigued.
>
> Best,
> *Trudy*

Next, she opened a new text from the real estate agent.

> LINDA HICKS: Checking in—have you decided about the house?

If Zoe sublet her apartment and this book deal happened—her idea was to write a book about Chana Rosenzweig, aka Eveline Martin—she might not have to sell the house at all. Her imagination drifted forward to what could happen after she left Vienna. She interpreted Wes's silence since she quit as if he had heeded her warning against blackballing her. If so, she could get by for a time writing freelance articles and tutoring while looking for a new job. Tonight, she would ask for Henri's blessing on the book. If he agreed, then when she returned to North Carolina, she would write a book proposal for Trudy

Tuffin. If she was lucky, Trudy would take her on as a client, and eventually a publisher would buy it.

They were big *ifs*, but she wanted to take the chance.

> **ZOE:** I'm holding off. If I'm ever interested in selling, I'll let you know.

A smile lifted her lips. When she left Vienna, she would move back to her grandfather's house. She went to the window, where the graffiti hummingbird's rainbow colors appeared more vibrant. As if in the night, the artist had swept in and touched up the paint.

◦

In the evening, an awestruck Zoe maneuvered between tables in the Empress Hotel's grand ballroom. The room sparkled—from the tables draped in ivory linens threaded with silver to the metallic-edged china. Flickering candles surrounded crystal vases that overflowed with white roses, creating stunning centerpieces.

Zoe had chosen a navy sheath dress with a V-neck and nude-toned heels, her lucky late-afternoon purchases from a consignment store a few blocks from the hotel. Her hair was especially curly tonight, and she wore it down except for the right side, which was swept off her face and held back by the same jeweled-wren comb Meyer had once given Chana. Henri had brought it to her room earlier.

"But this was in the gallery case," Zoe had said as she put it in her hair.

"It was only on loan," he said. "She had wanted you to have it. You are the spitting image of her."

Zoe beamed at the comparison.

"There you are," Liam said, dashing past others in the ballroom. He looked splendid in a charcoal-gray suit, crisp white shirt, and burgundy tie. His gaze flitted to her hair. "I like the wren on you." He offered her his arm, and she happily let him guide her to the front of the room. They arrived at table one, set for eight. The others were all there: Henri, Rose, Jack, and Oliver. Rolf smiled at her, and beside him was Jacques Simon.

Henri walked over. "I'm glad you're here."

"I am, too." Zoe decided now was as good a time as any to bring up what she'd been considering all day. "Henri, I've been thinking about writing a book."

He watched her warily.

"I want to write about Chana. About her bravery. I know I don't need your permission now, but I want you on board. She was fierce and did so much with her life, despite everything trying to hold her back. She's an inspiration."

"She was, and I think it's time. She'd be all for it." He whispered, "I never want to stand in the way of your freedom."

It was what she had hoped for, and it echoed what he'd vowed to Chana all those years ago. "Thank you." She couldn't wait to create a proposal for Trudy Tuffin.

"We have more to discuss. Perhaps I'll even entice you to visit us in Australia."

"I'd like that."

"Good. Now there's someone dying to talk with you." He waved for Jacques to join them. "Zoe, I believe you met Jacques before my speech." He whispered in her ear, "You would also know him as Elias Bohm."

She'd been so overwhelmed by Henri's last stories she'd failed to ask what had happened to Elias. It all came together in her mind. The farm—now a vineyard! Incredible! "But how on earth did you two become friends?" she asked.

Henri offered her a sly smile. "Through Ursula and Johan, Eveline corresponded with Elias in Switzerland. She would read his letters aloud, and I'd begrudgingly listen. Over time, I came to look forward to them as much as she did." He shook his head at a memory. "In one letter, he wrote he followed Tottenham Hotspur. Living in Sydney, I'd become an Australian footy fan. I asked her to tell him ours was a much more exciting sport. She told me to do it myself."

"She meant you should write to him?"

He nodded. "Eventually, I did, and he wrote back."

"You became pen pals," Zoe said, amazed.

"And then we became friends."

Jacques grasped her hand and kissed it. "When I met you the other day, I couldn't get over how much you resemble her. Like traveling back in time. It will be a pleasure to get to know the grandniece of my dear friend." Emotion filled Jacques's eyes. "I knew Aron as well."

"I know." Zoe grew teary. She noticed a necklace dangling above his open collar with a saint medallion and a Star of David. She wondered when he'd reclaimed that part of his history.

Henri's daughter, Rose, broke into their group and hugged Zoe, while Jacques promised to talk to her more later.

"Welcome to the family," Rose said. "I'm looking forward to spending time with you. I'm your cousin, but I hope you'll let me step in for my mother and be a *tanta*."

Zoe tightened her embrace at the Yiddish word for aunt. She'd never had one. "I would love that."

A tap on the microphone caught everyone's attention, and the Boucher president announced, "If you would find your seats, we're ready to begin the night's festivities."

Henri ushered her to a seat beside him, with Liam on her other side. Beside her plate was a snow globe of the Sydney Harbour Bridge, adorned with a red ribbon.

She picked it up and looked at Liam. "From you?"

"To tempt you to visit," Liam said.

She shook the globe and smiled.

The Boucher president gave a long speech about the Martin Baking Company before inviting Henri to the podium, where she handed him a hefty crystal award and directed him to the microphone.

"Thank you for bestowing this honor on us," Henri said. "It's hard for me to accept this award. The person who deserved it most was my wife, Eveline Martin. Our bakery was her brainchild, everything a result of her talent and passion. I miss her every day." He gazed out at the audience. "Tonight, I'm grateful to have my beloved family with me."

He introduced them all, including Zoe Rosenzweig, his great-niece. Then Henri looked at her and with two fingers he tapped his chest twice, right over his heart. She repeated the gesture and let her tears fall.

He raised a glass of water. "Please join me in a toast." Everyone lifted their glasses. "To family and *l'chaim*, which means *to life*, the two most important things on earth."

Reprises of his toast rang out around the room.

Zoe sipped her wine and wished her grandfather and great-aunt Chana could see them all here together. A pleasant warmth swept up her back, and she took it as the universe's way of telling her they already knew.

Author's Note

I'm often asked at what age I realized my mother was a Holocaust survivor. My answer is simply that I've always known. There was never an aha moment. I grew up aware that my mother, Evelyn, along with my aunt and grandmother, had lived through unimaginable horrors.

By the middle of elementary school, I knew those horrors were because of World War II, Nazis, and being Jewish. In our home, the adults spoke Yiddish so the kids wouldn't understand. Sometimes, my mother and her sister, my aunt Helen, discussed their impoverished childhood. "We were poor as mice," my mother would say of lives in a faraway city named Vilna. Their father's parents and his eight brothers and sisters had immigrated to America long before the war. "Our father was meant to go, too," my mother said. "Only, the doctor examining him for his visa application denied it, because of a harmless birthmark on his eye." His name was Aron, and my mother often showed me the framed 8×10, black-and-white photograph of this grandfather I'd never met. We kept the picture in our guest room, where my grandmother, Gita, slept when she visited. Mom told me that the only reason she had any picture of him was because it had been sent to his family in America before the war.

My mother sparingly spoke of her war experiences. Her tale went something like this: the Nazis overtook Lithuania, which at the time was part of Poland, and as a result, my mother and her family were forced to live in a

Jewish ghetto. After a couple of years, the Germans liquidated the ghetto, emptied the city of all Jews, and sent them to a concentration camp. My mother and her family hid in an attic instead, along with several families. By the time I heard this, I'd read Anne Frank's *The Diary of a Young Girl.* When I made the comparison, my mother said in a somber voice, "Yes, it was just like that."

These limited details were all I knew until my sophomore year of college, when I took a class on Judaism. For a paper, I planned to interview my mother about her war experiences. I was home on a school break, and one afternoon, Mom and I settled at the kitchen table in the suburban New Jersey house where I'd grown up, and we talked about the war. For the first time, I took notes . . .

My mother was fifteen, and her sister was twelve, when the Nazis marched into Poland in 1941. Upon hearing of the German army's approach, my mother and her family fled Vilna. They wanted to reach the Soviet Union and walked with thousands of others for several days. Bombs dropped all around them. Finally, they were told to turn back by others who were already backtracking. Apparently, the Germans were advancing and there was no way to get through to the Soviet Union.

With nowhere else to run, they returned to Vilna, and soon after, they were herded into a Jewish ghetto, as the Germans were already in charge of the city. They lived with several other families in cramped quarters, surviving several German *Aktions.* Finally, the Nazis liquidated the Vilna ghetto, sending all the Jews to concentration camps. My family didn't leave as ordered. Instead, they hid in an attic for months. Eventually, they were captured, and sent to the Kovno ghetto. This was the first time I'd ever heard of their being taken to a second ghetto. When Kovno was liquidated, my mother, aunt, and grandmother were imprisoned in the Stutthof concentration camp. My grandfather had been killed during the liquidation of the ghetto. My mother didn't tell me the exact circumstances, and I knew not to ask. It would be several years until I learned how he was murdered.

Mom wept as she told me about arriving at Stutthof. Usually, our conversations ended then because she couldn't go on, and I couldn't bear to cause her pain. Only, that day, my mother continued . . .

She told me the Nazis put them to work digging trenches for railroads.

Once a day, they were fed watery soup and a thin slice of bread. A Nazi captain favored her because of her blond hair and hazel eyes, and he kindly gave her his lunch every day for two months. That alone might have saved her life. She spoke of horrid conditions, cruel soldiers, jealousy among prisoners, and one day when my grandmother was nearly beaten to death. They somehow found the strength to stay alive. About nine months after they were imprisoned at Stutthof, they were liberated by the Allied forces. Mom was nineteen by then, and her sister was seventeen. After liberation, they ended up in a displaced persons camp somewhere in Europe.

I expected the story to end there. I'd naively assumed that once the war had ended and they were liberated, the Red Cross had swaddled them in blankets and tenderly transported them to their family in America. I couldn't have been more wrong.

My mother described their eventual escape from the displaced persons camp. She, Helen, and Gita, along with about ten others, were smuggled out. It was some kind of organized effort, though she never revealed who was in charge. It happened under cloak-and-dagger conditions with forged papers and a long, perilous train ride, constantly in fear of detection.

They ended up in Vienna for nearly two years, where my grandmother's mission was to reach my grandfather's family in America. While in the city, my grandmother went every day to a place my mother only called "the consulate" in her attempt to find my grandfather's parents and siblings in the United States. For a long time, her search proved futile, though she never gave up.

The three found work in a hotel kitchen, and I will never forget my mother telling me, "A man dealing on the black market took an interest in my sister. He was a few years older than us, and our mother encouraged it. She wanted us to date, because the city was dangerous and we were three women alone. She said we needed protection." My mother told me he was a nice enough fellow, who also "stole chickens from farmers at night, only to sell them back to those same farmers in the morning."

My grandmother's claim about the dangers in Vienna and the need for protection echoed in my mind for years. During the war, my mother, aunt, and grandmother had survived deprivation, torture, and imprisonment in two ghettos and a concentration camp where tens of thousands were murdered. Small acts of resistance had helped them survive. Now the war was over, and as refugees, they faced continued hunger, new dangers, and again, they were trapped.

I believe my mother spoke more openly that day because it was for my class paper. And how appropriate that our conversation took place in the kitchen. It was where all the important family conversations took place in our home. I also think it was the room where my mother spent the most time. I can still picture her reading the Newark *Star-Ledger* at the table. Or standing by the stove, often frying something, with a cigarette in an ashtray at her elbow, clad as usual in a cobbler apron over her blouse or dress. Her hair was still as blond as ever.

Over the following decades, I often wondered what was so dangerous about Vienna and postwar Europe. Why did my grandmother feel they needed the protection of a man? Why couldn't they leave Europe?

When my mother passed away in 2000, I worried that her untold stories had died with her. But in the decade following her death, my aunt and my father told me more.

Periodically, I would research the different cities, ghettos, concentration camps, and circumstances for postwar survivors. I discovered that my family wasn't alone in their plight to leave Europe. There were many Holocaust survivors who had nowhere to go. No homes. No countries where they felt safe or welcome. Thousands languished in displaced persons camps for years. Many were also desperate to get out of Europe.

In time, my research filled in the gaps in my mother's stories. I learned details that she never told me. I discovered it was likely the Brihah organization that had smuggled them out of the displaced persons camp. Vienna was a way station on one of Brihah's routes to the ports in Italy, where illegal boats transported refugees mainly to Palestine, and some to America and to Canada. I found that, in 1946, the lack of food and resources in Austria, and much of Europe, was much worse than I'd known. And because of limited and discriminatory emigration quotas, Jewish survivors struggled to find overseas relatives and were mostly denied visas. Like my grandmother.

Also, in Vienna at that time, there was a rampant black market, widespread poverty, continued antisemitism, and a devastating number of assaults against women. I finally understood the dangers and the reasons for my grandmother's directive to her daughters to date, so they'd be protected. I thought of the black-market dealer. Many what-if questions followed.

What if my mother and aunt had refused to date?

What if a woman in that circumstance didn't want to date at all?

What if a woman wanted something else for her life after years of war, torture, and deprivation?

I've wanted to be a writer since I was in elementary school, and I've always had a deep-seated belief that someday I would tell my mother's story. I struggled for many years with the best way to do so. It is from my grandmother's quest for safety and those what-ifs that *The Lost Baker of Vienna* emerged.

My mother, aunt, and grandmother were the strongest women I've ever known, and I've poured their strength into Chana Rosenzweig, the novel's main historical character. My family's resilience, during the war and after, inspired this novel. The Rosenzweig family's path through the war was my family's path: Vilna, Kovno, Stutthof, a displaced persons camp, and Vienna. The fate of Chana's father in the Kovno ghetto was the fate of my grandfather, and I've depicted it almost exactly as it happened in real life. It was the hardest scene I've ever written. Many of my mother's stories inform Chana Rosenzweig's life, from her childhood through the war and her work in a Vienna hotel kitchen.

In 2018, I went to Vienna to research this book. I stayed at the Hotel Imperial, chosen because it would serve as the inspiration for the Empress Hotel in this book. I toured the city, wanting to see it as Zoe Rosenzweig would. At the time, I—like Zoe—was working as a food writer.

I began writing this book in March 2020, at the beginning of the pandemic. As the world settled into lockdown, I feared what the next week, month, or year would bring. I also missed my mother deeply. Fleshing out my mother's experiences gave me strength and a better understanding of her. In a way, researching this book brought her back to me. For the next three years, I wrote and explored the past with a tightened focus: to tell my mother's stories while accurately depicting the Jewish refugee experience in postwar Europe. I gathered information from current and archived articles, books, and historical texts. I reached out to history experts at museums around the world, who generously reached back with guidance and information. Adina Seeger, a curator at the Jewish Museum Vienna, was particularly helpful in answering my questions on Jewish refugee immigration to the United States after World War II.

In early 2024, I returned to Austria. At the time, I was working on revisions with my editor and I was eager to revisit the places featured in the book. I traveled to the Wachau Valley to see Dürnstein for the first time; it was as charming and beautiful as I had imagined. The trip's highlight came when I toured the Jewish Museum Vienna and met Adina for coffee. We talked for several hours like we were old friends, which I suppose we had become.

Of course, my family's oral history was the backbone for the writing of this novel, and I often thought about that long-ago conversation with my mother. We were alone, and had talked well past when the sun set; the room's only light coming from a dim bulb over the stove. I listened in the dark, only recognizing decades later it was the most illuminating conversation of my life.

At the end, my mother said, "I tell you these things so that the world remembers what happened to us."

I imagine I told her, "I know," and that an unspoken promise passed between us, one where I would carry her stories forward once she no longer could.

I believe that my mother's storytelling stemmed from her hope for the future and her desire that our humanity would prevail. I wrote *The Lost Baker of Vienna* with that same hope in mind. This novel is historical fiction, inspired by my mother, and saturated with my family's experiences, which also makes it deeply personal.

Acknowledgments

I began *The Lost Baker of Vienna* in the solitude of pandemic lockdowns, yet there is a large community who helped make this book possible. I am infinitely grateful to them.

My first thank you is for my amazing agent, Wendy Sherman. Without you, this book wouldn't exist. You are the deliverer of dreams! I am so grateful for your belief in this story, and me, from our very first conversation. I'm the luckiest writer on earth to be partnered with you on this journey. To the brilliant team at Wendy Sherman Associates, with a shout-out to Callie Deitrick, your support for this book has meant the world to me.

My heartfelt thanks to Pamela Dorman for providing my novel with the perfect home at Pamela Dorman Books/Viking. It has been a privilege to have your keen attention on my work. I remain in awe of your brilliant guidance and revision notes, which made everything about this story better. So many thanks to Marie Michels for spot-on insights, suggestions, and for diving in on the sentence-level with me. You made me and my book shine our brightest. To Natalie Grant—thank you. After more than twenty years of writing, I am humbled and grateful to have landed with my publishing dream team. Thank you to all the wonderful people at Viking and Penguin who have touched my novel and ushered it into the world: Brian Tart, Andrea Schulz, Patrick Nolan, Kate Stark, Tricia Conley, Tess Espinoza, Nick Michal, Diandra Alvarado, Gabriel Levinson, and Claire Vaccaro. I want to thank Andy Dudley and the rest of the Penguin sales team. To the design team, Nayon Cho and Jason Ramirez, thank you for creating the book cover of my dreams. Thank you to my marketing team, Mary Stone and Chantal Canales, and my publicity team, Carolyn Coleburn and Yuleza Negron.

Buckets of gratitude to Jenny Meyer and Heidi Gall for bringing Chana and Zoe's story to the world. Jenny, working with you has been a tremendous gift. I am more grateful than I can ever fully express.

To each of my foreign translation publishers, editors, sales teams, and marketers, my heart is full from the enthusiastic way you have embraced Chana and Zoe. Your championing of this book to readers around the globe has meant everything to me.

To brilliant author and dearest friend Therese Anne Fowler, thank you, thank you, thank you for twenty-plus years of sage advice, mentorship, friendship, feedback, and unparalleled generosity. I am so lucky to have you in my corner and in my life.

This book found its early footing because of insightful beta readers to whom I am much obliged: Rebecca Hodge, Heather Bell Adams, Kerry Chaput, *the* Sharon J. Wishnow, and Mary Grant. Your feedback ensured that this manuscript was in tip-top shape. To Chelsey Emmelhainz at Keen Editorial, thank you for helping me level up my story.

I've been writing for well over two decades and my journey has included a collection of close friends who occupy the orchestra section of my life. Thank you to my writing friends: Maureen Sherbondy, Diane Chamberlain, Barbara Claypole White, Sheryl Cornett, Bernie Bro Brown, Rebecca Hodge, Monica Cox, Elaine Neil Orr, Janna McMahan, Robin Miura, and Michelle Taylor. I treasure our fellowship, laughs, and conversations. *Danke* to John Kessel for his translation assistance. To Sue Lucey, thank you for your support.

As a member of the Women's Fiction Writers Association (WFWA), I've gained writing and publishing knowledge, as well as dear friends like the TGIF Rogues. Throughout the pandemic, the Rogues met on Zoom, and I share my appreciation—with special thanks to Lisa Montanaro—for encouraging me as I wrote *The Lost Baker of Vienna*. A shout-out to Michele Montgomery for guiding WFWA Writing Dates, where I wrangled my first draft into existence. Thank you to Joan Fernandez for starting WFWA's Historical Fiction affinity group. So much gratitude to Kelly Hartog for answering questions in a heartbeat.

ACKNOWLEDGMENTS

Research plays a huge role in writing historical fiction, and I researched far and wide to flesh out my family's stories. Lucky for me, some extraordinary people responded to my cold calls. Adina Seeger at the Jewish Museum Vienna, I'm so grateful for your generosity. Your knowledge enriched this novel. Thank you also to Jason Dawsey, research historian with The National WWII Museum. Thank you to the Library and Archives division at the United States Holocaust Memorial Museum.

I was fortunate to have earned my MFA in Fiction Writing in 2019 from Vermont College of Fine Arts. To my faculty mentors Nance Van Winckel, Brian Leung, and Bret Lott, working with you helped me grow exponentially as a writer. Another round of thanks to my VCFA pals: Jennifer Pun, Tara Potter, Josiane Chriqui, Asena Mckeown, Sara McCraw Crow, and Liza Nash Taylor. A big shout-out to Anne Gimm, dear friend, and advocate for my book and me.

My life is infinitely richer thanks to friends who are like family. These women have always encouraged me: Jill Alper, Susan Pincus, Elizabeth Rubach, Jane Chesebrough, Lisa White, Susan Turner, Donna Kortes, Holly Robinson, Cindy Schwartz, Dr. Julie Weidner, Stacy Ross, and Jacqueline Fagan.

To Lisa Becker, my best friend since childhood, thank you for your unwavering belief in my ability to pull off this whole published author thing.

An abundance of love and thanks to Ellen Kurtzman and Martin Kurtzman for welcoming me into your family as a daughter. I want to especially thank Ellen Kurtzman for her never-ending patience as I queried spellings and comma placements. To Allan Rothspan, Tammy Rothspan, Stephanie Bungard, and David Bungard, thank you for always believing that this day would come. I want to thank my extended family—the Kurtzmans, Rothspans, Bungards, and Fishbeins—for always rooting for me. I am grateful to my cousins Jodi Erdman, Harvey Erdman, Jennifer Erdman Hajar, and Felice Goldberg for their support.

From early on, my parents, Herman and Evelyn Rothspan, fanned the flames of my writing ambitions. They were resilient, loving, hardworking, and the best parents. I only wish they were alive to see this book and my publishing dreams come true.

A very special acknowledgment to my mother, aunt, and grandmother, Evelyn Rothspan, Helen Erdman, and Gita Kraus—a courageous trio if ever there was one! It is my greatest honor to bring your stories to the world. To my maternal grandfather, Aron Kraus, murdered before I was born, if not for your strength, smarts, and sacrifices, I wouldn't be here today. Whenever I'm asked to name the historical person with whom I'd most like to have a conversation, my answer is simple. It's always you.

To my children, Gabby Kurtzman and Cole Kurtzman, I'm forever grateful for the patience of your younger selves and always allowing Mommy to finish writing one more sentence or paragraph when needed. You two own my heart and brighten my life; your laughter is my sunshine.

My last thank-you is not the least part of this story as it goes to my beloved husband, Warren Kurtzman. He has lived with an up-close view of the highs and lows in my writing life. Thank you for locking the windows every time I threatened to toss out my laptop. How gratifying it was to travel to Austria with you and explore the cities, streets, buildings, and meals that found their way into this novel. I have always wanted to write a great love story. As the years and our anniversaries have stacked up, I know that I'm living one—ours. I'm eternally grateful for the life we share.